PENGUIN BOOKS
1388

KNIGHT WITH ARMOUR
ALFRED DUGGAN

KNIGHT
WITH ARMOUR

BY

ALFRED DUGGAN

PENGUIN BOOKS
IN ASSOCIATION WITH
FABER AND FABER

Penguin Books Ltd, Harmondsworth, Middlesex
AUSTRALIA: Penguin Books Pty Ltd, 762 Whitehorse Road,
Mitcham, Victoria

—

First published by Faber and Faber 1950
Published by Penguin Books 1959

Made and printed in Great Britain
by Hazell Watson & Viney Ltd
Aylesbury and Slough

CONTENTS

I

SUSSEX

1096

OSBERT FITZRALPH held the manor of Bodeham in Sussex from the Count of Eu. But in the winter of 1095 the Count was in the King's prison, awaiting sentence for his unsuccessful rebellion last summer; his tenants in southern England, who had been too closely watched to dare to join in the rising, hoped they would soon hold direct from the King, after the land had been confiscated. Still, it would be blatantly unfaithful to go to the King's court while their lord was his prisoner, so Osbert and his two sons, Ralph and Roger, kept that Christmas of 1095 at the new and half-built Abbey of Battle.

During the Octave of Christmas a monk from Fécamp preached on the acts of the council recently held at Clermont, and the duty of all Christian warriors to go to the rescue of their persecuted brethren in the East. All the congregation of local landholders and idle peasants heard the sermon in silence, and said nothing afterwards to commit themselves, the Saxons because they could not understand a word of what was preached to them, the Normans because they were members of a cautious race.

On 7 January Osbert rode the ten miles home with his sons, through the deep tangled woods of the Weald. Conversation was impossible on the ride, as the horses struggled in single file, girth-deep in the muddy clay track; but in the evening they crossed the Rother at Bodeham Bridge, and rode up the hill to the timber-and-wattle hall that looked northwards to the endless woods of Kent. There were only servants to welcome them at the manor, for Messer Osbert's wife had died two years before, and he had no daughters. He got stiffly off his horse and limped into the hall, for he had received a spear-wound in the thigh at the second taking of York. He was an old man, creaking with the rheumatism of the Weald, and his beard was white, though his hauberk had long since rubbed the hair from his crown. His sons followed him, and all three stood warming their hands round the fire that burnt in the middle of the room, while the servants set out the table for supper. He glared at his sons under shaggy white eyebrows, and spoke in a complaining voice:

'Well, out with it. I suppose you two young fools are burning to fight for the Christians of the East, and all you want is a large sum of money from me to take you out there. The whole idea is nonsense, and that's flat. I very much doubt if those Easterners really want us, whatever they may have told His Holiness the Pope, and in any case we have quite enough to do here, holding down this half-conquered land. What do you think about it, Ralph?'

He sat down at the supper-table, and took a long drink of beer. His sons sat down in their places, and Ralph looked up to answer, with a nervous smile. He was a handsome youth of twenty-one, his fair hair worn long in the new fashion of the court.

'I think it is an excellent idea, Father. Now that my excommunication is lifted, I mean to keep on good terms with the Church. At this end of the kingdom we have no chance of winning new lands, and I don't want to die in Bodeham, without making any name in the world.'

'Stuff and nonsense,' his father answered. 'You young men are never content to stay at home. Let me remind you that your last campaign was nothing to be proud of; going off as a soldier, and then getting excommunicated too. You remember what it cost me to get that ban lifted. But you had better stick to the King's service. You may have to do some ugly things, as all soldiers do, yet the King will be grateful to you one day. You have arms and a horse already; go back to the King in the spring, and watch your chance to win his favour. I am an old man now, and when I die, I want a son to succeed me. Stay in England or Normandy, and you shall have Bodeham when I am gone.'

'You mean that, Father?' said Ralph, unable to keep the eagerness out of his voice. 'Of course it is a long time in the future, and you mustn't think of yourself as an old man; but could you swear before witnesses that I am to be your heir, and get a seal put to it? After all, you did not inherit this manor; it came by conquest, and you can leave it where you like. I suppose you want it to come to me undivided. You hear that, Roger?'

'Leave the boy alone,' said his father severely. 'The manor must all be yours, without division, for there is not enough to support two knights, and we don't want the family to lose its nobility. We have been knights for three generations now, and people expect us to keep it up. Roger will have to go into the Church, unless he prefers to be a merchant or a craftsman. There are some quite well-born young men taking up citizenship in London and Winchester.'

They both looked at the younger son, who had been busily munching cold salt beef without paying much attention to the discussion.

Roger was in his eighteenth year; he was short, though his broad shoulders and large hands showed that he would be burly later on. He wore his dark hair cropped close round his skull, and there was a patch on the knee of his chausse, though he was wearing his best. He gulped to empty his mouth, and looked up frowning.

'I will never make a clerk,' he said slowly. 'I am too clumsy to write well, and, besides, I want to marry some day. But I listened to those sermons and my mind is made up. Since the Pope calls us, I will live and die in the Eastern world.'

He picked up his knife, and cut another piece of salt beef, as though he was not interested in any answer he might get.

'Silly, you don't have to write to be a priest,' said his brother, 'and you can read as well as any of us; that is quite enough.'

'I still think the Church is the place for you,' said Osbert, answering him directly, and disregarding the elder brother, 'but if you are set against it I won't force you. I have seen enough of scandalous priests not to wish to add to their number. But if you won't pray for a living you must fight for it, or work for it, that is clear. We might fix you up in service as a soldier with the captain of a band of routiers. That is how my uncle went to Italy, and I heard that he prospered out there.'

'You don't understand, Father,' Roger burst out violently. 'I won't be a clerk because I am not worthy of the calling. I shall never have the money to be a merchant, and I am too old to be apprenticed to a craft. There seemed to be nothing for it but soldiering, fighting for a wage, burning churches and priests in Wales in the course of an unjust quarrel, as Ralph did. I have always dreaded that, for it is a road that leads straight to Hell. Have you ever known an honourable soldier? This pilgrimage that we have heard preached gives me a chance of an honourable life, and Heaven after death. I tell you again that my mind is made up, and if you won't help me I shall steal a crossbow in the village and set out on foot.'

'This pilgrimage is a new idea,' said Ralph indignantly, 'and nothing like it was ever heard of before. We don't even know if they are proper Christians in the East, or whether they deserve our help. Now I can give you an introduction to the captain of the King's routiers, and you may end with a castle of your own.'

'The Pope thinks these Easterners deserve our help,' his father said quietly, 'and we can trust his judgement in such a matter. Roger's idea is worth thinking over, and we can discuss it at length tomorrow. Now it is time for bed.' He rose from the table and climbed the ladder to the sleeping-loft, without another word.

*   *   *

The whole countryside was talking of the new pilgrimage, and so many knights said they were going that by February Osbert was brought to admit that there must be something in the idea. One Sunday they all stayed to breakfast with the parish priest of Ewhurst, on the opposite hill across the river, for Bodeham had no church of its own. Father Matthew was a Saxon of good family, a well-educated man who spoke Latin fluently, used by all the neighbouring landowners as an interpreter in the manor-courts. He was worthy of a better cure, but he would never get promotion, since he could not speak French. Roger listened to the talk, in grammatical but elementary Latin, where each speaker put the words in the order of his native tongue. He realized with a sudden thrill of joy that his father was talking about the prospect of the pilgrimage, and how to get money for it from his tenants, as though it was finally settled that he should go.

'I think I know as much of your law as you do, Messer Osbert,' the priest was saying. 'I seem to spend most of my week-days in one court or another. Now you can tallage your tenants (I believe I have the right word), you can tallage them to pay for the wedding of your eldest daughter, or to fit out your eldest son, or of course to ransom their lord from captivity. We didn't have these laws in King Edward's time, but we obey them quietly now. But in all this there is no mention of a tallage for the arming of a younger son, who is not even going to serve his lord, and therefore his tenants also, but proposes to go in arms on pilgrimage to the ends of the earth. Your tenants pay you to protect them, but what advantage will they gain from this pilgrimage? If you ask for a tallage they will refuse, and if you threaten to harry them for it, they will complain to the King's sheriff.'

'I agree, Father Matthew,' Osbert replied. 'I can extort nothing from the villeins for the arming of my younger son, and I don't want to set the King's sheriff against me. But this pilgrimage has been preached all over Sussex, and I thought that some of these men, who cannot go themselves for they are useless in battle, might give money to send a knight whom they know and trust. Thus they would share in the spiritual benefits.'

'Just what I was going to propose myself,' said the priest. 'They must make a spontaneous voluntary gift, and that will need a good deal of arrangement before hand. Your court meets on the Feast of the Annunciation, doesn't it? That's the 25th of March, and gives us plenty of time to plan things. How shall we go about it?'

Osbert considered for a few moments; then he spoke:

'How would it be if I followed the example of the old Duke, when King Edward died and we were preparing to come over here? He called a council of his vassals, and asked us to help him in the invasion. We answered, of course, that he had no right to order us to follow him to England, merely to win new lands for his own profit, as it had nothing to do with the Duchy. Then, after we had stood up for our rights, came the bargaining. We all followed him in the end, but voluntarily, not as a matter of duty.'

'That is an excellent plan,' said Father Matthew. 'Let them refuse first, and accept their refusal. That will make them see what a conscientious, law-abiding lord you are. Then, when the court is closed, but before they have time to go home, your son must get up and make an appeal for himself. I will talk to a few of the more prosperous tenants beforehand, and arrange that they give a good lead to the rest. Everyone will be eager to promise something, so long as it is really a voluntary gift, and not another tax. Now, who shall we put up to do the refusing?'

Roger was a good deal surprised at this peep into the way that manor-court business was arranged in advance; it had never entered his head that all the long-winded, formal speeches were rehearsed beforehand; but the important thing was that his father was reconciled to his going.

As they walked back towards the hall in the afternoon he began to speak his gratitude, but his father interrupted him.

'You can thank me when it is all over; and mind you, I haven't finally decided to let you go. But there is no harm in getting you a horse and armour from the religious feelings of the tenants, and once you are armed, you can always go fighting elsewhere. The important thing is to get a good sum of money out of them.'

'I think I can manage that, with a torch to their roofs if necessary,' put in Ralph.

'Oh no. You won't do anything like that here,' said his father, 'whatever you may have burnt in Wales. You young men must learn that no matter how ruthless you are in the field, you must be respectable at home.'

'But, Father,' cried Roger, 'I thought you had agreed that I should go on this pilgrimage. Surely you will allow me to use my arms for that, and for no other purpose. What have you against it, anyway?'

'There is a lot to be said against it,' his father replied gravely, 'and I will say it now, before you take any rash vows. In the first place, where are you going? It's no answer to say the East, and I haven't heard anything more definite. There are infidels from Constantinople to Spain, and you don't know which of them you are going to fight. In the second place, who is going to be the leader? The Emperor has set up a private Pope of his own, the King of France is excommunicate, and no one can imagine our King William doing anything for God's Church. The pilgrims will quarrel among themselves, and wander in small parties all over the infidel lands, unless you have very good luck. In the third place, do the Christians of the East really want you? That heretical Greek Emperor has fallen into a panic, and asked help from the Pope, whose authority he doesn't acknowledge. How can you be sure that when you get there he may not have made friends with the infidels again? The real trouble is that we know nothing at all about the lands of the East, not even the best way to get there. You will be riding into the dark.'

'All that is true,' Roger answered, 'but people have been on pilgrimage to Jerusalem. Didn't the Count of Flanders go there a few years ago?'

'He did indeed. He was three years on the voyage, most of his followers died, and he has been a sick man himself ever since. I don't regard that as a good omen.'

'And our ancestors under the first Duke Rollo,' Roger persisted, 'did they know the way when they settled in France? Or my great-uncle, when he went to Italy? Surely we Normans can march into any strange land, and conquer it, and settle in it, no matter what the customs of the people.'

'That's the spirit, little brother,' said Ralph, 'but what is the matter with Wales? It is so much nearer.'

'Well,' said Osbert, 'you may go if the expedition seems to have a chance of success, since you have set your heart on it. You can take a vow as soon as you like; it will make the appeal to the manor-court easier. But if the whole thing falls through, or if the first starters are massacred on the way, you will have to get your vow dispensed. The Abbot of Battle will fix that up for me. I won't let a son of mine lose his life in a hare-brained foray with no chance of success. Now you must spend the

13

spring learning the management of arms. I should be ashamed if you were killed in your first charge through bad lance-work or faulty horsemanship.'

*   *   *

The Welshman was set up in a water-meadow by the Rother. The Welshman was a stout post with a bag of straw for a head and straw padding for the shoulders; it used to be called the Saxon, but they had changed the name out of consideration for the tenants. Roger had been practising at it for more than an hour, and his right arm was beginning to feel numb; but battles lasted for many hours, and he thought he had better get used to the feeling. He wheeled Ralph's borrowed warhorse a hundred yards from the dummy, and sent him straight at it again. He wore his own helm and sword, and his own thick leather fighting-tunic, for he could not get his broad shoulders into Ralph's mail shirt, though he had borrowed his shield and lance. He cantered briskly towards the post; about thirty yards away he stuck in his spurs and set the horse alight. This was the tricky bit. As he lifted the heavy shield, and brought his head down till his eyes were peering over the shield-rim, the broad leather reins slipped through his fingers, and hung loose from the bit to the palm of his hand. Neither could he guide with his legs, for at the same time he must push his buttocks into the back of the heavy warsaddle, and stick his feet out level with the horse's shoulders. The lance tucked horizontal under his right elbow had only a narrow arc to move in, and the horse was in control. This particular horse knew his job, and went straight at the post, which fell flat on the ground as the lance caught the straw padding; Roger sat up straight and loose, and the warhorse checked of his own accord. A touch on the bit, and he stopped; Roger dismounted to pick up his lance, and to set the mark on its feet again. That charge had gone right, thanks to the horse, but he must work out some way to keep more control when he was in the proper jousting position. He looked at the river-mist rising all round him; soon it would be too dark to continue. He saw his father limping down the hill, and waited for him to come within speaking distance.

'Good evening,' said Osbert, leaning on his stick. 'That last course was well run, but how would you manage if the horse didn't do most of it for you? I wish you could have had more hunting; but no one, except the great lords, is allowed to hunt round here. Now walk that horse about to cool him off. When you have put him away, I want to speak to you at the hall. The manor-court is tomorrow, and we must decide what we are going to say.'

As Roger watched a groom rubbing the horse down, he reflected on how quickly his adventure was approaching. At Christmas a campaign in the summer had seemed ages in the future, leaving him plenty of time to learn how to handle his arms; now it was nearly the end of March, and he was certainly not a trained knight. But perhaps the tenants would refuse him their help, and in that case there would be no hurry at all. Later, he discussed his speech with his father; they decided he would make a better effect by talking baldly, yet sincerely, and touching the pity of his hearers; also, the speech would have to be translated by Father Matthew, and, as none of the family knew Saxon, they would be entirely in his hands.

Next day was the Feast of the Annunciation of Our Blessed Lady, and after dinner the court assembled. The hall was full of villeins, standing carefully in their complicated Saxon ranks, though no one paid any attention to that nowadays. Osbert and the priest faced the suitors across the fireplace, while Ralph and Roger stood at the upper end, behind their father. They were neither tenants nor landlords, and therefore technically not part of the court. Roger noticed with secret admiration how smoothly everything went; people spoke spontaneously, there were differences of opinion, yet everything fell out as his father had said it would.

After the ordinary business had been settled, Osbert spoke of the expedition to the East, and explained it carefully, though no one had talked of anything else for the last two months. Then old Sigbert, that year's reeve, denied his lord's right to tallage for such an object, and the suitors backed him in his refusal. Finally the court was closed, but before anyone could leave Roger came forward, and stood beside Father Matthew. He was nervous and

15

stuttering, but he had thought out carefully what he wanted to say and had already turned it in his mind into simple dog-Latin. He told them of his unfitness for the holy life of the cloister, and of his longing for warfare; he spoke with scorn of the life of the soldier, fighting without loyalty for pay and plunder; he told them how this expedition fitted his aims exactly, and that he would willingly risk death to free the Christians of the East. His brother Ralph blushed and looked away, as we do when we hear our relatives giving way to their emotions in public, but Father Matthew, as he translated, caught some of his warmth, and transmitted it. His elaborate, inflected, Winchester Saxon was rather above the heads of his listeners, but that was what they expected from a priest, and when he had finished there was a faint murmur of applause. No more was said, and the suitors shuffled out of the hall to their cabins on the hillside. Roger felt at a loss. Was this all that had come from his carefully prepared speech? But Father Matthew came up to him and spoke cheerfully:

'That went down very well, and I am sure they have taken it to heart. Next Sunday, after Mass, they will come up to me one by one, and each will have something to give, even after this bad year.'

His father was also smiling. 'It couldn't have gone better. After twenty-five years I ought to know what a manor-court is thinking, and they are all in your favour. As to the bad harvest, some of them had corn stored, and they sold it for money to the townsmen of Rye. I only hope they give it over before they hear that the Council at Westminster have agreed on a double Danegeld for the King.'

'Two Danegelds!' exclaimed Father Matthew. 'Two Danegelds at once! That has never been done before. What can your Red King want with it?'

'I happen to know what he wants the money for,' said Osbert. 'The Duke is going on this pilgrimage, and is trying to raise money just as we are. The King will make him a loan on the security of his land, and rule there till the debt is paid. I heard it at Rye from a knight who was going oversea to warn his cousins in Normandy. It is a very good thing for the pilgrimage;

a great many Normans will leave for the East when they hear that our King is coming to rule over them.'

*　　*　　*

On the Feast of Saint Philip and Saint James, 1 May, most of the contributions had been gathered at the manor, and the three Bodehams sat round a table by the fire, discussing how the money should be spent.

'There is enough here,' said Osbert, 'to send you out as a knight, and a well-armed knight too, if you don't waste money on provisions for the journey. It is years since I saw an army, unless you count that unhappy fyrd at Dover; but you, Ralph, have been in Wales lately; had the rich knights any new ideas in their armour? They are always thinking of something extra for more safety, as though they would live for ever if they didn't get killed in battle.'

'There are no new ideas, really,' Ralph answered, looking at the roof with a frown. 'Of course, the knights at court don't like scars that disfigure their beauty, so they cover their faces as much as they can. I have seen one or two hauberks of interlaced iron rings, without any leather backing; they are so light and cool you can fasten them over the mouth, and still turn your head. Also more and more people are wearing leather breeches, with over-lapping iron plates on the outside, like a mail shirt has. Then you can have your skirts shorter, and they say it is just as comfortable on horseback as cloth chausses, though of course more tiring on foot.'

'The old Duke and other great lords wore them at Hastings in the conquest,' said his father. 'It is not a new idea. But it needs a very good horse to carry all that extra weight, and if you haven't got plenty of servants, it is cumbersome about the camp.'

'Otherwise, there is nothing new,' Ralph continued. 'Except that everyone wears long mail sleeves down to the wrist, and ties them close with a thong at the end; but you have seen that on my armour.'

'Let us count up what we have already,' said Osbert. 'There is plenty of leather, and the Abbot of Battle has sent two old mail shirts, and promised to lend us his smith. We can make a new leather foundation to fit you, big enough to allow for growth; the smith can take enough iron from the old armour to make you a really good mail shirt, with long sleeves; but you will have to manage with a leather-backed hauberk. If we wait for him to make one of rings only, you will be dead of old age before it is finished. As to the mail breeches, what do you think yourself?'

Roger had gone off into a daydream. He was leaning back with his hands behind his head, and his eyes fixed on the smoke-hole of the roof. But what he saw was a dusty rutted road, climbing mountains, fording rivers, skirting great castles and enormous cities, running on south-east mile after mile, till it reached a hill with three crosses stand against the sky. He came back to earth with a start, and smiled at this new father who was being so helpful, seeking his opinion as if he was grown up at last.

'It really depends on how much we can spend. I must have money for the journey; but I have never had armour of my own before. I will take your advice, sir.'

'Well then,' said Osbert. 'I am not in favour of the mail breeches. You may have to fight on shipboard, or escalade a wall; and fighting on foot is largely a matter of getting out of reach of the enemy at the right time. I wouldn't have got that spear in my leg on the walls of York if I had been quicker on my feet. We will have the skirts of your mail shirt made long, with straps on the inside to go under your knee; that will keep your thighs safe, and you will find that you are much more active than you would be in ironbound breeches. It is not the expense I am thinking of; once you are fairly started you should not need a great deal of money. A well-armed, well-mounted knight, with a follower or two to forage for him, can live very cheaply when he is outside the King's Peace, as Ralph found in Wales.'

Ralph guffawed, but Roger frowned and kept silent. That was not the way he saw himself as a knight in the service of the Church; but it was all too difficult to explain to his worldly-wise father.

They went on to discuss horses and followers. The warhorse

was the biggest expense; and in France the price would go up with everyone buying for this expedition; but the breed of English horses had improved in the last thirty years. Eventually it was decided that he should take Ralph's trained French warhorse, Jack, and leave a sum of money behind; later on Ralph would go to the horse-fair at Moorfields outside London, and buy a two-year-old to train on for himself. Roger was not skilful enough to train a horse for war, and time was short. There would be a hackney to ride on the march, and a packhorse for the baggage. Osbert was insistent that this was enough, as forage must obviously run short wherever such an expedition passed. He also had clear-cut ideas about followers.

'You don't want to be cumbered with a crowd of footmen; they always start plundering friendly villages and set the local peasants against you. Take a good steady groom for your warhorse, and a servant to lead the baggage-animal; if one of them can cobble your armour a bit so much the better. There are plenty of peasants round here who want to go, but don't be led into making yourself responsible for a crowd of crossbow-men by the desire to cut a good figure. The leaders will put them with the other foot in the battle-line, and you will only see them at mealtimes. If you do win a castle in the East, you will have no difficulty in picking a garrison.'

Roger did not like these constant hints that he was going East to make his fortune, when he was really going to help the oppressed Christians of those parts; but he wanted to remain on good terms with his family, and he said nothing about it.

When it was known that young Messer de Bodeham could only take two men with him, there was a crowd of applicants from among the more prosperous of the free peasants and townsmen; for this pilgrimage made a much greater appeal to the lower classes than it did among the gentry. Osbert interviewed them personally for the whole of one day, and finally engaged two who seemed the most suitable. Peter the Fleming would lead the warhorse; he had travelled, and spoke good French, he understood horse-management, and it took a good deal of wine to make him drunk. Godric of Rye would look after the baggage; he had learnt leather-sewing in a bottle-maker's shop, and could do simple repairs to the armour; he only knew a few words of French, but as a townsman he was used to making himself understood somehow by incomprehensible foreigners. They were both young, strong, cheerful, and active, and though neither had any arms beyond knife and cudgel, Osbert said this was a good thing.

'The leaders won't take them to put with the archers in the battleline, and they won't feel safe if they go off plundering by themselves. You will get better service from unarmed men.'

*　　*　　*

By the beginning of June the expedition was taking definite shape. The Council of Clermont had fixed the Assumption of Our Lady, 15 August, as the starting day, and it was expected that most of the great lords who were going would be ready by that time. There had been no hesitation as to which leader Roger would follow; the Duke of Normandy had taken the vow, and pledged his lands to raise money; he was the natural head of the Norman race, wherever they might be settled, and any knight would be proud to serve a lord of such high lineage. The only question was, on what terms should Roger serve him?

'You will have to take some sort of oath,' said his father, 'but be sure to swear as little as you can. It would be absurd to set off for the East on your own without any leader at all, considering how little money you have, though that would be the best way to get rich lands when you arrive. The Duke must intend to feed all his followers on the journey, at least through the lands of Christendom; otherwise he wouldn't be borrowing right and left as he is. Your best plan is to get to Rouen on the Feast day, when they won't have time to haggle over terms. See the Duke's marshal and arrange things with him. You will have to swear to follow the Duke as long as he feeds you, that is only common sense; but arrange it that the time-limit at the end is left vague, so that you can transfer to another banner if it seems advisable when you are among the infidels. No knight may break his oath without incurring lasting dishonour, and it is also displeasing to God. The remedy is to be very careful about what you actually swear to.'

'Surely all this is not very important,' said Roger after a pause. 'We are going to help the Christians of the East, and we can count on them to look after us when we get out there. I intend to stay in the East for the rest of my life, but the Duke has arranged to come home after three years, I believe. I can swear to serve him until he begins his homeward journey, and then there will be no misunderstanding.'

'That would be all right,' answered his father, 'but don't make it too definite. Mind you don't let the Duke himself decide when the homeward journey has begun; he might force you to follow him back to the Loire, and the borders of Normandy. He is a better man than his brother, but all these fitzRollos stand on the letter of their rights against their vassals. Remember you go to Rouen as an absolutely free agent. You hold no land, and are not the man of any lord. Once you are oversea, neither the King of England nor the Duke of Normandy has any rightful claim on you, except what you incur by your oath. So, if you can't get good terms, you can go to some other lord.'

'Still, it would be more honourable to follow our own Duke,' Roger objected, 'and everyone says he is an easygoing leader. I shall be his man, for the duration of the pilgrimage only, if I can possibly manage it.'

There the matter was dropped. Osbert was generally faithful to his promises, but a keen bargainer beforehand, which was why he was well on the way to becoming a tenant-in-chief; but Roger was shy, and uneasy about the whole business. As a younger son and brother he was used to doing what he was told, and he felt that he would come off worst if he had to haggle with the Duke's clerks.

* * *

In the middle of June bad news came from across the Channel, and Osbert nearly forbade his son to go. Since early spring bands of peasants had been mustering, and marching vaguely south-east towards the Danube. Two badly equipped expeditions, under Walter the Penniless and Peter the Hermit, had fought their way through Hungary, and had been swallowed up in the mountains of the Sclavonians. They had not come back, so presumably the survivors had reached Romania, but other bands had met a worse fate. Father Fulkmar's band had been dispersed by a Hungarian attack, and Father Godescal's completely destroyed by the same foe at Merseburg. The Count of Leiningen, leading a well-found army, was stuck outside the same town. Hungary was really the boundary of geographical knowledge. Beyond lay the unknown lands of the Bulgarians and Sclavonians, mountainous and desolate, until you came out at the Christian and civilized Greek cities of the Thracian coast.

Osbert was appalled. These bands of plunderers had stirred up enemies in the path of the pilgrims, and made the normal overland route to Constantinople unusable for a law-abiding army. It was learned that the Duke of Normandy, in consequence, had decided to go south, to the Norman lands of Italy, and there take ship for the Greek Empire. It would be slower, for it was impossible to sail in the winter, and they would spend months in Apulia, waiting for the spring. Also, Osbert pointed out that it would mean putting all the horses on shipboard, and anyone who remembered the conquest of England knew what a frightful business that was.

'All the same, there is no other way now,' he said, 'thanks to that rabble who have made war on the Hungarians. The Duke is behaving sensibly for once, and you must promise to follow him, and no other lord; otherwise I shall forbid you to go. Now what do you know about the lands you are going to?'

'Not very much, Father,' Roger answered meekly. 'We shall winter in Italy in the lands held by the fitzTancreds. They are Normans, and I suppose their land is like any other Norman land. Then we shall cross the sea, and come to the dominions of the Greek Emperor. He is the richest prince in the world, by far, and as we are coming to help him, of course he will succour us. That land is Christian, and has been since the time of the Apostles. When we leave Constantinople we must cross a big river, and then at once we are in the lands where the infidels ravage. Beyond that is Antioch, and then Jerusalem, all Christian lands oppressed by devil-worshippers; and we are to free as much of them as we can.'

'When you put it like that it sounds quite simple,' said Osbert drily. 'But you don't really know anything about these foreign lands. Anyone who has been to Rome will tell you that Italy is not a bit like Normandy or England; and beyond Italy the whole world is strange. I have been making inquiries, and there is a lay brother in the monastery at Battle who served in the wars, when the Duke of Apulia invaded Romania. Tomorrow we shall ride over to see him, and learn what he knows about the country.'

The next day Roger and his father reached the Abbey in time for dinner. After a meal in the guest-chamber they sought the cellarer's workshop where Odo the laybrother was mending nets, for he was employed as a fowler. Odo was an elderly man, and his left ear and two fingers of his left hand were missing. He spoke well, in good French, helped out with an occasional Italian word. Like all retired fighting-men, he was delighted to tell the story of his life.

'I went to Italy as a lad, to serve the Count of Apulia (he wasn't a Duke then). I could tell you all sorts of adventures I had there, but you want to know about the war with the Greeks, and that was only a few years ago; about sixteen, I should think. It all began like this: there had been trouble in their great city Constantinople, and a new Emperor had turned out the old one, as they do quite often. Those Greeks have no loyalty to their lords, and an oath means nothing to them. But what can you expect from people who won't obey the Pope, and leave out bits of the Creed? Anyway, the old Emperor, Michael, was a friend of our Duke, Robert. So the Duke thought this was a good reason to invade the Greek Empire, and put the old Emperor back on his throne. However, you want to hear about the country and the fighting, not about who is Emperor over those heretics. Well, it is a great country of mountains and rocks, where the peaks in the distance are no nearer at the end of a day's march than at the beginning. The sun is very hot, and the springs few, and the water in them so cold that it gives the horses colic. A poor country, and very rocky; I wore out my shoes in a few days, and the horses were always going lame. But among those wastes are the most amazing cities, all made of hewn stone; stone streets, stone houses, and great steep stone walls set with towers; though there is nothing worth plundering in them, because they have all been sacked so often. Well, we landed there; I forget the names of the places, but it's always easy to land wherever you wish; deep water right up to the cliffs, and no tide like there is here. We conquered wherever we went, even the townspeople couldn't hold their great stone walls, but somehow we never got a grip of the country; there were always hired soldiers coming in behind us, and cutting up the stragglers. So we marched up and down, hungry men and lame horses, taking what we could find, and Duke Robert was always going back to look after his land in Italy, until presently he died, away from the army. We were left under his son, the Count of Taranto, a fine young warrior and an open-handed leader. He gave up, about six years after we first landed, and I came back to Italy with a damaged hand and no plunder to speak of. I got the Count's permission to go home to see my family; but my parents were dead, and my brothers still poor, and there were things I ought to repent of; in the end I came here.'

'Thank you,' said Osbert. 'I am sorry to hear that Romania is not such a rich land as I had been led to believe. Still, you may not have seen the best parts, for surely there is money somewhere in the Emperor's dominions. Now this son of mine is going out there, with the great pilgrimage. He wants to know all he can of the dangers of the way; tell us about how they fight in those parts.'

'Yes, sir, he ought to know that; but it isn't easy to tell, for we met so many different peoples, and each had their own way of fighting. You see, the Greeks are not warriors themselves, so they hire soldiers to do their work for them. Let's see, first there were the axemen of the Emperor's guard; they fought on foot in mail shirts, like Count Harold's men here.'

'I charged in that battle,' said Osbert. 'They fought well, but knights and archers together will always beat men on foot.'

'You are a true warrior, sir, if you fought in that battle. As you say, we Normans can always beat foot. Some of these guardsmen were Saxons, too; men who had been chased out of England, and gone to serve the Emperor as soldiers. Of course, we had crossbows, that's new since your time, and we could shoot harder than ordinary archers. The knights threatened to

24

charge and made them stand still, and we shot them down as safely as though we were shooting at a mark. But the Greeks had other warriors too, horse-archers mostly. There were Bulgarians, Turks, Cumans, Patzinaks, tribes and tribes of them, and very awkward they were to deal with. You can chase horse-archers away, but you can't very easily kill them.'

'I have never heard of a horseman using a bow,' Roger put in.

'You have seen Warrenne and his foresters out hunting,' said his father sharply.

'Yes, but their arrows from horseback would never kill a man,' Roger insisted. 'It doesn't sound very dangerous to me.'

'It is dangerous, all the same,' Odo replied. 'It is true their arrows are not shot hard enough to kill a man, especially a man in armour. But they get you in the legs, or in the face, and they cripple the horses.'

'What happened when you met them hand to hand?' asked Osbert.

'This!' replied the laybrother, lifting the stumps of his missing fingers to where his ear had been. 'The Cumans, at least, carried light, sharp swords, with a curve in the blade, and sometimes they would pluck up their courage and charge home. One day, about fifty of us crossbow-men, with half a dozen knights, were on our way back to the main army after plundering a village, when a party of Cumans came galloping round a spur of the hill. Our crossbows were unwound, and they dashed straight into us with their swords. But their horses are so small that they don't try to ride you down. One reined up beside me, and cut at my head. I ducked, and he got me in the ear; then I caught his sword with my left hand, and stuck the knife I had drawn with my right hand into his horse's shoulder. He shied away, and then our six knights drove them off. They won't stand up to mailed knights.'

Brother Odo had little more to tell them. It was clear that he had never seen a Greek, except when looking along the stock of his crossbow, and it was impossible to get anything out of him about their manners and customs. The Abbot had never met anyone who had been to Constantinople, though one of the choir-monks had once read somewhere the unkind remarks that

Bishop Luitprand had written about it over a hundred years ago. It was a very large, strong city, where all the gold money came from, and nothing else was known about it.

* * *

All over England knights were preparing for this pilgrimage. It was considered unwise for the English pilgrims to set out in a body; King William was nervous on his unstable throne, and would not let armed men gather together, for fear of another rebellion. As no great leader came forward in England to head the pilgrimage, and they did not all intend to follow the same lord, they crossed the Channel independently.

On 1 August 1096, the Feast of Saint Peter ad Vincula, Roger was ready to go. He and his two followers had taken the pilgrim's vow in the Abbey Church at Battle, and had sewn crosses of red cloth on the shoulders of their mantles as a visible sign of it.

The horses were in good condition. Jack, the warhorse, was ten years old, and considerably past his prime; but he was perfectly trained, ran straight at the mark without guidance from his rider, and, above all, could be trusted not to bolt in the charge, the most dangerous fault in a knight's warhorse. He was fat, but not too fat, and his wind and legs were still perfectly sound; he was a handsome, strong horse, chestnut with a white forehead and white socks, and his tail was long and flowing; that would have to be knotted up in battle, lest a footman catch hold of it to hamstring him, but it enhanced his appearance on the march. His fore-feet were shod, more as a weapon than as a protection against hard ground, but his hindfeet were bare. He led easily, was quiet with other horses, and knew both his rider and his groom. Of course, he was a stallion. On the march he would always wear his bridle, and the heavily-padded war-saddle, with its semicircular guardboards rising in front and behind to protect the rider's loins and waist. The heavy five-foot triangular shield would hang by its straps on the near side of the saddle; it was made of leather, stretched over a wooden framework, with a central boss of iron, and iron binding on the edges. It was a massive affair, much too heavy to be wielded by the left arm alone, and in action most of the weight was taken by a strap over the wearer's right shoulder, though he could direct it a little by movements of his bridle arm. Properly worn, it covered him from neck to ankle on the left side, and was proof against spears and arrows. Peter the Fleming, who led the war-horse, also carried the knightly lance, eight feet long and tipped with a sharp steel point. Lances had not yet become battering-rams, and the knight still tried to pierce his enemy in a vulner-able spot.

Godric led the baggage-horse. It was a sturdy pony from Devonshire, and carried its load in two large leather-covered panniers; these contained the best clothes of all three pilgrims, and Roger's supply of fresh linen. Balanced on top of the load was a light wooden cross the height of a man; the crosspiece was threaded through the sleeves of the mail shirt, and the hauberk and helm were fixed to the top. Godric carried a satchel for food and another for odds-and-ends, but he had to be watched lest he add these to the pony's load, or, worse still, climb on its back himself.

Roger rode the hackney, a common-looking brown beast, touched in the wind, but sound in all four legs; a verderer from Ashdown Forest had given it to him, as a personal contribution to the pilgrimage; it was quiet, with good paces, a comfortable ride for a long journey. Both hackney and baggage-horse were geldings, for greater ease of management in the crowd that was to be expected. Roger rode unarmed, in his second-best blue tunic, and thick blue cloth chausses, cross-gartered, but he wore his heavy, double-edged, blunt-ended sword, to show that he was a knight.

So, on this first of August, they heard Mass and took Com-munion in the parish church of Ewhurst, and after breakfast set out on the dusty pack-road for Rye. Roger embraced his father and brother in the little cobbled courtyard of the hall, then mounted, with an unfamiliar tug at his left hip from the unac-customed sword, and rode downhill to the long pile bridge over the tidal Rother. He knew that whatever happened in the future, whether he ruled as a rich baron in the unknown East, or died in vain among the mountains of the Sclavonians with nothing accomplished, he would never see Bodeham manor again, or any of his family. It was a depressing thought, but young men of eighteen look forward to the unknown, and he reflected that he was following the tradition of his race. Generations ago, his ancestors had left the barren heaths of the north, and, after years of wandering, had settled under the great Rollo by the fertile estuary of the Seine. His own father had sold his little patch of ground to buy horse and arms, and crossed the Channel to win a new home; his cousins had wandered into the rich and enchanted land of Italy, and prospered there. Everywhere the Normans went they became the ruling class; in Scotland and Wales they were expanding now, and every jongleur from the south told how in Italy and Sicily they were setting up a mighty kingdom. Why should they not rule the rich and mysterious East? If those Greeks wouldn't fight themselves, and hired soldiers to defend them, they would be better off under Norman protection. He began to sing as they dropped into the valley of the Brede River, and saw on the horizon the flats of Rye.

After a night in the town, they took passage on a big Sandwich ship, and after a smooth crossing marched towards Rouen by easy stages. They were well fed and lodged by the inhabitants on the way, who refused any payment; for all the world was going on this pilgrimage, and those who stayed behind suffered from a feeling of guilt. They reached the mustering-place outside the city walls on the evening of the 14th, a day too soon, but Roger was eager to celebrate the Assumption of Our Lady in the cathedral church, and some of his father's worldly-wise counsel had already faded from his mind.

There was a crowded encampment outside the city walls; burgesses had run up little timber huts for letting to the pilgrims, and every wandering pedlar, beggarman, jongleur, and whore between the Loire and the Somme had gathered to give them a good send-off. Roger had no tent, but he did not mind sleeping in the open air on a fine summer night, and rolled up in his blankets by a fire of brushwood.

Next morning, after Mass, he bought dinner in a cookshop of the town (the first money he had spent since leaving home), and after his meal inquired for the chancellery of the Duke's clerks.

He was directed to a pavilion outside the walls, for the Duke had lost Rouen to his brother in the last war, and King William had a garrison in town and castle. With some nervousness he joined the crowd that waited outside, and tried to remember his father's sound advice; but he had never spoken to a royal clerk at home in England, so that it was with trembling knees that at last he pushed aside the curtains and went in; for to him, as to all true Normans, the Duke was a more important man than his younger brother.

Inside, he found himself before a long, cloth-covered trestle table, with a row of clerks sitting on the opposite side. In the middle sat a young man, whose face was lined with wrinkles of bad temper, though he smiled politely at his visitor. Roger stated his business, in a stammering voice that sounded unnaturally loud, and the other listened coolly, playing with a penknife. When he had finished, there was a pause; at last the clerk cleared his throat and spoke:

'Messer Roger de Bodeham (I have your name right?), you have come very late. Today is the Feast of the Assumption, and the Council which was called by his Holiness the Pope fixed this day for our departure. As a matter of fact, unforeseen circumstances will delay our start until the end of the month; but you could not know that, and it is unmannerly of you to apply to serve the Duke at such a late date.'

Roger braced his knees to stop them trembling, and swallowed the first symptoms of nausea. But the clerk went on, after a pause and a stare:

'Yet it is not quite too late, and we must make allowances, for England is a long way off. You have a horse and full armour, but no followers except two unarmed servants? Hardly a very great reinforcement. Is your mount a trained warhorse? Ah, that is good. And you have mail shirt, helm, hauberk, sword, lance, and shield, but no mail breeches? H'm, that puts you among the knights of the second rank. If you had mail breeches, you could have ridden with the counts and great lords, but that is the best I can do for you. Still, even the lesser knights are worthy men of good birth; this pilgrimage hasn't attracted the soldiers. You will dine at the second table, and the Duke will provide food for your servants, and forage for your animals. Be at the pavilion next to this, the dining tent, in three hours' time, and you can take the oath when the Duke sits down to supper. You will find criers going round the camp who will tell you when to be ready to march. Now have you any question? There is a great deal of business waiting for me.'

This was the time to raise the question of the terms of the oath, but Roger felt himself tongue-tied. If he argued about conditions, this busy and bad-tempered clerk might tell him to go home again, and that would be the end of his vow. He bowed and withdrew.

When the horns blew for suppertime he was standing just inside the entrance of the dining-tent, trying to keep out of the way of the servants. The Duke entered with a train of counts and courtiers, and all stood while Grace was sung. Then the household sat down at table, and the Duke emptied his winecup and called for more. He was a short man, broad-shouldered, active, and in the prime of life; his black hair was cropped close, and from his red face and bushy eyebrows his grey eyes stared fiercely; his dress was shabby, and his hands, with their bitten fingernails, not over-clean. But he looked what he was, the Conqueror's eldest son, and with the Conqueror's fiery temper also. Roger shuffled his feet by the entrance to the pavilion, and realized the impossibility of haggling about his oath of service with such a great lord. Presently the same official whom he had met that afternoon came hurrying down to him.

'Ah, there you are, Messer de Bodeham. The Duke will take your oath now. Do you know the procedure? Go up to the table opposite his place, kneel on the right knee, place both your hands in his, and repeat the words after me.'

In a daze of shyness Roger walked forward. He realized that this hand-clasping meant that he was to take the full oath of homage and fealty; but he could not possibly back out of it in front of all these people. He lurched unsteadily on to one knee, and stretched out his joined hands, as the Duke rose to clasp them. From a great distance he heard the voice of the clerk, and repeated his words.

'I, Roger de Bodeham in Sussex in England, a free man, not

holding any land from any lord, swear by Almighty God, by Mary His Blessed Mother, by all the company of Saints in Heaven, and particularly by Saint Michael patron of warriors, that I will true allegiance bear, and true homage do, in field and court, to Robert, Duke of Normandy, my true lord; and this I shall do for the pilgrimage to the Eastern parts of the world, as long as he is out of his dominions. All this I swear on the faith of a true knight; and all you here present are my witnesses.'

Two knights standing by repeated: 'And all here present are his witnesses.' The Duke released his hands, and sat down again. Roger rose, bowed, and walked out of the tent, no longer his own master, but the servant of the Duke until his lord returned from the pilgrimage.

His father's advice had not helped him a bit, and altogether it seemed a good occasion to get drunk.

2

NICAEA

1097

ROGER was riding in his place, in the rear of the column of horse. He was mounted on his warhorse, Jack, for they were in enemy territory now, and he was fully armed. The day was very hot and the discomfort almost unbearable. The thick leather of his mail shirt was airtight, and the thinner backing of his hauberk was stinking with old sweat and clammy with new. Below the waist, the padded cloth of his riding-chausses brought runnels of sweat which collected behind his knees, and made them yet more tender for the saddle. The two straps, for sword and shield, pressed his wet clothes against his body, and caused twinges of rheumatism in his sword-arm. The burnished helm, crammed firmly on the hood of the hauberk, glowed from the reflected rays of the sun, and a regular succession of drops fell from his noseguard to the saddlehorn. A blinding cloud of dust enveloped the column, save for the leading files, where rode the Duke of Normandy, the Count of Blois, and the Count of Boulogne. There was a smell of woodsmoke, ordure, and petrefaction on the south-east wind. They were obviously catching up with the main army at last.

The head of the column halted when they reached the crest of a small saddle in the hills, and the rear hastily pulled up in a series of jerks, for fear of being kicked by the warhorses in front. Evidently the leaders were having one of their long and inconclusive conferences about where to go next. The dust blew away, for the wind was in their faces, and Roger looked about him for the first time for an hour.

The road was paved with cobblestones, and stretched straight behind them to another saddle which cut off the view; on either side were gently swelling hills, grassgrown and still green with early summer. In every direction, over the crests and beside the road, stretched ruined dykes and broken stone walls, while in the valley below two apple trees grew beside the scorched foundations of a group of stone buildings. The contours of the hills reminded him of his own South Downs, though in the south-west mountains rose behind them. Yet nowhere was there smoke, or growing corn, or grazing animals. This was the border of the Turks, harried for fifteen years.

The column of foot came over the hill behind them; since nearly every man led a packhorse it flowed towards them like an endless snake, the rear still out of sight. At last the horseman in front moved on. Roger put Jack into a walk when the movement reached him, and the cloud of dust rose again. Roger was in the left-hand file, and his right-hand neighbour, who was suffering from toothache, had nothing to say for himself; so he rode in silence, thinking only of the heat and his own discomfort.

About midday there was some excitement in the advance-guard, as they climbed the shoulder of another hill. Roger hoisted up his shield, and put his bridle-arm through the grips, but the news was quickly passed back; they were at last in sight of Nicaea.

Soon all the cavalry in the main body could see it, and Roger woke up and began to pay attention. Here at last were the enemies of God. The town looked smaller than he had expected, as all towns do seen from above, but the line of walls could be made out, completely enclosing it. High and straight, broken at intervals by tall square towers, they gleamed golden in the sun, as formidable as the Aurelian walls of Rome, though not so terrifying as the triple girdle of Constantinople. On the right stretched the lake, and north, east, and south were the camps of the pilgrims. This was the Holy War at last, and the long journey through peaceful Christian lands was over. It was 1 June 1097, eleven months since he had left Sussex.

Duke Robert, with the Normans of Normandy, rode right past the town and halted on the south side. Then the criers gave orders that the camp should be pitched where they stood, beside the followers of the Count of Toulouse. Roger dismounted where he was, stuck the butt-end of his lance in the ground, and waited for Peter and Godric to find him. It was hopeless to look for them in that crowd of men and baggage animals. Presently Peter arrived, leading the hackney; the horse bore a light sack of clothing, and after he had been disarmed, for no one could put on or take off a mail shirt by himself, he set off, in his best tunic and mantle, to visit the other camps. His bivouac would be complete when the baggage-horse arrived, since he had no tent.

It was only mid-afternoon, and he walked, since he was saddle-sore. This was the first time he had seen the host of the pilgrims gathered in one place, and the crowds stunned and bewildered him. The Provençal camp was large and well-organized, consisting chiefly of huts built of timber and roofed with brushwood. They had been encamped a fortnight, and the stench was appalling. So was the noise. The women were collecting grain from the Greek merchants who had brought the supplies promised by the Emperor; it was supposed to be free, but the Greeks were reluctant to give it over for nothing, and there was shouting and gesticulation. There seemed to be little military activity, though in front of the camp was a line of Greek balistas, with Provençal footmen at the winches, and a detachment of crossbows and spearmen stood at a respectful distance from the south gate, ready to repel a sortie. This was businesslike, and even the women seemed to be well fed. Evidently the Count of Toulouse could look after himself and his contingent.

But the language, so different from north French, made conversation difficult. He went on to the next camp, on the eastern face of the town. This was also stoutly built and well guarded, though the language difficulty was even greater, for it was the camp of the Duke of Lotharingia, and many of his followers spoke nothing but German. He inquired of a priest, in Latin, where the Normans of Italy were to be found, and was directed to the camp over against the north wall.

The camp of the Count of Taranto was quite different from the others, and did not look at all Norman, either. Many of the servants were dark-skinned, and spoke an unknown language; there were few wooden huts and many pavilions of cloth, some decorated with silk. The main guard consisted of fully-armed knights who stood holding their horses out of balista-range of the north gate. Since these men were not busy at the moment, while everyone else in camp was engaged in tending the horses or getting supper ready, Roger approached a young knight who stood rather in the rear, leaning on his lance.

'Good evening, sir. I am Roger fitzOsbert de Bodeham in England and I have just arrived with the Duke of Normandy. Will you tell me how the war is going?'

The other looked him up and down. He was a dark young man, in his twenties, and his white-toothed smile was gay and welcoming. He answered in good though hesitating north French:

'This siege, like me, is standing still. But something is up behind the scenes; the Greeks are making some preparations about the lake, and there is a suggestion that the Turkish commander may be bribed to surrender. What is the news from Normandy, and particularly from Eu; my grandfather William came from there, and my name is Robert fitzRalph de Santa Fosca in Apulia.'

'Then, sir, we are cousins. My father holds from the Count of Eu in England and was born his man in Normandy; his uncle William went to Italy, though we never heard how he got on.'

Robert put out his hand, sliding the reins to his elbow. They chattered excitedly of names and dates, and established that they were second cousins. Then, of course, talk turned to the war. From Italy they had followed much the same route to Constantinople, though Robert had been earlier by six months, and could give an account of the discussions and negotiations there; he seemed to be very full of inside information, for a simple knight, and always attributed the lowest motives to everybody. The thing that interested him most was the question of the pilgrims' future conquests, and their relation to the Greek Emperor. Roger had never given this much thought; he had supposed that he would help to conquer towns and castles from the Turks and other infidels, and would end his days holding one of them against the enemy, but he had never bothered who his overlord would be. Robert was eager to know what oaths he had taken, and he explained that in England he was landless, and no man's man, but that before setting out he had become the man of the Duke of Normandy, only for the duration of the pilgrimage. The Duke had taken the oath to the Greek Emperor, the same oath which had caused such trouble earlier, and that of course bound his men, though when the Duke left for home they would be free.

'But that is splendid,' cried Robert. 'The Count of Taranto is the Emperor's man, and he intends to stay out here; so I am bound to him, whether in Romania or Italy. But you will soon be as free as air, and if you can get hold of a castle, you may take it to the highest bidder. I know what Bohemund is up to; he is trying to get Antioch from the Emperor. If I hold from him, and find that I have to rebel for some good reason, I shall have your castle as a refuge.'

This was going much too fast for Roger, who explained that he probably would never get a castle to himself, that if he did he would get it from some lord, to whom he would owe suit and service, and that pilgrims under a vow should not talk of oathbreaking. Robert listened with a grave face, and agreed with everything he said, but didn't seem to be paying much attention. Then, as the night guard of crossbowmen were seen to be getting under arms, they parted, agreeing to meet the following evening, if they were both off duty.

Roger walked back towards his lines, too deep in thought to notice the hubbub of the camp settling down for the night. He recalled the eleven months' journey he had made. First from Rye by ship to the mouth of the Seine, and then by easy stages to Rouen; the six weeks' waiting in Normandy, getting to know the other pilgrims, and fearful that it would be all over without him unless they started soon. Then the always unpunctual Duke had set out, and they had journeyed south through France, Burgundy, and Savoy until they reached Italy. It had been a march from the confines of civilization to its centre, from barbarism to the seat of culture. Supplies had been plentiful in the closely tilled south, and the people had been glad to see them. The different languages, from north French to Italian, had melted gradually from one into the next, without any abrupt barrier, so that you could not help picking up a bit as you went along, and everywhere the literate clerks could speak Latin. The manner of living was the same as at home, in spite of the increasing splendour of the towns; each village was held by a knight, who held of a count, who held of a king or an emperor, the vines and olives were a new experience, but otherwise the pattern was unaltered. Even Rome was as he had expected, from the countless descriptions of pilgrims and ecclesiastics who crossed Sussex and Kent on their way to London. Southern Italy was part of the same world, a world where peasants, speaking various queer languages, were ruled by French- or Roman-speaking knights, who held land by military tenure. When Bishop Odo of Bayeux died in Palermo, he had not really wandered very far from home.

But after the olives and wine of the mild Italian winter, they had crossed the sea into a completely different world. That six weeks' ride from Dyrrhaccium to Constantinople had not been at all difficult or arduous, for strange Greek barons, in long silk robes like Mass vestments, had arranged the route and assembled provisions. But human relationships were so completely different, so unlike the sensible, everlasting foundations of the Christian life at home, that it was almost impossible to understand them. In the first place, there was the language difficulty; no one spoke Latin, the tongue that would carry a man from Spain to Norway, from Ireland to Hungary; the very letters of their writing were incomprehensible, and seemed to mock the pilgrims with a spurious likeness to the proper alphabet of civilized man. The troops of the Greek envoys, who guarded the pilgrimage from the savage mountaineers, seemed to be respectable men, but they were all soldiers. The churches were strange, too; so shapeless that a man could not tell from the outside where the East might lie, and so amazingly gorgeous within. He had ventured into one in Thessalonica, choosing the early afternoon when Mass would be over and Vespers not begun, as he did not wish to imperil his soul by taking part in a schismatic service. The height of the dome had astonished him, and the host of saints, angels, and armed men depicted on the wall cowed him like a living crowd; the altar was hidden by a carved and shining screen and the wheel-shaped candelabrum overhead seemed to

37

threaten like a suspended club. It was a jealous and secretive God who was worshipped there. A doorkeeper had come up and jabbered at him and he had been glad to leave.

Oddest of all was the whole economic and military organization of the Empire of Romania, as he had gradually realized it in the course of his journey. On the one hand were the mountaineers, who paid tribute when they had to and plundered when they could; that was normal enough, for an armed knight could never catch them on their hillsides, and the same thing happened in Wales. But the plain country was owned in a very curious way; most of it belonged to rich men who lived in towns, who took rent in money from their tenants, and paid taxes in money to the Emperor. Nobody did military service, and soldiers were hired to defend the towns. There was not a single knight in the whole Empire of Romania! All was guarded by soldiers; even the barons who conducted them were in a sense soldiers also, for they were not born to their positions, but served the Emperor for pay. Furthermore, the Emperor himself, though of noble birth and the son of a leader of soldiers, had no more right to his throne than Count Harold to the crown of England. He had won it in battle, and would hold it until he was overthrown by a stronger. No wonder these Easterners needed Normans to defend them, rebels, schismatics, and oath-breakers that they were.

So the march had continued, through the vineyards and the mulberry plantations, round the shining white towns half-hidden by their high straight walls, with the sea on the right hand, and the hills of Thrace on the left. Then as they rode over gently undulating green swells, with the red earth showing in the gullies and the roads, they were aware of a regular level line in the far distance, stretching seemingly from horizon to horizon. As they drew nearer, the line was broken by towers and roofs, then it dissolved into row after row of walls, running from right to left as far as the eye could discern, with the gleaming helms of sentinels reflecting the sun from the battlements, banners flying from the towers, and behind it the murmur and smell of a multitude – the Triple Walls of Constantinople.

It was not only the largest city they had seen, but of an altogether different order of magnitude, as Russia is larger than Middlesex; nor was it friendly. The gates were kept shut, and it was difficult to get permission to enter. Roger had not been inside; he had no wish to trust himself among this alien crowd, that showed so little gratitude for Norman aid. He had not even seen the Emperor, for when the Duke gave his oath at a meeting in the suburban camp of the pilgrims he had been absent collecting forage from a Greek village. All the other pilgrims had already crossed into Asia, and indeed the siege of Nicaea was already formed, so they had not lingered. A quick crossing of the Bosphorus, two days marching in the uplands of Bithynia, and here they were with the main arm. But what a strange land, how terrifying the queer motives and actions of these people, and what worlds away from Sussex!

With these sad thoughts clouding his mind, Roger wandered slowly back to his bivouac. Peter was absent, with one of the troops of grazing horses that strayed under guard on the nearby hills, but Godric had prepared his master's bedding, and told him supper for the knights of the second rank was arranged by the pavilion of the Duke.

The front of the Duke's pavilion had been looped up, and the high table faced the open air, while the lesser knights squatted at boards laid on the ground, running at right angles from it. Roger found himself sitting between a young knight from the Cotentin, and a middle-aged priest from Brittany. The high table was unusually full, and Roger asked who the guests might be.

'The Count of Toulouse,' answered the priest, 'and his courtiers. That is Count Raymond himself sitting beside the Duke, at his right hand; on his left is the Bishop of Puy, who ought really to have the highest place, since he is the Pope's Legate in charge of the pilgrimage. But the holy man is a vassal of Toulouse, and will not sit above his lord.'

The young knight on the other side joined in the conversation. 'The Count of Toulouse should always have the highest place among the pilgrims. Not only is he a warrior who has done great deeds in Spain, not only did he come the whole way here on his horse, fighting his way through the mountaineers of Sclavonia, but he is the only free prince we have among us, untrammelled by any oath. He could set up a third Empire in the Holy Land, if he wished, without leave of Alexius or Henry. If he stays, after the Duke has gone home, I shall take service under his banner.'

'All this endless talk about oaths!' said Roger. 'I wasn't there when the Duke took his, though of course I am his man and it binds me. But it seems to me quite a reasonable thing to have done. We are here to help the Christians of the East, and if they provide for us suitably, as they are doing now,' and he waved a mutton chop, 'I am willing to fight their battles for them.' He spoke more often, and more loudly, than he had done a year ago.

'Exactly. If they provide for us suitably,' agreed the priest. 'As a matter of fact, they are drawing up a treaty about it. The Bishop of Puy's archdeacon is writing our version of it this evening; I used to know him at Clermont and he told me so this afternoon.'

'That is bad news,' said the knight from the Cotentin. 'Everyone knows what an oath means; but once you get things written down, any clerk can twist it to mean what he likes. My uncle holds by a written charter from the Abbey of Mont-Saint-Michel, and I know by experience. In three months we shall be fighting the Emperor, if we argue on parchment now.'

Roger felt there was something in this. He remembered the discontent that was caused by the writing down of all the holdings in England in Domesday Book, and he was sorry all these Christian princes could not trust each other better. But he was anxious to know more.

'It is no good, Father, you telling me what is written in the treaty; I don't know the language of lawyers. But will you explain it in simple words. For example, what is going to happen to this town when we take it?'

'The treaty is quite clear on that,' said the priest, 'and so is the oath. This town will go back to the Emperor, and I suppose he will give it to some good knight to hold for him. Until quite recently the Emperor of Romania held lands stretching for hundreds of miles to the eastwards, up to Antioch and beyond. It has only been lost in the last twenty-five years. I don't know where the boundary was; though I hope the people did who drew up that treaty.'

The talk then turned to the prospects of the siege, and the difficulty of finding forage for the horses; soon after Roger went off to his bedding. He thought of the conversation he had listened to during this first day of war; there seemed to be too many legal arguments for warriors on pilgrimage. His cousin Robert appeared to know a good deal about feudal law; he would consult him tomorrow. He was soon asleep.

The next day he spent a lazy morning, though he heard Mass first. Some of the Normans overslept badly, and even missed that, which was rather shocking on such a pilgrimage. After dinner he was on the main guard before the south gate, but without his horse, as it was thought easier to defend the siege-engines on foot. He was interested in the work of the balistas, machines he had never seen before, which threw large boulders, always aimed at the same corner of one tower by the gate. They were directed by Greek engineers, excitable unmilitary men in cloth tunics, who pushed and slapped the crews composed of Provençal footmen and grooms. It disturbed him that schismatics should give orders to good Christians, but of course the war must be carried on. As far as he could see, no damage was done to the corner of the tower, and the garrison on the walls often cheered, and shot arrows which fell short. In the evening the guard was relieved, and after being disarmed he went to meet his cousin at the appointed place.

The sun was setting, but Bithynia is warm in the evening in June. Roger had spent all his money during the comfortable winter in Italy, and all he had left was a silver chain that his father had given him at parting. With one link of this chain he bought quite a large pottery jar of wine; the jar itself interested him; he was used to leather jacks or wooden casks, and it seemed sinful that such a well-made pot should be thrown away when it was empty. Robert found him without difficulty, and they sat on a pile of balista-stones, taking turns at the wine, and chatting till supper should be ready.

After family reminiscences had been discussed, Roger opened the subject that had been troubling him.

41

'You were at Constantinople for this oath-taking, and I think you know a good deal about law. Please tell me what you think of it.'

'I do know some law, as it affects people like us,' said Robert, settling himself to deliver a long speech. 'That is because I have been at the conquest of new lands in Sicily. Your manor was conquered before you were born, and you grew up knowing your father's rights and duties; but all these things have to be settled when new manors are given for the first time. In the first place, an oath has two sides; you swear to be somebody's man, and he swears to do something for you, either to protect what you already have, or to help you to conquer more. If the lord breaks his share of the contract, rebellion is justified. Now what are we doing for the Emperor? We are helping him to reconquer his lands, and to defend the remnant that he still holds. What is he doing for us? Well, we are going to eat his supper in an hour. He has fed and protected us, which is useful and, I suppose, kind of him. But so did the counts of Burgundy and Lombardy protect you when you passed through their lands, yet no one took an oath to the Emperor Henry, their overlord. In my opinion, he is not doing all that a lord should to protect his men. Where is his army? And where is he? He should be here with the whole army of Romania, not sitting on his throne at Constantinople. I think the Count of Toulouse was right, an oath to do nothing against his honour and dominion was quite enough. But I don't think you realize the fix we were in at Constantinople.'

'I suppose it was rather awkward,' said Roger.

'Rather awkward! We were in a bloody trap. Walter's miserable crew were sent straight across to Asia, but before we arrived they had come back with their tails down. The Emperor had the impertinence to arrest the Count of Vermandois, own brother to the King of France, and held him as a hostage. The Count of Taranto wouldn't bring us up to the city, for fear we should storm the walls in spite of him. We were left encamped at Rusa, with no ships to cross the sea and a Greek army of soldiers to see we did not forage, while the Count went on to the Emperor to arrange some sort of peace. Of course we were in no danger; we could have fought our way home at any time. But we couldn't cross into Asia without Greek ships, and we would have looked silly if we had gone back to Italy with nothing but a few Greek heads, when we set out to conquer Antioch. No, the Count had to take the oath for his followers, and that includes me, but I am not happy about the position.'

In his excitement Robert was using more and more Italian words, and waving his arms in a most un-Norman manner. Roger answered slowly, speaking distinctly in north French, to bring the conversation back to a language that he understood.

'It remains that your Count took the oath for you, and my Duke did the same for me. That binds us both, at least till our lords release us. Meanwhile we are engaged on a holy enterprise, and the least we can do is to keep our sworn undertakings.'

'There I agree,' said Robert more calmly. 'Oaths must be kept, for oaths bind this army together, and indeed all our livelihood rests on them. But your talk of a holy enterprise only brings more confusion. Your Duke has come here, meaning to go back home with increased glory and greater strength to fight his brother; but the Count of Taranto is here to live and die in Romania, fighting the Turks. You think of freeing the Holy Places, I think of beating back the unbelievers wherever they may be, and the two aims should be kept separate. The Count wants to hold some big city from the Emperor, Antioch for choice, and therefore he must keep on good terms with him. Let those who don't intend to stay go on to free Jerusalem, while we settle down in some border fortress, and defend Christendom from there.'

'I should like to free Jerusalem before I win a castle, and oaths should be kept on a pilgrimage,' said Roger with a frown.

'Well, let us leave things as they are, and keep our oaths as long as we can,' said Robert cheerfully. 'We will see what happens to this town, when it falls, and that will not be very long. That garrison cheers too much; they can't really be very happy, and there may be something in this story about bribing the commander.'

The wine was finished, and they got up to stroll over to the supper-place, where a crowd was already gathered.

That night Roger went to sleep with a buzzing head, after listening to many highly-coloured stories of the wars of Sicily. He was delighted to have a cousin and a friend in the most war-like contingent of the army, and he hoped to get good advice about fighting from him. The tangled question of feudal obliga-tion could wait till they got to Antioch. He woke late and missed Mass for the first time since leaving Italy.

* * *

For a fortnight the siege went on, and Roger settled into the habits of army life. The weather was dry and warm, and as he got used to the climate his armour chafed him less. The Emperor provided abundant food and wine, and Godric had built him a fairly wind-proof hut of turf. But the garrison still shouted from the walls, and the balistas still made no impression on the tower. The siege seemed ready to go on for ever, and he realized that war is nine-tenths routine.

The end came suddenly. On 17 June, Greek ships appeared on the lake, brought overland from the Gulf of Nicomedia, a tech-nical feat that only Greeks could have accomplished. These ships could batter the wall by the lake with their engines, and also cut off supplies that the Turks smuggled in by rowing-boat after dark. Then at midday on the 18th, while Roger was in his hut and Godric was helping him into his mail shirt, there was a sudden outbreak of shouts and cheers from the whole southern camp. Roger ran outside, without hauberk or helm, his mail shirt flapping unlaced. The tower, that had been so long the target of the balistas, had crashed outwards in a cloud of dust. Now was the time for an assault, while the defenders were still dismayed, but the opportunity was lost; the morning guard was due to be relieved in a few minutes, and many of them had slipped away to get good places for dinner; the afternoon guard, of whom Roger was one, were not yet armed. A half-hearted advance by the few knights who were ready was called off by the Duke's criers, and soon the garrison lined the breach in great strength. The Count of Toulouse rode through the crowd, in tunic and mantle, to show that no fighting was intended, and the attackers dispersed, leaving Roger with the new guard staring across the old familiar two hundred yards of dusty ground.

When he came off duty for supper he heard that a grand assault was definitely fixed for the next day, at the fifth hour (11 a.m.), when the garrison would have lost the alertness of early morning, and the sun would be behind the attackers. There was a good deal of heavy drinking in camp that night, but Roger was too excited by the prospect of his first battle to need wine to stimulate him further, and he wandered into the Lotharingian camp. There he found a strange priest to shrive him, which was much less embarrassing than confessing his sins to a comrade whom he would meet at meals.

In the morning Godric brought him his breakfast of bread dipped in wine. After living together for a year they could communicate easily in a mixture of ungrammatical Saxon and mispronounced north French. His servant told him the rumours of the night; that trumpets had been heard in the town, and the marching of troops; evidently the garrison was getting ready for an obstinate defence. He polished his sword and helm, while the other went carefully over his mail shirt, renewing any that looked frayed of the leather thongs that held on the overlapping iron plates. An hour before the time fixed for the assault, he was in his place behind the balistas, which still played on the curtain and the breach.

Knights were drifting up in ones and twos, so as not to alarm the defenders, while the poorer sort were kept out of sight behind the huts. As he glanced idly round, he noticed something different about the wall; he looked more closely: that was it! A banner was removed, and he saw that they were disappearing from tower after tower. Then one was replaced, but it looked different. Of course, it was not the same shape; instead of the flag streaming from a pole used by the Turks, this had a cross-piece, with the cloth hanging down the staff. Then another was displayed from a nearer tower, and he could make out the charge – the Saint Andrew's cross of the Labarum, the flag of the Empire of Romania. Suddenly a trumpet blew, the south gate opened, and there stood a party of Greek soldiers!

A roar of disappointment came from the crowd of watching

45

pilgrims. Without thinking they began to advance, brandishing their swords, while the footmen came running from behind the huts. But the gates were quickly shut, and Greek archers appeared on the wall. Then the Count of Toulouse appeared once more on horseback, in full armour but with his grey beard streaming over his open hauberk and his shield hanging from the saddle. He raised his arm for silence, and at last was able to make himself heard.

'Pilgrims! Our generous friend the Emperor of Romania now holds the good town of Nicaea. Respect his garrison. The plunder will be ours. Wise and discreet men from our camp shall enter the city to gather it, but the host will remain outside the walls. Return to your huts. There will be no assault.' Grumbling, the crowd slouched away.

What seemed most strange, in the whole strange business, was that no Turkish garrison came out; they would hardly have surrendered without the promise of life and freedom, since only one tower was down and the breach was strong. In the afternoon Godric, most conspicuously unarmed, managed to join a party of the poorer sort who were allowed to go and see the town. Roger thought it undignified to enter without his sword, and took Jack and his other horses out grazing. When Godric returned he had a strange story to tell.

'You know, sir, if you ask me the whole thing was a put-up job. They have restored the churches that the Turks used for their devil worship, and that's about all they have done. There are the Turkish knights, sitting in the doorways of their houses. None of them are going to be turned out, and by tomorrow I expect they will all be soldiers of the Emperor. The townspeople seem to be more frightened of us than of them; of course, they are all Greeks, anyway, and it seems they helped the Turks to surrender to the Greek commander, for fear they would lose their filthy possessions if it came to a sack. Serve them right if we burnt the town over their heads. All the same, it is a lovely place, better than any we saw in Italy. You should see the paved streets, and the pillars and the arches, and the shops round the market-place. At least, there ought to be some good plunder, if it's collected honestly.'

There was nothing to be done about it. So far, helping the Christians of the East seemed to mean helping the Emperor of Romania. Roger wandered away.

He was very lonely and homesick. There were plenty of other knights of his own class and upbringing with the pilgrimage, but most of them were older, and all seemed to have seen war before they set out. The Duke's following was the only contingent that had not been compelled to fight before reaching the Greek capital, and on account of it they felt slightly inferior. His comrades did not seem to have the interest he had in oaths of service and the mutual obligations of vassal and lord; they took their oaths willingly, but always with the thought of rebellion in the back of their minds. England was a long way over the horizon, eleven months away as they had marched, and many weeks' journey even for a messenger. England was a remote province of civilization, nearly surrounded by barbarians, Scotch, Irish, and Welsh; but on the south-east lay all the countries of the Franks, France, Spain, Italy, the Empire, with Rome at the centre; and the limits were everywhere expanding against the infidel (he had been brought up on tales of the wars in Spain and against the Slavs). Now he had marched clean through the lands of Latin speech and the Roman obedience, and come to this pale imitation of Christendom as he knew it, this land of mighty cities and wasted fields, where there were no lords or vassals, only taxpayers and taxgatherers, mercenary soldiers, and the mighty Emperor who held his throne by successful rebellion. He wanted to hear the monks singing in Battle Abbey, to see a manor-court or a tavern that sold beer, and they were all such miles away. He curled up in his blankets, and wept with longing for Sussex.

Next day, Roger idled about the camp. He saw an ox-wagon draw up at a ruined farm near the town, and a Greek family, with women and children, get busy at putting up a sod roof. Peasants spent their lives doing that, repairing the work of armies, but it showed that they thought the Turks were driven away for good. At dinner-time criers went round the eating-places saying that the plunder had been collected, and would be distributed by the leaders to their men an hour before supper. Roger

47

was early at the Duke's pavilion, and joined the crowd of knights who sat their horses in front of the foot; for every man had been told to come armed, so that he might be paid according to his efficiency as a warrior. The spoil was disappointing, though the older knights agreed that it always was, and that what made a city look rich came to very little when it was divided among thousands. At least, the Duke of Normandy would not keep back more than his fair share, whatever the other leaders might do; he was too notorious a spendthrift for that.

The Duke's clerks sat on a bench behind a trestle table covered with cloth marked off in squares, like the Exchequer at Rouen, and the valuables were handed to them by the Duke's servants; meanwhile Duke Robert, all unarmed, strolled about in the background, grinning all over his face. The Count of Blois and the Count of Boulogne were called up first, and each received several gold cups; then the barons dismounted and came to the table, leaving their horses with grooms. The knights with mail breeches came before Roger, who was one of the last to be called; he found his share was three large silver coins and a piece clipped out of a flat silver dish. One of the coins could easily be divided in two, as the full-length figure of Our Lady ran down the middle of it; so he gave one and a half each to Peter and Godric, who were unarmed and therefore received no share of their own. The bit of silver plate was quite small enough to go in his pouch, and that he kept for himself.

That evening there was much gambling, drunkenness, and rioting in the camp; but Roger was too poor to gamble, and he had seen enough to realize that the price of wine would be very exorbitant, so he spent another quiet night by himself. Next morning Godric called him at dawn as usual, and stood about waiting for permission to speak.

'It's like this, sir,' he began, in his awkward jumble of languages. 'I told you what a fine place the town is, and not by any means full of people. Well, the Emperor has set aside a quarter for the pilgrims who want to settle down in it, with a church and a building for monks, and they will live tax-free for the first two years. I met an English soldier from the Varangians

48

who are in garrison there, and he told me all about it; they have quite a lot of English in their army. Now I would like to settle there and start a shop for leatherwork. I have got the tools I brought with me, and hides are easy enough to get hold of. You will remember, sir, that I was a townsman of Rye before we started; I am not your man, and only followed you for protection on the road; you have paid me, and we can call it quits. Do you mind if I leave you here, sir?'

'You are no man of mine, and can leave me if you wish,' said Roger. 'But there are two things to think of. First, how will you get on, in such a strange land, with a strange language? The second is the matter of your pilgrimage. You are under a vow; have you fulfilled it?'

'As to the strangeness of the land, that will not upset me. England is a strange land to the English now, with new masters and new laws and a new language. Here I shall be as good as any other Latin, and everyone is equal under the Emperor and his law. The vow of the pilgrimage doesn't bother me at all; surely I have accomplished it. I swore to go to the Eastern world and help to protect the churches of the East from the infidel; but I am in Romania, and I have been at the taking of a great town which was infidel and is now Christian. There are not many Latin churches in these parts, but there will be one here. I can settle here with a good conscience, and live as a free man, with no lord but the Emperor. But I don't want to part bad friends with you, sir.'

'Very well,' said Roger. 'Go in peace and with my friendship. I am a knight, and must march forward as long as there is fighting to be done, but you are, after all, completely unarmed. From now on we go through the enemy's land, and if my armour breaks I shall be dead inside it, so I shall not want you to repair it. If you think you have accomplished your vow, I shall not dispute with you. Go with my good will, and pray for me.' He never saw Godric again.

* * *

It was given out that the pilgrims would march on 27 June, and Roger sold the hackney; a priest from Lotharingia gave a good

49

price for it, four pieces of gold; for horses were beginning to die from the heat and the foul water round the camp. The Treaty was working quite well, although it was a disappointment that Nicaea had not been given to some lord of the Franks to hold from the Emperor. The plunder had been collected honestly, and the Greeks were not keeping the town to themselves, but allowing pilgrims to settle there. No one could complain of the way the army was being fed. It was said that a Greek force was being prepared to accompany them, though the Emperor himself would not take the field.

Best omen of all was the ease with which the town had fallen. As Robert said one day when they were guarding the horses together: 'It only shows that the people of the Eastern world don't know how to fight. We were forty years conquering Italy, but the infidels overran this whole country, from Antioch to the sea, in less than five years. It was as easy as the conquest of England. They say these Turkish barons quarrel among themselves; when they are attacked by people who are not afraid of them, they surrender as soon as a tower crumbles. Also I am told the Turks can be bribed to go away. They haven't dared to meet us in the field; they have lost their chief town with hardly a fight; I think we shall be in Antioch in six weeks, and in Jerusalem by next winter.'

The army marched in high spirits.

3

DORYLAEUM

1097

AT dawn on 1 July the camp was already stirring. Peter was saddling the warhorse Jack and Roger had to get a passing cross-bowman to arm him; Godric's desertion was a great nuisance, but it was his own fault for taking a townsman to war; they never would stick it out to the end. He was stiff from sleeping on the ground, and his stomach was slightly upset. They were running short of supplies, and supper had been meagre; nearly everything they ate had to come across the straits from Europe, so harried was eastern Romania, and the cowardly Greek sutlers hung back now the pilgrims were deep in infidel territory. When he was armed he made his way to the Duke's pavilion, and was lucky to get for breakfast a lump of twice-baked bread dipped in watered wine. There was no time to hear Mass if they were to be on the march before the heat of the day, though everyone knew the Turks were near, and this was not a good way to begin a battle. There was also a slight shortage of drinking water, chiefly because the footmen were too lazy to fetch enough of it, and although he was not exactly thirsty he felt constipated and liverish. However, he bolted his lump of biscuit, and retired behind a hillock, where his nose told him many of the other pilgrims were also getting ready for the day.

After that he felt better, and when he had seen the pack-horse loaded, and Peter had led it to the baggage-column, he mounted and rode to the mustering place of the knights of the second rank. There were many hundreds of them, too many to count accurately, for the whole Norman contingent, from England, Normandy, Sicily, and Apulia, were marching together, and they formed about half of the host. They were more or less under the leadership of the Count of Taranto, so long as their lords were inclined to obey his orders. The Frenchmen, Provençals, and Lotharingians were a few miles to the south, ostensibly for better foliage, but really because everyone knew that the Count of Toulouse would not take orders from a Norman.

Roger had heard that a battle was likely that day, and to show his eagerness he trotted up completely prepared for war, shield an arm and hauberk laced; but he noticed at once that the others had not bothered to get ready yet, and hastily he hung his shield by his left leg, his helm from the saddlebow, and threw back the hood of his hauberk on to his shoulders; then he stuck the butt of his lance in the ground and sat his horse carelessly beside it, though he would have preferred to continue muttering prayers for success and his own safety. The Duke appeared, mounted and in armour, though his shield and weapons were carried behind him by a page. He rode among them, cheerful and courteous as always, and recommended rather than ordered them to form a column. The paved highway pointed straight at the gate of deserted Dorylaeum, another ruined town in that land of ruins, completely empty and not worth plundering. So they left the road, and marched south-east across the rolling grasslands, dotted with burnt-out remains of farms, and crossed in all directions by overgrown dykes. This was once the granary and recruiting-ground of Romania, now it produced nothing but the desert grazing of the Turks. Even the grass was scanty, and dried by the summer heat, and Jack was no longer in good condition.

They rode six abreast over the open country. Behind a screen of scouts came first the counts and barons, well-armed and well-mounted, the striking-force of the army; then the knights of the second rank, with hungry horses and unarmed legs; last of all straggled the baggage and the foot, with the clerks and women. There were also a few scouts on the flanks, but no rear-guard, for the enemy was known to be in front. Roger found himself between Ralph de Rendlesham, a knight from Suffolk, and Hugh de Dives, a Norman who was said to have been a routier in Flanders, but had made money, and now claimed to be a knight. They both seemed calm and not very interested, and Roger was comforted to think that in his first charge he would have a veteran riding at each knee. Hugh was a pleasant, well-spoken, middle-aged man, and in the long ride from Apulia Roger had found him fond of giving advice, so now he mentioned that he had never drawn a sword in earnest before.

'Not everyone would have told me that,' said Hugh. 'Half these lads would be boasting of the hundreds they had slain. I like your modesty, and I'll keep an eye on you. Try to follow me, and do as I do, and you won't come to much harm; it's the young knights who want to make a name for themselves in their first battle who get killed. In the first place, don't get ready too soon; we have scouts in front, and there will be plenty of time to put your shield on your neck when you see the enemy; some young men tire their bridle-arms before the fighting begins. Then, for the love of Our Lady, don't try to charge on your own; the trouvères are all back with the baggage, and no one can become famous in his first battle, don't throw away your lance in the first shock; if they stand and the fighting gets close you can pull out your sword when I do. Finally, remember it is the first duty of a knight to stand by his comrade who is on the ground. If you see me dismounted clear a space for me to get up, and if you come down yourself lie still under your shield till the hoofs have gone by, then go to the rear unless you can catch a loose horse. A knight on foot hinders his own side when we are charging.' But it was not to be that sort of battle at all.

They had been on the march for an hour, and the column had lengthened owing to delays in crossing the ruined dykes, when they saw the scouts come galloping back, not only from the front, but all along the left flank also. The army halted in a disjointed fashion, each man pulling up in turn to avoid the horse in front, and messengers were seen riding hard from the barons in the advance to the straggling baggage-train and foot. They were in a shallow valley, with a reedy lake to their right rear, and low hills forming the skyline a few hundred yards on either hand. The scouts had been on the crests of these hills before they were alarmed. Roger saw Hugh drop his reins and begin lacing his hauberk, and hastily he also arrayed himself. His fingers fumbled with the shield-grips, his bowels seemed over-full, dancing liver-spots were in front of his eyes, and all his bones felt stiff and awkward. His hauberk rasped the week's growth of beard on his chin, for now Godric had stayed behind there was no one to clip it, and a cold sweat formed on his forehead under the nose-guard of his helm, which itself felt insecure, at once too small and too heavy. He had never felt less like fighting. On the skyline of the left-hand ridge, only four hundred yards away, appeared several tall black objects, spaced out evenly from before the extreme front of the vanguard to beyond the hurrying clusters of foot in the rear; these objects seemed to grow suddenly taller, then below them appeared a solid line of heads and brandished weapons, and he knew them for the horse-tail standards of the Turks.

The long column of Norman knights was jostling in a stationary haze of dust, as each man turned left where his horse stood, and then tried to push himself into the foremost line. Jack had his muzzle in the tail of Ralph's stallion, and Roger hauled him back a pace, fearing a kick. But all the horses were wellused to crowds, after their long march across Europe, and they got into position without any casualties that he could see. He found himself in the second rank, with Hugh on his right hand, and a knight whom he only knew by sight on his left. By now the hill was crowned with the Turkish array, stretching along the skyline, its right far outflanking the pilgrims' rear, which had become their left. The knot of counts and barons had broken up, and the leaders were galloping down the front of the line towards the baggage. He saw the Duke, his helm pushed back so that the noseguard projected horizontally, cantering along while he shouted over the shield on his left shoulder:

'Pilgrims, stand fast where you are! Pilgrims, don't charge them uphill! Halt, pilgrims, and let them come down into the valley! No knight is to charge until I give the word!'

He cantered on, taking his helm right off his head that all might see who he was, his voice breaking into a shriek from the effort of reaching the distant ranks. The Counts of Blois and Boulogne followed, and the pushing, heaving line slowed down and halted, though a trampling noise still rose from the restless horses. Jack was covered with sweat, reaching at his bit and getting his back up, and Roger found it difficult to control him with the finger-ends that were all he could spare from his shield.

'Hold him!' cried Hugh. 'Hold him! Push your wrist through the shield-grips and get a hold of the reins! If you let him get away now we shall start a charge at the wrong time and lose the whole blasted battle. For God's sake, young man, if you can't control your horse, get off and lead him. Give the foot a chance to array themselves, or the Turks will snap up every bloody pack-horse before the fighting begins, and you won't have a clean shirt for Antioch. Steady there, didn't you hear what the Duke said!'

Roger dropped his lower shield-grip completely, and though the shield banged against his forearm he got a good grip of the stout leather reins, and quieted his horse. He looked at the enemy. The Turks had halted on the crest of the swelling hill; he could see four or five ranks of them, but in such loose order that it was hard to count their numbers. Their horses were small, no more than ponies, but obviously handy from the way they weaved in and out; and they were ridden with the reins very short, their heads up and their noses poking out in an un-balanced fashion; the bridle-hands were held high and crooked, and he noticed with a shock of surprise that the riders had no shields; from their fluttering draperies it appeared that they had no armour either. In fact, they did not look to be very formid-able foes, though their sudden appearance had rattled the nerves of the pilgrims.

His breathing became easier, and he looked up and down his own battleline. He was to the left of the centre, about the middle of the Duke's own following; on the right were the Normans of Sicily and Apulia, and on the left some of the Flemings, though most of these were with the second division of the army, some-where in the south, which was now their rear. Beyond the Flemings he could see a fluttering like the sails of a fleet of ships in a gale; the foot were putting up their tents at the edge of the marsh, to form an obstacle to horsemen and safeguard the left flank. The sun was shining, and the increasing heat brought out the shrilling of the cicadas. Roger had expected a battlefield to look different from any other piece of ground, purged of nonessentials, but he found it hard to drag his attention from the cloud of flies that hovered over the immobile horses, and when Jack staled he had an overpowering urge to do the same thing himself.

Suddenly there was shouting from the left, and the clouds of dust with a drumming of hoofs. 'Watch for it,' muttered Hugh. 'They are going to charge all down the line. No, they aren't, though; they are only attacking the camp. Stand fast and wait for our turn. They can't gallop through those tent-ropes.'

Word passed up the line, with all the swiftness of rumour in battle, that the Turks had caught some belated stragglers, spearmen, women, and clerks, out in the open plain, and massacred them before they could reach the shelter of the tents. But the marsh, and the solid obstacle of the camp, gave them pause, and the attack was not pushed home. Meanwhile the Turkish line on the slope opposite was growing thicker and thicker, as more horsemen rode over the brow of the hill, and already they outnumbered the battle-line of knights several times over.

'But where are their foot?' Roger heard his left-hand neighbour say. 'I don't believe they have any. Thousands and thousands of woollen-clad ruffians on ponies, and not a knight or a spearman among them. This is the queerest army I have ever seen.'

Now the infidels seemed to be growing individually bigger; this was because the line was advancing, though as they still came over the hill the rear of the huge array was not yet in sight. And they were advancing at a walk!

Roger could see the upper part of one of their own leaders, he thought it was the Count of Blois, sitting his horse at right-angles to the line, with his lance held horizontal, his whole posture giving the order to stand fast. Roger was well set now, with his shield and reins held properly, and though he was sweating all over, his eyes had cleared. But he was in a dream, looking around him as far as his hauberk would allow him to turn his head, and telling himself: 'This is what a battle looks like. This is my first battle. I mustn't miss anything of it. I must get a clear picture and remember it always.' So that when the Turks reached the bottom of the hill a hundred and fifty yards away, and the Count whirled his horse round and flourished his lance, he was left half a length at the start of the charge.

In a moment they were all galloping, with a thunder of hoofs. Roger carefully lowered his lance, till the point was level with Ralph's right knee in front of him, and he felt the calf of his own leg jostled by the acute end of Hugh's shield; Jack was out of control, with his ears back and his tail up. His teeth set, his toes far forward, and his eyes blazing on each side of his nose-guard, Roger waited for the shock. Nothing could withstand this impetus; the infidels on their light ponies would be swept out of the path. But there was no shock. Instead he saw the lean hindquarters of the Turkish horses labouring up the hill, and suddenly there came a shower of arrows. Two shot past his eyes before he could duck his head under his shield-rim, and one tapped his right shoulder with a breath-taking shock. 'Is this my death-wound?' his mind had time to ask with inconceivable rapidity, before the arrow dropped harmlessly from his mail. There was nothing within reach of his lance, and the shafts continued to whistle by. Suddenly Ralph in front of him disappeared completely. He felt Jack leap and buck unexpectedly, banging his rider's fork against the high pommel of the saddle, and then all the horses round him were pulling up, and so was he. They were on the crest of the hill, and he was in the front rank, while halfway down the slope in front were the Turks, facing them now, and shooting as fast as they could draw arrows from their quivers. The whole infidel army was composed of horse-archers, a form of equipment unknown in Western Europe, which even the wisest of Norman veterans had never met before.

They could not stay where they were, an easy target on the sky-line, and though a few angry men prepared to charge again, the leaders were wheeling their horses and shouting to them to get back. Luckily, the configuration of the ground had made the horses check at the crest of the hill, and they were saved from a scattering, unlimited charge, which would have left small parties on blown horses to be shot down one by one by the infidels. Roger was beginning to get frightened. Many knights had been unhorsed, not a Turk had been harmed, and there he was on top of the hill, with every hostile arrow seeming to converge on his face. Thank God the leaders wanted them to retreat, and he could get down the hillside without loss of dignity. He rode back with all the other knights at a slow trot, and the rise in the ground mercifully cut off the arrow-shower. He saw that Ralph was on his feet, stripping the saddle from his dead horse, and he pulled up beside him.

'Do you want any help?' he called out.

'No, thank God, I have nothing worse than bruises. Just stay by me while I carry this saddle back to our battleline. I may pick up a horse after this is over, but I shall never get a saddle that fits me as this does.'

They went slowly back to where the knights were forming up in their original position. Roger took his place in the front rank, and the dismounted stood about in rear of the second line. His neighbours had been differently affected by the failure of the charge; most were simply in a frantic rage at the cowardly infidels who wouldn't stand and fight, but a few were trying to think things out, and find a way of beating the enemy's tactics; among them was Hugh de Dives, who was now behind him in the second rank.

'Look here, Roger,' he said, 'we must get to close quarters with those infidels. Can't we make them charge us, instead of the other way about? Instead of trotting slowly down the hill we should have galloped here. A feigned flight is the oldest trick in the world, but it always works the first time you try it against strange enemies. Do your best to catch the attention of the Duke the next time he rides by, and I will suggest it to him.'

Meanwhile the enemy had crowned the hill again, and were walking down it towards them; when they reached a line about a hundred yards away, they halted, and the front ranks began to shoot. That was evidently about as far as their short horsemen's bows would carry. Roger could see the arrows coming in time to shelter behind his shield, and in fact they were not shot hard enough to penetrate mail, so that only his face, his lower legs, and his right hand were in danger; but the horses were completely exposed. He could hear the thud of arrows striking home, and the squeals of the warhorses. So could Jack, and he was nearly unmanageable, rearing up and staggering forward on his hind legs, screaming with rage and struggling to fight in the only way he knew.

The Duke came riding along the line from left to right, crouched behind his shield. He also had thought of trying a feigned flight, the favourite ruse of Norman armies in a tight place.

'Now, brave pilgrims,' he cried, 'when I give the word charge as fast and as suddenly as you can, and we may catch some of their front rank. Then, when you arrive at the crest, halt, and fly back in disorder. When you reach the dismounted knights here, turn round sharp; we may lure some of them within reach. But for God's sake keep control of your horses; no farther than the crest and no farther back than here; and keep all together. Watch my lance for your orders.'

He rode on, and Roger heard his voice, very faint, repeating the order farther to the right. Jack was still fighting his bit, and taking more out of himself at a stand than he would have done at a gallop; a wet mess of slobber from the bridle hit Roger in the face, and made it hard to keep an eye on the Duke's lance. But at last he saw it wave in the air, and then point at the enemy. He dug in his spurs, and Jack jumped straight from a stand to a sprint.

This charge was more fiery and determined than the last; also the Turks had settled down to their shooting, and were not so alert. As he sped forward Roger saw in front of him an infidel whose horse had been baulked as he swung round; he aimed his lance-point between the shoulder-blades and sat back for the shock; the Turk saw him coming and lay flat on his pony's back, the lance passed harmlessly overhead; but in the next stride they were up with him, Jack had reared up, and his ironshod forefeet crashed down on horse and man. Then they were on the crest, and looking down on the reserves of the Turkish army massed below; Roger had a glimpse of an endless multitude of ponies scurrying over the ground as far as the eye could see, and he was thankful that it was his duty to gallop back as fast as he could. He had time to notice that Jack's Turk was wriggling on the ground with a broken back.

The feigned flight did not tempt the Turks to charge, but it had been a partial success, all the same. The enemy had lost a number of men who were not quick enough in getting away, and they realized that if they sat still, their horses facing forward, some more might be snapped up in another surprise attack. Accordingly, they halted on the hilltop, and there was a pause in the main battle, though the clamour on the left showed that fighting was still going on at the camp.

Roger found himself again in the front rank, and now Hugh de Dives was beside him once more. The veteran was as talkative as ever, and discussed the fight with a detached interest, as though nobody could possibly be hurt in such an absorbing game of chess. Jack was blown now, and tired enough to stand still without being incessantly ridden.

'What happens now?' Hugh was saying. 'It seems we can't catch them, and they are too cautious to do us much harm. You will notice that they have hardly killed a man of ours here, whatever they may be doing to the foot, and we caught quite a few of them. That is a well-trained horse you are riding, by the way; he smashed his man very nicely. If only our horses last out, we ought to win this fight after all. Those ponymen are under good control, but we are deep in their land, and their patience can't last for ever; they must charge eventually, to get rid of us. If only these knights can keep their tempers and stand still. Remember what happened to the Count Palatine of Suabia, and the Count of Teck, when they were with Walter's lot outside Chalcedon, and don't try to charge till we all move together. If we sit tight and keep our order we ought to reach Antioch yet.'

This was the first hint Roger had heard that a more experienced warrior thought they might quite likely lose the battle, and it disquieted him considerably. He wondered how far Jack could carry him in a fast gallop towards Nicaea; the horse was getting his breath back, but he was no longer fresh. There was an arrow sticking in the front of the saddle-bow, and another in his shield; he dug the butt of his lance in the ground and pulled them out; where he sat he could see no blood on his horse, except by the off-fore fetlock, and that was probably Turkish. Hugh confirmed that Jack was so far unwounded.

The lull in the fighting was not of long duration. Presently a clamour arose on the right of the line, and was taken up nearer and nearer; then Roger saw a band of Turks riding down the ranks at a hand-gallop, shooting arrows as they came. Their reins hung on the ponies' necks, and, with the bow in the left hand and the string in the right, they could shoot almost as easily to the left as in front. Luckily, they had not realized yet that Western mail was proof against their arrows, and they shot at the men and not the horses. They swept down the line, shouting and twanging their bowstrings, without doing any damage that Roger could see. The Duke was riding round his men, first in front of them to the right, with his shield towards the enemy, then to the left behind the line; he called out incessantly that they should hold their ground and not charge without orders. A second party of Turks rode by, and now they were learning from experience, and shot low at the horses; many beasts were wounded, though not mortally, for the weakly impelled arrows could not penetrate from the breast to the heart, or split a skull. But a certain number were hit in an artery, many more were lamed, and all the injured animals shrieked and threw themselves about, causing gaps in the ranks. Some knights also were hit in their unprotected legs. Following his neighbour's example, Roger inclined his horse to the right, crouched very low in the saddle, and guarded his left leg with the tail of his kite-shaped shield. He heard Hugh muttering beside him :

'This can't go on. We must do something now. Here we are, being shot down one by one without striking a blow. We must frighten these Turks away, or we shall all leave our bones here. I've seen many a battle, I've fought for my bread all my life long, and I won't wait to be shot like a strawfilled mark on a post. To Hell with the Duke! Will you follow, youngster, if I go after the next gang of bowmen?'

Roger was getting more and more frightened; it was wrong to disobey the Duke's orders and break the line, but Hugh must obviously know a great deal about fighting; furthermore, he

was talking sense, and something had to be done. He was terrified of leaving the protection of his companions, where he could
only be shot at in front, but he was also frightened of showing
his fear. His throat was dry, and his eyes smarting from the
dust, his left arm ached from managing the heavy shield, and
his sun-heated helm seemed to be eating into his scalp. Anything
to finish this suspense, he thought; if he got moving again his
stomach would either be sick or quieten down at last. He nodded
agreement to Hugh.

The next band of Turks came along, about fifty of them,
straggling in column at an easy canter, mocking at the pilgrims
while they shot their arrows. As the tail of the band passed,
Hugh pulled his horse out of the ranks and galloped diagonally
to the left to cut them off from their main body; Roger and
eight of his immediate neighbours followed him. Instantly the
Turkish line on the hill was in motion; by the time they got
abreast of the cantering archers there was a crescent of Turks
hemming them in, and shooting at them from all sides. Hugh
saw the danger, and swerved again left-hand, to regain the ranks
of the pilgrims; this exposed his unshielded right side to the
arrows, and a moment later he went down, with two shafts in
his horse's belly, and one in his own ankle. Roger knew he ought
to stop and succour him, but he also knew that he was in deadly
peril; Jack was at full stretch, excited by all the other horses
galloping round him, and some of his rider's fear had crept into
the hysterical brain that all mettlesome chargers possess; Roger
gave a tug at the reins, but when this had no effect he let his
fear control him, and thundered back towards his own battleline. The skirmishing party was still in the way, and he saw that
by hard riding he would just catch the last man; remembering
how the previous infidel had avoided him, he aimed his lance
low, and it was nearly wrenched from his hand as it entered the
enemy's body above the hip; they were riding at right angles to
one another, and Jack swerved to avoid the pony's quarters; as
the Turk fell to the ground Roger raised the butt of his lance to
clear it. Then he was through his own ranks, which made way
for him, and trotting behind them to his place in the line. Of
the ten who had ridden out, two more came back on their pant-

ing horses, and four on foot, but Hugh and two others were lying in front with their throats cut, and the Turks were back on their hilltop.

The Duke rode up to him; his face was black with dust, save where the red of recent sunburn glowed through the channels cleared by sweat, and his voice, from much shouting, was a husky croak. He thrust his horse up against Roger, and leaned out of the saddle towards him.

'You blasted baby knight! You rash, disobedient fool! Three good knights, and seven warhorses, lost for one unarmed infidel. Don't you see that is what they wanted you to do. You should be blinded and castrated for murdering your comrades. If we weren't all so near death I'd make an example of you this very minute! Now stay in your place, and if you charge without orders again I'll ride you down myself!' and he passed down the line, croaking encouragement to his men.

Roger sat his horse with a heavy heart. The Duke evidently thought he had led the charge, and would hold it against him if lands and castles were given out in the future; but worst of all was the feeling that he had been craven, when he might have saved Hugh de Dives. What had the older man said only that morning? 'It is the first duty of a knight to stand by his comrade who is on the ground.' Certainly Jack had been difficult to stop, and he got the Turk he had been aiming at, but all the same he had left his old friend, unhorsed and with an arrow in his leg, to have his throat cut by an infidel in dirty woollens. All he could think of was that Hugh was dead, and by his fault. Then he began to remember that he had never heard of Hugh a year ago, that on the march he had regarded him as a long-winded bore and a social climber, pushing himself into the society of born knights. After all, he was not Hugh's man, or bound to him in any way, and it had been impossible to pull Jack up. Furthermore, the Duke had not noticed that part of it at all; he obviously thought Roger had led the charge himself, which would have been rather a dashing thing to do. So he comforted himself – till an even more disturbing thought struck him. If an experienced veteran like Hugh could fall into a Turkish trap, so obvious when you saw it, what chance of life had he, or even the rest of the pilgrims, mostly young and vainglorious knights?

The agony of the Christian army continued. It was two hours since they had met the enemy, and still the arrows flew, and still there was no hope of closing with the lance. The clamour from the camp now had a shriller tone, more of panic than of defiance, and the shrieks of women could be distinguished. The Turks must be getting in amongst the followers. Horses dropped continually, and the line of dismounted knights in rear grew thicker, many of them seated on the ground nursing a wounded leg. If the whole infidel army had advanced within arrow-range, the pilgrims must have been overwhelmed; but they still tried to tempt the knights into partial charges, and only small bodies of them galloped along the line, while the rest watched from the hillside. The Duke and the other leaders rode round their men, keeping the ranks in order, but there was a note of desperation in their voices; they no longer promised victory, but appealed to honour to make their followers stand firm. A band of Turks, riding close, suddenly slung their bows, drew their little curved swords, and dashed into the front rank a hundred yards from where Roger was sitting; the unarmed men were easily repulsed, but it showed that the enemy was getting bolder. A young, white-faced knight, a few paces to the left, pulled back from the line with a curse, and began to walk his horse towards the camp. The Duke galloped after him, and seized his bridle. Roger could not hear what was said, but the knight returned sullenly to his place in the line. This was a revelation to him; this was the first battle he had seen, and he had no standard of comparison; now he knew that not only was it a stalemate, but that other people, just as sensible and brave as he, thought it was time to slip away. It was the right thing to do to be afraid just now, and therefore his fear increased. He had killed a Turk, which not many of them had done, he had taken his fair share of the front rank, now he must begin to look for safety before he was left unsupported.

Passive defence gives the novice too much time for thought about his own peril, and in a few minutes Roger would have been riding to the camp, in a surly mood of fear and self-pity, but at that moment orders and movement came to distract him.

The right flank was in the air, and had suffered most from the Turkish arrows on the unshielded side; now the leaders were trying to wheel the whole line back through a slight turn, pivoting on the camp; at the same time they closed to the left, shortening the front and filling up the gaps. This meant that the Turkish left wing had to come down from their hill if they were to follow up, and the numerous dead horses made an obstacle in front of the Christian army. But it was not an easy manoeuvre to accomplish; wheeling in line is always difficult to undrilled troops, and when men are frightened, a movement to the rear is hard to halt. In fact, a few knights rode away, but the leaders were in the rear watching out for this, and a bunchy, crooked battleline was formed again. The difficulty of backing his horse, and then making him passage to the left, filled Roger's mind and for the moment drove out fear; the wary Turks, suspicious of every tactical movement, hung back to see what was coming, and there was a lull in the arrow-shower. Someone had thought of another expedient for prolonging the defence; the cry went up for the dismounted knights to stand in the front line, and they moved forward willingly enough; they preferred to see the enemy and, anyway, if the line broke they had no chance of escape. Their long shields did something to protect the horses, and their lances kept off a Turkish charge. Roger immediately felt braver; there is an enormous difference between standing in the front rank, feeling exposed and naked, and seeing the shoulders of a comrade between oneself and the enemy. The line was thicker, too, and it would not be so easy to turn Jack round for flight. He considered the future quite calmly; it was now midday, and they must hold out either till darkness fell on one of the longest days of the year, or till the Turks were out of arrows; at nightfall, if he was still mounted, he could try the long and dangerous ride to Nicaea and its Greek garrison; if Jack was shot, there was still the camp and its crossbowmen; water was near, there were plenty of dead horses to eat, and they ought to be able to hold out for several days. With the knowledge that he need not die today, his spirits lifted.

The infidels had realized that the Christian retreat was not a ruse to trap them, but a genuine admission of defeat; they came on boldly, and pressed closer to shoot their arrows. The dismounted men in the front rank prevented them from charging into the pilgrims, and also hindered insubordinate counter-attacks; but few knights had the spirit left to expose themselves more than was necessary. The Turks still concentrated on the right wing; they were edging round it now to outflank it, and this made things quieter where Roger sat, on the left centre. He looked over his shoulder at the camp. Half-pitched tents still flapped like sails, but more of them were flat than when he had looked last; a pack-horse galloped towards him with an arrow in its rump; there were riders among the tents, and unless they were knights deserting from battle, the infidels must have broken the defence. If rout came, he must flee at once, there was now no question of holding out in the camp. What would he do if he saw the Duke unhorsed before his eyes? It was a vassal's duty to give his horse in battle to his lord, but no dismounted man would get away from this field. He prayed that nothing of the sort would happen, or that if it did there would be someone braver and more willing standing by. He was no longer hoping to fight well and make a name, only to see tomorrow's sun; and still he had not drawn his sword or taken a blow on his shield.

The right wing was still hard pressed, and the leaders tried to repeat their manoeuvre. If they could bring it off, the line would be at right angles to its original position, and the battered flank would rest on the marsh. He saw the Duke behind him, waving his lance, and shouting to his men to form up on the new line; they all turned their horses and went slowly back. But the order to halt was not obeyed; three hours of being shot at without a chance for a blow in return, three hours of heat and dust and thirst, three hours under shield on a wooden warsaddle, had drained all courage from the knights. Most of them pushed on towards the camp in a disorderly mass, and among them was Roger. His heart was full of rage and misery; damn his oath and blast the Christians of the East; their leaders had dragged them into a wilderness to be a mark for arrows, but at last he had found more sense; this wasn't how battles should be fought. Jack still had a few more miles in him, and he would get to

Nicaea somehow if the infidels stayed to plunder the camp; he would take service under the Greeks, and attack the Turks where they stood behind stone walls, and couldn't retire out of reach; suicide was a mortal sin. His lord could die fighting if he liked; the battle was lost and a man must look after himself; besides, so many were running away that it must be the right thing to do. He rode on, tears washing the dust from his cheeks, and tried to shut out of his mind the cracked shouts of the Duke and his horseless knights who still faced the enemy.

As they reached the camp a cloud of Turks galloped out at the other side of it, thinking that the fugitives were a rescue party. Roger was horrified by what he saw; the tents had been pitched hurriedly as the baggage animals came up, the big pavilions huddled as close together as possible, that their guy-ropes might make a barrier. Packloads had been thrown down higgledy-piggledy, and forage was mixed with clothing underfoot; many wineskins lay about, all empty. Here and there were knots of crossbowmen ensconced behind the tent-ropes, with clusters of women and clerks hiding among them, but many of the un-armed grooms and pages had been cut down as they fled for shelter. For the first time, he saw the ghastly slashing wounds of the Turkish sabre, so different from the deep bruises of the Western sword. A man was cowering against the belly of a dead pack-horse, and sprang to his feet when he saw the knights approach; Roger recognized him as the Breton priest who had sat next to him at supper on the first evening at Nicaea, in an earlier and happier life. Climbing stiffly out of the saddle, he dropped on his knees.

'Shrive me, father. This is the last day of all our lives, and I beg for absolution as one in peril of death.'

'You are not excommunicate, I suppose,' said the priest quite calmly, 'and you haven't committed any sin reserved for a bishop's absolution? Oh no, I remember you, the good little Eng-lishman. *Absolvo te*, etc. etc. . . . that is a conditional absolution, you can confess your sins when we have more time. Now, for your penance, you can go back to your lord's banner, and fight the infidel. If you see another priest, ask him to come here, by the red pavilion with the dead horses; I should like to make my own confession. Be off with you now, I see I have a lot more customers.'

In fact, a number of knights were crowding round, now that they could identify the Breton as a priest, for there was then no distinctive clerical dress, other than Mass-vestments. Roger was calmed by the other's courage; if an unarmed priest, who could not shrive himself and might die unabsolved, faced certain death so bravely, he should do as much in a state of grace, and with the chance to be killed on the field with his sword out. He hoisted himself on to his horse's back, and rode slowly to the remains of the battleline; once he got there he would charge into the enemy, and all this waiting would be over.

He reached the Duke's side, and the thin line, chiefly of dismounted men, who still made a front against the Turkish arrows.

'Good boy,' said the Duke. 'Wait until there are a few more of us, and then we'll try and drive these infidels back again. They must be short of arrows, and they're just as tired as we are.'

His face was drawn and hopeless, but he kept his voice cheerful. Roger lined up beside the Duke and his half-dozen mounted followers, and a few more knights came slowly back from the camp, as their minds climbed from panic-stricken love of life to the self-possession of despair. Then there was a stir on the extreme right flank, quickly running down the line. He looked to the right, which the Count of Taranto had kept in slightly better order than the Normans of Normandy; knights were couching their lances and catching hold of their horses, though the Turks pressed as closely as ever. This must be a preparation for a general charge, though there was no more reason for it now than there had been all the last three hours; perhaps they were all tired of this hopeless fight, and seeking death together. The Duke saw it too, and waved his lance in the air.

'Close up to the left, you footmen in front; when you see me give the signal, horsemen, charge! *Deus Vult!*' and he pointed his lance to the front, shortened his reins, and set off.

As Roger spurred Jack into the lumbering unbalanced gallop of a tired horse, he suddenly saw, behind the Turks on the crest of the hill, the unmistakable shields and pennons of Western knights, and heard the war cry of the pilgrims, 'Deus Vult!' above the trampling of the horses and the cries of the wounded. The second division, the Lotharingians and Provençals and French, had come to the rescue in the nick of time. Everyone saw them at once, and the dismounted cheered and danced as the Duke's following thundered past, squeezing their horses without thought for the future. The Turks were aware of them also, and drew their curved swords since flight was impossible; but their light ponies and woollen-clad bodies were no match for the heavy charge of the pilgrims. Roger ran his lance into a pony's shoulder, and it was nearly wrenched from his hand; he drew it out and flourished it round his head; then he was through the Turks, and riding beside a Brabançon follower of the Duke of Lower Lotharingia; he had a sudden longing to kiss him on both cheeks, but only grinned weakly. He settled down to ride more quietly in the pursuit.

The Turkish left wing had been caught back and front, and annihilated; the right wing fled north-west, away from their homeland and towards the Greeks, but the centre tried to retreat in good order. Every horse on the field was blown, for the Lotharingians had done a six-mile gallop and the others had had three hours fighting, so the flight and pursuit moved slowly on, in spite of the desperate excitement of the riders. Roger and the Brabançon cantered side by side, their horses sobbing and floundering. They passed a knight who was dismounting from a completely lame horse, and Roger recognized his cousin Robert; a sudden inspiration came to him, and he pulled up.

'I'm glad to see you alive, cousin,' he said. 'Now that you are out of the hunt, will you do me a favour? Disarm me, and look after my mail shirt till I get back. There is no more fight left in these men, and I shall be safe enough with a shield.'

Soon he was mounting again, many pounds lighter, and his sweat-soaked shirt felt deliciously cool against his body. Robert grinned, and shouted after him that the Turks carried their gold in a belt round the waist. He had lost ground, but Jack went much better now, and soon he was overhauling the leaders.

It was a nightmare chase, the horses staggering at a trot up and down the rolling hills, while frantic men flogged and spurred them. Many of the Turks carried riding-whips, and this was their undoing, for they beat their horses to a standstill in the first miles; those pilgrims whose horses foundered led them back to the camp, but every Turk who came to a halt was a dead man. Roger marked one, a big man in baggy white clothing, whose little horse was lame in front. As he overtook him the other spurred and beat his pony, and finally pulled a dagger from his waist-cloth and pricked the beast in the flank; Roger's lance was not six feet from its bushy tail; slowly he gained and the point was over the pony's quarters; then, so nearly equal was their speed, it dug the Turk in the buttocks and could go no further. With a squeal the fugitive leant forward and buried his teeth in his pony's neck; slowly the lance travelled to his bowels, and he fell to the ground; he had been too panic-stricken to shoot, though he carried bow and quiver.

Roger dismounted, finished him off, and took the pouch from his waistband; without opening it he trotted on. The pursuit continued for three hours, till the pilgrims' horses, with quivering tails and outstretched necks, could go no further. Then Roger began to lead his horse home to camp, the reins over his arm. He was desperately thirsty and tired, and all his clothes were drenched with sweat; the shield-grip had galled his left wrist, and at some time he had banged his right leg against another rider; Jack was so stiff that he could hardly walk, but he appeared to be sound, and there was not a wound on either of them. Fatigue and hunger had affected his brain, which with the ingenuity of exhaustion made every bush and rock look like a church or a Turk to his red-rimmed eyes. The same circle of thoughts raced through his mind. He had killed at least six Turks, and two of them facing him in fair fight; he had gone far in pursuit, and even unarmed to go farther; but he had deserted the Duke at the crisis of the battle, and before that he had failed his fellow-knight Hugh in his utmost need. He remembered how he had galloped past, and how Hugh had looked at him from his knees, with the arrow in his ankle and his sword half-drawn. He had murdered him as surely as if he had stabbed him in the back. Moreover, he had received conditional absolution, and must confess his sins as soon as possible; would he have to confess that coward's deed, or was a failure in courage not a sin? And what of his honour? Of the three feudal breaches of honour, he had at least never thought of treachery; but he had fled from his lord fighting in the field, and he had made up his mind that he would not give up his horse if it was called for. On the other hand, he had killed six Turks. . . . He had plenty of time to repeat this circular train of thought many times before he reached the camp.

Nor was this the end of his trials. There was no sign of Peter, and he had to water Jack, rub him down, and picket him, before he could look for supper; but the camp had been so thoroughly fought over that nearly all the food and wine were spoiled. He could get nothing from the Duke's kitchen but a bit of bread, some half-roasted horseflesh, and a jack of water faintly tinged with wine. He slept on the ground, wrapped in a dead man's cloak, among the unburied corpses.

Next day there was a certain amount of reorganization. Roger searched for Peter the Fleming, and had him cried through the host; but he could get no news of him or the pack pony; both must have been killed by the Turks. He was left with his horse and arms, and fifteen pieces of gold that he had found on dead Turks in the pursuit.

The whole army now set out for Iconium, the capital of the infidels, following the line of the Turks' retreat. The pilgrims had lost four thousand men, chiefly foot, and very many horses, but few of the killed were knights; if they could capture more horses they would be as strong as before.

4

ANATOLIA

1097

THE Turks had reduced this land to the condition that suited their economy; a grassy plain, unpeopled, where stone threshing-floors and bramble-covered dykes were the sole relics of past prosperity. Nowhere was there a smoking chimney, or a cultivated field. The enemy had fired the sun-dried grass, and the pilgrims marched through a cloud of black dust with no grazing for the horses. On the fourth day after the battle Jack the war-horse died of hunger.

Roger was quite alone, without a servant or even a change of clothes; at the beginning of the march the Duke had distributed hackneys and captured Turkish ponies among his unhorsed followers, but they had all been given out, and Roger dared not ask for one. In his first battle he had deserted a comrade, and then fled shamefully from his lord's banner, and he felt a deep sense of guilt; he plodded among the despised unwarlike foot, and hoped no one would notice him. He could not march in mail, and put his armour and shield on an oxcart; he still carried sword and lance, to show he was a knight, but if he could not get a horse he would not long remain one. Every man's social position depended on the place he could take in the line of battle, and a dismounted knight was worth less than a crossbow-man. He walked beside the oxcart, and his surroundings deepened his misery; he was hungry, he was thirsty, he was tired, dirty, and ashamed. All day he must loiter at the pace of the plodding oxen, arriving late in camp, when the streams were already fouled, and the best food had been given out. The sun shone from an unclouded sky, over everything was a thin film of ashes, and the stench of the host rose in an almost tangible cloud. Round him crowded the poorer pilgrims, who had walked all the way from the Rhine or the Loire; they shuffled along with downcast eyes, muttering in their incomprehensible dialects, but they bore the accustomed toil better than he. He set his teeth, and determined to show that a knight could go as far as a peasant, even on foot.

The host followed the Imperial road to Iconium; this had been in good repair thirty years ago, but the Turks had destroyed every bridge and culvert, and the rare streams delayed each vehicle. On the third day the cart which bore his armour was checked at a ravine where a narrow passage had been dug by the pioneers. In the bed of the stream a covered chariot was stuck among the boulders; the four oxen that drew it stood each at a different angle, their heads kept together by the yokes, and a crossbowman heaved ineffectually at a great stone that lay against a wheel.

Such incidents were common on the march, and as a rule Roger would not have interfered, lest he compromise his dignity as a knight. But the crowd was impatient, and if something was not done quickly the peasants would overturn the obstacle. He saw the heads of two women peering out from the canvas tilt. That decided him; only ladies still had wheels to carry them. He scrambled down the bank and put his shoulder to the stone.

In Sussex he had often helped to extricate harvest-wagons from the muddy Wealden bottoms; as soon as the stone was out of the way he went forward and pushed the oxen into line, then darted back and helped the crossbowman to manhandle a wheel. The chariot moved, and presently lurched up the farther bank. Rather nervously, he walked round to the rear opening of the tilt, to see what kind of passengers it carried.

Sitting on a box inside the tailboard was a large weather-beaten middle-aged lady, her face scarlet and peeling from the sun; she wore a grey gown and hood of coarse material, made even less attractive by dark stains of sweat. Her companion was only a dim shadow in the interior of the chariot. Roger was disappointed. He had hoped for thanks from a pretty girl, and perhaps the offer of a seat in the chariot. Nevertheless, he bowed, smiling, and waited for her thanks.

73

He had forgotten that he was wearing the very dirty shirt and wadded riding chausses that were all the clothes he possessed; his hair was much too long, and his fluffy adolescent's beard had not been trimmed since he had lost his servant; even with his lance and his great sword he looked like the lowest kind of foot-sergeant. The lady beckoned to him, while she fumbled in a purse.

'I am a knight, Domna,' he exclaimed, in an agony of shyness. 'My name is Roger fitzOsbert de Bodeham, and my father holds land in England. I lost my servants and baggage in the last battle, and then my horse died.'

The other lady came to the tailboard.

'My poor Alice!' she called in the langue d'Oc of Provence, which was near enough to French to be understood by a Norman. 'Of course our deliverer is a knight. Can't you see the sword he carries? Climb in, Messer Roger, and let me thank you properly. The oxen will not notice your weight.'

This was what Roger had hoped for. The second lady was beautiful. She was in the prime of life, perhaps nearer twenty than fifteen, but then her maturity should make her easier to talk to; her eyes were a very dark brown, and her hair black; that was not the colouring that was in fashion, when poets sang of ladies fairer than snow. But in that climate it was an advantage, for the sun had given her skin a golden bloom. Her limbs were long, and her high-breasted body slight. Her gown, laced tight at each side to show off her figure, was of fine green cloth, unwrinkled and well-brushed; the long sleeves came halfway over her hands, and the full skirt hid all except the toes of her red leather slippers. Her hair hung in two plaits, and instead of a hood she wore the black silk kerchief of the Greek women. To Roger, surrounded by stinking peasants, she looked like an angel in an altar-painting.

His feet seemed unusually big as he hoisted them over the back of the chariot. He had very seldom spoken to ladies of his own class; a younger son could not expect to marry the daughter of a landholder. At the abbeys and castles where he paid formal visits for Christmas and Whitsun he had met ladies, but the Normans of England did not understand courteous love, and their men had not allowed them to talk with strangers. In his journey through Provence and Italy he had come to understand that foreigners allowed their wives more freedom, and he hoped he could make conversation without angering the husband who would be riding in the advance.

But the ladies were without a protector; for the beauty answered his greetings:

'I cannot be gay and courteous, for I am newly widowed. I am Anne de la Roche, wife of Messer Giles de Clary in Provence, and my husband was killed in the battle. This is **my** waiting-lady, Domna Alice de la Roche; she has been a widow for years, and is showing me how to behave as one.'

In the widespread homogeneous society of western land-holders strangers identified themselves thoroughly; quite possibly they would find some common tie of marriage or descent. It was therefore natural, as soon as Roger had given an account of his ancestry, that Domna Anne should tell the story of her life. Her husband had held from the Count of Toulouse, but the fief was small; he had mortgaged all he possessed, and brought his family to Romania, intending to settle in the East. It seemed that his marriage had been part of his preparation; for she said they had married in the spring of 1096, and her dowry had been spent on equipment. She was a daughter of the Lord Odo de la Roche, who held a castle somewhere on the Aquitanian border.

Now they both knew where they stood in a class-conscious world. Roger saw that she was of slightly higher birth, but her marriage had brought her to his level, as often happened to the younger daughters of barons. She had thanked him prettily for his assistance, and he knew whereabouts he should go to have the obligation repaid; there was no need for the interview to continue. But, to his surprise, he was enjoying himself; he wanted to go on listening. It seemed only polite to ask Domna Anne how her husband had met his death.

He expected a eulogy of the prowess of Messer Giles de Clary, and a stirring account of the slaughter he had dealt among the infidels before he was vanquished by overwhelming numbers. But Domna Anne replied baldly:

75

'I didn't see it happen, for we were in the Provençal column, six miles from the battle. Someone told me his horse stumbled as he galloped to help you Normans; he fell, and broke his neck, before he had even couched his lance. It's the sort of silly thing that does happen sometimes, and poor Giles was not a good horseman. He had spent his life in siege-warfare, and he was very clever with scaling-ladders; but when his horse pecked he always shot over its head.'

Roger was abashed by this frank obituary; but it gave him a comfortable feeling of intimacy. Naturally, he could think of nothing to talk about in reply except himself.

'It's surprising that it doesn't happen more often. I had a nasty fall when I was a child, and sometimes I get a feeling that another is coming in the next few yards, and it is all I can do to keep my horse galloping. Still, Messer Giles died fighting the infidel, as truly as though he had slain them by thousands. He gained all the spiritual benefits of the Pilgrimage.'

'That is a comfort, of course, and it will look well on a memorial at home. But he had no chance to win land. I am wondering what to do next. There are Franks in Nicaea, and I might find an Italian ship at Constantinople. But no one is turning back, and we dare not go alone. For the present we must remain with the army.'

'Surely it is the duty of the Count of Toulouse to protect you,' answered Roger.

'Oh, he gives me food, and my crossbowmen march with his foot. But I would rather not draw his attention until I have to. He would maintain a de Clary against any perils; but by birth I am a de la Roche, and he might use me as a hostage against my father. Our family are not obedient vassals.'

Roger murmured in sympathy; tenants should not defy their lords without reason, but occasionally they must stand up for their rights.

'The best thing is to march with the host until we come to a seaport,' put in Alice, the waiting-lady. She sat beside her mistress, and took little part in the conversation; but of course it would be fatal to the reputation of a young widow if she were alone with a man, so her presence was necessary.

'Yes, that is what we must do,' said Anne sadly. 'I wonder when we shall find the sea? This is a much larger country than I had expected. Do you know its boundaries, Messer Roger?'

'No, Domna. But there are mountains to the south-east; you can see them at dawn, before the host stirs up this cloud of ashes. The coast lies to the south, and perhaps we shall turn towards it presently.'

'Yes, the sea bounds every land. But I was forgetting. Alice, this knight helped us when the crowd would have overturned the chariot. We must repay his kindness. Get out the chest with my husband's clothes. We can at least give you a clean shirt, and some thinner chausses. Of course you must take them. Presently, when you have taken others from the infidel, you can give them back, if you like. A towel also, and blankets. It is ridiculous that I should carry a knight's baggage while you have nothing.'

Roger did not attempt to refuse her generosity. One reason for his loneliness had been shame at his personal appearance. Soon the chariot came to a rise, and he got out to spare the oxen; but for the rest of the day he walked beside it, and when they halted in the evening he brought his armour from the baggage-cart.

He made up his bed in unaccustomed luxury. He had been long enough in the field to live from day to day, and to seize every chance of comfort as it came. But he was surprised to find, as he composed himself for sleep, that he thought of Domna Anne not merely as a timely provider of bedding and clean linen, but as a delightful companion.

Next morning he sought out the chariot, and greeted the ladies as old friends. There was plenty to talk about, as they skirted at a safe distance the closed gates of Iconium.

'Isn't it wonderful to think of that ridiculous King of the Turks gnashing his teeth in there, unless he has fled to the desert he came from,' said Anne cheerfully. 'The Greek Emperor will be annoyed that we are leaving the city uncaptured, but who cares? We need a land with plenty of castles, not this sea of burnt grass, without peasants to till it. Have you learnt our future plans, Messer Roger? Giles would have found a way over the wall of Iconium. He was a marvel on a scaling-ladder, although he couldn't ride.'

Roger was a little shocked. It was right that a freshly bereaved widow should talk of her husband, for he must be continually in her thoughts; but her references seemed to lack respect. He kept the conversation to matters of business.

'Since we are leaving Iconium untaken in our rear, and there is no food in this part of Galatia, we shall have to get supplies by sea. Soon we must turn south and occupy a harbour.'

'And then I shall find a ship to take me home. Are you so eager to be rid of me?'

That was a tiresome trait in the character of this beautiful lady, Roger reflected; in Sussex no one spoke except to convey information, or to ask a question; these southern ladies made conversation into a game, a game he did not understand. They seemed to have a limitless appetite for compliments; composing them on the spur of the moment made him stutter, and no one was any wiser at the end of it all. However, he mumbled something in north French, which she did not understand fluently, and was pleased at the smile he received in reply. The trouble was that he wanted to be near her and to hear her speak, and yet he could not think of anything to say. Sometimes he walked in front, and helped the crossbowman to manage the oxen, but then he felt he was wasting a golden opportunity; soon he would be back at the tailboard, racking his brains for a pretty speech. He measured the day's march by stages; when we pass that rock I shall fall back and admire her kerchief, then at the rough place half a mile on I shall move up and twist the tail of the leading ox. It seemed to have been arranged that he should manage the chariot.

By afternoon the mountains showed like a wall in the south-east, though no doubt a pass would appear when they were closer. The oxen strained at the first long rise, and both ladies got out to walk. Here the ground was damp; the grass had not burned, and there was less dust; it was pleasant to walk with a lady on either side, even at the maddening mile-an-hour pace of the tired oxen.

Domna Alice was apprehensive when she saw the tumbled

78

blue-grey ridges ahead. Her fears made her forget that she was only there to preserve the proprieties.

'More mountains! Anne dear, do you think it will be like the terrible country of the Sclavonians? You have no idea, Messer Roger, what we endured in that barbarous land. As soon as we slid down one precipice we had to start climbing the next. And the inhabitants! They are called Christians, but they had no respect for the Holy Pilgrimage. They hurled rocks from the cliffs, and murdered the stragglers. Other pilgrims went round that country by sea, and I think our Count was wrong to take us through it.'

'It was a very bad time,' said Anne with a shudder, 'but I am proud that we Provençals accomplished what no other knights in Christendom dared even to attempt. It must be more honourable to ride straight to your goal than to put yourself in the hands of a gang of barefooted sailors, separated from your horses, at the mercy of every wind. The Count of Toulouse has made war on the infidel for twenty years, and he rides where he wills.'

Anne threw back her head as she spoke, and her eyes had the hard look of a warrior peering over the shield-rim. But Roger would not let it be thought the Normans had chosen an easier route for fear of naked barbarians.

'Our Duke wished to bring all his power to Romania, without losing horses by the way; and we took oath not to make war on Christians during the journey. Besides, we are accustomed to seafaring. My father was a conqueror of England; that is an island, and they went in ships. They landed on a hostile shore, dismounted, with every warhorse unsaddled in the holds. That was gambling against odds!'

'Of course, it takes courage to venture on the sea, far from land, as you did when crossing from Italy to Romania,' said Alice, in a soothing tone; she was old enough to be bored by the boasting matches of the young. 'But these mountains will be difficult. Are there any weak spots in the chariot?'

Roger walked round the rough, sturdily-built vehicle, examining the wheels and axletrees; when he came back to his companions they talked of other things.

79

It was a new experience for him, this making conversation and changing the subject when there was disagreement. He found it a strain on the mind, but amusing; these southerners had made an art of companionship, and the weary routine of marching passed more quickly than if you merely exchanged information, and contradicted every statement with which you did not agree. But what should be the next move in the game? Apparently every knight who spoke to a lady must imply that he was dying for love of her. In Sussex such expressions might be taken at their face value, but Domna Anne would not mistake them. He gathered that she had been married to an elderly stranger, to fit in with a plan of her father's; therefore marriages in Provence were arranged on the same commonsense lines as in England; she would not take him seriously. Besides, he was absurdly presumptuous; a young widow had taken pity on a dismounted knight; there was nothing more in it than that. A landless man from barbarous England would only make himself ridiculous if he went about thinking ladies valued his devotion. He ought to march in some other part of the column, before people began to gossip. But that would be giving up a harmless pleasure. Anne was an amusing companion, full of unconventional opinion wittily expressed; talking to her was a little frightening, but even the fear was pleasurable, like riding a horse that was just too hot to hold. While she wanted a man to look after her chariot he would stay with her; all too soon they would be parted, in this confused throng of many tongues.

That evening he walked over to the Italian cooking-fires; there he found Robert de Santa Fosca, sitting with his hauberk on his knee, mending a thong. He seemed glad to see a visitor.

'There you are, cousin. I heard you had joined a young lady. All the better if you are alone, for I have a proposition. Come for a walk, and I'll tell you all about it.'

He led Roger aside, and began to explain.

'So far we have marched through a desert, with nothing in it but Turks and sheep. But among these mountains things are different; Christians still live there, and though they pay tribute to the Turks they are good fighting-men. Armenians they are called, and they have their own church, quite distinct from the Greeks'.

Some of their leaders joined us outside Nicaea, and the Count of Taranto has kept in touch with them ever since. Well, the scheme is this: the Turks are afraid, and anyway their horse-archers are no good on a mountainside. Young Count Tancred, Taranto's nephew, is raising a force to go into the hills, chase out the Turks, and set up a county of his own. Will you join us?'

'I have no horse,' said Roger, 'and that puts it out of the question.'

'Never mind. We shall be storming cities and climbing mountains, which means fighting on foot; we can fix you up with a pack-horse to ride on the march. Do come; and if you can bring some crossbows so much the better; they are useful in sieges.'

'It sounds attractive,' said Roger. 'I suppose we take an oath to Count Tancred, and he gives us land if we succeed? At the moment I am still under oath to the Duke, but I will see him tomorrow, and ask him to release me.'

Robert gave an impatient shrug. 'You seem to attach too much importance to this oath. That isn't how we won Italy, with no help from our own Duke. Count Tancred won't bother to take an oath from you; we follow him because he is a warrior, and he keeps us in order with his sword. But see the Duke in the morning, and let me know your answer tomorrow. The more we are, the more land we shall conquer. Now tell me about this young lady.'

Roger had little to say, except that she was a lady, and always had her waiting-lady with her. He did not realize that the quickest way of starting scandal is to protest that the conventions are observed.

Next morning he waited on the Duke. He could not have chosen a worse day. There had been rain in the night, and the pavilion leaked; breakfast was scanty, and the shortage of wine frayed tempers accustomed to deep drinking. The Duke was famous for courtesy to his followers, but he was weak, and like other weak men enjoyed putting his foot down. He sat behind his trestle-board, with a clerk beside him, and frowned at Roger.

'So you want to recover the fealty you gave me in Normandy. You don't say where you intend to carry your service, but I suppose you want to go plundering with those Italians, who should be my subjects. Let us see how we stand. (Clerk, take this down.) You were not born my man, and joined me for the Pilgrimage, which makes you free when I go home. From Nicaea you have fought for your keep, but if you want freedom now you must pay for your food and forage in Burgundy and Italy. I did not pledge my land to bring men here for the Count of Taranto. You can pay the money, or stay with me; and whichever you choose will be written down. If you desert I shall have you cried through the camp as an oath-breaker, and your family will find me a bad neighbour when I get home.'

There was no more to be said; Roger could not pay for eight months' food. He bowed, and left the pavilion.

When the march began, up a steep rise which the paved road attacked in zigzags, he walked with the two ladies. He was discreet about Count Tancred's proposed expedition, but otherwise he told them the whole story. Domna Alice agreed that the Duke had been harsh, but said that he was within his rights; the solution was for Roger to get money at the next sack to pay his debt. Anne thought he had been too conscientious.

'You are a good young man, to be so true to your oath, like the paladins of Charlemagne. Do oaths hold good all over the world? Here in the East no one would know what you are talking about. If you win a little castle you could commend it to the Greek Emperor, and hold it against any pilgrim; poor Giles discussed doing that, if our Count didn't give him what he wanted. But, of course, we had a castle at home, and were used to the idea of defiance. You knights from open manors get in the habit of obeying your lords, and then you are imposed on.'

'That may be true,' he answered, 'but my father was a conqueror of England. What would he think of a son who left his lord in the field? One day the Duke will go home, and I shall remain; then I can set up for myself.'

'Spoken like a true knight!' she smiled. 'And now, sir, will you see that they lock a wheel of the chariot before we begin this descent.' Though he was the elder by two years, Anne sometimes spoke as though he were a child.

* * *

These were the mountains of Lesser Armenia, settled not long before by exiles from the plains dominated by Turkish horse. On the hilltops were walled towns, and the few Turkish tribute-gatherers fled at the pilgrims' approach, while the townspeople opened their gates. Still, there were difficulties; horses continued to die, and in many places the Armenians set up lords of their own, instead of showing gratitude to the host that had marched so far to free them. They seemed to be as independent as the Greeks, and as attached to their absurd religious practices. Roger wondered if the Christians of the East really wanted Western help. Easterners, whether Christian or infidel, got on well enough together; they were used to buying land and selling it, and paying taxes in money to a distant tyrant, rather than inheriting from their fathers and doing service with their swords. One day he mentioned his doubts to Father Yves, the Breton priest who had absolved him in the battle. The priest was interested; it was a point that had not occurred to him, and he enjoyed thinking out new situations.

'At present the Eastern world is held together by money. That is the old way of doing things, as it was at the Incarnation; then there were soldiers and centurions and tax-gatherers, as you have heard in the Gospel at Mass. Now we Westerners have found a better way, with oaths and services taking the place of perpetual payments of money; when we have shown it to these poor foreigners they will see it is better, since all men are brothers and they are at bottom the same as us. As for religion, they are ignorant and oppressed. When they understand the position of the Pope they will obey him like reasonable Christians.'

It sounded very simple, and Roger looked to the future in a hopeful spirit. He saw himself as not merely a champion of the Faith, but a missionary of a more decent way of life in this world.

Meanwhile there was his friendship with Anne de Clary. As a matter of course, he now walked beside her chariot on each day's march; though since they drew their food from different sources, and to avoid scandal, they separated when they reached camp. But the evenings were dull without her, and each night he looked forward to the toils of the next day in a manner that would have surprised his weary and footsore companions.

He was content to go on for ever in his present mode of life, gazing all day on her beauty, and occasionally provoking her to conversation for the pleasure of hearing her voice. He put from his thoughts all hope of greater intimacy. He was still a landless man, with nothing to offer; in any case, marriage did not occur because two people were attracted to one another; it was arranged by the parents to unite neighbouring estates, or to gain an ally. The thought of seduction never entered his head; Provençal ladies had been known to take lovers, but there was no reason that she should choose him. He had disgraced his knighthood in his first battle (the anguished face of Hugh de Dives, abandoned among the infidel, recurred frequently in his dreams), and he was not handsome or amusing. He must enjoy this exquisite but transient pleasure; it was foolish to inquire how long it would continue.

Nevertheless, as no man can forbear to press on an aching tooth, so he must find out how long he would enjoy Anne's company. Tarsus had fallen, and there were rumours of Western ships on the coast. But it was late in the season to start a voyage, as she pointed out.

'I haven't made up my mind. I should like to complete the pilgrimage; we shall probably keep Christmas in Jerusalem, and then I can decide. I am in no hurry to be home. Giles's land goes to a cousin, since I am childless; my dowry is spent, and my father would not give me another. Here I am with ten crossbows and a good chariot, and in Provence I would not have so much.'

'You have also one knight to serve you, though a horseless one,' said Rogert, in what he hoped was a gallant tone; French was not the language for these expressions.

'Thank you, Messer Roger, but you are mistaken. While you are bound to the Duke of Normandy I have not one knight.'

An idea awoke in Roger's mind. Anne thought him unnecessarily scrupulous in his fidelity; but suppose that was because she did not want to lose him? After several weeks she was still not tired of him; perhaps she really liked him, as a person. Yet to make a definite declaration of love was to run an appalling risk. If she were offended, worse still if she laughed at him, the companionship of the march would be ended. But a true knight never shirks a crisis. He gulped, and went red to the roots of his hair. Then, forgetting Domna Alice, who was listening with interest by his other shoulder, he spoke in a husky voice :

'Domna, I am on God's holy service, and I owe a duty to my lord. But after those I serve you. I have nothing to offer save my sword, but if you will be my wife I shall win land, and maintain my lady against the infidel.'

She looked at him steadily, from his patched shoes to the helm, too large without its hauberk, that wobbled on his head. Then she laughed happily.

'That was a very Norman way of saying it, dear Roger. You must never propose marriage to anyone else, but if you should, take care not to put the lady in third place. None the less, I will be your wife, and serve you faithfully, as you shall serve me.' This last sentence sounded formal, but Roger knew that the acceptance of an offer of marriage was an extremely formal undertaking; no doubt she had used the same words when she accepted Giles de Clary. She held out her hand. In that throng of strangers he was too shy to kneel; clumsily, as they walked, he bent his head over it. Domna Alice had witnessed everything, and now they were as formally betrothed as though parchments had been exchanged. It was not a contract recognized by the Church, and if they anticipated the religious ceremony they would be committing grievous sin; but in law they were bound, at least not to wed another.

Then Anne held up her face to be kissed, and told Alice to go back to the chariot; there were congratulations from the cross-bowmen, and from other pilgrims. The day passed in a dream, as they walked hand in hand, and spoke of the splendid life they would lead together in some castle of the East.

At night there were practical arrangements to be made. Roger knew that his father would never learn of the marriage; but if parental consent was out of the question it was still his duty to inform their separate lords. He asked for an interview at the pavilion of the Count of Toulouse. When the Count had finished supper he was admitted, and stood before his chair.

Count Raymond was the eldest of the leaders, almost too old for warfare; but he had lavished his wealth on this Holy War, and preserved his dignity and independence in his dealings with the Greek Emperor; nor as yet had he tried to seize any castles for himself. For all this he was widely respected by the lesser knights.

Roger told his story briefly, and the Count considered for a moment; then he spoke:

'You are the peer in blood of Domna Anne de Clary, and I accept your word that you are free to marry. It is true that you have nothing at all, but many pilgrims are in the same condition. Do you acknowledge two things: that as she is the widow of my man the lady's marriage belongs to me; and that neither she, nor any children she may bear in future, have a claim to the lands of Clary?'

Roger agreed, and a clerk put it in writing. 'Then it seems there is no obstacle in the way. You may marry with my blessing.'

The Duke of Normandy's consent was a formality; he gained ten crossbows and lost nothing. He was in a good temper after supper, and Roger realized how foolish he had been to ask for his release in the morning. It was arranged that a clerk from the Duke's chapel should marry them in two days' time, and the bridal pair were invited to sup at the Duke's own table on their wedding night.

Roger could not sleep for thinking of the future. For weeks he had been deeply in love, and in two days that love would be satisfied. That was a glorious prospect. But he wondered uneasily whether he could cope with the purely social duties of a husband. Anne knew many ladies in the Provençal contingent; she would expect him to go visiting with her when the army halted; perhaps he might even have to compose verses. No, she could not expect that, for quite literally they did not speak the same language; that was a barrier between them, though it often happened when great lords made dynastic marriages. Anyone who spoke French could understand the langue d'Oc, and the other way round, so long as the conversation was confined to serious matters; the long abstract words were practically the same. But the jokes and catch-phrases were different; sometimes he had been disconcerted when he quoted a well-known Norman proverb, and found she had never heard of it.

But these were slight matters. Anne was lovely, high-spirited, and capable, the ideal wife for a landless adventurer on such an enterprise. He did not deserve her, but in future he would risk his life as rashly as any hero, and win fame on the battlefield. Their past acquaintance drifted through his mind, as he tried to make out why a lovely woman had chosen an undistinguished warrior like himself. That brought a disturbing suspicion. Obviously life was difficult for a virtuous widow, adrift without a protector in this lawless host; it was necessary for her to find a husband. He remembered the way she had looked at him, before accepting his proposal; had she been seeking any respectable man to take care of her, and decided after some hesitation that he would do? But he put the thought from his mind. She had shown by a thousand words and actions that she loved him truly, as the high-born princesses in the poems loved their lowly suitors; she was beautiful and kind, and in two days he would be holding her in his arms. At the thought of it he ached with longing and desire.

Next morning Domna Alice sat among the baggage, while he walked with his future bride. They told of their early lives, and he described his childhood in wooded Sussex, and the paradoxical peace of newly conquered England, with its rebellious nobility and uncertain line of succession, controlled by the mighty king in Winchester. Anne had been born in a more stormy land, the youngest daughter of a small baron on the Provençal border of Aquitaine; her father had defied his lord, and was not sure of holding his lands; as a gesture of peace, he had married her to a middle-aged but loyal knight, a trusted castellan on the Spanish March. She had met Messer Giles de Clary for the first time on the day of their betrothal, and did not pretend that she had ever loved him. They had been married only a year, and most of her talk was of her childhood.

Until he set out on the Pilgrimage, Roger had been ruled by his elder brother, and the company of so many experienced warriors had increased his inborn feeling of inferiority. Now a number of people took his orders without argument, a novel and pleasing sensation. Anne was obviously happy and relieved, willing that he should shoulder her troubles. As he called to the driver to keep away from the edge of the road, and steered his lady over patches of loose stone, he felt his self-esteem growing in the most comforting manner.

He loved Anne, and would have married her if she were penniless. But he was a Norman, with a Norman passion to climb in the social scale, and this marriage would add to his importance. Ten crossbows would garrison a tower, if he could get hold of one; and there was wealth in the chariot, silver and weapons and fine clothes, though at present there was little he could buy with it. He was a very lucky man, who could follow his heart and still advance his prospects.

At sunrise they heard Mass and were married, in the tent that served as the Duke's private chapel. A knight of Toulouse gave Anne away, in the name of his lord; and when it came to endowing his bride with gold and silver Roger produced a satisfactory handful, though it was all he possessed in the world. The Duke of Normandy was not present, for he disliked early rising, and often heard the morning Mass in his blankets; but he had paid the priest's fee, and he sent a truly magnificent wedding-gift. This was a captured Turkish pony, an ugly little brute and quite untrained as a warhorse, but a comfortable ride on the march. So many horses were dead that this was a lavish piece of generosity, worthy of the Duke's reputation as an open-handed spendthrift. Roger was married in full armour, for he had no other clothes. Anne wore her best gown, of close-fitting wine-red cloth, and Domna Alice attended her, showing suitable emotion. Immediately after breakfast the army marched, and Roger rode his new hackney among the Normans of Normandy.

That evening they supped in the highest place among the knights, just below the barons; the Duke was in a good humour, and sent down a big loving-cup for them to drink together. There were the usual ribald jokes, especially from the ladies; but Anne was a widow, and did not seem put out, although Roger blushed. The Duke made a speech, beginning by wishing them good fortune, and then wandering off into the difficulties of the campaign. They spent the wedding-night in the chariot, and Roger felt peaceful and secure for the first time since leaving England.

Next morning there was a crossbowman to wait on him, and Domna Alice heated wine to restore them, as was the custom. The army still marched through unending hills, and when the narrow way permitted he rode beside the chariot. It was long since he had taken a turn at scouting or foraging, but there was little need for it; the Greek and Armenian towns expelled their garrisons on the mere rumour of the pilgrims' approach, food was given willingly, and here, in Cilicia, the inhabitants seemed not merely grateful for liberation, but eager that knights should stay behind to protect them. Roger rode happily beside his moving home, and the crossbowmen managed the hills without his supervision.

Speech was impossible above the noise of the chariot-wheels, but that evening they discussed the nebulous future, on which Anne held decided views.

'You know, Roger darling, it is possible to be too much in the power of your oaths. Other people don't guide their conduct in the same way, and this is the world as we have to live in it. Could there be a more sacred promise than that we all gave, to live in peace with our fellow-pilgrims? Yet the Lotharingians and the Italians came to blows outside Mamistra. It was wrong, of course, but Tancred needs a county of his own, and so does Baldwin; and instead of being shocked, people admire their spirit. Your Duke is charming, but he hasn't made a wonderful success of his life, has he? One could call him a landless man, for he will never turn his brother out; and you, darling, are his landless follower. You swore to serve him on the pilgrimage, but now that knights, and good knights too, are settling in this country, couldn't we say that the pilgrimage is finished? You have a household to support, and you could provide for us better under another leader.'

'My darling,' said Roger gently, but with a frown, 'an oath of fealty should be as sacred as a wedding-vow. But what should a woman know of the duties of a knight? Count Tancred is a brave warrior, I grant you, but all those Normans of Italy are a turbulent, forsworn gang of freebooters, and I believe the great

Duke William would have nothing to do with them. In England we keep our vows. We should never have conquered the land otherwise, and in fact we got it by the judgement of Heaven, because Count Harold was an oath-breaker. Let me hear no more of this; the Duke is my lord, because I freely gave him my allegiance.'

'Very well, my dear. I am foolish to talk of these things, of which, as you say, a woman can know nothing. Tell me about the palaces of Italy. We went straight from Lombardy to the land of the Sclavonians, and never saw Rome.'

Roger did his best, for he had been impressed by the wonders of the Italian cities; but he was not naturally talkative. When it had been a question of making an impression on a beautiful lady he had racked his brains; but now Anne was his wife, he had won her until death should part them, and there was no need to woo her. Besides, he wanted to go to bed. By the second night of their marriage they were beginning to jar on one another.

* * *

A different spirit ran through the host, now they had passed the barren zone. Tancred was organizing Cilicia into a county, and Baldwin of Lotharingia was trying to do the same on the Euphrates. The land was rich enough to support a class of knights and nobles, and everyone was eager for a share. But the march continued. The battle of Dorylaeum had been fought on 1 July, and in September range after range of mountains still showed to the south-east. Then the chariot broke its back in a rocky ford of the Anti-Taurus. This might have been a terrible disaster, but in these Armenian lands the pilgrimage was accompanied by a crowd of merchants, and Roger was able to exchange the oxen and some of the heavy gear for a pair of riding-mules. He knew he was cheated, but there was no time to haggle.

Now Anne could ride beside him all day. He loved her companionship, but sometimes her talk angered him. She had not been convinced by his exposition of his duty, and continually tried to change his mind.

They passed a little town, perched on a shelf of the mountain-side; it was very small, but the walls were Roman limestone, clear cut and impregnable. Anne could not take her eyes off it.

'What a dear little town!' she began. 'And what a fine dome over the church! I wonder how many people live there? Look, do you see a steep roof in the angle of the walls? That must be the hall of its ruler. The fathers of these Greeks were rich, to fortify a little town so strongly. I wonder why they built it there? Oh, because it overlooks the road. In Aquitaine they build castles by the road, and merchants pay a toll to the lord. Wouldn't it be lovely to hold a town like that? Ten crossbow-men could defend the hall, and these Armenians will man the wall against infidels. The tolls would make you rich, and you could serve the Greek Emperor, or some Count of the pilgrims, whichever you preferred. Shall we make an excuse to stay be-hand, and try our luck when the army has passed?'

Roger did not interrupt; he was angry, and that made it all the more important that he should observe the courtesies. He was beginning to regret the privacy he had guarded all through the crowded march; he was not used to talking all day, and this temptation had been put very crudely.

'My darling, I am under oath to follow the Duke. People don't always keep these promises, and I would not defend the Duke's every action in his quarrel with the King of England; but he has treated me fairly. While I eat his bread, and ride his horse, I have no excuse to desert him.'

'Of course you are bound by your oath, and I could not love a husband who was forsworn. But that is a dear little town, all the same, and I hope we get something like it. Perhaps we can come back later, after we have won Antioch and freed these Christians of the East. Tell me, what do you think of these Easterners? They don't seem the sort of people I would like to protect.'

'Quite true. They are not attractive people. They prefer to pay taxes instead of fighting; and I hear they take their disputes to a paid magistrate, instead of being judged by their equals in open court. They have no honour. But they asked for our help, and we shall get along with them somehow.'

It was true that some local Christians did not welcome the pilgrims. For thirty years they had been under infidel lords, who exacted heavy tribute but otherwise left them in peace; now they found themselves on a dangerous March, exposed once more to Turkish raids, and they preferred security to independence.

Anne was extremely capable on the march, always ready in time to start, knowing the whims of the mules, and able to keep the servants up to their work. At the same time she deferred charmingly to her husband's judgement, though sometimes he wondered if this was only because she had been thoroughly trained in courtesy. All their disagreements ended in the same way; she would say prettily that it was the duty of a wife to obey, and that anyway a man knows best; but he had not really convinced her, and soon she would raise the same question again.

'Which lord will you follow, when at last Duke Robert goes home? Bohemund is a great warrior, but I don't think he would treat his vassals well.'

'I don't know the Count of Taranto well enough to drop his title, and I wish you wouldn't,' Roger answered wearily. Was it going to start all over again? 'They say he has been promised Antioch, but he will have to provide for all the Normans of Italy. We might push on to Jerusalem, if anyone goes so far. We can make up our minds when the time comes.'

'Oh well, you know best. But I am sorry. This country is rich and full of strong castles; and the desert begins beyond Jerusalem. My father used to say that a vassal should strengthen himself, for that strengthens his lord; he is entitled to disregard commands that make him weak.'

'That is not how I was taught to keep faith.'

'It is only what Father used to say, and of course it is you I obey now. ... Wouldn't the Duke be pleased if you had more men? We have money, and if you gave some to the groom he might buy horses; then you could lend them to your friends, and have knights to follow you. We should be quite important.'

'It would be pleasant to have knights to follow us, but you know as well as I do that no pilgrim has a horse to spare. You really want Mark to steal horses, by bribing some other groom. That would be against the laws of the host, besides being wrong in itself. Never mention such an idea again. In battle I may win some Turkish ponies; if not, we must continue as we are. Remember, Our Lady had only a donkey, and Saint Joseph walked.'

'As you did, dear Roger, before we were married. In truth horses are rare in this country. Yet all the Greek soldiers outside Nicaea were mounted; why can't they send us theirs? What has become of our gallant allies?'

'Their Emperor has taken them off to Caria and Lydia, to win the towns he lost twenty years ago. We can manage without him, and it all helps the Christians of the East.'

'The poor dear Christians of the East! Of course we must help them. But I wish their horses would stray.'

Anne's malicious grin was so attractive that Roger's heart was softened. In his plodding, literal mind he was often puzzled whether to take seriously her infamous proposals. He was glad that she was only joking. Women were mysterious creatures, and from the pulpit you always heard that they were more wicked than men. Perhaps they all talked like that in her castle at home; he must make allowances, but his point of view was more in keeping with a holy pilgrimage. The trouble was that Anne did not think of it as a holy pilgrimage, but as an expedition of conquest, on an equal footing with the winning of Sicily. He could not say she was badly brought up, for she was charming, discreet, and outwardly extremely obedient to her husband; none the less, her parents had given her wrong ideas, and he would have to instil his own principles into her mind. He was nineteen, and that is the priggish age.

Domna Alice might be a bad influence. She was fond of Anne, and wished her to be rich and successful; possibly she encouraged these predatory suggestions. Altogether, the woman was a burden. It looked as though she would be with them for life; she was too old for marriage, and there were no nunneries in the Eastern world where she could be packed off with a corrody. He resolved to have a talk with her.

The opportunity came at Michaelmas, when the pilgrims halted to celebrate the feast. After Mass Anne went to play blind man's buff with the young ladies, and the more fashionable knights; the game was all the rage in France, but Domna Alice was too old, and Roger, who had to wear armour to appear well-dressed, would not play in a mail shirt. He took the waiting-lady for a walk, and found her talkative.

'When my husband was killed in Spain I was left very badly off. Messer Odo is my cousin, and he gave me hospitality as waiting-lady to his four daughters; little Anne is the youngest, and she was the last to marry. That wedding was a sad business! Poor cousin Odo was in a fix, for we had been raiding once too often; and Messer Giles had influence with the Count. We had to make peace before the castle was besieged. Messer Giles managed that, in return for a young maiden with a dowry in cash. He was preparing for this pilgrimage, and he was so high in the Count's favour that he would have gone far if he had lived.'

'Why was Messer Odo in such an unfortunate position? Did he often wage war without leave of his lord?'

'His whole life was spent in war, and sometimes the Count wanted peace. Besides, the merchants complained of his tolls, and a Bishop excommunicated him for sacrilege. My poor cousin had a great many difficulties, and his friends did not stand by him.'

This sketch of his father-in-law's activities explained a good deal about Anne. But many a disturber of the peace could argue his own conscience into approval, and Roger wished to know more about Messer Odo's way of life.

'England is a peaceful country; only great lords have castles, and my father lives on an open manor. But I know things are different in the south. I suppose Messer Odo would only fight in a righteous cause? There are robber-knights in the world, but they don't have well-behaved daughters.'

'My cousin was not a robber; he never took anything that was not his own, even though he had to raid for it. You see, there were disputes about the boundary of the fief, and those wicked Aquitanians would not render service. Merchants ought to pay toll to the knights who guard the roads, and it is cheating his vassals when the Count grants them free passage. The trouble with the Bishop was a misunderstanding; some monks owed service, but they denied it, and their monastery caught fire during the argument. Yet our castle was respectable. Little Anne was strictly brought up, and even when we were ex-communicate Father John offered Mass in the chapel every day.'

'He should not have done that. I know, since my brother suffered the same misfortune.'

'He did, all the same. There was nothing he wouldn't do for Messer Odo. I wonder what became of the poor man; the Bishop had him in prison when we left. But it shows the castle was properly run; you need have no anxiety about the virtue of Domna Anne.'

'I am not anxious on that subject,' said Roger, stiffly, 'but her childhood was unlike mine. Now I see why she is so eager to win a castle in these mountains, and live by raiding her neighbours. But I don't like raiding, and I doubt if I should be any good at it. I want you to speak to my lady privately. Remind her that, for women at least, peace can be better than war; and that one way of getting on in the world is to keep sworn engagements. Tell her, if you like, that we have had a talk, and that you are obeying my instructions.'

He thought Anne would heed advice from the waiting-lady, even if she rejected the counsel of her young and untried husband. As for Domna Alice, she must obey him or be turned adrift; there was no oath between them.

Dinner was a happy picnic. It was long since the pilgrims had enjoyed a hot meal in the middle of the day, and all were in holiday mood. In the afternoon there was a little half-hearted jousting, though the trained warhorses were to precious to be risked in hard courses. Roger did not compete. He sat on the ground, with his wife beside him, and watched the sport.

Anne had been playing 'Hot Cockles', and other games that involved smacks on the behind; and she sat carefully. But the exercise, and even the bruises, had brought a glow to her cheeks and a sparkle to her eyes; she looked more beautiful than he had ever seen her. But presently the happiness died out of her face; she shivered slightly, and spoke:

'We used to watch jousts at home. How long ago that seems! Shall we march through these mountains for another year?'

'I don't know, my darling, nor does anyone else in the pilgrimage. But we shall probably halt when Antioch is won.' Roger had never before seen his wife depressed; he spoke his mind, without thinking of her fears. She was angry at his indifference.

'You don't understand,' she answered unhappily. 'You travelled through peaceful Italy, and wintered with your cousins; when at last you reached Romania there was a treaty with the Emperor. But we marched through the mountains of the Sclavonians; it was autumn, and the torrents were full. The mountaineers rolled great boulders down at us, we were always hungry and cold, and the horses were lamed by the rocks. When we reached Romania the Greeks treated us as enemies, and we had to pillage or starve. I have been among bitter foes since we left Lombardy – and Giles is dead – and we grow fewer every day – and each step takes us farther from Provence.'

She sobbed, and Roger had no idea how to comfort her. But there was a bright side, and he tried to put it.

'This land is hostile now, my sweet, but that will soon be altered. When all the pilgrims are settled in their castles this will be a second France. The Turks are afraid to face us, and the stone walls of these cities will keep them out. Now forget your fears, and watch that fat Brabançon fall off his horse when he meets our Norman.'

'Of course I'm not afraid. I am a baron's daughter! It's just that we are so far from home.' She spoke in short gulps. 'I am miserable, too, because of what Alice has told me. She says you think I am a pagan, and that my father's castle was a den of thieves. We only defended ourselves against our enemies. And I am not excommunicate now, whatever happened to father years ago. Poor Giles arranged things when I was betrothed to him. And what do you mean by complaining to my waiting-lady, behind my back?'

Roger fought down a feeling of exasperation; his wife could change in a breath from a frightened child to a lady standing on her dignity, and he must answer both at once. But perhaps he was in the wrong, and he smiled as he spoke in a humble voice:

'Please, darling, don't imagine I think ill of your family. Your

96

father is a conscientious man who stands up for his rights, and I dare say the Count was at fault. You were brought up a good Christian, and Domna Alice tells me you never missed Mass. I love and respect you, and I know you are as brave as one of your birth should be. Now do stop crying, and look at the joust.'

The appeal to pride of race did not fail. She hiccupped, and set her lips into a wavering smile.

'Oh dear, this journey has got on my nerves, and when we do have a holiday I waste it in tears! Alice is a stupid old woman and I expect she misunderstood what you said. I shall be quite safe with you to protect me, and all these brave knights. But they are not so many as they used to be. Is the army getting smaller? I notice it now we are all in one place.'

'Armies grow smaller every day, I suppose,' he answered, with a frown; he had noticed it also. 'People die of diseases, and others desert, like my Godric at Nicaea. You know I started with two men and three horses? But there are plenty of brave knights left. Soon we shall be riding round our own fields.'

That completed Anne's recovery; she could not be unhappy when she thought of the fief that would soon be hers. Next time she spoke it was about the points of a horse in the joust.

Roger remained uneasy. Nothing could alter Anne's opinion that this Holy Pilgrimage was a device for endowing all the landless knights of the West, however she might acquiesce when he spoke of their duty to the Christians of the East. As for her fears, they were a passing fancy; all the pilgrims were in great danger, and had been since they left Europe, and they must get used to facing it.

He loved his wife, but he was happier when he was not called upon to talk with her. Other men did not listen politely to female advice. But then his marriage had been unusual, for he was in love with his wife. All round him were the best trouvères of the West, and they sang of Love nearly as often as they sang of War; but never of love between husband and wife. It was a most unlikely subject, in a world where marriages were arranged by the parents for financial or diplomatic reasons. The conventions of courtesy enforced certain forms of politeness on the man, which disguised the real subjection of the woman; but they had met as strangers, and reasonable couples planned their lives so as not to interfere with the privacy of the other partner. Roger rode all day beside his wife, shared her bed at night, and was hardly ever out of reach of her voice. Life would have been more enjoyable if she had been content with his company in silence.

*　　*　　*

As they approached Antioch the pace grew slower. The road was even steeper than before, and parties of infidel horse hovered in the path of the advance. Roger was ordered to ride in the van, with other knights mounted on local ponies. They were called Turcopoles, since they were supposed to fight in the Turkish fashion; their shields and lances were left with the baggage, and they carried short bows. They were incapable of shooting behind them, or even to the right, as the Turks could; but their armour was arrow-proof, and the enemy, not realizing their limitations, kept at a respectful distance.

The host was stronger than it had been; many local Christians joined the foot, and small detachments of knights and crossbow-men returned from Cilicia, now safely garrisoned by Count Tancred, and even from Baldwin's tentative and half-conquered county of Edessa. A decisive battle was imminent, and every pilgrim gathered for the final effort.

On 19 October Roger rode back to camp at sunset. All day scattered Turks had ridden before the advance, just out of arrow range; now the local Christians took over piquet duty, and the Turcopoles were free until tomorrow. Anne always chose a good place for the night, and he quickly found the little fire, near the kitchen and out of the wind. As he dismounted some-one called his name, from the confusion of the crowded road. It was his cousin, Robert de Santa Fosca, wearing a long tunic of red silk, and looking sleek and prosperous.

'Welcome, cousin,' called Roger in great delight. He was always glad to pick out a familiar face in the noisy anonymous crowd. But as they embraced he recollected himself. He envied Robert, who had left the army to better himself, yet he despised him as one who had chosen the easier service; he forgot that he had wanted to go too, and only remembered that he had done his duty. He meant to be stern with the shirker, but his voice betrayed his affection. 'Welcome cousin. What a beautiful tunic, and how well you fill it. I see you have not gone hungry. I also have won a prize in this campaign. Domna de Bodeham, may I present to you my cousin from Italy, Robert de Santa Fosca. Robert, this is Domna Anne de la Roche, my wife.'

Robert kissed her on the cheek, as a cousin should.

'How delightful, Domna, to meet a beautiful lady in these desolate wastes. You must tell me your adventures. But perhaps French is not your language? Do you prefer Italian?' For Anne had been listening to his quickly-spoken words with a slight frown of concentration. 'Ah, you were bred in Provence, the land of poets. Well, I can speak a little in that tongue also. But how do you manage, Roger, or are you a silent and masterful lord?'

He had hit on a sore point. Many Frenchmen of the north could speak the langue d'Oc, the most elegant language for love-making and poetry, and Roger always felt a little boorish when he failed to understand a phrase; but it was his wife's duty to learn the language of her husband. He was determined not to be left out of the talk, and he interrupted in slow clear north French:

'We had no adventures. We stayed with the host, and that means hard marching and scanty food. Tell us instead about Count Tancred, and how you won that silk tunic. You have been conquering counties and delivering cities while we plodded through these hills.'

Robert settled himself, hand on hip and leg out-thrust, like a trouvère beginning a poem.

'We delivered cities, all right; but some of them did not welcome us as deliverers. Can you imagine four men playing chess on the same board, each against the other three? There were the Turks and the Armenians and the Lotharingians and us. The wretched Turks didn't stand a chance; all they thought of was surrendering to some Westerner who would protect them from the local Christians. Count Tancred led us first to Tarsus, where the infidel garrison were quite willing to hand over the town, though we were only a hundred knights; but Count Baldwin turned up with a much larger force, five hundred knights at least. The Turks galloped away in the dark, and the local inhabitants manned the wall. They would have liked to set up an Armenian lord, but there were too many Western knights about, so they began to treat with the weaker side, which was us; but Count Baldwin threatened to besiege the town if we occupied it, so we very sensibly retired. Next we tried Adana, but the Turks fled too soon, and the Armenians wouldn't let us in. At Mamistra the Turks lingered, and ran out of one gate as we got in by another; as we were settling down Count Baldwin came up, and began to shoot arrows at the wall; but that was really going too far, and his own men cried shame. In the end we made a treaty; we were outnumbered, but we were behind stone walls, and Count Baldwin left us in possession. Now Count Tancred is lord of Skanderoon, and the Lotharingians will set up their county at Edessa when it surrenders.'

'It does not sound like a pilgrimage,' said Roger, slowly, 'but at least you made peace before the fighting had gone too far. I am glad my Duke was not mixed up in it.'

'What strikes me,' said Anne, 'is that the Turks ran away wherever you went. Those towns could have been held for a long time. Our troubles are over; we have only to walk up against Antioch and Jerusalem, and then settle down to grow rich.'

'I hope so, Domna,' Robert answered. 'But the local Christians say Antioch is stronger than any city that we have seen, and the Turks are gathering to hold it. They don't know how far we mean to chase them, and they feel they must make a stand somewhere. The leaders should send word to them that Antioch is the end of our journey; they might give it up quietly if they could keep the rest of Syria.'

'We can't do that,' Roger put in. 'Too many pilgrims want to go on to Jerusalem; and how can the leaders stop us while there is land for the taking?'

'No,' said Anne, 'this army will never halt so long as the infidels run away. Anyway, we need land, though I hope Roger's castle will not be right on the March.'

'I understand, Domna,' said Robert with a smile. 'Near enough to raid the enemy, but far enough back for your own cattle to graze in the open. That is the right position for a castle.'

'Quite so, but I have no castle,' said Roger. 'And unless we see more fighting I may never be given one. In the end I may guard the walls of Jerusalem, for whichever lord rules there.'

'That would be a noble occupation,' said Robert politely, 'though not well paid. But I must get back to supper. No, I won't stay. You can't feed chance guests on these rations. Perhaps I can dine with you later, when we are halted in fertile country.'

He swaggered away, swinging his tunic.

'A handsome scoundrel,' said Anne, looking after him. 'But those Normans from Italy are the worst brigands unhung. I wonder how he came by those silken clothes?'

'He is, after all, my cousin,' said Roger mildly. 'He talks a lot of wild nonsense, but I think it is only talk. They led a very unsettled life in Italy.'

'Whereas you were brought up on your father's unwalled manor. But that is the type who will prosper here. You heard what he said about an agreement with the infidels; Bohemund leads the other leaders, and that young man has heard a rumour of negotiations. We must get a castle at once, before it's too late.'

'My dear Anne,' Roger spoke mildly, and forced himself to smile; but he was very weary of this topic, 'if no one gives me land we can live in a town; my father would see no disgrace in that, whatever they think in Provence. Or I can defend Jerusalem. That would be almost the same as entering religion; I would fight no one except infidels, and it would be an honourable livelihood.'

'It may come to that, but it is not an occupation for the husband of a de la Roche. While there is no fighting you have no chance of making a name. Can't you do something about it? Get into a skirmish when you are scouting, and kill a few Turks. You are drifting, my darling; you do your duty, but you don't look for a chance of distinction. You are too honest to take a castle by force, and we won't go into all that again. Now try to earn one.'

She looked at him with the conventional languishing appeal

of a lady begging her knight to perform an exploit. It seemed odd, coming from his own wife; but then he was husband and lover combined.

'Very well, sweetheart. Tomorrow I shall try and catch up the infidels who watch the advance. I might kill a few; but I may lose my only horse, and the Duke would not give me another.'

He was nervous that night, and slept badly. He had taken part in one great victory, and the advance had continued unopposed for so long that everyone despised the Turks. But he could not forget the despairing face of Hugh de Dives.

Next day the infidels hung more closely round the Turcopoles. They were only a day's march from Antioch, and the enemy wanted information about the numbers and composition of the army. Roger edged his pony to the front; he had never used a bow, except the toy with which children scared birds, but it seemed fairly easy to shoot to his left front, and his mount had been trained to carry an archer; it trotted straight, and did not shy at the twang of the bow-string. Presently he took a long shot at a solitary Turk, and missed. He cantered forward and dismounted to pick up the shaft, for he had only ten in his quiver. As he went down, an arrow whacked against the skirt of his mail, and another passed below the belly of his pony. Two Turks had ridden out from behind a rock; they knew Western mail, and had aimed at his legs and his horse. He threw himself across the saddle and urged the pony to a gallop. The Turks did not pursue, for he was riding straight to the main army; but it had been a narrow shave. He was not going to risk being dismounted with a battle in prospect, and for the rest of the day he rode in line.

As he rode back that evening, trying to compose an explanation of his failure that would satisfy his wife, he met a small body of knights setting out to drive away the lingering Turkish scouts. Among them he recognized his cousin; Robert still had his European warhorse; he wore high Greek riding-boots and a red linen cloak over his armour; his horse was fat, and his helm polished. So that was how a knight fared who followed Count Tancred for his private gain, while those who were true to their lords rode untrained ponies and ate dry biscuit in the saddle.

Roger decided that he had a grievance against the world, and therefore he might righteously be angry with Anne.

But Domna Alice was helping her mistress to heat supper when he arrived, and he could not lose his temper before her. Also Anne was looking even more charming than usual, with a gay silk kerchief that he had never seen before. It suited her golden face, and she was evidently very pleased with it.

'I see you have a new headdress,' he said at last. 'I hope it was not expensive. You know I must save to buy a proper warhorse if we are to get on.'

'Oh, I didn't buy this. Your cousin gave it to me when we halted for dinner. He said he owed me a wedding-gift. It's handsome, don't you think? Of course, he got it off a Turk, but it was woven by the Greeks.'

'Well, I can't object to your taking wedding-presents from a cousin. I hope he doesn't get married himself, or expect a present in return. But it was handsome of Robert, and I must not grudge him his good fortune.'

'He seems a very gallant knight,' said Domna Alice, 'and he speaks good langue d'Oc, though you can tell he is a foreigner. It cheers me when a knight serves the ladies as they do at home. He said he would compose a poem to my lady during the siege.'

'He expects a siege, then, not a battle,' Roger said quickly, 'and he always knows what is going on. Still, that is obvious, or the infidels would have stood before. Yet there may be fighting tomorrow, and I shall go to bed early. Don't wake me, Anne, when you come.'

Nobody had asked about the failure of his attempt at single combat, and that was something to the good. As for cousin Robert, one must remember that envy is a mortal sin, and that some people are by nature luckier than others.

5

OUTSIDE ANTIOCH
1097–8

ROGER sat outside his hut, and stared across the marsh at the city of Antioch; it was November, and the pilgrims had been in front of the walls for three weeks. From where he sat he could see the interior of the town, climbing the hillside of Mount Silpius in close-packed acres of whitewashed stone walls and vivid red-tiled roofs, with the domes of the desecrated churches standing out clearly in the pale winter sunshine. It was an enormous city, rich and well-built, and the taking of it would make many fortunes; but that taking would be a laborious and dangerous task. On the north-west the town wall ran along the left bank of the Orontes, broken by the great Bridge Gate and the massive embattled bridge, which was held by the infidels; west and south-west it climbed the mountain, with St George's Gate in the narrow plain at the foot, from which issued the south-western road to Daphne and the coast; exactly opposite him, across the whole breadth of the town, he could see the double walls of the citadel, the highest point of the enceinte, crowning a spur of Mount Silpius; thence the wall dipped into a ravine, climbed out again, descended the hillside to St Paul's Gate and the Aleppo road, and swung round behind the marsh to the Dog's Gate immediately opposite. The curtain was forty feet high, sheer stone unbroken by any window or loophole, but at intervals of fifty yards were square towers, overtopping it by twenty feet, projecting into the ditch, furnished with engines and pierced by slits for arrow-shot. The pilgrims' camp was built on a narrow neck of land, south of the Orontes and north of the marsh that served as a moat to the northern wall; east and south stretched the endless empire of the infidels, and while they held the great Bridge Gate the Turks could sally out at will to the west and north also. The pilgrims were nearly surrounded on their narrow peninsula; they had no skilled Greek carpenters to make catapults, and in any case the marsh was too broad for siege-engines to be used with effect; in three weeks they had not scratched a stone of the defences, and Roger thought gloomily that they could sit there till Doomsday without inconveniencing a single Turk. The siege of Nicaea had been easy, with Greek workmen and Greek supplies; then the miraculous deliverance at Dorylaeum had given them a moral ascendancy; but they had extracted the last ounce of prestige out of that victory, as they pressed the Turks back and back from Bithynia to Syria; now they had come to an impregnable barrier, the final high-water-mark of the expedition.

It was evening, and he sat on his rolled-up blankets with his head in his hands and his elbows on his knees; he was on watch that night against the Bridge Gate, and he was already fully armed, for the warmth of the leather under the iron outweighed the stiffness and chafing of the heavy mail shirt. A yard down wind an iron pot simmered over a small fire, which he watched anxiously. Firewood always became scarce when an army sat down long in one place. Domna Alice came out of the little hut behind him, and walked over to inspect the pot.

'I think it is ready, Messer Roger,' she called, 'and you don't want to be late for your guard. Shall we begin?'

'Where is Domna Anne?' he inquired.

'She went over to the Provençal camp, while you were sleeping after dinner. I took her there, of course, but it was a party of young ladies and I didn't want to stay; they will send her back with a crossbowman. The ladies had a goat, and they asked her to share their supper.'

'I don't like my wife wandering round the camp, cadging hospitality that we can't return,' grumbled Roger. 'Why can't she stay here to look after my meals? What is it this time? Boiled millet again? Certainly the Count of Toulouse looks after his people better than our Duke. What's the good of the Count of Blois being made Governor of the Camp if he doesn't distribute the food equally?'

Domna Alice brought out two wooden bowls from the hut

and ladled the hot porridge into them; years of dependence had made it a habit for her to soothe her employer's temper.

'You must remember, Messer Roger,' she said, 'that these Provençal ladies are Domna Anne's neighbours at home, and were her companions in that awful march through Sclavonia. I believe they all put their money together to buy the goat, and my lady paid her share. It is not part of the army supplies; a Syrian smuggled it into the camp under his cloak, and sold it to them.'

'It should have been army supplies, all the same.' Roger went on grumbling. 'The Count of Blois ought to get hold of all the goats round here, and distribute them equally; if people buy smuggled food the rest of us go short. I expect those Italians and Lotharingians, with their castles in the north, are living as well as they do at home.'

'It is only fair that those who pay money should have better food than the rest.'

'No, we are on a pilgrimage, and should share equally. Besides, Domna Anne cannot afford it.'

'I am very sorry, sir. Domna Anne seldom goes out to supper, and I will tell her you don't like it. Now, please eat your porridge before it gets cold.'

He felt better-tempered when his stomach was full, and thanked Domna Alice as she fastened his hauberk and put on his helm; the crossbowman who acted as groom brought up his pony, and taking lance and shield he rode to the light wooden bridge that Syrian workmen had built in the rear of the camp.

Opposite the great Bridge Gate, on the north bank of the Orontes, was a low but steep-sided hill; on this was an infidel burying-ground, and a small stone building where in peace-time they worshipped their devils. Every evening it was occupied by dismounted Turkish archers, to guard against a surprise attack on the Bridge, and to cover the raiding-parties that crept out in the darkness to the north of the Christian camp. Every evening the pilgrims sent out mounted patrols north of this Cemetery Hill, and clashes were frequent in the dark. It seemed to be the only way of getting to close quarters with the Turks, who otherwise sat safely behind their impregnable stone walls. Tonight there was a special reason for extra precautions; Count Tancred of Cilicia was taking a force of crossbowmen and Syrian workmen over the hills and right round south of the town, to build a fort on the western side, opposite the Gate of Saint George; if he was attacked the night guard must assault the Bridge, to distract the defenders.

When Roger joined the other horsemen of the night guard he found that his luck was in; he was attached to a small group of nine other lesser knights, all mounted on country-bred ponies; but the Duke of Normandy himself, on his great warhorse, was to command them. It was unusual for one of the leaders to take on such a tiresome duty as the night guard, but there had been little excitement in the last fortnight, and there was the Duke, with a thick cloak over his armour, slightly drunk and in very good spirits. When it was dark enough the patrol set off westwards at a quiet walk, and drew up a bowshot to the west of the great Bridge. The night was dark and cloudy, but the native ponies could pick their way over the stony ground without mishap, and the Duke's warhorse was behaving calmly. Roger was praying hard that the Turks should come out, and give him the chance to distinguish himself in the presence of his lord; if he now did well in a fight his castle would be secure.

The winter night drew on, and nothing happened except that they grew colder and more hungry; the ponies, used to night-raiding, stood and shivered without a sound, and they could hear the infidels talking in their fortified cemetery. All was quiet on the hillside across the river, where Count Tancred's party worked in silence, and the other patrols to the north made only an occasional noise. Presently Roger's pony raised his head and blew softly through his nostrils; Roger could just distinguish in the darkness that his ears were pricked. He whispered to his neighbour.

'Tell the Duke my horse hears someone coming.'

The Turks in the cemetery were making more noise than usual, chanting their prayers to the devil to ward off the ghosts of the night; but soon all the patrol were listening, and something seemed to be moving on the Bridge. The Duke led them quietly forward. They halted, peering into the blackness, and suddenly there shone a spark where a horse's hoof had struck against a stone; the Duke shouted *'Deus Vult'* with all the force of his lungs, and they were all galloping hard for the Bridge-head, a hundred and fifty yards away. They were not riding knee to knee, and the ground was rocky and uneven. Roger suddenly had that desperate terror that his horse would come down in the next stride which is as unnerving as the paralysing fear of heights; he rode loose, ready for the fall, keeping his spurs and knees well away from the pony's sides, and his nervousness made him tighten the reins. They could just see a cluster of mounted Turks when Roger's bad riding took effect on his pony, carefully trained for a very different kind of warfare. He felt the beast check and turn to the right; then he trotted sideways to the enemy, waiting for his rider to shoot his arrows. In a blind rage, Roger turned him with his knees and spurred after his companions, but he was too late; already the Turks had turned back into the safety of the Bridge, and the knights were pulling up. A flight of arrows came blindly over them from the cemetery and they cantered out of range.

The Duke was very pleased with himself, for there was blood on his lance, though no one else had been quick enough to reach the enemy; like most leaders of fighting-men, he had eyes in the back of his head, for he spoke to Roger.

'I saw that horse of yours pull out, young man; you've been acting as a Turcopole, haven't you? Don't forget how to use a lance, just because I have given you a bow. See that you have your horse under better control next time. Now, gentlemen, we shall stay here till dawn, but you may dismount; they won't send out another raiding party in a hurry.'

Roger was sick with rage and shame; his pony's behaviour had taken him by surprise, but it was his own nervousness that had provided the opportunity. All his life he had been terrified of the way the ground comes up to hit a rider whose horse trips at full gallop; it had happened to him once when he was a child. For the rest of the night he raged inwardly, and vowed to himself that the next time he charged he would stick in his spurs and go straight on, if the river Orontes was in the way.

When the late November dawn reddened the sky the patrol

rode eastward to the temporary bridge that served the camp. Roger gave his pony to the waiting groom, and called into the doorway of the hut for Anne to disarm him. She came out half asleep, and shivering in the cold air.

'Good morning, Roger. What a climate! Were there any excitements in the night? I hear the Duke of Normandy was out there with you. Did you have a chance of bringing yourself to his notice, and winning that castle we must get out of him?'

'I attracted his attention all right, in the worst possible way. A gang of Turks tried to get out across the Bridge, and the Duke charged them without a word to any of us. I had a bad start, and then my pony took fright and wouldn't go in. The Duke rebuked me for bad horsemanship in front of the whole patrol. He noticed me most particularly, and the castle is farther off than ever.' He flung his hauberk in the direction of the hut, and swore. That was the version of the charge that five hours' brooding had implanted on his mind; it was all the pony's fault.

'Oh dear, I am sorry,' said Anne, opening her eyes wide with a startled look. 'What bad luck, and how tiresome of the pony. You must practise at the mark again. Do it this afternoon where the Duke can see you; that may impress him with your keenness.'

'I'm damned if I will take riding-lessons in front of the whole blasted army,' Roger burst out. 'I have no hope of impressing the Duke, and I had better keep out of his way. I'm sick and tired of this foolish pilgrimage. I shall sleep all day. I'm worn out. And do something about padding the inside of this helm, it has given me another filthy headache. When is breakfast?' It was the first time he had lost his temper with Anne, and he already felt better for it.

He woke at midday, quite refreshed in body, but something in his mind told him that he ought not to be happy; for a moment he could not remember the cause, then recollection came of the awful mistake he had made last night. However, he had slept off his sulks, and he could not recapture the angry mood. He came out of the hut whistling and kissed his wife as she knelt by the cooking fire; she turned a sullen face towards him, but smiled when she saw he was in a good temper. The clerks of the Count of Blois had sent them a piece of strange meat, said to be camel, though the camp joke was to call it dead Turk; at least it was more sustaining than millet porridge. Domna Alice joined them for the meal, and they were quite gay together. The whole camp was in high spirits, for it seemed that Count Tancred had succeeded in building his fort during the night, and this should help to cut off supplies from the Turks. Antioch was built on the northern slopes of a steep hill, and there was no road into it over the crest from the south. The pilgrims' main camp more or less barred the north, and now the new castle was opposed to the western gate. The Turks were all horsemen, and they had thousands of horses in the town; when these began to die for lack of forage the enemy would probably ask for terms.

But there was a disappointment in store; in the afternoon Saint George's Gate was opened as usual and the horses of the garrison came out to graze. Tancred's castle was built on a hillside, divided from the western side of the town by a steep valley, in which a brook flowed northward to the Orontes. A few Turks picketed the fort, and there was plenty of room for the grazing horses on the river plain to the north. Of course, the pilgrims could have formed in battle-array and driven the Turks within the walls; but they would have tired their own horses, who also needed grazing, and no one felt like getting under arms every time the enemy opened a gate. The stalemate was allowed to continue.

The routine of the siege went on. Roger was only needed for duty every third day, and was free to spend the rest of his time sitting in the camp and looking at Antioch. The whole army was bored and despondent, for it was easy to see the attack made no progress, and food was growing scarce. A Genoese fleet was in the harbour of Saint Simeon, a day's march to the west near the mouth of the Orontes, but the Greeks of southern Anatolia were reluctant to empty their magazines so long as the infidels might return unexpectedly. In fact, the arrival of the ships reminded the pilgrims that it was possible to go home in comparative safety, and weakened their resolution for another winter abroad. It was difficult to kill time. Roger disliked the endless crowding and lack of privacy of the camp, there were not enough supplies for feasting, and horses were too precious to joust with. He was happy in the company of Anne, but she had her housekeeping to do, and that tiresome Domna Alice shared the hut. The most cheerful person he met was his cousin, Robert de Santa Fosca. He had not yet been given a castle by Count Tancred, but the Count of Taranto had promised to do something for him when Antioch fell; he wandered about the camp in his silken tunic, usually with a flask of wine, and composed songs to the ladies in north French, langue d'Oc, or Italian.

One evening Roger strolled up to his own hut after hearing Compline in the Duke's chapel. Robert was singing a sirvente to Anne, but he jumped up and, taking his cousin's arm, drew him aside.

'Cousin Roger, I have secret news for you. You know the Count of Taranto can speak Arabic? He learnt it in Sicily. Well, he has spies out in the country, and one of them says that a Turkish army will leave Harenc tomorrow, to raid our camp. The Count intends to lay an ambush for them and the Duke of Normandy and the Count of Flanders will go with him. It is only a small party, because we depend on secrecy, and only knights with warhorses are going. But your pony is up to your weight, and he can gallop. Go to the Duke and ask to come with us; it's a chance to earn some glory and get into his favour. You can say I told you in confidence, but remember it is supposed to be a secret.'

Roger was excited; the expedition would break the monotony of the siege, and he might win some renown. He hurried off to the Duke's tent. There was the usual crowd of petitioners, but he felt the occasion was important enough to warrant a handsome tip to the doorkeeper and he was soon admitted. The Duke was as private as any great lord could ever be; that is, there were only present three or four clerks, a page, and two sergeants as guards. He seemed anxious and impatient, and his temper was short.

'It's quite impossible. We are going to ambush these people, and charge right home before they have time to scatter; for that you need a trained warhorse, though God knows we have few enough left. I am only taking fifty knights myself, and those the best mounted and armed. If you want to kill infidels there are plenty of chances when they take their horses out to graze. In any case, this is supposed to be a secret attack, and I'd be glad to know how you heard of it.'

Roger did not wish to give his cousin away, but he tried one more appeal.

'My lord, the last time I fought behind you my pony carried me clear of the charge, and I was shamed before the other knights. Since then I have trained him at the mark' (this was a lie) 'and I must have a chance to redeem my honour. Let me come with you tonight.'

'No! and that's final,' said the Duke. 'I remember that last time now you speak of it, and it's just the sort of thing we don't want to happen; one horse flinching upsets the ranks and makes the others hesitate. If you like, you can go round to Tancred's absurd castle tomorrow, and have a go at the horse-guard. That is all your pony's fit for, but don't bring on a battle by calling out the Italians to rescue you.'

Roger bowed and withdrew, angry and disappointed, while the sergeants pretended to have heard nothing, and one of the clerks smiled to the page. He found Robert still gossiping to Anne, and at once poured out an account of the interview. His cousin found it amusing.

'Duke Robert is getting very military these days,' he said with a smile. 'For the first time in his life he has found someone who obeys him, and he delights in giving orders. It wasn't wise to ask permission first; perhaps you should just have tacked on to us in the darkness. What do you think of a trip to Tancred's castle; it doesn't sound a very good idea to me. You won't bother the enemy, and you might lose your only mount.'

'Of course he must go,' Anne broke in eagerly. 'If he is so careful to obey the Duke, he can take this as a command. He must make a name, or we shall never get our castle.'

It never seemed to occur to Anne that knights might be killed in these encounters. Or else she thought the chance of winning a fief was worth any risk.

'If you think it's a good plan,' Roger said, 'I'll ride round there tomorrow morning. I will say the Duke sent me and the Italians can't object then. At least it will get me off night-patrol in the evening, and that will be clear gain. I'm sorry I can't come with you, Robert, and I wish you the best of luck. Shall I come to your hut and arm you?'

At this hint Robert took leave of the ladies and went off, singing to himself, towards the Italian encampment.

Next morning, after Mass and a leisurely breakfast, Roger was armed by Anne and Domna Alice, and set out at mid-morning with a lump of biscuit for his dinner. With the walls of Antioch on his right, he rode south-east across the deserted Aleppo road, and soon his pony was climbing the ridges of Mount Silpius. The Turks usually kept their horses inside the walls during the middle of the day, and though he rode cautiously he saw no one until he came to Tancred's castle from the south, as the garrison was finishing dinner. They were chiefly crossbowmen of mixed south Italian stock, and he could not understand their various languages, but there was a Norman-Italian knight in charge; to him Roger explained his errand, stressing that it was the Duke's command.

'If the Duke of Normandy sent you, I suppose it is all right, but I don't know what you think you can do. When we try to raid the herd the Turks just bring more men out of the city, and we are not strong enough to drive them in by main force. Of course, you might catch one of their guards by himself, and ride him down, though that won't really help on the Holy War very much. I can't send out my crossbowmen to support you, it would endanger this fort; but we will cover you if you come back in a hurry. That bush marks the farthest range of an arrow from here, and the Turks won't pursue past it. I hope you brought your own dinner; it's shameful the way the Count of Blois neglects this place.'

Roger was slightly disappointed that this tough old warrior did not think him a hero, and he was in two minds whether to ride back to the camp; but that would look altogether too foolish, so he dismounted and munched his biscuit. Almost at once, the Gate of Saint George was opened in the plain below, and a body of about a hundred Turks rode out, followed by an enormous herd of loose horses. Ten of the infidels came straight for the drystone walls of the castle, and sat their horses without moving about two hundred and fifty yards away.

'That is what they always do,' said the captain, 'and we can't harm them if they don't come any nearer. Still, any day they may grow careless, and at sunset most of them dismount to worship their devil. One of my men will hold your horse ready by the entrance at the back, where they can't see him; a lance shows over the top of this wall, so keep yours couched as you ride round. Go straight out when you see your chance, don't stop to consult me or you may be too late. Good luck! Now it's time for my nap,' and he stretched himself, wrapped in his cloak, in the lee of the flimsy wall.

Roger stood in an embrasure, beside the sentinel, for two long hours, and the Turks sat outside, waiting. But their ponies were getting cold, and after that time they began to walk up and down, not in a group, but in twos and threes. A dun-coloured stallion, with three mares in attendance, was grazing up the hill, and as the little troop of horses drew nearer to the fort six Turks rode to turn them back; another had dismounted to look at his pony's foot, and only three were left to guard against surprise. Roger stiffened; was this his opportunity? He dreaded to make up his mind. He had never given an order in battle, and the only time he had used his judgement, at Dorylaeum, he had clearly been wrong. But he had been growing more and more nervous, and with a sudden resolve to get the waiting over, he ran silently across the fort to his horse. The crossbowman grinned as he helped him into the saddle, and handed him shield and lance; he looked old enough, and wicked enough, to have been at war for many campaigns, but, like all footmen, he obeyed the orders of any untried young knight.

Roger wheeled his pony out of the entrance on the far side of the fort, turned sharply round the walls, and galloped as hard as he could downhill towards the three Turkish sentinels. They were watching their comrades turn the straying horses, and the ground of the hillside, softened by the winter rains, muffled the noise of approaching hoof-beats. Luckily it was close turf, without boulders, and the paralysing fear of a fall was driven from

Roger's mind by his taut, screwed-up resolution. He had gone a hundred yards before the Turks were aware of him, and then they behaved as he had hoped; instead of galloping away and shooting over their horses' tails, they drew their ridiculous little curved swords and rode towards him, calling loudly on their devil. He dug his spurs deep, in a way his pony had never felt before, and holding the beast straight with his knees, thundered down the slope. In a few seconds he was into them, his lance thrust deep into the chest of the man on his right front, while his gallant pony charged into the opponent in the middle as though he was a trained western warhorse. The Turk on his left cut with his sabre as they all pulled up in a milling, stamping knot, but no swordsman can do much damage on the near side of his horse, and the blow was turned on the leather of the shield; he dropped his lance at the first shock, as the Turk whose chest he had pierced rolled out of the saddle. The pony he had knocked into was sitting on its tail like a dog, while its rider clung to the saddle, dazed by the collision; the only Turk still in action was on his well-protected left side. He plucked out his sword and swung his horse to the left. But as the heavy, straight weapon was heaved up into the air, the Turk whipped round and bolted, the other when his horse scrambled up did the same, and for a moment he was alone with the dead man's pony, which had been trained to stand while its reins trailed on the ground. He had to be quick, for six Turks were riding towards him, bending their bows; but he just had time to thrust his sword-blade through the loop of the riderless pony's reins, and then he was galloping back towards the fort. A few arrows came past, but the enemy had been taken by surprise, and they did not dare to pursue within range of the Italian crossbows. Breathless and sweating, without his lance, and with a long bright scar on his weatherbeaten shield, he rode into the fort with his captured pony. The garrison were standing to their embrasures, but when they saw that there was no pursuit they crowded round him, admiring the new horse and congratulating him in their unknown tongues. The captain smiled and helped him to dismount.

'You did that very nicely,' he said, in the sing-song French of

Italy. 'Of course, they played into your hands by trying to meet you sword to sword; they wouldn't have done that just after Dorylaeum, but with the siege going so badly they have got above themselves. All the same, I think it is enough for one day; look how careful they are now it's too late. You had better not go back until they drive their herds home for the night, which won't be long now. There is a little jug of wine I keep for emergencies; will you have a drink?'

Roger felt like a hero, a very pleasant sensation. He had conquered his dread of a fall at full gallop, and he had been quick and dextrous at getting hold of the riderless horse; best of all, until he got back to the fort the remembrance of Hugh de Dives had not once occurred to his mind. This was what real war was like, meeting your enemies in full career and hurling them to the ground; and all before a crowd of admiring spectators. He coughed modestly, and said it was nothing and what about that drink.

In the evening the Turkish herdsmen went back into the city, driving the horses before them; and as darkness fell Roger set out on his long ride back to the main camp. The Duke was bound to be pleased with him, the Italians could be trusted to exaggerate his exploit, and furthermore he had regained his self-confidence. He was almost sorry that he met no enemies on the way home, and he trotted briskly through the chill of the evening; the new pony was used to being led, and he seemed a sound, good-moving horse, though common and not up to very much weight.

There was no one to welcome him at his own lodging, except the crossbowman who acted as groom.

'Where is Domna Anne?' he asked, 'or Domna Alice? I am tired, and I want someone to disarm me.'

'Everyone has gone to watch the Duke distribute the spoil he won in the battle,' said the man, 'and I expect, sir, that the ladies are there. I see you have been fighting also, and successfully; is there anything damaged that I ought to repair?'

'Take the shield,' Roger told him, 'and smooth it down where that scar shows. Also I lost my lance; we have spare lanceheads among the baggage, and you are sure to find an Armenian pedlar with shafts for sale. I won't disarm now. I shall go and look for Domna Anne as I am.'

He felt a strong sense of grievance. Whatever victories the Duke might have won, his wife should have been there to see her husband return with his spoil from single combat against odds.

There was a large crowd outside the Duke's pavilion, and knights were clustered by the entrance. But Anne stood out, with her slender upright figure and golden face; she was full of excitement when he came up to her, and put up her cheek to be kissed very prettily.

'My dear,' she said rapidly. 'I am so glad to see you back safe, though you must be tired and hungry. Isn't it splendid news? Your Norman ambush was completely successful; they took more than thirty horses and killed I don't know how many Turks. The Duke is just giving out his share of the captured horses now.'

Indeed, that was what the knights by the pavilion were waiting for. Roger decided to see the Duke, though he sent his wife back to prepare supper; he was angry that she had not shown more interest in his doings, and he told her nothing of his fight below Tancred's castle, or of his own prize. For the first time in his life he had performed a brave deed of arms, and everyone was too busy talking of the Duke's ambush to hear the story. When at last he was admitted to the pavilion he was boiling with rage; he came straight to the point.

'My lord, you told me yesterday that I was unworthy to ride with you to the ambush, and that if I wanted fighting I could go to Tancred's castle. I went there today, killed a Turk, and took his pony. Now I have two ponies; would you, my lord, like one of them?'

The Duke was in excellent spirits, for he loved to make presents, and ten knights had been very glad to get their ponies.

'Ah yes, young man, I did say something of the kind; but you mustn't take everything I say too seriously; you might have got yourself killed. Now you have an extra pony and you very loyally offer your lord the first chance of buying him; that is very good of you. But I'm, h'm, a little short of actual gold, h'm, at the moment. When I sell I get promises, and when I buy they make me pay cash; it's just as it was back home in Normandy.' He paused, wrinkled his brow, and went through a pantomime of desperate thinking.

'Could I buy this pony with anything else?' he continued. 'Not gold, but wine say, or a pretty slave girl? No, I see you are not that sort of man; besides, I remember, you have only just been married. I've got an idea, my second warhorse. I never ride him now, while we are encamped for this siege, and it is a shame to keep a warhorse idle when so many knights are on their feet. You can give me both your ponies and take Blackbird, my second warhorse, in exchange. How does that strike you?'

Roger was delighted, but this talk of horse-dealing automatically brought a surly, wooden expression to his face.

'It all depends, my lord, on what you think of the ponies and what I think of the horse. Perhaps I could examine him in daylight.'

'Of course,' said the Duke heartily. 'Bring your animals here tomorrow after breakfast, and I'll tell them to have Blackbird ready. I'm sure you will like him; he's not young, but he's sound, and I trained him myself.'

Roger went back to his hut, and over a late supper told Anne and Domna Alice all about his adventures; they had both had years of practice at listening to knights telling their achievements in battle, and showed a suitable interest.

In the morning the exchange was effected; Blackbird was a big, powerful horse, not very fast, which made him safe in the charge, but sound in legs and wind, and with the deep ribs that mean staying-power; he was about twelve years old, but good for two or three more campaigns, and he had been carefully trained by the Duke himself. The shortage of warhorses in the pilgrims' camp made it hard to calculate his value, but even in Normandy he would have been a good horse.

Roger found that his new acquisition altered his status considerably. In the West, as armour and weapons were improved, the gulf between lords who could equip themselves with the best that money could buy, and simple knights who relied on the fighting gear of their fathers at Hastings, was tending to widen. He had always been regarded as a knight of the second rank, but now, though he still had no mail breeches, the possession of a warhorse put him on an equality with dukes and counts.

*   *   *

As the siege dragged on into December, Roger was glad he had only one horse to look after, for it was a difficult job to keep even Blackbird fed; in midwinter the fields gave little grazing, and it was not easy to compel the liberated peasants to give up their grain for fodder; there was also disease in the transport-lines, and the mules that had carried his wife and her companion died of it. The groom wandered all day in the plain of the Orontes valley, cutting rushes and sun-dried grass for the war-horse, and Roger had to spend several gold pieces to buy oats from the Syrian merchants. Yet the horses must be kept alive somehow until the spring, for without them the pilgrims would not be an army.

Food also grew more and more scarce; their Turkish overlords had effectively discouraged the Syrian peasants from hoarding grain, and there was only the last autumn's harvest to feed both the countryside and their deliverers. Of course, warriors were used to seeing peasants starve in wartime, but in this strange, mountainous country, where their language was not understood, it was difficult to ferret out the buried grain from the hill-top villages. As one of the better armed, Roger was not called on for these unpleasant foraging parties, and the susceptibilities of peaceful Sussex were not harrowed, but every burnt-out farm-house meant more spies for the Turks, or more useless starving non-combatants hanging about across the river from the camp, begging from every passer-by. The Count of Blois still managed a small daily distribution of grain, but the price of meat, or any other extra, rose to fantastic heights among the pilgrims, still stuffed with gold from the Greek Emperor's largesse.

In the middle of the month the council of the leaders caused proclamation to be made that all non-combatants, women, clerks, and other useless mouths, should leave the camp to winter in the Greek towns or at the port of Saint Simeon. Roger heard this with mixed feelings; since his wedding he had not been parted from his wife for a single day, and he would miss her dreadfully. But she had grown much thinner, and the leaky hut had given her a cough. It was lucky she had not started a baby. He sent her off to the port, and Domna Alice and two sickly crossbowmen; they had ten gold pieces to last until spring, while he kept only a handful of Greek small change, queer coins of copper washed with silver on the outside; but the local merchants knew the tricks of the mint at Constantinople, and valued these coins as copper only. There was no transport, and Anne had to make the journey on foot; Roger felt a pang as he watched the two gently-reared ladies shouldering their bundles across the stony plain, but all the pilgrims had come down in the world during the last year, and even the Duke of Normandy often went hungry to bed.

He discussed the situation with his cousin Robert, as they strolled on the riverbank.

'I don't see that we are doing any good, sitting here,' he complained. 'It was stupid to start this siege so late in the season. This is my first campaign, but I always thought one went into winter-quarters by November at latest. What do we gain by grinning at the Turks across this marsh; we can't get at them, and they don't bother to chase us away.'

'There is a reason, all the same,' said Robert in a low voice. 'Perhaps you don't realize quite how bad things are. The leaders are afraid that if they let us disperse now, they will never get an army together again in the spring. Nothing keeps a disheartened army together like the constant presence of the enemy; that is why they dare not let us go to the Greek towns.'

Roger was taken aback by this despondent view from his cousin, who was usually so sanguine.

'Do you think we are any nearer taking the town than we were two months ago?' he continued. 'They still get in convoys of provisions by the Gate of Saint George, and send their horses to graze under the wall.'

'Oh come, you never know how badly the enemy are feeling. They must think we are the sort of people who never let go.

And remember these Turkish rulers hate one another just as our kings do in the West. None of them like the present lord of Antioch, and they may leave him to his fate; in that case we can starve him out in the summer if only we hang on here. After all, we have done pretty well so far, marching from Nicaea to the Orontes in spite of anything the Turks could do.'

'We shall starve first,' grumbled Roger. 'Why can't we get supplies from the Greek Emperor? We have liberated a lot of his country, and we are fellow-Christians, whom he promised to support in this Holy War; otherwise what was the point of that oath the leaders took in Constantinople?'

'That oath, yes, we mustn't forget that, or all the obligations he undertook in return for it; he is back in his city now, after mopping up all the towns in the south-west, when we had put the fear of God into the Turks. That will be important later on, when we come to share out the fiefs. But in the meantime I don't think there is much he can do for us; the road we came by is a bit rough for convoys of supplies, and I shouldn't be surprised if it's closed now by the local inhabitants. We weren't very popular by the time we had gone through, even if we are fellow-Christians. No, we must rely on ourselves, and get food up from the port if there is any there. Otherwise we can manage on dead horses and the leather from our saddles. But we must make a front against the city.'

Roger was surprised at his cousin's determination; he did not look the sort of man who would starve rather than retreat, but after all, it was by that sort of toughness that these Normans had won Italy. They walked on, looking for driftwood by the banks of the river.

*　　*　　*

That Christmas was a very miserable feast, the second the pilgrims had spent away from their homes. Horses were dying daily from hunger and disease, and there was very little to eat; many knights left the camp, and went to neighbouring towns to celebrate the holiday, leaving the crossbowmen to hold the camp. Roger decided to go to Saint Simeon to spend the first Christmas of his married life with his wife. Robert de Santa

Fosca had nowhere particular to go, and cousins should stick together in a strange land, so he asked him to come also. The Turks were snug behind their walls, with plenty of provisions, and were unlikely to sally out and provoke a battle during the shortest days of the year.

The two cousins rode their warhorses gently towards the coast, spending a night on the road, and reached Saint Simeon in the evening of the second day. The haven at the mouth of the Orontes was normally nothing but a fishing village and customs station for the great town up the river, and consisted of a few stone-built cottages inside a feeble rampart of earth. Now the harbour was packed with shipping from all over the Western world; square unwieldy merchantmen from Flanders and the ports of the North Sea, towering three-masted ships from Provence, swift feluccas from Sicily, and galleys from the Adriatic. The village itself was crowded with noble ladies, clerks, and Genoese merchants from the ships. Many of the peasant women, their husbands dead in battle or from famine, had turned to prostitution as their only means of livelihood, and starving crossbowmen and sailors menaced unarmed travellers. Robert hardly noticed the condition of the town, since for him it was the accustomed background to war, but Roger was shocked; this was not how the army of the Holy Pilgrimage should behave.

They found Domna Anne with her waiting-lady installed in the upper room of one of the stone-built houses, for the Count of Blois had tried to make provision for the better-born ladies. One of the crossbowmen who had accompanied them was dead of disease, and the other had deserted to the footpads outside the town, but Domna Alice did the marketing, carrying a fully-wound crossbow, and they had some money left. There was an occasional free distribution of food, for alms had come in with the ships from the West, and sometimes a ship from Constantinople braved the wintry seas with a load of corn.

His second Christmas abroad was the most miserable Roger had ever known; most of the firewood within reach had long been burnt, and it was too cold to go to the Midnight Mass; but they crept out, wrapped in blankets, to the Missa in Aurora, and then came back to their lodging for dinner. The night before

Robert had gone foraging, and returned with a bundle of sticks and seaweed, so they could have the treat of a fire with their dinner; biscuit and watered resin-tasting wine had been given out by the Count of Blois, and Domna Alice had bought a little piece of smoked bacon. As they sat round the smoky, spluttering fire, munching the feast, Anne burst into tears, and her misery was infectious; Domna Alice sobbed quietly to herself, and Roger felt his eyes watering. Only Robert was unmoved, and he looked at his companions in surprise; then he began to sing a ridiculous and rather improper Italian song, beating time with his hands, and calling on them to join in the chorus. Anne tried to sing through her tears, and became hysterical, but Robert would not be denied, and presently their voices quavered together. When they had finished he spoke:

'You should be gay, cousin Roger. We are both Normans, and neither of us has ever kept Christmas in Normandy; it is our nature to go into strange lands and rule them, as you conquered England and we conquered Italy. Now we are on the best conquest of all, a very rich land and the Kingdom of Heaven to follow. Dry those tears, cousin Anne, or you will weep away your beautiful eyes. With two such knights to protect you, you will be wearing a golden coronet next year. And you, Domna Alice, this is a better land even than Provence; we will make you Queen of Babylon, or Abbess of Mount Carmel if you don't want to marry again.'

'Oh dear, I shouldn't behave like this,' sobbed Anne. 'At home we always heard the singing of the troubadours at Christmas, and the knights would make vows about how much they would win in the next year; and here we are starving on biscuit round a smoky fire. Year after year we go on with this pilgrimage, and never find peace. Where is that dear little castle, with warm beds and good food, that is waiting for me somewhere in the East?'

Now Roger tried to comfort her. 'That castle is ready for us, just beyond Antioch. We must endure this winter, and we shall win it in the spring; cousin Robert says so, and he is an experienced warrior. Meanwhile we must do something to get warm. What about blind man's buff?'

'I've got a better idea,' said Domna Alice bravely. 'Christmas isn't Christmas without dancing, and there are four of us. But what shall we do for music?'

'I know,' Robert cried. 'There's a man with a bagpipe on the Genoese ship by the hard. Let's go out and ask him to play for us.'

They went down to the waterside and called out to the ship; presently they were dancing slowly up and down, bow, curtsey and back again, so that other knights and ladies joined in, and the strumpets and crossbowmen too, until half the town was dancing. The few Greeks looked on in wonderment; what did these strange foreigners have to be happy about just now, and if they must rejoice, why not keep it until the Epiphany, the really big feast of the winter?

On Saint Stephen's Day the two knights started back for the camp. Robert had insisted on giving Anne five gold pieces, and she still had two left from her original store; with that, and the occasional free distributions of the Count of Blois, she would have to keep herself and her companion alive until the city fell. Roger hated to leave her behind him; the evenings were lonely in his hut, and the knowledge that she had not enough to eat made his hunger more unbearable. He now loved her gallant spirit as much as her beautiful body. Robert was also silent and depressed; he had taken leave gaily, with plentiful assurances that food must soon come from Romania, or even the West; but these were obviously forced, and deceived no one. They rode their horses at a slow walk, through the muddy wasted plain by the river, and spoke only at long intervals.

On the following day, the Feast of Saint John the Evangelist, they reached the camp in time for dinner. The pilgrims before Antioch had got over their Christmas headaches, all the more easily because there was little wine in the camp, and a new purpose and activity seemed in evidence among the crossbowmen and grooms who wandered about collecting what they could find. A busy clerk came up to them before they had time to separate.

'Two knights with Western warhorses, that's good; I am looking for people like you. Go at once and see your lords; a big raiding party is being prepared and you will be in time for it.' He bustled away and caught hold of a crossbowman.

Roger gave Blackbird to his groom, and had himself disarmed, with a pang as he watched Anne's neat and delicate knots untied from the hauberk; no one armed him better than she did, and he wondered when she would be there to do it again. He went to the Duke's pavilion to find out the orders, but the clerks could tell him little; only that all knights with warhorses must appear fully armed an hour after sunrise next day, and that if he could bring two days' food with him so much the better. On Holy Innocents' Day he was there in plenty of time; he could not bring food, but he had eaten a good breakfast of the biscuit that was meant to provide his dinner. Rather to his surprise, a large number of crossbowmen were waiting also. The Duke came out of his tent, mounted his warhorse, and addressed them as they stood in their ranks.

'We are trying a new departure; the Turcopoles and the other knights with light ponies have often been out foraging to the north; they have harried the country bare, there is no more to take, and the peasants now band together to resist us. Our only hope of getting more food is to ride south, where the Turks are thickest. The Count of Taranto is in general charge of the undertaking, and the Count of Flanders and I have agreed to follow him, of course saving our rights on all other occasions. The Count of Taranto says he wants to take a crowd of foot with him; why I don't know, when there is plenty of work for them in the camp; so I have picked out my strongest crossbowmen, and they must do their best to keep up with us. Don't forget them, or go galloping about the countryside leaving them behind. We will now ride out to join the Italian and Flemish contingents; keep your ranks, and hold your horses together, and we shall show them what the Normans of Normandy can do.'

The Duke was always touchy about accepting a subordinate position; by inheritance he was the greatest man in the army, except possibly the Count of Vermandois, brother of the King of France; but everyone knew he was not good at getting himself obeyed, while the Count of Taranto was an exceptionally cunning warrior.

When they rode out of the eastern entrance to the camp and formed up on the Aleppo road, Roger was surprised to see how many crossbowmen were coming with them; there were at least two thousand foot to four hundred knights, a very large number of second-rate fighting men to drag about the countryside. The Count of Taranto marshalled them all according to his strange but very definite ideas; footmen in front and behind, and even on the flanks, with the knights in the middle of what was practically a moving square.

They left Antioch on their right, and marched south all that day at an easy pace, because of the foot; in the evening they halted by a mountain torrent, and went supperless to sleep; evidently their leader wished to get into unravaged country, and do the plundering on the way home; a sound idea with a swift-moving band of raiders, but risky when they were encumbered with all these unmounted men. On the 29th, still fasting, they pressed south until midday, when they swerved aside to a large village on a hilltop. They were beyond the limits of the Greek Empire even as it had been thirty years ago, and the inhabitants were infidels; they fled down the hillside to the west as the pilgrims approached from the east. There they dined. and fed their horses, before scattering to comb the valleys for hidden cattle. The afternoon went pleasantly; it was a hilly, fertile land that had not been ravaged since the infidels took Antioch more than ten years before, but the peasants, from old habit, still stored their food in or under their houses; as they did not stand to defend their homes this made plundering easy, and all the pilgrims, even the foot, had full bellies for once.

On the 30th the ravaging continued, with little bloodshed save of the very old and very young who could not get out of the way in time; the pilgrims wanted food, not conquest. In the afternoon they turned north, and plundered slowly along the road they had come by so quickly on their outward march; they had a large flock of sheep and a few oxen for the camp, and so far they had not seen a single mounted Turk. On the 31st, the Vigil of the Circumcision (not then the last day of the year, which began in March), they were late in starting, and moved slowly; one or two of the horses had colic, from too sudden plenty after long weeks of semi-starvation, and the foot were stiff and lazy. The hollow square of crossbowmen now enclosed a multitude of sheep and cattle, each ox bearing a sack of grain on its back; they made slow progress through the mountains, for one party was nearly always climbing a steep hill, and the rest had to conform.

Shortly before midday the beasts and the horsemen were jostling along a narrow valley while the flanking-parties struggled across the steep hillside, when there were shouts from the rear. Roger, in the middle of the column of knights, could see nothing, but the leaders began to gallop about, and the vanguard was induced to halt; soon all the mounted men were urging the herd up the slope to a grass-covered ridge that bounded the valley on the west, and the Count of Taranto rode up and ordered them to hold this ground. Twenty knights on ponies were told off as a cattle-guard, and the rest formed up in their ranks. Roger was surprised at the array; a strong detachment of crossbows was drawn up on the ridge, facing south, flanked on each side by another body of similar size, halfway down the slope to left and right; a fourth company barred the ridge to the north, and the knights were left with the plunder, almost encompassed by the foot. Why had the Count of Taranto chosen well-mounted men, with nearly all the trained warhorses, to fight a defensive battle on a ridge?

Turkish horses were in the valley, and breasting the slope to the south; more and more of them came into sight, but as usual it was difficult to estimate their numbers in that loose formation. Presently the southern end of the ridge was a mass of fluttering cloaks and wheeling horses, and a black horse-tail standard appeared in their midst. The centre approached slowly, while the wings advanced at the bottom of the slopes until they were level with the Christian knights; then there was a sudden horrid clamour from the infidel cymbals and kettledrums, and the whole force closed in at a canter. As they came within range, those on the ridge began shooting with their short horsemen's bows; but a bolt from a crossbow carried straighter and hit harder, and the front rank of the Christians kept up a continuous discharge, while those behind wound up the weapons and passed them forward; to Roger they looked like men digging in a cabbage-patch, as their backs bent and straightened. The Turks in the centre could not bear the shower of bolts, and drifted back out of range; but the wings crept forward, and now the pilgrims were encircled on three sides; soon enemy arrows were falling, nearly spent, among the knights and the animals. The Duke of Normandy, whom Roger had not noticed since they left the valley, rode up to his followers. He called out:

'Now, gentlemen, our part of the battle begins. We are to advance down the western slope, at a trot and keeping our ranks. It is NOT a charge, and you must all control your horses; the Flemings will do the same down the slope to the east. Then, when we see a signal from the Count of Taranto up here, you must wheel left about and charge uphill at the Turks in front of the crossbows. The Flemings will be coming up from the other side, so don't go for anyone you can reach; first make sure it's a Turk. When we meet again on this ridge the Count of Taranto will be in command, and you must follow him till your horses drop or he tells you to halt. Watch, and advance when I do.'

Roger hitched his shield higher on his bridle-arm, and took a good grip of the reins; the Duke edged forward, then waved his lance and trotted towards the enemy wing. As the Normans followed him the Turks withdrew; they knew that the shield of a Western knight was invulnerable to their arrows, and they waited to shoot when the Christians turned their backs to rejoin the main body. Roger was in the middle of the front rank, very happy to be riding Blackbird into battle for the first time; it was a joy to be mounted on a trained warhorse, who knew that his rider's bridle-arm was busy with the shield, and who could be controlled as much by posture of body as by pressure of knee; so long as the lance was held upright, and not couched, the horse knew he was not charging, and trotted with his companions. The Duke looked all the time over his shoulder at the crest of the ridge; suddenly he wheeled his horse, and waved his lance in the air. Instantly the ordered ranks turned into a milling mob as each knight pulled his horse short to the left-about; then they were galloping up the steep hill, each rider leaning forward as far as he could reach, and praying that his saddle would not slip.

The Turks on the ridge did not realize they were being attacked from two sides, for each individual could only see down one slope; as they closed into the centre they formed a dense mass of horsemen. The Christians laboured uphill towards them, and when there was only twenty yards to go Roger couched his lance. Blackbird could see the point out of his right eye, and bounded forward, neck stretched out and quarters labouring; he might be past middle-age for a horse, but he knew his job. As they reached the enemy, he collected himself and jumped in, clear of the ground, as though there had been a ditch in the way. Roger's lance went clean through the ribs of a Turkish pony that tried to turn at the last minute, and he dropped it to draw his sword. Charging uphill, the knights had not the impetus to gallop straight through the enemy, as they would have done on the flat, and for a few minutes they were trampling about, all mixed up with the Turks; Roger swung his sword, and sometimes felt it meet resistance, while Blackbird struck out with his forefeet, and worried with his teeth the thigh of a screaming infidel. Other shouts of 'Deus Vult' sounded in front of them, where the Flemish knights pressed forward, and very soon the Turks found that their unarmed bodies and light swords could not avail against these heavy horsemen; the remnant turned desperately along the ridge to flee, and Roger arrested his sword in mid-blow before a Fleming's shield. There was a shout from the Count of Taranto; he was urging his horse through the midst of them, bareheaded, his hauberk lying on his shoulders, and his scarlet face spotted with mud and sweat. He called on every knight to follow him, and swept on after the Turks towards the southern end of the ridge. The infidels had panicked, and their ponies, accustomed to delicate manoeuvres under the arrow-shower, were terrified of the screaming stallions of the West. But at the southern end the ridge fell away in a steep and rocky descent. Down this rock-face no horse could gallop, and complete disaster overtook the flying enemy; some tried to ride straight down, and rolled head over heels to the bottom, some hesitated on the brink and were caught by the Christian lances, the more level-headed jumped from their ponies and scrambled down on foot. Soon the Count of Taranto was leading his knights down the easier eastern slope, and into the valley where they had marched before the enemy overtook them; still at a gallop, he led them south over the road of the morning's retreat. His guess proved right; the Turkish force had not been merely a sudden gathering to repel raiders, but a relieving convoy for besieged Antioch. Two miles further back they found the cattle and the corn-wagons, abandoned by their terror-stricken guards when the survivors of the flight rode by. They sent a message for the crossbowmen to come and gather the spoil.

As they rode slowly behind the lowing oxen, their ranks relaxed in safe consciousness of victory, Roger searched the column for his cousin, to make sure he had come through unharmed. He found him among the other Italians, with a Turkish waistcloth tied to his lance in imitation of a banner, and a leather bag hanging from his saddlebow.

'Good evening, cousin Roger,' he called with a happy grin. 'I am glad to see you safe and sound. How did you get on in that little skirmish? I haven't done so badly myself. But isn't our Count a wily leader; don't you wish you could serve under him always?'

Roger was a little annoyed at this. 'The head of the whole Norman race is my lord,' he answered, 'and I am his man with no mesne vassal between us. As for the Count of Taranto, it was brave of him to charge bareheaded, and he led us fast and far; but the victory was won by our swords and armour against those woollen-clad archers. I haven't been off my horse all day, so I won no plunder. I suppose this convoy will go to the Count of Blois, as provisions for the pilgrims in general.'

'So it will, and that will make things easier for all of us. But I thought you knew these Turks carried money in their waistbands. I dismounted at the top of the cliff, while you were riding down the valley, and I got this bag off a man with a silk cloak, who looked more prosperous than the rest; it's so heavy that I would have baptized him before I cut his throat, and sent him straight to Heaven, if there had been water handy. You must use your opportunities if you are to last out this pilgrimage, but I don't mind giving a handful of silver to Domna Anne since you have been so unlucky.' Roger was bitterly angry and disappointed at his missed opportunity, but if Robert was going to be generous he needed the money so badly that he must not quarrel.

'You had a more thorough training in the Italian wars than I in peaceful England,' he said calmly, but with rage in his heart. 'Still, I don't see that the Count of Taranto did anything special, beyond charging in front, as a leader should.'

'Don't you?' said his cousin, smiling. 'What about his eye for country? We were riding along that valley, with no thought of fighting, and we hadn't picked a position to stand in if we were attacked. Then the moment the Turks appeared the Count hustled us on to that ridge; he spotted the precipice at the end, and knew that in both valleys we could see a signal from the top; he had it all worked out before the Turks could get into battle array. Everyone knows that the brutes can be bowled over if we get a fair charge at them, but the whole art is to put them in a position where they can't get away. Our people agree that it was one of the neatest things ever seen.' And the other Italian knights grinned and nodded.

* * *

The captured food did not go far among the multitude of pilgrims and soon everyone went hungry again on a diet of barley bread and millet-porridge. After nearly three months' occupation the camp was stinking abominably, for though the Orontes flowed past on the north, nothing could stop the footmen from dumping rubbish in the marsh that lay between them and the walls; there were deaths every day. It was no consolation to learn from spies that the epidemic had spread to the town, for the Turks could get limitless reinforcements from the south or east, while the Western recruiting grounds were on the other side of the world. One day, in the middle of January, Roger was surprised to find his cousin waiting for him when he returned to his hut after supper. He could not remember a previous occasion when Robert had sought him out; it had always been the other way round in the past, except when Anne had been the attraction. His cousin began to speak at once:

'My dear Roger, I have bad news for you. Domna Anne is well, or was when I left Saint Simeon yesterday; but Domna Alice is dead. Apparently she ate a piece of goat that had been dead too long, and caught this flux that is killing so many people. She had a priest, and they buried her properly on the seashore. But it leaves your wife quite alone, without any female companion, and you know what that port is like. She is very worried, and doesn't know what to do. She asked me to tell you this, since she can't write very well, and she would like you to go to her at once.'

'You are sure she is in good health herself?' asked Roger.

'Oh yes, and as cheerful as she should be. We are all used to sudden death by now.'

'Then I shall start tomorrow morning. But I don't know what to do when I get there; I can't stay and look after her, unless I hand over my warhorse to someone else, and that is asking too much of me. If I bring her here she will be alone most of the time just the same.'

'Still, she will be better off here than in that rowdy place.'

'Very well, I shall go tomorrow, and see what she wants. I agree that she will probably be better off here.'

Once again he took the dreary mud-bound track to Saint Simeon, and tried to make plans as he rode. He was not used to responsibility, and he dreaded to make a decision that might be wrong. Perhaps he ought not to have married, while he was engaged on a Holy War. But then what would have become of his darling Anne, without a protector on that difficult march through Galatia? She was a fellow-Christian, and her peril had been as great as that of any of these Easterners whom he had sworn to rescue. Women were a hindrance to a single-minded warrior, but none the less her safety must come before the Pilgrimage. That was clearly his duty, and in any case he could not bear to think of his sweet, capable, courageous wife, exposed to all the dangers of a demoralized and starving seaport.

He found her in the same lodging, sitting hunched on her rolled-up bedding, staring at the wall; there was no furniture in the room except an empty charcoal-brazier, and a leather sack for clothes. She started up with a cry of alarm as he pushed open the trapdoor at the head of the ladder from the ground floor; when she saw who it was she ran across the room and flung herself into his arms.

'Darling Roger,' she sobbed. 'I have been longing for you to come, and I have been frightened some drunken sailor would find his way up here. Please take me away with you. I hate this place, and I never want to be parted from you again.'

Roger manoeuvred so that he could see out of the unshuttered window and keep an eye on Blackbird, who was tied to a ring in the wall below; although he longed to give all his attention to comforting his wife, it would be an appalling calamity if the horse were stolen now.

'I am very sorry to hear of your sad loss,' he said, as he embraced her. 'Domna Alice was faithful, and she served you well. Come down with me while I find a safe stable for the warhorse, and then we will discuss what to do next. Have you had enough to eat lately?'

'Do let's go and find some supper,' said his wife, stepping back out of his embrace. 'For the last two days I've tasted nothing but their beastly bowls of porridge. I was afraid to go out marketing by myself, and there isn't even any charcoal left to cook with. Look, there is a ruffianly crossbowman hovering round Blackbird; get down the ladder straight away, and I'll join you in a minute.'

Roger was soon in the street, where he stood by the horse with his hand on his sword. In a few minutes Anne joined him with her sack of clothes, and leading the horse they wandered down to the beach. At the warehouse the clerks of the Count of Blois gave them biscuit and a little watered wine; they sat on a rock by the sea, munching the bread softened in salt water, while Blackbird sniffed despondently at the sand. Anne hated Saint Simeon, and wanted to get away at once, anywhere; but back at the camp she would still be alone. Very few wives had come out from Normandy, for the Duke meant to go home at the end of the campaign, and so did most of his followers. Neither Roger nor Anne knew any Norman ladies.

'I have never felt so lonely,' said Anne, 'and you must never leave me again. I thought that all of us were in this holy enterprise together, but you can't call the scum that rob round this port pilgrims in a Holy War. In Provence the troubadours made songs about the rich, hot East, where gallant knights could live in peace and comfort when the infidel was overthrown; and here we are, without fire or food, sitting on a rock eighteen month's journey from home. Why did I ever come to this Godforsaken land?'

Roger did not quite know what to answer; he had come out expecting danger, discomfort, cold, and hunger, for war was always like that, as his brother had told him; but he had never thought that the second winter of the campaign would find them still on the borders of Romania, with all Syria unconquered before them, and an unending prospect of more fighting in the future. There was really nothing comforting to say, since Anne would not be consoled by the thought that they were all warriors for God's Church, and if they kept their vows would earn remission of sins; for one thing, she couldn't fight. He did his best.

'My darling, you must be brave. It would be shameful to go back to the West with Antioch untaken, and my father's manor in England would seem rustic and uncouth to a lady from Provence. Things are better now in the camp, and you will be safer among the brave knights who face the foe than with this rabble of marauders at the port. Come back to our little hut. We shall still be hungry and cold, but I can stay with you much of the time; and when spring comes we shall take that city from the infidel.'

Presently she sobbed herself to sleep in his arms, and they spent the night wrapped in her blankets on the beach, with his armour for a pillow.

Next morning they rose at dawn, and Anne, who knew her way about the town, stole a feed of oats for Blackbird from a poorly guarded storehouse. They had only the one horse between them, so Anne rode, with Roger's mail in a bundle before the saddle and her leather sack behind. The clerks in the warehouse, impressed by the warhorse, gave them a bag of grain for the journey; properly equipped knights must be kept fit for battle, no matter who else starved. Then they set out on the familiar two-day journey, where every slough in the road, every stinking corpse of a pack-animal, was to Roger a well-known and well-hated landmark. The unpleasantness of the road made the camp seem more welcome, and it was with a sense of coming home that he reached his old stick-and-turf hut, and found his groom with a fire going and the day's food set out; it was still millet-porridge, but they were all so used to it now they would have been surprised at anything better.

Next morning Roger went round to the Duke's pavilion to arrange that his wife should be fed, and to see if there were any orders for himself. The rule that non-combatants must leave the camp was now a dead letter. For the commands of the leaders, grudgingly obeyed when they were first proclaimed, were soon forgotten; and thanks to recent raids the besiegers before Antioch were now as well supplied as the port. There were no duties for him; the fighting stood still, and no warhorses were to leave the camp until the grass grew in the spring. Every hut and path in the camp was now boringly familiar; the walls of Antioch frowned unchanged across the marsh, the Orontes flowed in its old familiar bed, and the refuse of the thousands of inhabitants stank as ever; luckily it was too cold for flies to breed. The green damp of Sussex was a dimly remembered background to childhood, and Roger found it hard to imagine they would ever leave this crowded spot, that combined the disadvantages of a desolate country and a closely packed town.

Most of the time he was alone with Anne. They saw little of the other women, for they were too poor to mix with the barons' wives who still had money, and Anne was too proud to drift into the dependent position of a waiting-lady. Roger was still awkward and shy with his fellow knights, and had practically no men friends except his cousin; Anne complained that he believed the boasting of any idle warrior, and always assumed that a man who laid down the law must be an expert; but it was not easy to change the life-long habits of a well-snubbed younger brother. So they were both pleased to see Robert de Santa Fosca when he called round in the evenings. He was one of the lucky men whose warhorses had stood the journey from France to the borders of Syria, and he did not know by experience the sense of uselessness and frustration that attacked a dismounted or badly mounted knight. He got on very well with Anne, and it amused him to compose ballads and sirventes about her. Roger liked to see him also, for he always had the news of the camp, and told all the secrets of the leaders' councils as though he had been present at them. It was common knowledge that the Count of Taranto was very friendly with his followers; in his position he had to be, for the whole Norman realm in Italy was new, and the succession of its rulers not really determined; in many cases these vassals were the first of their families who had followed the house of Hauteville as lord, and Bohemund had none of the prestige of a hereditary Duke of Normandy. Robert was always telling his praises as a warrior and leader of men, and running down the other chiefs who were supposed to be too cautious for his daring plans; Roger sometimes suspected that the Count was using his knights to influence opinion in the camp at large.

The close confinement was hard on Anne, though she never complained; it was not safe for a young woman to walk about the camp alone, and of the ten crossbowmen who had once followed her late husband only the groom who looked after Blackbird remained; all the others were dead, or sick, or had deserted to some other lord. Roger had nothing to give them, and their desertion was only to be expected, for they had not the faithful sense of duty of a knight. A groom he must have, and he kept that one man in his service by the occasional gift of a silver piece, and by promises of more when at last he had his castle. Roger himself had few duties, for there was nothing left to plunder in the parts of the countryside that a Christian raid could reach; the irregular issues of coarse and scanty food were brought from Saint Simeon, and there could be no more raids until the grass grew and the crops began to ripen.

No one was really busy, or even fully occupied, and to boredom was added unceasing hunger; the chief task of the footmen was to dig graves for those who died of sickness. All day long Anne had nothing to do but boil a little porridge, and Roger only went on patrol once every three or four days. In a sense, all castle and manor dwellers were used to killing a great deal of time, but in this camp it was hard to pursue the ordinary winter diversions; all the game had been scared away, and hunting might damage the precious horses, the songs of the trouvères and jongleurs were stale, and life was too depressing for them to compose new ones; even love was not amusing to a hungry man. The only way to pass the time was in gossip about the failings of the leaders, and on this topic husband and wife could not agree; Roger took to spending as much of his time as possible at the long religious services and processions organized by the Bishop of Puy, who hoped thus to counteract the moral deterioration of the pilgrims. He struck up a close friendship with Father Yves, the Breton priest, frequently served his Mass, and then breakfasted with him. Father Yves had his own view on the reason for the failure of the campaign; he thought it was the judgement of God on the wickedness of the pilgrims. But to Roger this seemed an inversion of cause and effect; they were wicked because they were demoralized, and they were demoralized because they could not take the city.

In his efforts to keep Anne amused and cheerful, he took her to Mass and breakfast with Father Yves. The priest was glad to meet a cultivated lady, and did his best to be pleasant to her. Both agreed in abusing the Greeks, and by a natural transition went on to hope that the conquered land would be settled by true Christians.

'These people are attached to their liturgy,' said the priest, 'but they are ignorant of the teaching of their own Church. If we can leave their services unaltered they would never notice when the priest taught them the True Faith. What we should do is to drive out their bishops and theologians, and tell the inferior clergy what changes they must make. But every parish must have a French lord, to see that they don't slip back into their old wicked ways.'

'Of course we must have plenty of French lords,' Anne agreed, 'and it is the duty of those pilgrims who mean to live and die out here to get hold of a village as quickly as they can. My husband has sworn to follow the Duke of Normandy for as long as the pilgrimage lasts, but it was always understood that Duke Robert will go back to Normandy presently; if he keeps on and on, fighting infidels towards the ends of the earth, is it Messer Roger's duty to follow him for ever? Surely he can break his oath, if it will be a means to the conversion of infidels or heretics?'

'Do you think you are competent to advise on this?' asked Roger. 'These oaths of fealty have very little to do with the Church. If I wanted to wriggle out, I am sure I could get an excuse from some lawyer; but I wish to be true to my word for my own private satisfaction, and because my father, who fought with the Great Duke William, would want me to keep it.'

'God forbid that I should tell you to break an oath that you want to keep,' said Father Yves. 'All the same, homage is a thing altogether outside the Christian life, and I should prefer not to advise you. If you think you have been hardly treated, why don't you ask the Duke for your release? He has the reputation of being an easy-going man, and certainly his followers did not obey him very faithfully in France.'

'He is a very much sterner leader out here,' answered Roger. 'He governs more strictly on this pilgrimage than he ever did as ruler of Normandy. Unfortunately, I asked him to release me in the autumn, when I was getting married, and he refused. If I ask again the answer will probably be no, and if I leave him after that it is open rebellion.'

'Then why not rebel,' put in Anne, 'and get as many landless knights as possible to follow you? What could he do? You have no manor to be harried, and if they refuse us food in the host we can seize a castle, and live on our plunder. But probably the Italians would be glad to have us.'

'I certainly shall not do that, and Father Yves must agree that it would be wrong. We don't want the pilgrimage to dissolve into robber bands, though perhaps the Count of Taranto would not mind if it did.'

'Messer Roger is right,' said the priest. 'The Duke has brought you here, which is all he promised to do in return for your service. He never guaranteed you a castle, and you should not leave him while he fulfils his obligations. We are eighteen months' journey from home, among strangers whose laws and customs are quite unfathomable; unless we obey our own Western customs, which we understand, the army will become a leaderless mob. We are not Greeks, whose rulers fight among themselves for the throne, and perhaps that is why we have come so far.'

'I think that is absurdly scrupulous,' Anne said angrily. 'Father Yves says we ought to rule this country, and you want a castle to live in. Yet you won't do anything about it. You should listen to me, and remember that a man's first duty is to provide for his own family.'

'You are forgetting your duty yourself,' Father Yves said sternly. 'A wife must submit to her husband, since women, by the natural weakness of their minds, cannot understand the workings of human law. My advice is that you must obey the Duke as long as he supports you, and there is no more to be said.'

Anne was silent. When men began to talk of the natural inferiority of women, every sensible wife knew she had been too clever, and that someone might take a stick to her unless she kept quiet.

*　　*　　*

For the rest of January the siege dragged on, if such it could be called when no harm was done to the enemy. The miserable allowance of food was still distributed by the Count of Blois, and in the absence of any hope of success, this alone kept the army together. Horses continued to die, and the shortage of baggage-animals had made the whole host immobile, so that for the poor there was no way of retreat. The garrison of Antioch still pastured their horses outside the wall, in spite of Count Tancred's fort, and received supplies of provisions through the unblocked gates of Saint George and Saint Paul. At the end of the month disquieting rumours were brought in by the country-people; the Turks of Syria were gathering an army of relief. The pilgrims were really in no condition to fight, but without transport it would be a disaster to abandon the camp, and in any case it would be dangerous to sail from Saint Simeon at that season of the year. By Candlemas (2 February) there was a good deal of panic among the non-combatants, and even the knights, many of them dismounted, were anxious and worried. Anne was certain of approaching defeat, but she faced it bravely; it was known that young women taken by the Turks were not killed, but sold into slavery, and she discussed with Father Yves and her husband what she should do if the camp were captured. Honour demanded that she kill herself, before she was defiled by the infidel, yet suicide is a mortal sin; she asked Father Yves about it as calmly as if she was discussing her plans for a picnic in the summer.

'Of course suicide is a sin,' said the priest, 'and in these cases the women usually get round it by asking their men to kill them. That is quite permissible, and then the men themselves fight until they fall; and if they die fighting the infidel anything like wife-murder in such excusable circumstances will surely be forgiven.'

'But the chances are that I won't be here,' said Roger. 'I am one of the few knights left who still has a warhorse, and the leaders are not likely to waste Blackbird by setting me to defend the huts.'

'In any case it seems to me rather degrading to be destroyed like any other valuable property, so that the enemy can't get hold of me,' said Anne, in an unmoved voice. 'I should like to have a dagger always in my girdle, or I suppose I could cut my own throat with my eating-knife, though it hasn't much of a point to stab with. Yet I don't want to be damned, however good the company in Hell. You must find some way out for me, Father.'

'This is a difficult problem,' the priest answered, 'and some clerks might tell you differently. But a long time ago there were certain Christian ladies who killed themselves rather than submit to the embraces of their pagan rulers, and the Church has always honoured them as martyrs. Perhaps you would fulfil the same conditions, if you killed yourself for fear you would be compelled to worship the devil, and not from mere knightly pride and the honour of this world. Still, I don't want to put thoughts of self-murder in your heart. Wait and see; it is even possible that we might win the battle.'

'Well spoken, Father,' said Anne. 'We nearly lost hope when we were in the Sclavonian mountains, but we came through, and here I am. I see Messer Robert de Santa Fosca coming to tell us the news, as usual. Cousin Robert, we were discussing whether I should kill myself if the infidels storm the camp, but Father Yves here says it might be a sin. What do you think?'

'Domna, it would be a very great waste, to take so much beauty from the world. Perhaps you might find a Turkish household not so bad after all. They are men like ourselves, and the fairest of their wives bears rule over the rest; you might be Queen of Antioch. I remember in Sicily some of the infidels killed their women as we took their towns, but those who escaped were not sorry to find other brave warriors to love them. Besides, what is all this talk of losing the battle? Things looked just as black for those of us in the Norman camp at Dorylaeum. We shall chase those Turks for miles, and take the city as soon as the sun gets a bit warmer. Will you come for a walk with me, Roger? There is something I want to discuss with you.'

The two knights strolled away from the huts down to the bank of the Orontes, Robert still in his rather tattered silk tunic, and Roger in the patched and faded clothes that he wore under his mail. When they were alone Robert turned on his cousin.

'You should be ashamed of yourself, allowing Domna Anne to talk like that. I know that the foot are panicking, it is just what you would expect from creatures like that; but the knights and their ladies should never give up hope. We can beat the Turks whenever they come out to fight us, and you know it in your heart; we shouldn't be here otherwise. But what I came to say is this. You still have a warhorse, haven't you? Well, Count Bohemund has a little grain hidden away in a safe place that the Count of Blois knows nothing about. We are going to give it to the warhorses in the next two or three days, but if the poorer pilgrims heard that we were feeding animals while they starve they would make an unpleasant outcry. Don't let your groom know, but ride out to a place across the river that I will point out to you, and there you will find some Italian knights guarding the sacks. Will you please swear, on your honour as a knight, that you will give it all to your horse, and not keep any back for Domna Anne or yourself? I know you wouldn't think of such a thing, but it is a rule we have to make.'

'Of course I swear, if you wish it,' Roger answered. 'If the grain must go to Blackbird it shall, though it seems to me wrong to hoard food for the horses when the poor are dying of hunger.'

'Nonsense, the horses must come first, though we can't trust all the pilgrims to see it; in this war every trained warhorse is worth ten rascally crossbowmen. Remember we are all fighting for our lives, and the poor will face death or slavery if the knights are beaten. You see how frightened they are already, and they depend absolutely on us. I am sorry you are so doubtful of success.'

'I am trying to face the facts,' said Roger with indignation. 'I think we must face certain defeat, and I will do my best to meet death bravely. You know as well as I do how little hope there is, and I always thought that you Italians put very little faith in the inevitable victory of a holy cause, just because it is holy. After all, you have seen the Pope chased out of Rome often enough.'

'Oh, I don't think we shall win by a miraculous intervention of Heaven, if that is what you mean,' said Robert soothingly. 'But no battle is lost until it is won, and these Turks have run away before. All the same, have you thought about what you will do if we do happen to lose? Their arrows can't pierce a good coat of mail, and a lot of us will be taken alive. It can't be very unforgivable to change your religion to save your life, otherwise those who refuse and are martyred for the Faith would not be so highly thought of.'

'That is a very wicked idea, and quite unworthy of a knight,' Roger said with a startled look. 'But I know you well enough now to realize that you say the most appalling things just to shock me, and your actions are better than your words. We shall both fight our hardest, and face death like true knights, but I confess it is more difficult for me, with my wife in the camp.'

'I think Domna Anne will be able to look after herself, whatever happens,' Robert said dryly. 'Concentrate on coming out of the battle alive, and you will make a good warrior. These knights who vow to die fighting the infidel are apt to fulfil their promises too speedily, and it doesn't help the army as a whole.'

Three days of feeding on oats and barley, instead of the miserable hay that could be found near the camp, made a great difference to the warhorses, though the secret could not be kept from the non-combatants, who grumbled as much as they dared. But there was nothing they could do against the knights, and though the policy was ruthless, from a military point of view it was sound. By 7 February it was known that thirty thousand Turks had assembled at Harenc, only sixteen miles east of Antioch, and all mounted knights were advised to muster in the plain to the north of the river. Blackbird had been groomed till he shone, and was lively and fit, and Roger was armed by Anne, which reminded him of all that was at stake. He still had no lance; the one he had lost in the fight south of Antioch could not be replaced, for lack of suitable wood for the shaft; but his sword was specially sharpened, and in the sort of skirmishing fight that the Turks preferred most of the other knights would drop their lances in the first melée. Many of those barons who had taken refuge at Saint Simeon had been brought back by a threat of excommunication launched by the Bishop of Puy, who openly accused them of being false to their pilgrims' oath; among them was the Duke of Normandy, who was no coward, if he did like to keep his belly filled. Roger was glad that he would have another opportunity of fighting under his lord's eye, and perhaps earning his admiration.

When they were assembled it was announced that the Count of Taranto had again been given the chief command. Roger heard one of his neighbours grumble: 'We all know the proverb, "three times makes a custom". This is twice running that the Duke has agreed to serve under that Italian. I didn't come all this way to learn warfare from a jumped-up thieving Hauteville.' But most of the knights seemed to think it was a good idea that the most cunning warrior should command them in such a desperate emergency.

The Count inspected them and their horses very carefully, and it was discovered that many knights, eager to play their part in this crisis, had come on donkeys or mules, or on Turkish ponies so famished that they could never carry an armed man into

143

battle; all these were sent back to guard the camp, and then it was found that there were seven hundred properly mounted men left, of all the mighty host that had started from Europe a year and a half ago; they were divided into six more or less equal detachments, as far as possible under their own leaders, and then dismissed, to assemble again that evening.

Roger rested and ate, and tried to snatch a little sleep, while Anne rearranged the padding in his helm, which gave him a headache when he wore it for hours. Then it was time to muster again, and she armed him carefully. When he kissed her good-bye she bravely kept an unmoved face, and it was he who nearly broke down. Not only did he love her for herself, but she was a habit, a substitute for his far-off home, and probably the only person in the world who knew him through and through. With tears in his eyes, he clutched her to his mail-clad bosom until she gasped with pain, and kissed her fiercely. Then he mounted, and rode to join the Duke's detachment.

The small expeditionary force crossed the temporary bridge behind the camp in twos and threes, so as not to alarm the Turkish garrison which covered the northern end of the City Bridge. They drew up on the plain north of the Orontes, and all the leaders were summoned to conference with the Count of Taranto; presently they came back to explain to their men the plans for the coming battle. The Duke of Normandy sat his horse in the darkness, just visible as a darker lump against the gloom, and addressed his hundred-odd followers in a voice that was raised to carry over the shuffling and coughing of the unfit horses.

'Knights and pilgrims, you all know the situation. If the in-fidels of Syria can bring their army here, to this plain where we stand, they will join with the garrison of the city and attack our camp from all sides. Even if we could defend the camp against them, and that would not be easy, we should be unable to feed ourselves with the northern bank of the river in enemy hands. Many people, of whom I am one, thought that our wisest course was to retreat to Saint Simeon and get away by ship. But if we tried to do that all the foot and the baggage must fall to the infidel for lack of transport, so, as a last desperate resort, and our only chance, we have decided to meet them in a spot that the Count of Taranto has chosen. I tell you this so that you will realize how serious is our plight, and that only the utmost exertions on your part can bring the army to safety. You could not have a better cause to fight in, and I shall be charging in front of you. Now march on slowly, and spare your horses all you can.'

As they picked their way cautiously over the stony ground in the dark, the knight riding on Roger's left spoke to him quietly.

'The Duke of Normandy should not try to make speeches on the eve of battle. I know he is a good enough warrior in a charge, but before he sees the enemy he is frightened, and he shows it. Now King William would never have let on that he had advised retreat, and was fighting against his better judgement.'

'He didn't tell us anything we didn't know before, and he may have thought that fear would make us charge harder than ever. It has that effect on some people, I believe,' said Roger in what he hoped was a calm voice; he had been praying mechanically to get his courage back, after the Duke's disheartening address. 'But you spoke of King William as though you knew him. Do you come from England, or did you mean the late King and Duke?'

'I come from England, all right, and lucky to get away from it. And I meant the King who reigns now, William Redface, curse him. I saw enough of him before I left. My name is Arnulf de Hesdin, and I was a vassal of the Count of Northumbria; does that tell you anything?'

'I am Roger de Bodeham in Sussex. I think I know what you mean. There was a rebellion in the North about a year before we left, wasn't there?'

'I followed my lord, Count Robert, and no one can call that rebellion,' the other answered. 'But he had a grievance, and made war on the King. When we were beaten they called it treason, under some ridiculous Saxon law. I was lucky, and won my trial; I think my accuser knew it was unfair to put a man on trial for following his own lord, and he didn't fight his hardest. But I knew that afterwards the King and his judges would always be watching me, and I thought it safer to leave the country. Were you in trouble at home, or did you come just because you were young and foolish?'

'My family has had no bother with the law since we settled in England at the Conquest. But my father is a poor man, with only one manor, and I have an elder brother. It was this or the Church for me, for I wouldn't like soldiering. I thought at the time that the Christians of the East wanted our help, though they don't seem so eager for it now we are here.'

'Oh, they are a shocking crowd of heretics, and they don't know what it is to be faithful to a lord. The whole pilgrimage is a mistake, but it has taken us out of the reach of King Red-face. I thought I could win land over here, and settle down, but I am afraid this looks like the last battle for all of us.'

'No, there doesn't seem much hope, does there? Of course, I had never drawn sword before I left England, and the leaders know more about it than we do. Still, things looked very bad at Dorylaeum, and we came through all right. We are lucky, as it is, to have horses at all. What do you think of this one? He used to belong to the Duke himself.'

They settled down to discuss horses they had known, until they had marched about seven miles. Roger reflected that he had come up in the world. He had left Normandy as a knight of the second rank, but now his possession of a trained warhorse put him among counts and barons.

They were riding over open rolling country, with no obstacles for a horseman, where it seemed that the Turks could easily carry out their usual tactics of encirclement and partial flight; but after marching for about an hour and a half the head of the column halted, and they were told to dismount and wait for the morning. Roger saw that they had reached a good position, and his hopes revived. They were in a small dip of the rolling plain, which hid them from an enemy approaching from the east; on the south flowed the Orontes, and on the north a marshy lake protected their left flank; the whole position was less than a mile wide, and seven hundred knights, with intervals between the detachments, should just be able to fill it. They loosened their girths, took the bits out of the horses' mouths, and sat or lay about on the ground; there was a little of last year's grass, dead and turned to hay, so the horses had something to pick at, and plentiful water. The knights themselves were not so well off; no fires were allowed, for fear of warning the enemy, and most of them had nothing to eat. It was too cold for sleep. Roger had no cloak, and he lay on the ground, pressed close to his new friend for warmth. Everyone was in better spirits, for they could all see the advantages of the position they occupied, and like all warriors in all times, now there was hope they grumbled more freely.

Arnulf was complaining of their hardships:

'I do think the leaders might have seen to it that we had some grooms and cooks here with us. After all, what are they for? They are no use in battle, and their job is to make the knights as comfortable as possible before we meet the enemy.'

'Perhaps they are not fit for a seven-mile march,' answered Roger. 'And I don't agree that they are no use in battle, at least in the sort of battles we have out here; their crossbows can shoot farther than the little horsemen's bows the Turks use, and if we trained them to it, they could learn to stand firm against a charge from those little ponies. Probably the leaders don't want to weaken the camp too much. If we are beaten, they might just manage to retreat to Saint Simeon over the open country, if there are enough dismounted knights with them to make them stand firm in their ranks.'

'Nonsense, my boy,' said Arnulf. 'I have seen footmen try to stand against a charge of horse; where I come from the North-umbrians and Scots are always trying to fight us on foot. It may just be possible if they take up a position and refuse to budge from it, but once they get moving the Turks will split them up and cut them down one by one.'

'They say that the Turks are thirty thousand men,' Roger put in thoughtfully, 'and we are seven hundred.'

'Don't let that worry you too much. Who says so? Only a few Syrian peasants, who would be quite glad to see the last of us, and who can't count above ten, anyway. If this country can't support us pilgrims any better than it has this winter, thirty thousand Turks can't live on it either, and they are all supposed to have come from this side of the Tigris. Three thousand would be nearer the mark. No, I am a good deal less frightened than I was, now I see the position we have taken up. That Count of Taranto is a cunning warrior with a good eye for country.'

'Then you think we have a chance of victory?' Roger asked hopefully.

'Yes, we have a chance; I won't say more than that. But I tell you that I feel much happier now, before this battle, than when I fought at York, with my eyes and my manhood at stake. If we lose it will be a good clean death; and I need something to wipe out all my sins, as the priests say it will.'

Roger was not sure on this point; as far as he knew death in battle against the infidel remitted the pains of Purgatory, but did not avail against mortal sin. However, there were no priests in the little striking-force, and no chance of getting Absolution that night, so he did not depress his comrade by contradicting his hopes. They huddled close together, and tried to get warm enough for sleep.

By the time the first streaks of dawn showed in the eastern sky he had given up the useless attempt, and was walking about to restore his circulation; the jackals stopped howling as the new day appeared, and the birds in the marsh set up a chatter. When full daylight came everybody was wide awake and felt fresh and rested, for the time being; a sleepless night does not tell on hardened warriors until the middle of the day.

The army was divided into six small 'battles', the universal name for any division of troops, from fifty men to ten thousand. Five of these formed a single line of two ranks each, while the Count of Taranto held the sixth in reserve. Roger was in the second battle from the right, under the immediate command of the Duke of Normandy, and since he had neither lance nor mail breeches he was in the second rank, behind Arnulf de Hesdin; there was a gap of about two hundred yards between each battle, but they had to fill the ground between the river and the lake somehow, and it was the best they could do; everyone knew that two ranks was the absolute minimum depth for a charge. It might have been worse, he reflected; at least he was not in the right-hand battle, which always suffered heavily from being outflanked on its unshielded right side. He noticed what another lanceless knight had done, and busied himself tying the hilt of his sword to the baldric of the scabbard, with a length of cord that he used to picket Blackbird; if his weapon was knocked out of his hand he would have a chance to recover it.

Each battle was concealed in a hollow of the ground, so that the line was not absolutely straight, and no one could see very far ahead. The skyline was not more than a hundred yards in front of the Duke, and a dismounted knight stood where his head just showed over the top, watching for the enemy. The wildfowl in the marsh were restless, and continuously circled over the strangers who had disturbed them; but it was still the time of the dawn flight, and the Turks might not notice the warning.

Sunshine was staining the tops of the ridges, but the hidden battles were still in shadow, when they were aware of a steady drumming, pulsing through the puddled clay of the plain; at the same time the scout ran back crouching for a few yards and vaulted on to his horse. He trotted up to the Duke, and Roger, only a few feet away, could hear his report. 'Here they come, my lord. The main army is half a mile away, but they have patrols out in front, and they may find us in a few minutes.'

'Very well,' said Duke Robert, 'but we will stay hidden as long as we can. Let us all say a Paternoster and two Ave Marias, then we will ride to the top of the ridge; and when the other battles have shown themselves we will all charge together.'

Roger closed his eyes, and prayed aloud; it was the best he could do, since there had been no Mass that morning. Many knights did not join in the prayers, busied with getting their equipment in order and tightening their girths; but as a measure of time it was known to all of them, and as one man they advanced up the ridge, knee to knee, and in line. Roger felt the newly risen sun strike full in his face and was blinded for a moment, as Blackbird stopped at the top of the slope. Then he looked again, and saw the enemy; a broad column of horsemen rode through the middle of the defile, more or less on the line of the old Roman road, while nearer the whole space between marsh and river was filled with a loose cloud of horse-archers. There were a great many Turks in sight, but they didn't look like thirty thousand. A cluster of sparkling lights on the right showed where the Count of Vermandois' Frenchmen had swung into position, with the low sun reflected from lancepoints and polished helms. Roger crammed his own helm down on his head; in a short time he would have another headache, but that was better than exposing the soft leather top of the hauberk to a Turkish sword. What were they waiting for now? He drew his sword, and his toes curled with impatience; the Turks had seen them, and the column was already beginning to deploy into a wider front. Ah! there were the Flemings on the left; now they must all be in line; how much better I could fight if only I had some breakfast inside me, he thought, as his nervousness made him belch from an empty stomach. Then the Duke waved his lance, the man in front of him bent low in the saddle, and they were all pelting down the hillside, shouting and brandishing their weapons.

Blackbird stiffened his neck, and plugged along with a wrenching twist of his quarters that Roger could feel up his spine all the way to his ears; there was no checking the horse now, but he was old and sensible, and knew enough to keep clear of the hind legs of the front rank. Roger wondered for a moment why he had no fear of a stumble and fall, which in their close-packed formation would certainly be fatal; he decided that it was because he could not see the ground, hidden by the riders before and on each side of him; there was no chance to swerve to avoid tripping, as they galloped knee to knee, but the dangers were hidden also; in any case, that particular terror came in unexpected gusts, and now it was absent. He kept his eyes on the back of the man in front of him, and gradually sank his head lower as he lifted his shield; his throat was already sore, though he did not know he had been shouting; in this particular 'battle' the long-drawled cry of 'Deus Vult', common to all the pilgrims, had given place to a high-pitched staccato yapping of 'Dex Aie', the Norman warcry, sharp and keen as a fox's bark. Then he saw the man in front straighten his legs level with his horse's shoulder, while his body bent forward till he was in the shape of a horizontal V with his rump sticking out behind; the frenzied horses quickened into a final spurt, and the first Turkish arrows flickered across the sky. There was nothing he could do, wedged into the second rank of a solid mass of galloping flesh, but sit tight and wait for the shock; his eyes, focused close on his own front rank, did not even pick out the enemy in the middle distance, and he wondered dully why the collision was so long delayed; they seemed to have been charging a long time. Then Blackbird made a sudden leap, jerking him against the cantle of the saddle, and looking down, he saw an overturned pony flash past under his right stirrup; they had met the first fringe of the Turkish horse-archers, but the pace was not checked. The Turkish scouts had attempted to retire on their main body, but they were hampered by their own numbers, and many who had turned too late were caught and overthrown. As the charging knights ploughed on they were gradually slowed up by the frequent collisions, like huntsmen who ride into a bog; it was at a slow trot that they met the main body of the infidels. The enemy scouts had suffered heavy losses, but they had acted as a cushion to their own supports, and when the two armies finally collided the impetus of the Christian charge was lost. Not many warhorses had been brought down, for the Turks, seeing there was no room for their usual tactics, had thrust their little bows into their felt boots and drawn their curved swords; but the front rank had extended into many little packets, as knights sought out individual antagonists, and Blackbird, boring on the bit with the purposeful drive of a horse who runs away at the trot, carried Roger forward until he was on Arnulf's left, and as far up as anyone in the Duke's battle.

The Turks were a solid but everchanging mass of excited ponies and yelling men, as far as his eyes could see, and he felt a sudden nausea from the wave of stink, mutton-fat, and sweaty woollen clothes, that came from them; the horses of both sides, all stallions, were squealing and striking out with their forefeet, and uplifted swords and tall fur caps filled the horizon. Roger marked a man who seemed to be within reach on his right front, and cut down with all the strength of his arm, but the Turkish pony bounded sideways, and he nearly toppled from the saddle as he felt a heavy blow on his shield. He dropped the reins, and heaved the heavy five-foot shield outward with all his force; it hit something, but blocked his vision on that side; he swung his sword in a circle, to clear a space, but Blackbird at once pressed forward, and was up on his hind legs, boxing with his forefeet. The horse plunged down again, trampling a Turkish rider, and as he swiped blindly to the right he felt his sword caught on an unmistakable Western shield.

'Whose side are you on, comrade?' panted Arnulf beside him. 'You nearly had me over that time. Come on and kill some Turks. This is the fiercest fight I have ever seen, but it looks as though I shall die unblinded after all.'

Roger pulled himself together, and kept his sword swinging on the horse's near side, trusting Arnulf to guard his right; but no man born of woman could wave the knight's heavy sword at arm's length for long; when he hit someone the blow sent a shock up his arm to the shoulder, such as a woodman feels when he hits a stout tree trunk with a blunt axe, and when he missed his stroke the weight nearly pulled him from his seat. Then he held his sword obliquely over his head as a guard, and crouching behind his shield let Blackbird do the fighting. Since they had begun to charge, he had kept his spurs rammed into the horse's side without noticing what he was doing, and he was gripping as tight as he could with his thighs; the maddened war-horse, blood streaming from his flanks, still pressed forward, biting everything he could reach; but he was beginning to tire, and the weight of the armoured rider kept him from rearing on his hind legs. In front, the heavy horses of the big Western knights still pushed back their opponents, but there had been wide gaps between the battles, and now each group was split into fragments; the Turks in the gaps thronged round the flanks and rear, and each body of knights slowly buried itself in a sea of enemies. All lances had been cast away, and swordarms were tired out; the fight was becoming a pushing-match, with few casualties to the enemy, and some Turks were already riding out behind the Christian line, pulling out their bows, and seeking a chance to shoot without hitting their own friends. Soon the pilgrims would come to a stand, and then they would be shot down one by one.

Few warcries came from the panting and exhausted knights,

and Roger was whispering a prayer; a memory of the great abbey-church at Battle flashed through his mind; that was building for the souls of men killed in a mere secular struggle to decide who should spend the taxes of England; what could man build worthy of these pilgrims who were about to die in Syria for the welfare of all the faithful in Christendom? This was the best possible death, and the one he had sworn to face, eighteen months ago in Normandy. With a feeble croak of *'Deus Vult'* he shortened his sword and jabbed the blunted end into the eye of a Turkish pony. The whole struggling mass of men and horses was still drifting eastwards, to the narrowest point of the defile between the river and the lake. Now a Turk rode up behind him and cut at his left leg; the skirt of his mail turned the blow, but he realized that it meant that the Duke's battle was surrounded. He tried awkwardly to look over his left shoulder, always a difficult move for a horseman, but the shield blocked the more usual peep under the armpit; it was never easy for an armoured man to look behind him, since the hauberk fitted too tightly for him to turn his head far; meanwhile he lowered his shield, so that its tail covered his left ankle. By twisting as much as possible he could just make out the Turk, who had now lifted his sword for a cut at Blackbird's quarters; driving in his left spur he swung the horse round and presented his shielded side to the new attack from the rear. Yet if the knights must now form a front in all directions they would be brought to a standstill, and that would be the end. He lifted the heavy sword in the air, with a twinge from his aching shoulder, and the Turk pulled back out of reach.

But something was happening behind the Christian rear; the Turks there were massing together and crowding into the intervals between the battles as though they wished to rejoin their comrades in front, and as they drew together into separate clumps Roger saw a thin scattered line of armoured men galloping towards him; they carried lances, so they could not have been fighting hand to hand already, and he realized that this must be Taranto and the reserve.

For a moment Roger could see the battle as a whole, since Arnulf and his companions of the Duke's battle had advanced a few yards, and there was no enemy within his immediate reach. He saw the Turks behind him riding hard to get out of the trap, he saw the Italians fall upon them as they piled up, a struggling crowd of kicking horses and frightened men, in the gaps of the battleline, and he heard the slow-drawled chant of 'Deus Vult'. Then he picked up his reins, and flung his horse at a gallop into the flank of a party of infidels who were riding by on the left. In a few moments every horse on the field was galloping eastward in a blinding spray of mud and small stones, pilgrims and Turks mixed together without rank or order, striking with their swords as they raced for the open country beyond the lake. It was the pursuit after Dorylaeum over again, but this time the enemy had no start. The Turks knew the country, and their ponies were always easier to control than the warhorses of the West, so they kept on the main road to Harenc, and the pilgrims thundered among them; all the horses were excited or terrified, and ready to gallop till they dropped. Roger was surprised to see that there was little fighting, for swordarms were tired, and the riders needed to give all their attention to keeping their beasts on their feet; pilgrims and Turks galloped together like a herd of frightened cattle. He knew that at that speed he could never get his sword back into its scabbard, though he longed to have both hands free for the reins; so he rested the blade on his shoulder, and concentrated on guiding his horse. There were many collisions, and every horse that checked at a ditch or a body in the path was likely to be struck into by ironshod hoofs from behind; if they came down the Turks were trampled to death, but the knights in their armour could lie under their great shields, as every jouster was taught to do, with a good chance of safety.

When at last they were past the lake the Turks might have scattered, and at least the well-mounted would have escaped; but they were struck with panic, and had no thought but to reach the walls of Harenc, nine miles away. Both armies remained together in one stampeding herd of horses, leaving behind them a wake of flattened and disfigured bodies. Roger was in an agony of fear. This mad gallop across unknown country in a mob of enemies raised all his terror of a sudden fall; but it was hopeless to attempt to pull up, and his comrades would have seen his efforts if he had tried, so he continued, hunched in the saddle behind his shield, with a grin of despair frozen on his face. Blackbird was a very good warhorse indeed, worthy of the Duke of Normandy, and he kept his feet admirably in the throng; after four or five miles he and the other horses began to tire, and the pace slackened. Roger found himself riding with an Italian knight on his left, whose lance kept a space free on that side, and a Turk on his right; the infidel had thrown away bow and sword in his flight, but he had a short knife in his right hand, and glared fiercely from side to side; he was visibly getting his courage back, and might decide to stab Blackbird at any moment. Roger lifted his sword, and leant over with his weight in the right stirrup; the Turk's nerve broke, and with a squeal of terror he slipped off his horse on the offside, to vanish under the hoofs behind. Roger had an inspiration; letting go his sword, which then dangled from his waist, he reached out and caught the pony's bridle; soon he transferred the reins to his left hand, and rode on leading the captured horse. The success of this move brought a glow to his heart, and the fear which had controlled him vanished. Other knights saw what he had done, and soon were catching ponies for themselves; after the next three miles nearly every Christian had a led horse beside him.

At length they reached Harenc, whence the Turkish army had set forth that morning. It was a walled town, but the walls were built against robbers rather than armies, and the gate had to be left open to allow the fugitives to enter. The whole mixed band of riders pushed their horses through the gate in one mass, and the grooms and servants of the Turkish baggage-guard fled to the east as they entered from the west. By common consent the pursuit ceased here; and indeed the weary horses could not have been driven any further. Those infidels who were still mounted escaped out of the east gate, under a shower of stones and roof-tiles from the Christian and Arab inhabitants, who both hated their Turkish masters; the pilgrims dismounted and scattered to see what there was to plunder.

The spoil was more than they had expected, and exactly what was needed by the army; the town had been the base for the forces of all the infidel barons of Syria, and was stocked with food, clothing, and arrows for the relief of Antioch; besides the ponies captured in the fight there was a vast number of baggage animals, mules, and camels, and for the first time the pilgrims got possession of blooded Arab mares, the property of the inhabitants, since the Turks used only their common ponies in war. Messengers were sent to the camp before Antioch for grooms and crossbowmen to come and fetch the spoil, and the knights settled down to a pleasant afternoon of sacking the private houses. Unfortunately there was little gold or silver to be found, naturally enough in a town that had been under Turkish rule for more than ten years; most of the inhabitants were Christian and could not be robbed of everything they possessed, and the few infidels were merely driven out to the east. They had made no attempt to defend the town and were entitled to quarter. That night everyone feasted in the main square, and next morning, after priests sent hastily by the Bishop of Puy had sung Mass in the reconsecrated church, they rode back to camp on their stiff and weary horses. Roger's share of the spoil, though it contained no money, was yet valuable enough; he had several linen shirts, a camel-hair cloak to wear over his armour in the new fashion that so many pilgrims had adopted, and several lengths of silk for Anne. Best of all, food supplies were now assured for the whole army for the next few months.

*   *   *

The rest of February was a holiday for everyone in the camp, though Roger was worried to note that the wickedness and flouting of God's laws that had begun when they starved did not diminish now there was plenty for all. The pilgrims seemed to be worse men than when they had left Europe, and it was easier to fill their empty bellies than to make them forsake robbery and fornication. Anne questioned him anxiously, to find out whether he had done anything to win the Duke's approval, but he had to admit that, though he had done his duty, he had not been amongst the most forward in the charge, and that no one had noticed his exploits. But he had sold his pony for a good sum of gold, and she was pleased with the money and the new

clothes. The whole army was in high spirits, convinced that the
Turks could always be beaten in fair fight, and everyone talked
of ways to take the city. It was clear that to breach the walls
would be a very difficult undertaking, but something might be
done to shut in the infidels, and starve them. At the end of the
month a fleet from the English Channel and the North Sea
reached Saint Simeon. The pilgrims were encouraged to hear
that all Europe was talking of their prowess, and that plans
were being made to reinforce them. Better still, the ships
brought timber, tools, and skilled workmen, who could build
siege engines.

On 1 March the Counts of Taranto and Toulouse set out with
knights and footmen to bring the carpenters and other workmen from Saint Simeon to the camp. The Count of Toulouse had
played a very small part in the siege hitherto, keeping to his
pavilion with a sickness of some kind; though gossip said he was
not really ill, only too jealous to serve under Count Bohemund.
Now the rumour was that he had bestirred himself to watch
Taranto, and see that the command was divided The Duke of
Normandy stayed behind; Roger was glad to stay with him, for
Blackbird had never really recovered from the hammering his
old legs had taken on the road to Harenc, and was still stiff and
lame in front.

On 5 March, the Vigil of Saint Perpetua, the convoy was expected back from the port, and the pilgrims before the city were
ready to welcome them; the foot were preparing huts to shelter
the newcomers, and Roger, with several other knights, strolled
across the bridge behind the camp to meet them on the north
bank of the river. Winter was nearly over, the sun was shining,
and the ground fast drying out; it seemed that the campaign
was about to make a fresh start. About midday the column came
in sight, the Provençal knights riding first, then the footmen and
the wagons, with the Italian cavalry in the rear. He heard a
pilgrim say how glad he was to see the Count of Taranto in the
place of lesser honour, and turned to rebuke him; for, like all
who had fought there, he knew that Count Bohemund had
saved them in the battle by the lake. But before he could speak
he heard an outcry from the other watchers; the great Bridge

Gate of the city had been flung open, and horse and foot were pouring across the river.

It was long since the infidels had dared to ride on the north bank, and the convoy had carelessly come too close to the enemy bridgehead; while dismounted Turks took ground in the cemetery which covered the northern approach to the Bridge, horse-archers spread out and prepared to charge the baggage-wagons. Taken by surprise, the Count of Toulouse made a false move; he brought the van-battle at a gallop to the northern end of the pilgrims' wooden bridge, evidently fearing that the Turks would swing right, cross the river again, and attack the unprepared camp. Meanwhile Roger and the other unarmed spectators were running back to the camp, to arm and mount. The alarm spread quickly, and he found Anne waiting, with his mail shirt in her hands.

'This is your chance,' she whispered fiercely as she knotted the laces of his hauberk. 'Jeannot is now saddling Blackbird, and you will be one of the first knights ready. I shall watch myself from the south bank of the river, and the whole army will be looking on. For the sake of your honour and the duty you owe to me, you must do some deed today that will make your name known. Come back a baron, or remain on the field.'

Roger was a little dazed; things had moved much too quickly for him. In his other battles he had been keyed up beforehand, and the charge had actually come as a relief from the tension of waiting; but only twenty minutes ago he had been looking forward to his dinner, and now he was pressing over the temporary bridge, with his bladder full, a dangerous thing on horseback, and his mail shirt most uncomfortably disarranged under the arms. On the north bank he drew his sword, and then put it back again to set his helm more firmly on his head; but, this done, there was no further excuse for waiting. He drew it once more, stuck in his spurs, and set Blackbird cantering in a lumbering stiff-legged gait, on the wrong foot, towards the nearest infidels.

The Italians in the rear-battle were held by a dense mass of Turkish horse, and the Provençals were halted to guard the pilgrims' bridge. Small parties of horse-archers were riding among the scattered foot and wagons of the convoy, and though most of the crossbowmen had climbed into the carts, where they could well defend themselves, many of the precious carpenters were already slain. Roger bowled over a Turk who didn't see him coming, for he was shooting at a wagon; he charged on downstream, with the river on his left; there were no knights in front, for he had been one of the first out of the camp, but he could hear the Provençals galloping behind. The Turks knew by experience that they could not withstand the charge of armed knights, and they began to withdraw towards the mound. Roger galloped on; Blackbird's joints were warming up, and he was going better. He saw with surprise an infidel galloping towards him, as though he wished to joust. The enemy had a steel cap on his head, and seemed to be wearing a light mail shirt; he had a little round shield on his left forearm, and carried a curved sword. Roger was puzzled; the man was not armed or equipped like a Turk, but he was clearly one of the foe, and here was a chance to do a deed of arms between the two armies. He tightened the reins, and squeezed Blackbird with his thighs, determined to knock the other over by the charge of his horse; but the infidel was well mounted, and at the last moment his handy pony swerved, so that the two riders met swordarm to swordarm. Roger cut down heavily with his sword, but the weapon glanced off the little round shield, held cunningly at the right angle, while his opponent coolly buried his sharp sabre in Blackbird's unprotected neck. Roger was horror-struck, but he had no time to think; the horse blundered on for a couple of paces, and then collapsed quietly on to his off side, just giving his rider time to get clear of the stirrups and stagger to his feet. The infidel was wheeling his horse, and preparing to charge his dismounted antagonist, but the Provençal knights were thundering up from the rear. With a mounted enemy bearing down on him, while he stood in the track of his own friends' charge, Roger took the safest but most unheroic course; he lay down flat beside the body of his horse, and tucked his feet under the point of his shield. The infidel tried to ride on to the shield, but the pony would put no more than one forefoot on such unsafe ground, and after one ineffective jab with his sword at Roger's hauberk, his foe galloped away. The ground shook as the Provençals charged by, and one hoof spurned the shield with a mighty blow, but then they were past; bruised, dazed, and very frightened, Roger staggered to his feet. Shock and fear brought tears to his eyes, and as he bent to pick up his sword from the ground he suddenly vomited. He looked dully round the battlefield, but he could see nothing except the hindquarters of the warhorses where they charged the infidels at the bridgehead, and a few crossbowmen rallying round the carts. There was no place in this battle for a knight without a horse, and he limped slowly to the bridge leading to the camp.

He felt stiffer every step he took, and the enemy's thrust had bruised his neck through the hauberk so that he could hardly move his head; he longed to disarm, to rest, and eat some food, yet he dreaded returning to his wife and the others in the camp who must have seen his downfall. Almost worse than the disgrace was the change in his military, and therefore his social, position. An hour ago he had been equipped to fight beside a baron or even a count, now he was worthless, a mere hoverer on the outskirts of battle, who must beg from some more fortunate warrior the gift of a miserable pony that he could never afford to buy. He could not bring himself to cross the bridge, with Anne waiting on the other side; wandering a little way upstream, he sat down by the river-bank. He took off his helm, and filled it with water; after he had drunk he tried to bathe the bruise on his neck, but though he could get the hauberk off the top of his head, he could not undo the fastenings, or reach the tender spot. His left arm was numb, and his hip swollen and stiff, where the Provençals had ridden over him. He wondered how bad the damage was. Perhaps he was really wounded, and in that case no one could blame him; but it was unlikely; after all, armour was worn to prevent that sort of thing happening.

Presently the clamour of the battle down river died away. With difficulty he turned his head, and saw knights riding back to the bridge, in small groups at ease, their shields and helms hanging from the saddles; evidently the pilgrims had been victorious. With a burst of resolution he got stiffly to his feet and hobbled back to meet them; he must face his home-coming some time, and perhaps if he slipped in with them it would look as though he had been fighting hard all day.

But when he reached his hut Anne's first words showed that she had seen all his misfortunes. 'My poor Roger, are you hurt? Let me disarm you and bathe your wounds. I'm afraid I asked too much of you, when I suggested that you should do some deed of arms between the armies and attract the notice of the Duke. My God, you did make a fool of yourself! If you can't manage a warhorse in full gallop you are better off on foot. That infidel would not have come out to meet you unless his pony was up to all sorts of tricks. Well, no lord will give us a castle after this. When your Duke goes home you will end up guarding a wall for some rich lord, even though you think soldiering beneath you.'

By this time they were inside the hut, and she was undoing the lace that fastened his mail shirt at the back, between his shoulder blades. He had begun to listen meekly, for he was at fault, and Anne knew enough about warfare to be entitled to criticize; but when he heard her speak of soldiering, the one thing which he disliked and despised above all others, he could stand it no longer, and fairly ran out of the hut. He caught hold of a passing groom, who was terrified at his angry scowl and blazing eyes, and made the man disarm him; then, throwing his mail shirt into the door of his quarters, he strode away, unwashed, in the sweaty clothes he wore under his armour, and with his hair on end from the ruffling of the hauberk.

Father Yves could have calmed him down, but he was not hanging round the Duke's chapel as he generally did. Roger walked on, his stiffness struggling against his impatience to give him a very curious gait, until he reached the camp of the Normans of Italy. His cousin Robert de Santa Fosca was at the door of his hut, with a comb in one hand and a bronze mirror in the other; evidently he was just getting ready for dinner. He exclaimed at Roger's appearance, and fussed round him more tenderly than would be expected of a warrior.

'Are you wounded? The Arabs at Salerno say it is a good idea to wash wounds clean as soon as possible. Would you like some clean clothes? Nothing but knocks through your armour? Then take this comb and tidy up. Come to dinner with me at Taranto's table, and tell me all about it.'

He bathed his cousin's neck, lent him a clean cloak to cover his disarray, combed his hair, and took him on his arm to the canvas open-sided pavilion where the Italians were already at dinner. Roger was so in need of sympathy that he poured out the whole story of his misadventures, and kept pretty strictly to the truth; Robert was kind, and set himself to restore the self-respect of his cousin.

'You had very bad luck indeed. Of course you were right to charge by yourself, it's the only way of winning renown among these trouvères who only appreciate blows, and never notice wise planning. I think that man who came to meet you was not a Turk at all, but a Saracen knight from the south. The Turks haven't spurred against us since the spring of last year, and no man of them would start it now; but the Saracens will fight hand to hand, as we learnt in Sicily. Yet it is a serious loss. Forgive me for asking, but will Domna Anne take this very hard?'

'She saw it all from the bridge,' confessed Roger bitterly, 'and when I came back to her to be disarmed she mocked me, and said I was only fit for a soldier. I couldn't bear her voice, and now I daren't go home. Damn all women. I've got no money with me, but I should like to get drunk tonight.'

'So you shall,' Robert agreed heartily. 'You have been very hardly treated, and you deserve something after all your bad luck. We are celebrating the victory tonight and there should be plenty of wine going round, but in any case I have a friend among the butlers. Have you heard that after we in the rear-battle had linked up with the Provençals we stormed that mound outside the bridgehead, where their cemetery is? We caught a lot of Turks, too, because some bloody fool on their side had shut the town gate behind them, to make them fight harder, I suppose. The foot were taking the heads of the slain when I left, and they say we are going to hold the cemetery permanently with crossbows. It is all our Count Bohemund's doing; he knows just where to attack. The other leaders should put him in charge of the whole siege. Hi! you with the wine-skin! fill up this knight's cup, and I will see you after dinner.'

The meal had begun late, after the battle, and there was no disposition among the feasters to get up and leave the table before supper-time. They sat and yawned and told stories, while the Count of Taranto watched from his high seat at the head of the table, and sent the wineskins round. Roger was not used to heavy drinking; at home in Sussex they only had wine on great occasions and the ordinary table-beer was very small. He soon grew loud-voiced and talkative, and would have been quarrelsome if Robert had not agreed with everything he said. Presently he felt sleepy, and dozed with his head on his hands and his elbows on the table, while a trouvère sang of the sack of Rome, and the deeds their fathers had done for Pope Gregory; the Count took pride in being a loyal son of the Church, and encouraged his followers to remember the north French tongue. Then supper was placed on the board, and though Roger did not feel hungry, he woke to drink again. Dazed with wine and fatigue, he became aware at last that Robert was talking persuasively in his ear.

'. . . so you see we have always fought for the rights of the Church, which is more than your house of Rollo has done, if I may say so. Now is our chance to extend the borders of Christendom, and bring all these Easterners into obedience to the Holy See. But to do it we must cut loose completely from this schismatic Greek Emperor, and that some of the leaders are not at all inclined to do. The only leader who wants to rule out here as an independent prince, and who is brave enough and rich enough to do so, is our Count Bohemund. But the other leaders won't give him a free hand, and he is not strong enough to defy them with his own following alone. In fact, we want friends among the vassals of the other lords, and that is why I am asking for your help. The Count will find a horse for you somehow, and all you have to do is to promise some little oath; nothing against your duty to your lord, but just never to bear arms against us, and to do our best to make Taranto the ruler of the Christian East. If you agree, we can slip away to the chapel now, and after you have taken the oath a horse will be waiting outside the door.'

Roger sat up stiffly and rubbed his eyes, which would not

focus properly. He did not quite grasp what it was all about, but he knew he was being asked to swear something to a new lord, and firmly implanted in his mind was the conviction that all his present troubles were due to the oath he had taken to Duke Robert in Normandy. He shied away from any more promises with instinctive repugnance. Beside, why should he want a horse; what was the matter with Blackbird? Then he suddenly remembered the events of the morning, and burst into tears.

'Leave me alone. I am no warrior, and not fit to serve any lord in arms. I would rather be a clerk, and leave fighting to my betters. Anyway, I won't promise anything; all I want now is sleep.' He put his forehead on the table, and shook with sobs.

Robert was annoyed; he had misjudged the correct dose, and now it looked as though he might antagonize a prospective recruit. He filled his cousin's cup again, made him drink it off quickly, and took his arm to lead him to his hut; the cold night air took away the remnant of Roger's senses, and he never remembered how he stumbled into bed.

He awoke next morning with a sick headache, and his stiffness was worse than ever. Anne's face was unsmiling, and she did not talk; but she took trouble to make him comfortable; she got hold of a large tub of hot water from the Duke's cooks, and after his bath gave him enough wine to quieten his nerves; all with the barest minimum of words. He was relieved that there was not to be another angry scene, and he was in no mood for talk. But how were they ever to become friends again? Only if he redeemed his honour by hard fighting.

In the afternoon Robert called round and asked him to come out for a walk.

'We could go and look at the new castle that is building on the mound before the Bridge Gate. Bring your sword and shield; it is quite close to the enemy and a few arrows come over, but I don't think they will sally out today, after the beating they got yesterday; you need not put on armour over your bruises.'

They strolled across the camp bridge, and down the north bank of the Orontes until they reached the mound. Footmen and camp followers from all the continents in the host were carrying stones and timber, to build up the cemetery wall where the crossbowmen were sheltered; when the castle was finished no one would be able to issue from the Bridge Gate of the city without being shot at, and the north bank of the river would be safe in the possession of the pilgrims.

'Of course, this was the Count of Taranto's idea,' said Robert proudly. 'It should have been done long ago, but now we are really starting the siege. He is building another castle to block the Gate of Saint Paul, on the east, and Count Tancred is enlarging his little fort on the west. The enemy won't be able to pasture their horses outside the walls any longer, nor to run convoys into the town; they will soon begin to feel hungry, and then they will ask for terms, as they did at Nicaea. When the city is taken, it will be thanks to Count Bohemund.

'Do you see those men with javelins and leather tunics?' he went on. 'They have been sent by the Marquis of Armenia to help in the siege, and they are as good as crossbowmen at close quarters; the Count fixed that up too. It's all nonsense to say that he doesn't get on with the natives. They admire him all the more because he stands up for his rights to the Greek Emperor.'

'I thought a Marquis guarded a March for his lord,' said Roger. 'If this ruler of Armenia has to keep back the Turks in the east, and defies the Greek Emperor in the west, then all his land is a March, and he will be raided from both sides at once. That is not my idea of a useful ally.'

'Don't be faint-hearted, cousin. He will have the pilgrims on the south, when we found a kingdom of our own, and anyway his highlanders are raiders themselves, and they must have hostile cities to plunder. If you live on top of a mountain, enemies on both sides only make you richer. We learnt that in Sicily.'

They cautiously approached the bridge, holding their shields before them, until a Turk on a gate-tower shot an arrow that fell at their feet, as a hint that they had come close enough. 'That wall is within easy reach of machines on the mound,' Robert said, as though thinking aloud. 'But it is so strongly built that we shall never batter it down. If we did, there would be time for them to build another behind it. Mines are impossible, with all this water on our side, and solid rock to the south. No, we shall have to starve them out. I wonder how much the Turks really want to keep this city. If they make up their minds to eat their saddles before they surrender we shall be here for months. But, after all, they are savages who live by plunder, and they can't like being shut up here, growing poorer day by day. We may come to some arrangement.'

They continued to gaze at the wall, which frowned, square and solid and sharp-cut, up to the blue spring sky; then they turned and withdrew out of arrow-shot, since it was stupid to take risks without armour. The drystone walls of the Bridge Castle were rising swiftly behind them; the workers had smashed the infidel temple, and were amusing themselves by digging up the corpses in the cemetery, adding the old skulls to the heap of severed heads that had been erected to mark the victory of the day before. As they stood watching the men at work, Robert looked sidelong at his cousin, drew a deep breath, and began a set speech.

'I made a proposal to you last night, but I think you were too tired and upset to appreciate it properly. In any case, I realize that it was not the right sort of scheme for a high-minded knight like you; it may not be quite honourable to swear secretly to obey the Count of Taranto, without telling your rightful lord. But I have another offer to make, and this comes from Count Bohemund himself; I spoke to him this morning. These three castles are all close to the walls, and they will have to be held by something better than crossbowmen; they will need plenty of good knights. Now it isn't easy to get knights to volunteer to man stone walls, when they might be riding and plundering in the countryside; but you, cousin, have no horse, and it seems an excellent employment for you. The Count of Taranto is afraid the Turks may surrender suddenly, after secret negotiations, as they did at Nicaea, and that some other leader may take the city for his own property, as did the Greek Emperor. Therefore he wants men in all the castles who will watch what is going on. His own followers are known, and any secret traitor would keep his designs from them; but if you will find out all you can, say in this castle here, and promise to tell it to the Count, he will pay you a regular sum once a week. There is

166

nothing in that against your duty to the Duke, and I am sure the money would come in very useful just now.'

Roger paused before answering. It was certainly a good idea for a dismounted man to offer to serve in a castle, but the part about reporting to a leader who was not his own lord seemed on the face of it an underhand trick. What exactly was his duty to the Duke? In his mind he ran through the terms of the ordinary oath of fealty and allegiance.

'You spoke well, cousin,' he answered at last, 'and for the sake of our grandfather I know you would not try to dishonour me. But one of the duties of a vassal is to keep his lord's counsel, and it would be wrong to tell his secrets to the Count, and even more wrong to do it for money. I must refuse your offer.'

'You are more innocent than I supposed,' laughed Robert, 'if after serving him for more than a year on this pilgrimage you think Duke Robert might take a city for himself, to keep it from the other leaders. Nobody is plotting against your Duke, or expects him to plot against anyone else. The man we are all afraid of is that foxy old rascal, the Count of Toulouse. Count Bohemund thinks he is trying to get Antioch for himself, when he has done nothing to take it except lie in bed. Surely you can keep an eye on his followers without doing anything against your duty to your lord?'

'The Count of Toulouse is a good knight,' said Roger in surprise. 'We all know he fought the Moors in Spain, and no one has spent more treasure on this pilgrimage, or brought a better following. He is an old man, and may have been really sick.'

'Then if he does nothing secretly you will have nothing to report; but the Count of Taranto will pay you just the same,' Robert answered quickly.

Roger had to make up his mind; there was no getting away from the fact that he was being asked to do something sly and underhand, or there would have been no need for secrecy; on the other hand, it was not disloyal to his own lord, and there was nothing in his oath to prevent him spying on a third party. The strongest reason of all was that he had been miserably poor since he lost his first warhorse in Anatolia, and money would make all the difference to Anne's comfort during the siege. He told his cousin that he had decided to agree, subject to an adequate recompense, and they spent an enjoyable afternoon bargaining about terms. Eventually they agreed on one gold piece every Sunday; which would have been an enormous sum in Sussex or Apulia, but would not go very far in this camp, where the Emperor's gold still circulated freely, and supplies were scarce.

Roger found no difficulty in joining the garrison; knights were not eager to sit behind walls for the months of a long blockade, and the Duke of Normandy was quite pleased to get rid of a dismounted man, who was a liability to his following. In three days the castle was finished and he was ready to move in. He would have to live there permanently, and that meant leaving Anne alone; that was the only difficulty. Their relations had now settled down into a sort of guarded friendliness, made up of duty and politeness combined. He loved his wife, and hoped wistfully that soon they would be back on the old terms of comradeship, as they had been on the march. But he could not bring himself to apologize for his failure in battle, and she could not forgive it. Perhaps his absence would in time heal the breach, and in any case he was going into danger to earn money for her, as a true knight should.

He was afraid to leave her alone in the hut, not only because the camp was full of robbers, but also for fear of damage to her reputation; the pilgrims in general were not leading a very holy life at that time, and Provençal ladies were well known for their love-affairs. Father Yves was unwilling to take her in; he was not an old man, and many clerks were living in open concubinage with women of the country; no one would believe in the honesty of his motives if he took a young lady to share his quarters. Robert de Santa Fosca offered to solve the difficulty, so that nothing should stand in the way of the service of his Count; he made arrangements for her to share the lodging of an Italian baroness. She would still be fed by the Duke of Normandy, and otherwise could pay her way from her husband's secret wages, so she would not be in a degrading position of dependence.

There was danger that she would make too much of her new freedom, especially as she had no waiting-lady to keep an eye on her. Roger gave a good deal of thought to this, and in the end he told her that she must obey his cousin Robert in all things, as her husband's representative. After all, Robert shared in the family honour, and he would be shamed also if his cousin's wife caused gossip in the camp.

Life in the Cemetery Castle, as it was called, was uncomfortable and dangerous. The castle itself was not a strong work; the mound had been scarped by the pioneers, and a ditch dug below it; running round the crest was a seven-foot wall of unmortared, unshaped stones, supported by timber framework, and pierced low down by loopholes for crossbowmen; three feet below the parapet was a wooden staging for the defenders to fight from; the only entrance was a wooden gate in the rear, too narrow to admit more than one person at a time. Just across the river, within extreme arrow-range, was the mighty Bridge Gate of Antioch, whose towers were furnished with balistas. The garrison of the city should have been able to smash it to pieces with stones from their engines, but the Turks were barbarians who knew little of siege-craft, and their Christian subjects, who hauled on the ropes, were disloyal; most of their missiles went wide of the mark. Still, the castle was at very close quarters to the enemy, who could mass behind their gate unobserved, and charge across the Bridge at any moment. Unexpectedly, the Turks had left the Bridge undestroyed when they lost the cemetery, probably to intimidate the pilgrims by threatening a sally; the besiegers were unwilling to break it down, since it might be used for a surprise assault on the city-wall. This meant that the Christians in the castle were exposed to a sudden attack every moment of the day and night, and never knew when a stone or a bolt from a balista might arrive in the unroofed interior. But they were really getting on with the siege at last, after all the weary months of winter, and hope kept them at their posts.

One afternoon in May Roger sat on the staging of the fighting-gallery behind the drystone wall. His head showed over the top, and he could see if there was any activity round the Turkish balistas, and duck if an arrow or a stone came over. Below him a crossbowman, his fully wound weapon at his shoulder, stared without blinking through a loophole, along the Bridge at the closed gate; the rest of the garrison were lying in the courtyard, asleep in the sun, for the nights were cold and wakeful. He was comfortably replete, since the men in the advanced posts were better fed than the mass of the pilgrims in the camp, and the warmth of the spring sun made him drowsy; but it was vitally important to keep awake, and he muttered to himself what he could remember of the penitential psalms. He heard steps on the wooden ladder that led to the fighting-gallery, and looking round, saw Father Yves climbing up to him.

'Good afternoon, Messer de Bodeham,' said the priest. 'It is a long time since I have seen you, and I thought I would pay you a visit. I forgot that most of you have to watch at night, and I am glad to have found you awake.'

'Come and tell me all the news, Father,' said Roger eagerly, for in that isolated place they did not hear much of the camp gossip. 'Lie down beside me, and keep your head low. It is tempting the enemy to show an unarmed head above the parapet.'

Father Yves propped himself on one elbow, and squinted into the sun. 'This is not a bad place in warm weather,' he said. 'It seems that your hardships have been exaggerated.'

'You ought to be here on a nice dark night, with cold rain, and the gale making a noise like Turkish ponies,' Roger answered. 'But tell me how they are getting on at the castles by the other gates.'

'I believe things are going very well. Tancred's castle now blocks Saint George's Gate, and the Count of Taranto is building another near Saint Paul's Gate, called Bohemund's Castle. We are shutting the Turks in nicely, and they must be beginning to feel hungry. But I really came to have a quiet talk with you; can you get away and come for a walk by the river?'

'I am supposed to be on watch till suppertime,' said Roger, 'but anyone would be glad to change places with me, and sleep at night instead of in the daytime. Go and wake Messer Hugh de Belmont over there, the fat knight in a green cloak, and when he comes up here I shall be free to go out for an hour or so.' He was feeling uneasy; priests didn't call you out to tell you good news in private.

Soon they had squeezed through the narrow wicket-gate, and were walking side by side on the river-bank. 'We seem to have got ourselves into a very silly position,' Roger said. 'We came out here to help the Christians of the East, and our knights are a force of charging cavalry such as they never possessed before, ideal for winning pitched battles; but in all the time we have been overseas, and it seems to be most of my life, we have only fought one really big battle, at Dorylaeum; and we have sat at this siege all winter and spring. Meanwhile those Greeks, who can't fight a big battle but are really clever with their machines, mess about in western Asia, taking towns by capitulation, when they could be really useful here. If the Emperor would send us food, and thousands of engineers and workmen, we could protect them while they batter down the walls. After all, they built the damned place, and they must have men in their army who garrisoned it only fifteen years ago. They could find a way in, if only they would come and help us.'

'They might come and take the city,' said the priest, 'but would that be helping us? Everyone fears that if the Greek Emperor got his men inside he would keep it for himself, and never allow any of us inside the walls.'

'But I thought it was all arranged, that Antioch was to be held by the Count of Taranto as a fief of the Empire?' said Roger in surprise.

'That may have been arranged at one time,' Father Yves said with a sigh, 'but the arrangement doesn't seem to be valid at the moment. I am told there was a Greek army hovering about near Cilicia in the winter, but the Armenians didn't encourage them and Count Tancred wouldn't have them on his land, and I believe they went home again. The Emperor doesn't really think we can take this city, and he is seizing the opportunity to finish off the Turkish towns nearer his capital, while we hold the frontier for him.'

'That is very unknightly and un-Christian.'

'The Emperor is not a knight, and I am not so sure that he is really a Christian. Some of his clergy, at least, prefer the infidels to us.'

'But we are really going to take the city now, at last. I assure you, Father, that while we hold these castles they can't get any food in, and Turks can't starve as we can.'

'Well, Messer Roger, are you sure that we can hold the castles? They can't get any food in, but they can always get messengers out over the south wall up those mountains. There are rumours that they are raising an army of relief among the infidel barons to the east, and if that army gets here we shall have to pack up and retreat to Saint Simeon. We could not carry on here with the city untaken and an army on the north bank of the river.'

This was the first Roger had heard of the rumoured army that was gathering at Mosul. It was very serious news, and his heart sank.

'For God's sake, Father, we must do something at once. We can't beat a new army in the field, unless we leave this position, and if we do that the garrison will get in more provisions, and we are back at the beginning again. Did you hear what plans the leaders have made?'

'The leaders are too busy quarrelling to make plans,' the priest answered bitterly. 'Some people would rather the infidels continued to hold Antioch, than that it should go to some Count they are jealous of. I really came to tell you this news, and ask if you had any commands for Domna Anne. There will be a panic soon, and the women would be better off on board the ships at Saint Simeon.'

'What does she think?' Roger inquired.

'Oh, she is quite calm, and not a bit worried,' Father Yves said soothingly. 'We have been in so many tight places before, and come out safely, that a great many people think we are invincible; but I know enough about war, in spite of my tonsure, to see exactly how dangerous this is. Some far-sighted or cowardly person will presently run off and get on board ship, and then all these valiant non-combatants will crowd after him as fast as they can. If I was responsible for a lady, I would get her safely on a Genoese or Pisan warship before the rush starts.'

'That might start the panic,' was Roger's retort. 'My wife should not be the first to run away, and she is not frightened herself, I understand. Let her stay where she is for the time being. Domna de Campo Verde, whose hut she shares, will not remain longer than is safe, and it will be time to run when she goes off to Saint Simeon. But tell Domna Anne from me, that she is to save her money from now on, and turn into gold any possessions or gear that is not absolutely necessary. If she has a bag of money she can always bribe a sailor at the last minute. Also tell her from me that I am determined to stay here as long as any of the pilgrims remain. Something may turn up in the end. I cannot believe that all these thousands of pilgrims would have come as far as this, and survived so many dangers, to turn back now with so little accomplished. What we have done so far was only done by miracle, and we must rely on God's favour.'

'That is a very wrong point of view,' answered Father Yves, 'and if you held it seriously I would denounce you as a heretic. During this winter the pilgrims have not behaved in a way to win the favour of God, as you very well know, and it is always wrong to demand a miraculous intervention in furtherance of our own affairs. But if you are determined to expose Domna Anne to these dangers, you are her husband, and the responsibility is yours. At least, I will give her your message, to gather what money she can.'

Roger could not believe that this camp, where they had lived for so long, was really in danger, and he knew that in a crisis Anne would keep her head better than he. During supper, the knights around him talked of nothing but the rumoured army of relief. As with so many other camp rumours, no one had heard of it yesterday, and no one thought of anything else to-day. If the army from Harenc had been estimated at thirty thousand, popular opinion made the army of Mosul innumerable, and even the stoutest warriors were estimating their distance from the sea, and the carrying capacity of the ships.

When supper was finished, and those who were to be on watch that night were wrapping themselves in extra clothing to keep out the chill, a groom appeared at the gate asking for Messer de Bodeham. When he was admitted he handed over a package, saying that it was a cloak sent by Messer de Santa Fosca, who particularly hoped his cousin would wear it that night. Roger was a little puzzled. Cousin Robert had not been to see him since he went into garrison, and he was so thoughtless of others, and so indifferent to climate himself, that this solicitude was very unlike him. Roger was straightforward, and very slow to suspect cunning in others; but at last he realized that the cloak would probably conceal a message from the Count of Taranto. He had entirely forgotten that he was being paid as a secret spy. Sure enough, when the cloak was unfolded at a discreet distance from the fire, he saw writing stitched in black thread on the border. He sat down to puzzle it out, sketching the forms of the letters on the ground beside him, and trying to remember all that the parish priest of Ewhurst had taught him when he was a child. The message was in Latin, for it was hazardous to write in French unless you knew the sort of spelling your correspondent employed. But it was brief, and easy to understand.

'Expect a message from the city. Give it this man, who will call every morning with a flask of wine for you.'

Roger unpicked the thread, wrapped the cloak round him, and climbed up to the fighting-stage, which was his post for the night. So the Count of Taranto was trying to win the town by treachery; it was the only way it could be done in time, before the relieving army appeared, for the walls were completely undamaged. But it was obviously a desperate gamble; the besieged had no reason to ask for easy terms, when the town was about to be relieved by the army from Mosul. He realized that he was being drawn deeper into these Italian schemes, whatever they might be; first he had been asked to report if any other lord was trying to take the town for himself, now he was to help the Count of Taranto to win it alone.

He stared across the river all night, occasionally shifting his position when an arrow came near, and watching closely for a swimmer, or someone climbing down the wall on a rope. But nothing out of the ordinary happened.

Next evening at supper the talk was all of a council of leaders that had been held in the pavilion of the Count of Blois. Every knight had a highly coloured version of what had happened at the council board, how the Count of Vermandois had been for instant retreat, and the Count of Toulouse for a strong appeal to the Greek Emperor; he was proud to hear that all the Normans, of Normandy, England, and Italy, had been firm for fighting another battle to the eastward before they gave up and retired, but it was obvious the ambush by the lake could not be used a second time. Most knights thought retreat unavoidable, though they would charge once more if their lords rode in front.

Next day the walls were crowded with the infidel garrison, who hurled many stones at the castle, and shouted taunts and insults; evidently the story of the army of relief was now public property within the city. Another council had been held among the leaders, and he heard their speeches recounted at supper. They had nearly come to blows on the question of retreat, and a last urgent appeal had been sent to the Greek Emperor, begging him to come with his army and take the city himself. Of course, this was just what most of the leaders didn't want, but it was better than giving up the whole enterprise; the question was whether the Greek army, last heard of in Caria, would get there in time. Some of the crossbowmen were getting a little hysterical, and saying that their leaders, for some unexplained reason, secretly wished the whole pilgrimage to fail. Panic was not far off, and the rumour was widely spread that the Turkish army had already set out from Mosul.

Roger kept his watch in a very depressed state of mind. He wondered whether to get himself killed in the retreat, and so earn at least the spiritual benefits of the pilgrimage; but it was his duty to protect his wife. He had not seen Anne for weeks, and sometimes he forgot her for hours together; yet she ought to come first in his plans.

He was the only knight watching from the fighting-stage on the river side, though three crossbowmen crouched at their loop-holes below. The Bridge Gate across the water was still and silent, and there seemed little need for him to keep awake; if he curled up in his new cloak and went to sleep where he was, it was likely that he would not be punished. He lay down, with a guilty conscience and a beating heart, on the planks below the parapet, and was spreading out the cloak to wrap over him when an arrow came silently out of the black sky, and pinned its outflung edge to the wood below. His stomach turned over at the sudden shock, but he realized that his armoured body was safe, close to the wall, and he reached out to free the hem. As he plucked out the arrow the moon shone from behind a cloud, and he saw that something was tied round the shaft. He brought it close to his eyes, and could just see in the dim moonlight that it was wrapped in a piece of paper, tied round with thread. At once a hundred tales of besieged garrisons and secret messages flashed through his mind; so this was the answer the Count of Taranto was expecting so eagerly! In great excitement, he teased the paper out of its thread, and waited trembling for the moon to appear again. But when a beam of light shone forth, he saw with disappointment the strange squiggles of an unfamiliar alphabet; it was not the Greek, which was sufficiently similar to the Latin to be recognizable, though of course he could not read it, nor yet the devil-marks of the unbelievers; perhaps the whole thing was an elaborate joke, or worse still, a spell that brought bad luck to the possessor. But his duty was clear; Count Bohemund paid him to deliver any message from the city, and here was a bit of writing from the mysterious stronghold of the infidel. He tucked it in a crack where the leather of his shield gaped from the iron binding, and lay down to sleep with his mind at rest.

In the morning the groom, now known in jest as Bodeham's butler, was waiting as usual. He took the flask of wine, and slipped the folded paper in the fellow's hand.

He was roused from a nap in the afternoon with news that Robert de Santa Fosca wanted to see him in private. As they walked together his cousin first spoke of Domna Anne, until they were out of earshot of the castle. Then he turned towards him with a broad grin: 'You have done splendidly, cousin Roger,' he exclaimed. 'That message you sent in is as good as a key to the city gate, and the Count is very pleased with you indeed. He told me to give you these gold pieces.'

'The Count is generous, and I am glad he is pleased with my service. But you must tell me more. How did you read the message, and what did it say? Is the city betrayed to us, and when shall we enter it?'

'One thing at a time,' said Robert, still smiling. 'You are the knight who said it was wrong for a vassal to betray his lord's secrets, aren't you? But I will tell you what the Count's followers know already, for I reckon you as one of them. In the first place, no wonder you could not read the message, for it was written in Armenian, and that language has an alphabet of its own. The writer is an Armenian renegade who sees a chance of making his fortune by going back to his old religion. That is really all I know for certain.'

'But there must be more that you suspect,' said Roger eagerly.

'Your guess is as good as mine, dear cousin,' Robert answered with a deprecating wave of his hand. 'But I think you can be sure of this. The Armenian is not just a common archer in the garrison; if he was, and he thought the pilgrims were about to win, he could slip over the wall like other deserters. He must have something more to offer, the command of a tower or a gate, or it wouldn't be worth buying him now. I really believe we shall be sacking this city before the month is out.'

As a matter of fact, 1 June found the pilgrims still in the same positions, which they had held for eight months. The relieving army was only a few days' march away, and the city must be captured immediately if they were not to be crushed against its walls. At the same time, men whispered to one another that something was up; that the walls would fall flat like those of Jericho, or the Turkish barons inside accept the True Faith; for all could see that the leaders were counting on success. It was hard to believe that in a week at the longest they must leave the camp where they had dwelt for eight months, and either enter the city or retreat to the port; it seemed a bigger move than leaving Europe in the first place. The garrisons of all the castles were increased, especially with Normans from Italy, and the women and non-combatants packed their belongings, and got as much stuff as the few baggage-animals could move down to Saint Simeon. The Italian baroness went on board a Genoese ship and took Anne with her; Roger was relieved that one responsibility was off his shoulders, though the separation was depressing. A final, and very quarrelsome, council of the leaders was held, when the Count of Vermandois despairingly offered the city of Antioch to any baron who could take it. This was the chance the Count of Taranto had been waiting for, and he was said to have closed with the offer.

On the evening of 3 June Roger woke from his afternoon sleep and prepared to take his place by the supper fire. He saw immediately that the whole garrison was ready for something to happen; all except the actual watchmen on duty were sharpening their weapons or going over the weak places in their mail, and the courtyard was crowded with new arrivals, nearly all of them knights. One of these soon told him what was expected.

'There is definite news that the relieving army is only one day's march away; the leaders expect it to arrive some time tomorrow evening. Meanwhile this is our very last chance to take the city, and they are going to attempt an escalade on the southern wall, where it climbs the highest hill. Some say there is treachery also, and we shall be helped inside the wall. All the greatest warriors in the army have gone round by Tancred's Castle to lead the attack, and if they get in they will make for the Bridge Gate, and try to open it from within. We are to be on the alert, and as soon as we hear fighting across the river we must charge over the Bridge. If we aren't in by dawn, the leaders have agreed that everyone may retreat to Saint Simeon as best he can. Have you any baggage in the camp? If so, you should go out and get it started for the coast before it is quite dark.'

'I have nothing at all but my bedding here,' answered Roger. 'Thank God my wife is on ship-board already. If we retreat I must carry my shield and walk. Do you know if there is a priest in the castle? I must have Absolution before the fight.'

'The Bishop of Puy himself will be round before we finish supper. We can make as much noise as we like, for the enemy will think we are packing up to retreat. But I should think there are dozens of priests round about, helping themselves to the good food meant for the fighting-men, before they start for the coast!'

Roger did not like this last remark, for the priests had certainly faced as much danger as anyone else in the pilgrimage, and many of them had fought well; but some pilgrims had only come to the East to avoid excommunication, and to get away from public opinion at home, and these were always sneering at the clerks and holy men. He soon muttered a brief confession to a priest, who probably understood little of it, for he was one of Duke Godfrey's German-speaking Lotharingians; but he got his Absolution, and then settled down to eat as much as he could hold; if things went badly he would not get another meal before Saint Simeon, two days' journey away. He decided to leave his bedding in the castle; he could not carry it with him on the retreat, and if they took the town he ought to win something better in the sack.

After supper he took his place on the fighting-stage. It was impossible to conceal from the Turks inside the city that the besiegers were going to make some sort of move, and the town wall that looked over the river to the north was crowded with the garrison. But they evidently thought the pilgrims were packing up to leave, which was true enough; and they shouted and sang to celebrate their triumph. All the better, thought Roger, for it would leave fewer men to hold the southern wall.

At midnight many of the infidels had gone home to bed, and the north wall was quieter; Roger felt his supper dying away inside him, and wondered what it would be like to march and fight for two days on an empty stomach. Surely the escalade had been cancelled; no one would betray a town on the morning of the day that relief must appear. He tried to make out the white streak of the southern wall, where it climbed to the citadel on the sky-line; but his eyes could not pierce the darkness. The town was quiet, save for the eternal barking of the dogs, swelling to a chorus and then falling to isolated yaps, that he had heard every night for the last eight months. Then to the south-east he heard a shout; it was not the falsetto wail of the unbelievers, or the nasal whine of the Greeks; it sounded like a deep-voiced Western war-cry. The men in the courtyard behind him began to stir, and someone unbarred the door at the back of the castle. Then lights could be seen coming down the hill, and Roger went quietly to the ladder and joined his comrades inside the castle; no more need to watch the Bridge Gate from across the river; soon they would be hammering their swords against its wooden doors. Now men were filing through the narrow gate, and a small (pitifully small) body of horse could just be seen drawn up in the darkness at the north end of the Bridge. He heard someone pronounce a Latin blessing in an ecclesiastical voice, and remembered the rumour that the Bishop of Puy was to lead this attack himself, for all the Counts and Dukes had gone to the escalade. He took his place among the dismounted knights who stood in front of the horsemen; their task would be to ascend the gate-towers as soon as the gate was won; nearly everyone in the army except himself had taken part in the sack of many a town in France or Italy, and they knew their business without further orders. He bent down to tighten the straps that bound his chausses to his legs, and the man behind him pushed forward and nearly knocked him over. All the time the clamour inside the town was rising, and the lights drawing nearer. Then above the confused noise could be heard one clear call of 'Deus Vult', and with an answering shout the dismounted knights stumbled into the darkness.

Roger shuffled along, his shield high over his head, and in a few moments he had joined the crowd who banged on the doors and shouted defiance at the Turks above them. Arrows, and stone merlons from the battlements, hurtled down among them, but the defenders had had no time to boil pitch or water, and the great Western shields made an arrow-proof penthouse for the attackers. Then he was suddenly blinded as the doors swung back, and torches shone in the vaulted passage that pierced the wall. A great shout of 'Ville Gagnée' rose from all the pilgrims near the Bridge, the signal that the assault was finished and plundering could begin; Roger, jumping for a dark stairway on the left of the Gate, heard the thunder of hoofs as the Bishop led the mounted men into the town.

He was the first man up the winding staircase, which of course twisted right-handed, to expose an attacker's unshielded side. At the head of the stairs a closed door barred further progress, but other pilgrims were pressing up behind him, and a groom with an axe came to the front and broke it down. Roger leapt through, his sword upraised, to find himself in a small square empty room, with a similar door opposite and a ladder leading up to the roof. The defenders had already fled, but the bolts of the other door were on the inside, facing him, and could not be closed by the retreating enemy. He dashed through, and found himself on the rampart-walk. The top of the wall was in shadow, and he hesitated to advance, but at that moment someone set light to a cresset on the roof of the tower above, and he could see that the rampart stretched empty before him to the closed door of the next tower. This was soon beaten in with the axe, to reveal another deserted chamber, and he realized that the enemy had abandoned the defence of the wall, and were retreating along the rampart-walk to the citadel, shutting the doors behind them. The walls of Antioch had been built on an ingenious plan, with these stout doors barring the way from the ramparts to the interior of the towers, which contained the only staircases. This had been planned so that if attackers managed to escalade the curtain-wall, they would still be cut off by a sheer drop from the houses inside, and could be shot down from the topmost stages of the towers; but now that the pilgrims had opened the great Bridge Gate all these precautions were in vain.

The defenders were unlikely to halt before they had reached the safety of the citadel, but it was as well to take definite possession of the walls, and Roger with his small party pushed on, past the marsh and Saint Paul's Gate, until they descended the ravine from the other brink of which frowned the citadel. Then, by common consent, they felt that they had done enough, and that it was time to look for plunder; a crossbowman who had twisted his ankle in the darkness agreed to stay behind the barred door nearest the enemy, and give the alarm if they attempted a sally, and the rest descended the stairway into the town.

Roger edged cautiously along a narrow alley, his back to the house-walls, and his shield over his head; although the defenders of the wall had quickly seen that all was lost, and had fled faster than they could be pursued, in the town itself things were different. Some of the townspeople were infidels, and many of the garrison had been sleeping in private houses. These, suddenly awakened by the sound of fighting, had instinctively picked up their weapons and dashed into the streets. In the narrow, twisting alleys and courts that rambled up the hillside a sullen murderous war-to-the-knife was being waged. In his journey along the ramparts Roger had gone faster than the pilgrims who were taking the town house by house, and he found himself behind the fighting. He looked behind him, and realized that he was alone in the narrow street; suddenly he felt frightened and backed into an angle of the wall, his shield held just below his eyes. He could hear the roar of the fighting below him but the immediate neighbourhood seemed to be deserted. Then a casement in the wall of the house opposite was opened, and an arm thrust out two sticks tied together to form a cross; it was equalended, and he knew that the holder of it must be a Greek. In reply he held up the cross-hilt of his sword and the arm was withdrawn, but a minute later he saw by the light of the fires below him that the door across the way had been silently opened. He hesitated; it might be a trap. But he reflected that the infidels were curiously reluctant to make use of Christian symbols, even to deceive their foes, and in any case he would get no plunder worth taking if he dared not enter a house. In three strides he was in the doorway, peering into a narrow corridor, whose painted plaster walls reflected a light that must be just round the corner. As he advanced towards the light he heard a piercing female scream, and went forward more boldly. He came out into a little paved courtyard, not ten feet across; a three-wicked metal lamp hung from a bracket on the wall, and a frieze of polished tiles reflected its flames. In an alcove at the far end was a low couch, and on it an elderly woman clothed in silk, who screamed again and again as a man wearing a short coarse tunic thrust a lighted torch into her face. Hearing the sound of Roger's feet on the pavement the man looked round, and he saw him to be a eunuch; in that case he probably had every reason to revenge himself on his mistress, and Roger saw no reason to interfere; at the same time, it would be better to have a guide while he looked for plunder. After a moment's hesitation he strode across the court, pushed the other back with a sweep of his shield, and split the woman's smouldering head with the edge of his sword. The eunuch's blazing eyes went blank for a moment, and he held the torch aloft and stared stupidly at the knight; then he grinned, and pointed at a curtained doorway in the left-hand wall, making strange mewing noises, and opening his mouth to show that he had no tongue. Roger thrust the curtain aside with his bloody sword, and saw a small inner room, barely furnished but gleaming with coloured tiles, and a small boy of about eight years of age crouching in terror in a corner. The eunuch crowed gruesomely at sight of the child, and waved his torch, but Roger seized his shoulder, shook him, and then pointed to the little money-wallet he wore dangling from his sword-belt. The other understood, went to a corner, still chuckling and crowing to himself, lifted up a loose paving-stone, and drew out a small leather bag, from which he emptied a heap of coins. With his foot Roger divided the money into two roughly equal piles; then he withdrew his left arm from the shieldstraps, went down on his knee, and cautiously picked up one pile, still keeping his eyes fixed on his ally; no Norman ever laid himself open to a stab in the back while he gathered plundered money. When he stood upright again he backed towards the door; he remembered that he would need some bedding now, for the bundle he had left by the castle gate must surely have been stolen. But he preferred to seek it elsewhere; Christian slaves were entitled to revenge on their infidel masters, but he did not want to see, or hear, what the eunuch intended to do to the boy. He left the other stalking towards the child with a little eating-knife he had picked up from a table in the corner.

Outside in the street the noise of fighting was nearer. Everything was going well, and the light of a few burning houses enabled him to see where he was walking. He picked out a substantial-looking house a few yards away, and began to hack at the wooden lattice of a window with his sword. The house had been silent when he approached it, but the noise of his blows stirred the inmates to activity. He heard the bolts withdrawn from the door, which was opened by an elderly man with a white beard, unarmed. The householder must have been accustomed to sack and pillage, for in his hands he held a copper tray with money, silver caskets, and a gold cup, while behind him three closely veiled figures carried small bundles. Such cooperation pleased Roger, and he decided to see if he could save the women from anything worse than robbery; he stepped into the doorway, shepherding the infidels before him, and pointed to an inner door, making the gesture of turning a key. It was the larder and storeroom, so the small window was strongly barred, and the walls thick; he motioned the family inside with his sword, turned the lock, put the key in his belt, and went on to explore the bedrooms. He found a little bread; not much, for the town was hungry; but upstairs was a sleeping-room with a magnificent pile of quilts and cushions. He barred the outer door again, after plastering on it a cross made of mud from the gutter, to show that it was already in Christian hands, and went to sleep as dawn was breaking.

At midday his stomach woke him by complaining that it was dinner-time. The street outside was quiet, but in the distance he could hear trumpets, and the monotonous voice of a crier calling out orders. He had slept in mail and hauberk, for there had been no one to disarm him, so now he picked up his shield, set his helm on his head, and went out into the street to see what was doing.

Every alley was crowded with rejoicing pilgrims, but there was very little wine in the town, and most of them were sober and had their swords back in their scabbards. The raping and killing were finished, and a few humble infidels sidled by with apologetic smiles. Roger made his way to the Cathedral, whose dome showed clearly above the surrounding houses, but the reconsecration and the Mass was already over, and he was getting hungrier every minute. At last he came to a crowd round a bakery, where flat loaves of unleavened bread were being handed out in an orderly manner. While he ate, leaning against a wall, he heard the crier and his trumpeters approaching. They announced at every street corner that all spoil was to be taken to the front door of the Cathedral for equal division and that this was the order of the Count of Blois. He wondered what he ought to do. The town had been taken by the skilful negotiation of Count Bohemund, not by the pilgrims as a whole, and he

184

had been one of Count Bohemund's followers; still, he had only taken a minor part, and it was fear of the whole army that had made the renegade betray his post. Finally, he decided to compromise; there was already a little heap of valuables in the Cathedral square, guarded by foot-sergeants, and he went boldly up to it, holding his gold cup aloft, but concealing his wallet behind his shield; with a flourish he placed the cup on top of the pile, and walked away amid sympathetic cheers from the bystanders. It was the most valuable piece of plunder that anyone had been honest enough to hand over, but just because it was so valuable it was an awkward thing for a simple knight to keep in his possession.

Contented and well-fed, with a clear conscience and a heavy purse, he strolled back to the house where he had spent the night. As he went in the sound of battering on the larder door reminded him of the existence of the original owner and his family. He still had the key tucked in his belt, so he unlocked the door and shooed the infidels into the street; they were hungry, thirsty, and very frightened, but the women had not been dishonoured, and he felt that he had amply repaid any debt that he owed to the householder for handing over his money so quietly. They crept away towards the Gate of Saint Paul, and the greybeard even thanked him in his unknown language before he went.

Roger went upstairs, and stood looking at the disorder of the sleeping-room; he could make it a comfortable bed-chamber for his wife and himself; but he could see now that it was too close to the citadel, where the Turkish garrison still held out. Eventually he decided that his wife and his money would be safer in the Christian camp, and that he stood a better chance of getting supper if he were nearer the Duke's kitchen. Outside in the street he found a young native Christian boy, staring wide-eyed at the Western pilgrims; he caught him by the shoulder, took him into the house, and loaded him up with all the bedding he could carry. He drove the lad straight down the ravine, and out of the town by the Gate of the Dog. As he picked his way round the marsh he heard the criers again inside the town, but it was too far to make out what they were calling; probably no more than a proclamation that the sack was over, and robbery must cease; they would be crying that every few hours for the next two or three days, and in the end they would be obeyed.

There were no ladies left in the tents of the Provençals, all had taken refuge on the ships; but he found a clerk who wrote a letter for him, telling Anne to come back as soon as possible. He gave it to a groom who was riding to Saint Simeon on some business of his master's. He then wandered towards the Duke's pavilion, looking for Father Yves; but before he reached it he heard a crier going round the camp, while a crowd of non-combatants scurried up to hear what he said, and remained following him about. Roger pushed through the throng to learn the message, for there was no need to restore law and order in the camp, and this must be something new. It was indeed.

The crier shouted after every trumpet-blast : 'All fighting-men to muster at once round the banners of their lords. Arm, fill your quivers, and fall in. The banner of the Duke of Normandy is displayed outside the nearest city gate. Arm and muster.'

Roger had been armed for the last forty-eight hours; his neck was chafed by the hauberk, and his shoulders stiff with dry sweat, but there was no chance of a wash now. The situation must be serious if they were calling out the shirkers and non-combatants who comprised most of the population of the camp; bitterly he realized that he had only eaten a bit of bread for dinner, and now he was called to go fighting at suppertime. He muttered angrily to himself as he stumbled across the uneven rubbish-strewn ground towards what was already called the Duke's Gate, a small entrance opposite the west end of the camp. As he came under the wall he saw that already every tower had a Christian banner flying from it, either the great embroidered standards used by the leaders in battle, or hastily improvised pieces of painted cloth; such a display of colours was unusual unless a city was besieged, and suddenly he remembered the Turkish relieving army.

The Duke was standing at a window over the gateway, looking worried, hot, and tired; he wore his mail shirt, but his hauberk was thrown back on his shoulders and he was bareheaded, that all might recognize him. When his followers were assembled, he addressed them in a weary, crushed voice:

'Pilgrims of Normandy, by God's help we have taken this mighty city, but the war is not ended. The King of Mosul, with a great army of Turks from the utmost East, has reached the Iron Bridge, and will attack us tomorrow. We have decided, in the council of the leaders, that the Count of Taranto with the Normans of Italy, and the Count of Toulouse with his followers, shall make themselves responsible for the defence of the city. I, with the Count of Flanders, will hold the camp, and the Count of Vermandois and the Duke of Lotharingia will give help wherever it is needed. Now I know you are tired and hungry, but the emergency is desperate. All dismounted knights and crossbowmen will go immediately to Cemetery Castle and hold the northern end of the Bridge until further orders; all knights who have horses, stand by them here, ready to charge out if the enemy attack. God has brought us this far in the face of many dangers, and we shall emerge victorious from this encounter also.' The last sentence was said in a perfunctory tone, and it was clear to his listeners that the Duke did not believe it himself.

When he had finished the crowd of Normans stood for a few minutes, while groans of disapproval and angry discussions filled the air. It seemed that the Normans of Normandy must always take the forefront of the battle. As he walked dejectedly back across the Bridge, Roger meditated whether to give up the whole pilgrimage and take ship from Saint Simeon to Europe. Surely he had killed enough infidels to have fulfilled his vow, and now he had money. But what future was there for him if he returned home? He had a wife to support and even his well-filled purse would not buy a manor after he had paid the expenses of the journey. He reminded himself again that he loved Anne very dearly, and that he was very lucky to have won her. But it seemed that a married man must always be thinking of money.

Wearily he re-entered the door of the castle, which he had left with such high hopes. Of course his bedding had been stolen, and the new silken coverlets from Antioch were somewhere in the Norman camp; he sat by the fire and wolfed a meagre and long-delayed supper in a very mutinous frame of mind. Luckily, after the plunder of the town there were plenty of blankets about, and he was able to borrow some from a neighbour. He was wakened in the middle of the night by shouts of defiance as the first Turkish scouts were driven off by the crossbows.

Then followed days and nights of misery, broken sleep, no chance to get out of his armour, incessant standing-to. The Turks did not try a general assault on the walls at any point, for the fortifications of the town had not been harmed by its treacherous capture; but they overran the whole north bank of the river, made hazardous the communications with the port, and sometimes crossed the Iron Bridge, eight miles upstream, to ride round the walls to the south and get in touch with the infidel garrison who still held the citadel. To make matters worse, the food supply failed after a few days. Antioch had been hungry before it fell, and there was always a great deal of waste when a city was sacked; the infidel citizens had all fled, except a few who had been sold into slavery, and the native Christians hung round the defences, clamouring to do a day's work in return for a little bread. Always there were masses of Turks hovering just out of arrow-range, so that the defenders could never relax.

On the morning of 13 June Roger was resting in the courtyard of Cemetery Castle, with his hauberk thrown back on his shoulders and his aching feet in a tub of hot water; he saw Robert de Santa Fosca enter through the new gate that had been cut in the wall facing the Bridge. His cousin looked tired, thin, and dirty, as of course they all did, but he still walked with his old swagger, and showed his white teeth in a grin.

'So there you are, cousin,' he said, standing with his hands in his sword-belt, which confined the gay silk tunic he wore over his mail. 'I knew I should find you at the post of danger and duty. I am glad to see you have no troubles worse than sore feet. I shall want that tub myself when you have finished with it, for my poor old horse has died at last. I am not broken in to marching on foot like some of you. But I really came to see you at the request of a fair lady. Domna Anne had this written for her, and told me to give it to you.' He handed over a twisted piece of cheap Egyptian paper, secured with an untidy seal.

With the burden of hunger, physical weariness, and never-ending danger, Roger had buried the thought of all his family responsibilities at the bottom of his mind; his shoulders drooped under the almost tangible weight of this further problem. But it must be faced. He unfolded the letter, and both cousins put their heads together to puzzle it out. Luckily the clerk who had penned it knew it was to be read by a layman, and he had spaced the writing out, with clearly drawn letters and no contractions. It said (in Latin): 'Domina Anna sends greetings to Dominus Rogerius, her husband. She fears to return to the camp, or the city of Antioch, as her Lord has commanded, until the army of the infidels has been driven away. She will remain at this port of Saint Simeon. She is in good health. She has no money.' Roger muttered the words to himself, and easily translated the simple Vulgate Latin into French.

Robert laughed. 'The lady doesn't waste words when her mind is made up. She is quite right; Antioch is no place for a woman just now. But how she thinks you can send her money with the Turkish army holding the road, I don't know.'

'When did you get this letter? Have you been down to the port? The road must be open, or the letter couldn't have got through.' Roger was talking eagerly; he always cheered up at the prospect of a gossip with his cousin. though he was a little annoyed that someone must have been calling on his wife without asking his permission. But, of course, he could trust Anne absolutely.

'Oh, I saw Domna Anne two days ago. Count Tancred took a strong party of us down there to try and catch deserters on the road, and the Turks gave us a clear passage. They are still afraid of mounted knights, if there are enough of us. She is camping in a deserted warehouse with a lot of other forlorn wives, watching the ships sail away one by one, and the wharves filling up with panicky clerks, and some knights who ought to know better. It reminded me of the time we had to fetch back the Count of Melun, and that ridiculous hermit Peter. That was an undignified business, but this was worse. At least our old hero, the Carpenter of Melun, had the grace to pretend he was going to fetch help from the Greek Emperor, but these people are just frantic to put the sea between them and the Turks. Unfortunately their betters are not setting them a good example. Have you heard who is the latest deserter? The Count of Blois, no less.'

'Good God!' exclaimed Roger. 'A Count, and a tenant-in-chief of the King of France, running away when we are in this fix! Did you Italians fetch him back?'

'We are not Italians, we are the Normans of Italy,' Robert reminded him. 'And we couldn't bring him back, unless we were prepared to start a civil war among the pilgrims. There is nothing so bloodthirsty as a really frightened man, and he was ready to organize the other fugitives and cut his way through, if we barred his escape.'

This was news to be discussed seriously. 'Tell me about these desertions,' said Roger. 'On this side of the river we are too near the enemy to hear the gossip of the camp. Are many good knights leaving us? The Count of Blois was in the council of leaders, wasn't he? So he must know exactly what our chances are. Do you seriously think it is foolhardy to hold the city?'

'There are more deserters every day,' answered Robert with a sober face, 'and some of them are brave and experienced knights. The Count of Blois is rather a special case. He is not a great warrior, but he has been in charge of food supplies since the beginning of last winter, and a job like that fills the whole of a man's mind. Food is our weakest point at present, and I suppose the fear of hunger preyed on his mind more than the danger of a Turkish arrow. As to its being foolhardy to stay here, isn't the whole pilgrimage a little crazy? But here we are, and we have taken Antioch, in spite of everything the infidels could do to hinder us. A fortnight ago I was much more ready to give up than I am now. God must be on our side, or we would not have come so far.'

'I never believed very much in miraculous help,' answered Roger dubiously. 'I don't think we deserve it, and it is always wrong to count on it, though Dorylaeum was rather like a miracle. But I have taken an oath to serve the Duke of Normandy as long as he is on the pilgrimage, and there are no signs of him giving up yet.'

'That's the spirit,' said Robert heartily, 'and I shall stay here while the Count of Taranto needs me to fight for him. After all, even if all these Frenchmen, Provençals, and Flemings run home to their own firesides, we Normans can conquer this country by ourselves. Do you know this is the last Turkish army we shall have to beat? Farther south the infidels hold from the King of Egypt, and the Greeks say they are not nearly such formidable warriors as the Turks. But what answer will you send to Domna Anne?'

Roger brought back his thoughts from the heroic regions of high policy to the sordid question of food and shelter for the wife he must support. He longed to see darling Anne as soon as the fighting was over, but he wished that in the meantime she could find herself a comfortable home, by her own efforts.

'I suppose she is right to stay at Saint Simeon,' he said, after a minute's hesitation. 'When I wrote to send for her I thought we were in peaceful possession of Antioch, and I had forgotten about the relieving army. I had better tell her to use her own judgement. I don't trust letters very much. In any case, though I know the alphabet, I doubt if a lady could read my writing. Can you write clearly and well, cousin?'

'Certainly not, it isn't a knightly accomplishment,' said Robert firmly. 'But if you will tell me what to say I can dictate it to one of the clerks in the city, and send the letter down with the next large detachment that goes to the port. Count Tancred is in charge of the road to Saint Simeon, and if I don't go next time one of my friends will. But what about the money? You can't leave her there penniless; if you are short at the moment, I could lend you a little, though I didn't do as well in the sack as I had hoped.'

Roger was in a quandary; he did not trust his cousin where money was concerned, but he could not possibly say so to his face. 'I have some money, as it happens,' he said slowly. 'I was lucky in the sack and found an untouched house. But how am I to send it to Anne? It isn't fair to send it by some knight I don't know, in case some of it were lost on the way; then he would be suspected of having helped himself.'

Robert burst out laughing. 'How very tactfully you put it! You are quite right not to trust a Norman of Italy with a bag of silver; we are all strong thieves, and proud of it. But there is a way of sending money in charge of the biggest rogue unhung, though you may not have heard of it in your remote and honest island. I will bring a Greek merchant here, and if you pay the coins over to him he will send a written bond to his Italian partner at the port, and the correct sum will be paid to Domna Anne. Do you agree? Then tell me what to say in the letter.'

Roger told him to explain that he himself was staying in Antioch as long as possible, and that he would welcome his wife if she thought it safe to come. Unless she had definite news that he was dead she was not to go farther than Saint Simeon, except to save her life or honour. He sent all the money he had, but it must last for a long time, for there was no more in prospect. Finally, he prayed every night for her safety, and asked her to pray for him. Robert repeated all this, and went back to the town, leaving Roger proud of the ingenuity he had shown in getting a message to his wife, two days' march away, as efficiently as if he had been a royal clerk.

The next day passed as usual, standing on the fighting-stage of the flimsy wall, sweating as the hot sun glowed on the metal of his armour; the Turks rode up and down the river bank, and occasionally came close to shoot arrows at the wall, but mostly they confined themselves to shouting abuse in their strange language, and displaying the heads of a few deserters they had caught on the road to the port. They were not to be tempted into a general assault, the pilgrims were too short of horses to go out and charge them, and it seemed the blockade must go on until the town was starved out. At sundown he was relieved, and went down to the courtyard to find his supper. A Norman groom had brought a basket of twice-baked loaves from the town, of which each one was split with a cleaver, and half given to each knight or crossbowman. The defection of the Count of Blois, who had a good business head, had disorganized the supply of rations, and the first-line fighting men were not getting the extra food that was their due. However, on this occasion their grumbles were cut short by the exciting news the groom brought from the town. Roger only heard the last part of it, but that was stimulating enough.

'. . . and so the holy priest had men dig all through the night behind the high altar of the Church of Saint Peter. Twelve work-men had been tired out when he stepped into the hole himself; of course, no vision had promised to them that they should find the holy relic, but it was soon revealed to Father Peter himself. He wrapped it in a silken veil and gave it into the keeping of the Count of Toulouse. Soon we shall go into battle behind it, and of course we shall win easily.'

Roger inquired eagerly as he wolfed his biscuit, and soon heard the full story; how a Provençal priest, Father Peter Bar-tholomew, had seen a vision of Saint Andrew the Apostle, who had told him that the head of the very lance which had pierced Our Saviour as He hung on the Cross had been hidden under the altar of Saint Peter's Church, to save it from profanation by the infidels; how that now Antioch was again in Christian hands the time had come for the Lance-head to be revealed by the agency of Peter Bartholomew, and that it would infallibly lead the pilgrim army to victory over all unbelievers. This was very good news indeed. Roger had never thought of Antioch as being part of the Holy Land, and Our Redeemer had never been in the city in his earthly life, but it reminded him that they were already in the cradle of Christianity, in fact in the place where that name was first given to the followers of Christ. Obviously the first step for any God-fearing man was to go and reverence the relic, with all adoration short of Latria. He heard that a de-tachment of the garrison from the castle would be allowed into the city next morning, when the relic would be displayed after High Mass in the church where it had been found, and he was lucky enough to be included in the party.

Next day, the Feast of Saint Vitus and 15 June, he washed as much of his face and hands as showed outside his armour in the muddy river-water, cleaned his shoes himself, and walked across the bridge with a dozen other knights of the garrison. They were fully armed, even to their shields, and had promised to come straight back if there was an alarm; but it was felt that the Turks would not dare to attack, now this holy relic was fighting for the pilgrims, and in any case it would be grossly un-fair if its discovery made things more difficult. Roger had not been in the town since the day of the sack, and he found things sadly altered for the worse; many of the great stone houses had their doors and casements burst in, and walls had collapsed where men had been digging for hidden treasure. He wondered idly if Antioch would ever be a thriving town again, but what did that matter so long as it was Christian?

Certainly the Church of Saint Peter was gay enough, though the animated and gaily-dressed congregation that filled it was hungry and tired at a second glance. After High Mass the Count of Toulouse ascended the altar-steps, dressed in a gorgeous silk mantle over his mail shirt and mail breeches, and holding a small silk-wrapped object. The whole congregation sang Te Deum Laudamus, then knelt as the Holy Lance was unwrapped and displayed, much in the same manner as the Sacred Host at Benediction. This was a Relic indeed, at least as holy as the True Cross that the Greek Emperor guarded so carefully at Constantinople, and it had been revealed, by the direct miraculous intervention of the Blessed Apostle Saint Andrew, to help the pilgrim army in its utmost need. Roger knelt and prayed in ecstasy, as he had not prayed since the day he took his pilgrim's vows in the Abbey Church at Battle, so many life-times ago.

Gradually the less devout and the busier of the congregation melted towards the doors of the church, and at last the Count of Toulouse, who had enjoyed himself in what was rather a queer position for a layman, placed the relic on the High Altar and withdrew. Roger came out into the sunlight with his mind at peace; there need be no more striving now, no more fears of defeat, no more petty planning to win some slight advantage against the infidels; God had intervened on their side, in spite of their many sins, and he would give them victory by a miracle if they only followed his standard.

All the same, he was still very hungry; was there a chance of buying a sausage or something like that from a Greek before he went back to his post? Down a little side-street he saw a green branch hanging over the door of a small but undamaged house. His companions had tired of praying before he had, and he was alone; it was not a good custom to enter a wine-shop by yourself, particularly with such a very empty stomach, but wine was cheaper than food in Antioch at that time, and he walked quickly down the alley and through the open door of the tavern.

Coming from the blinding June sunshine outside, at first he could make nothing of the room he had entered; there seemed to be a great deal of noise, and it sounded as though most of it was made by people speaking French. Then somebody hallooed, like a huntsman sighting a deer, and Robert de Santa Fosca strode out of the gloom and embraced him. Robert was flushed and excited, like the rest of the party that occupied a long table at the back of the room, but he was still reasonably sober, and Roger, in spite of the religious feelings that filled his mind, allowed himself to be led up to the board.

'Here is my young cousin, Roger de Bodeham in England,' Robert called at the top of his voice. 'He has come, like all true Normans and true knights, to drink the health of our noble Count, and celebrate the good news in a fitting manner. Find a cup, someone, and pass the jug. Inn-keeper, another wine-skin!'

The Italian sutler brought a great leather skin, and filled the jugs that stood scattered on the table; everyone cheered and drank Roger's health, and there was such a din for a few minutes that he thought it useless to speak. He leant his shield in a corner, sat down, and swallowed a large cupful of the bitter and adulterated Greek wine. Presently the noise moderated, and he was able to make himself heard; the wine had quickly gone to his head, and it made him talkative.

'I see you are celebrating very thoroughly, cousin Robert, but this is not the usual way to give thanks to God for the finding of a relic.'

'We haven't been worshipping that silly ox-goad, or venerating the Count of Toulouse in his armour, if that is what you mean, and I am surprised at a man like you doing such a childish thing. No, the really important news of today has nothing to do with crooked priests from Marseilles, or any of those horn-wearing Provençals. We are drinking the health of the Count of Taranto, Commander of the whole army of the pilgrimage, and soon to be King of Syria, please God. At last the council of the leaders has learnt a little sense, and they have agreed to appoint the wiliest leader in Christendom, and the bravest knight, to command us all, Normans, Flemings, Provençals, Lotharingians, and French. Here's to Count Bohemund, and to Hell with the Count of Toulouse!'

'Well, cousin, that is certainly something to drink to,' answered Roger with a slight hiccup, 'though I am not sure it is fitting for the Duke of Normandy to take orders from the grandson of his grandfather's vassal. Do you take no interest in the Holy Lance, which has revealed itself to lead us to victory? Surely that is important also?'

'Oh, that be damned for a lying priest's tale,' shouted Robert, very red in the face. 'The whole thing is a put-up job by that lazy, shirking malingerer, Count Raymond. He thinks he has the Church in his sleeve since the Pope's Legate is his vassal. Why should the Holy Lance be in Antioch, instead of in Jerusalem, and why should Saint Andrew appear to a double-faced Provençal when there are so many honest Normans in the army? These Provençals have no business here anyway. Everyone knows that Antioch was promised to us, the Normans of Italy. It won't be long before we turn the silly cuckolds out, and their sanctimonious Count as well.'

Gradually his voice died away in a sulky mutter, but Roger had heard enough to be worried. The Provençal ladies were allowed more freedom than most others, and they certainly had love-affairs in plenty; but that made their lords all the more sensitive, and if they heard themselves called cuckolds a battle would start in the city. Luckily everyone in the tavern was a Norman, and he realized that by the time his friends left they would be in no condition to insult anybody. Meanwhile here was a chance of getting really drunk in a moderately good cause, and he had not had much enjoyment in the last few months.

Thanks to nearly two years' service in the army of the pilgrimage, his legs carried him almost unconsciously back to his post when at length the party broke up, and someone had remembered to hang his shield round his neck.

Next day Roger sat at his look-out post, and thought back to the conversation in the tavern. On the whole the change of command was a good thing; any one leader would be better than a council, and the Count of Taranto was the best choice, if skill in warfare was what mattered. He was a bitter foe of the Greek Emperor, and that meant that the Greeks would not come to their help; but probably the leaders had known that they could expect no assistance from that quarter in any case.

The insults to the Holy Lance were more serious. He felt that he must clear up that question before the next battle. If they were going to be led by a miraculous relic, miraculously revealed, then he could concentrate on coming out of the fight with a whole skin, certain that the army would be victorious; but if the whole thing was a fraud, invented by the Count of Toulouse for some mysterious purpose of his own, then they must all fight their hardest. He worried about it so much that finally he sent the groom who brought their dinner to look for Father Yves, and ask him to visit Cemetery Castle that afternoon.

There were not many clerks left in the city, and those who remained took their turn in armour on the wall. Father Yves was not free until the evening, and he came after supper; with food so short no one came uninvited to a meal. He listened with a grave and serious face to all that Roger said to him, but smiled before he answered.

'Oh, bless you logical Normans. So you want to know if we have the aid of a miracle, because then you won't have to fight so hard? As to that, I don't know what to say. Bishop Adhemar has given it his countenance, and he is Legate for the Pope; but he is not, after all, the final authority. I shall be happier when the Curia at Rome has pronounced on it definitely, with all the facts before them. The whole thing strikes me as too lucky to be true. I had never heard of this Father Peter Bartholomew before, and he does not seem to be a man of very striking holiness. Still, God sometimes chooses very strange instruments. No one else saw the vision, and it may have been only an ordinary dream.'

'No, it couldn't be that,' Roger pointed out quickly. 'He was told where to dig for a lance-head, and he found it where he expected to. The lance was there, so it must have been a genuine vision, or else the whole thing was a deliberate lie from start to finish. Do you think Father Peter is wicked enough to do a thing like that?'

'Yes, that does make it harder,' admitted the priest. 'I see him occasionally nowadays. He takes his elevation quite well, and is certainly not outstandingly wicked. I wish I was more sure of the Count of Toulouse; he gains by being keeper of the relic, and if there is a trick he must be at the back of it somehow. One thing puzzles me, if it is genuine. This city has been Christian since the time of Constantine, up to only fifteen years ago, and the lance must have been buried after Saint Peter's Church was built; yet the Greeks have no tradition that it was in Antioch at all. That puts it in quite a different class from the other relics of the Passion, which were always known to be in Jerusalem until the Blessed Saint Helena found them.'

'This priest says that Saint Andrew told him it was buried here,' Roger pointed out, 'and Antioch is not an impossible distance from Jerusalem. Longinus might have settled here after the Crucifixion, as we know that Saint Peter did. He might reasonably bury the relic in the ground, in time of persecution, and afterwards a church might be built over it. As to the Greeks knowing nothing about it, why should God reveal such a precious relic to a set of schismatics who disobey the Pope, and won't even defend themselves properly against the infidel? They didn't deserve it, but now this army of pilgrims does. It's quite simple if you look at it like that.'

'Indeed, that is quite a simple explanation,' said Father Yves with a smile. 'Though I am sorry to hear you so bitter against the Greeks and their ancestors, for they were not always heretics, you know. But really it is impossible to argue about miracles; they defy the laws of reason, and therefore reasoning is a waste of time. Yet you must remember that it is a dubious relic at best, and don't relax your efforts to beat the infidels just because you think you have a miracle to help you. Now I must get back to the city; I go on watch at midnight. God bless you, and fight as hard as you can.'

When he was alone, Roger went up on the fighting-stage to think things out by himself; it would be comforting if God sent a miracle every time the Christian army was in a tight place, but he had to admit that it had not happened in the past. It was their own courage that had taken them so far into Asia. Yet in fact God's Providence had, in a sense, watched over them, and twice they had been saved from what looked like certain disaster; once when the Norman column had been at its last gasp at Dorylaeum, and the Provençals had arrived in the nick of time to rescue them; once when it seemed that they must be crushed between the relieving army and the walls of the city, and Bohemund had discovered a timely traitor literally on the last possible day. He thought again of how the pilgrimage had appeared to him at home in Sussex; he had expected a long march, for the journey to Jerusalem always took at least a year; he had looked for one or two fierce battles on the borders of the infidel; what he had not expected were these time-wasting sieges, the months of hunger, the great stone walls round every town and village, the innumerable hosts of Turks who kept out of sword-reach and shot their arrows by night as well as by day, and the sullen hostility or guarded neutrality of the native Christians they had come to rescue.

That night the Turks were bolder, and one of the knights on the fighting-stage was killed by an arrow that hit him in the mouth and penetrated to the spine. The enemy shouted and screamed, and came very close to the wall, but they never actually launched an assault. Next day for dinner there was nothing but a small piece of donkey-meat for each man, and the servant who brought it told them that Bohemund's Castle, outside the Gate of Saint Paul, had been evacuated by its garrison in the darkness of the previous night. The official explanation was that the wall of unmortared stone was weak, and that the Turks had started a mine nearby, but rumour said that the defenders had refused to stay there any longer, and had marched back into the city without orders. In any case, it was the first fortification that the pilgrims had lost to the enemy, though the Aleppo road which it blocked had no more importance now the city was taken. It might be the beginning of the turn of the tide, and the knights in Cemetery Castle went about with long faces, swearing, too emphatically to carry conviction, that they at least would hold their post to the last man.

Fortunately, the Turks were reluctant to face armoured men at close quarters in the streets, otherwise they could easily have entered the citadel by the southern wall, and charged down the hillside; they did not attempt this, but many pilgrims had to stand-to, night and day, on the improvised barricades that walled off the citadel from the rest of the town. It was obvious that things could not go on like this for much longer, and every day the number of desertions increased.

6

CHRISTIAN ANTIOCH
1098

ON 27 June the defenders of Cemetery Castle looked in vain for their dinner. Every day the meals had grown smaller, but up to now they had at least been fed twice a day. In mid-afternoon hope was revived when they saw a man cautiously picking his way across the rubbish-strewn Bridge, keeping a sharp look-out for stray arrows. At last he entered the southern door, amid ironical cheers from the hungry onlookers, and was seen to be one of the Duke's clerks. He conferred with the commander of the castle, and then mounted to the safest part of the southern fighting-stage; a trumpet blew for silence, and the discontented, idle, bored, and hungry men gathered in a crowd below him. They were muttering angrily, but after he had given the preliminary cough of the experienced preacher, and made the sign of the Cross as though he were in a pulpit, his first words caught their attention.

'Pilgrims of Normandy, I bring important news. Tomorrow we shall all march out of the city, to deliver battle on the plain north of the river. Every knight who can get hold of a horse of any kind must come mounted; the others will serve with the foot, wherever the leaders direct. Tonight this castle will be handed over to the followers of the Count of Toulouse, who is unable through sickness to take part in the battle, and therefore is undertaking the defence of the town.' This brought an outburst of groans, for though the Count of Toulouse was an elderly man, and seldom in good health, his sickness did seem to incapacitate him whenever danger was to be faced. The clerk continued :

'The dismounted knights will be arrayed among the common

foot. The Turks will attack us as soon as we cross the Bridge, therefore we must cross it in good order, formed up to fight. For this reason the Duke commands that all fighting-men come back into the city as soon as they are relieved by the Provençals; then the army can be arrayed by the leaders before daybreak, in the street. I know you have had no dinner today, the food just isn't there, but the Duke has arranged a good supper for you tonight; in fact, all the food that is left. The Holy Lance will lead us, and God will defend the right. Now get what sleep you can, and don't warn the enemy by cheering and shouting.'

As a matter of fact his speech was received in dead silence, for the tired and hungry men were in no mood to cheer; but they revived at the prospect of action. Roger, like most of the others, was glad to get into his blankets and rest on the shady side of the courtyard. His last thought before he fell asleep was that in another day it would all be over, and that by tomorrow night he would indeed be at rest; either victorious or with the jackals mauling his carcass.

He was aroused at sundown, as the cheerful, chattering, impudent Provençal crossbowmen filed in through the narrow door. There were one or two sick knights with them, who exaggerated their weakness to extenuate the position they had taken up in the rear, but most of the sick who were able to stand were left to block any sallies from the citadel. The Normans plodded silently across the Bridge, and sat down on the cobblestones inside the gate; none of them felt particularly warlike. Roger's feet were tender and inflamed, from long standing under the weight of his armour, and his whole body felt stiff and clumsy, caked with grime and sweat. He had not undressed for the last ten days, or put on clean clothes for a month; his hauberk had chafed his jaw into a line of sores, as he continually turned his head to watch for Turkish arrows, and his right shoulder was deeply calloused and stiff from the weight of his shieldstrap; he felt dizzy from hunger, and, of course, constipated from lack of exercise. No one else was in any better shape, and many suffered from dysentery as well. On the whole they were none of them really fit for battle, and the entire army was not one-tenth as efficient as it had been a year ago at Dorylaeum ... and they had been nearly beaten there. He consoled himself with the thought that his armour was sound, his shield whole, and his sword sharp; but there could be no retreating from a lost field with his feet in their present condition.

Presently great kettles of hot stew were brought round, and everyone could for once eat his fill of the soaked biscuit and the strange joints of miscellaneous baggage-animals of which it was composed. At midnight the Duke himself rode up, and ordered the dismounted men to an open space higher up the hill. There he joined them, and the pitifully few cavalry who stood by their horses a little to one side. All the Normans of Normandy could only muster about a hundred knights on European war-horses or Turkish ponies, with about the same number on baggage-animals, a few even on donkeys, to form a second line; the foot, and dismounted knights, were altogether about two thousand. The Normans of Normandy were usually reckoned one-tenth of the whole army, which at this rate would only muster about twenty thousand strong; and rumour said that the Turks were a hundred and fifty thousand.

The Duke and his companions began to array the detachment; the men, of course, had never been drilled, and their low morale made them slack and uncooperative. All down the long sloping street other contingents were getting into order, sullenly and in silence. Immediately downhill were the Flemings, and near the Gate the French followers of the Count of Vermandois, while up the street a corps of Lotharingians shuffled and grumbled. The Duke and his great barons had dismounted, and were pulling their men by the arm to get them in their places; they were forming a column of six files, with crossbowmen on the right and the less efficient spearmen and half-armed but able-bodied grooms and servants on the left; evidently the column was to perform a right turn before fighting.

The Duke saw that Roger was a knight, and told him quite politely to take his place between two crossbowmen in the right-hand file; other dismounted knights were scattered singly all along the line, but there were not as many of them as there should have been, for most knights had some money, and there-fore it had been easier for them to desert. When at last they were in position the Duke mounted again, to be seen by all, and gave them his final instructions.

'Pilgrims of Normandy, at sunrise we shall march out across the Bridge. The French are commanded by the brother of the King of France, and naturally they must lead the array; as soon as they have all passed Cemetery Castle they will turn to the right, and stand fast. The Flemings will march behind them, also turn right when they have gained enough ground, and continue the line on their left. We follow the Flemings, and come into line when we have passed them. The Lotharingians are behind us, and will take post on our left. No one is to move forward until the array is complete, which will not be until Count Conan of Brittany has brought the last contingent into line on the extreme left. The mounted knights will form up behind the foot; I shall be with them, and can see from my horse when the line has been formed. Then I shall give the order to advance; so remember, footmen, stand fast until you hear me behind you giving the command. Now you can sit or lie down in your ranks until it is time to move off.'

His speech was received with dead silence, and all the footmen flopped down where they stood. Roger was between two veteran crossbowmen, who were evidently old friends, and talked rudely across him as though he wasn't there.

'What a tricky way of getting into battle, Tom,' said one. 'Why don't we all march out in one column, and do our right turn when the last man is across the river. This way the people at the back have farthest to go, and we shall be all day waiting for them to come up. That isn't how the old Duke, his father, would have planned things.'

'You're right there,' said the other. 'Taranto, or whoever is the leader, must expect the Turks to stand still while he gets all his men into line. All this waiting about may be the right thing for Italians, but I am accustomed to going straight at the enemy, and putting in a few arrows before the knights charge. We should all march out together.'

'Oh well,' answered Tom, 'we have done a lot for the pilgrimage, and those Provençal cuckolds can watch from the castle while we are being cut down by the Turks. I never expected to end up a holy martyr when I took my vow for this expedition, but we will get one or two before they kill us; you can be sure of that!'

Roger thought it his duty to encourage these veterans, who must be depressing the spirits of their comrades sitting near, so he spoke out loudly. 'I never drew sword till I came on this pilgrimage, and I don't know how things were in the old Duke's time, but I can see that this is the only possible plan. In Europe you never fought in an army made up of a dozen different contingents, each under its own leader, and some of them speaking unknown and barbarous languages. If all these men came out in one column, who would give the order to turn to the right, and how could he get us all to obey him at the same time? As to the Turks attacking us before the others have come out of the city, you know they always hover round and shoot their arrows for a long time before they can pluck up their courage to charge home. With this plan we shall win, and remember that we are led by the Holy Lance.' The two crossbowmen were silent, rather sulky that their interesting technical conversation had been interrupted by a knight, whom it was unwise and insubordinate to contradict. Roger felt that perhaps he had encouraged some of his hearers, though it might be unwise to bring up the doubtful and untrustworthy Holy Lance.

At length the moon set, and boys came round with wine-skins and baskets containing small fragments of biscuit. Each man had a swallow and a mouthful; a few, exceptionally lucky, fell out to relieve themselves in the gutter, but the majority were still constipated from lack of food and irregular hours. Then grooms were to be seen tightening the girths of the bony warhorses, and Roger got an obliging crossbowman to run over the fastenings of his mail shirt and hauberk. As the light grew the chaplains appeared at every street corner and muttered through a short Mass; then, as the sun rose, the great Bridge Gate was thrown wide open with a loud creaking of hinges and the army began to march down the street.

Roger limped along on his inflamed and aching feet, hoping that exercise and excitement would soon make them more active; he found that if he carried his shield correctly on his left arm the point of it banged irritatingly against his scabbard, and threatened to trip him; so he slung it on his back until he should arrive within range of the enemy's arrows. It was the first time he had marched on foot, fully armed, in the midst of a dense column, and even though he was in the right-hand file he found it awkward and enraging; those in front were always too fast or too slow, and he could not see the rough places in the street in time to avoid them. But very soon he was through the Gate and on the Bridge; here a breeze was blowing, and though it brought the stench from all the refuse of the long-occupied pilgrim camp it was reviving after the foetid and stagnant air of the city. He was in the centre of the Norman column, and if they had got so far the French of the Île-de-France must be already across and formed up on the northern bank. They all moved more briskly as they crossed the Bridge, and the breeze blew away their early morning headaches and sleepiness; one or two men began to sing marching-songs, and everyone laughed when a donkey ridden by a lame knight behind them brayed fiercely. Perhaps they would go into battle in better spirits than had seemed possible during the long night in the stuffy town.

They marched past Cemetery Castle, and filed behind the little body of mounted knights of the French contingent, who were drawn up facing to the right in rear of their own foot; they could see no enemy, and hear no sound of fighting. Then they were abreast of the Flemings who had also taken post unopposed, and the spirits of the whole Norman contingent rose higher every moment that passed; so far this tricky manoeuvre had not been opposed by the enemy, but Roger hitched his shield round, and put his arm through the handles, for they would be within reach of the infidels in a few moments. The head of the column made an S bend to get into line with the troops already formed up, and Roger could see the Duke's banner halted on his left front. As he passed the last of the Flemings he looked eagerly to his right, where lay the Turkish camp; but he could not see so far, since the whole plain between the river and the hills was filled with dense masses of infidel horsemen, and towering clouds of dust rose to obscure the sun. Yet the enemy, though not at all taken by surprise, were not ready to charge, or even to come within range and shoot their arrows. They were scampering about, collecting into solid bodies and then scattering again, and did nothing worse than shout their warcries, and wave their bows, to intimidate the pilgrims. Suddenly there was an outburst of shouts and trumpet-calls from the head of the column, and the Norman contingent came to a halt; immediately every man turned to his right, as it had been explained to them in the town that they should do. Roger looked down the ranks, and saw that they were abreast of the Flemings. He gave a sigh of relief; the awkward manoeuvre, so difficult for undrilled troops, had been safely accomplished, and they were in line of battle, ready to receive the enemy's attack.

Now came a long and unnerving wait, while the other detachments crossed the Bridge to take post. He drew his sword and his hand sweated in the hilt as he gazed at the infidels three hundred yards away; he felt very naked and helpless, standing in the front rank on his own feet, and he trembled with nerves and excitement as he had done a year ago before his first battle. The trampling and neighing of the horses behind him made him apprehensive of being ridden down by his own side from the rear, and the swiftly moving Turks in front seemed hopelessly out of his reach; he appreciated why footmen were so panicky and unreliable in battle. When the Lotharingians, with the Burgundians and a detachment of miscellaneous French who preferred not to serve under the brother of their King, had prolonged the line to the left, the Turks at last made a move. A great mass of horsemen came forward from the foot of the hills, and ranged themselves across the end of the pilgrims' line, facing towards the river. Tom the crossbowman was keenly interested in all that went on, and he grunted to Roger on his right:

'They should have done that in the first place. Then we would never have got across the Bridge. I suppose they thought they could outflank the whole army whenever they wanted to, but if our rear column fight their way into line we shall stretch from the hills to the river bank, and they will only be able to attack us in front. Could you tell me, sir, what nation is in the rear-battle? Now it all depends on them.'

Roger did not know, and looked eagerly over his shoulder to see for himself. He could make out a large body coming up behind, and one of the banners he recognized as that of the Legate. 'I don't know who those men are,' he said, 'but they seem to be under the Bishop of Puy, so there must be Provençals among them. Yes, look. The Flemings are kneeling as they go by; that thing on the pole must be the Holy Lance. Surely we need all its help. Yet it will lead us to victory today if we all do our utmost. We must kneel, too, when it passes us.'

He had quite forgotten his doubts of the relic, and a surge of love for the menaced and oppressed Church of Christ filled his heart; he saw it battling to hold its little homeland in Western Europe, ravaged by Moors and Lithuanians, and he burned to attack the infidels who defiled its holiest shrine. He flung himself on his knees as the Legate passed, then sprang to his feet and joined in the mighty shout of *'Deus Vult'* that ran along the line. As he brandished his sword, and filled his lungs to shout again, all his weariness seemed to drop from him; his feet no longer ached, his empty stomach no longer gaped deep inside him, even the stiffness left his shoulder; the whole tired and hungry army was filled with a miraculous confidence and longing for battle. With many others, Roger turned his back on the foe, and watched to see whether the Bishop's men would be able to fight their way into line. He saw all the mounted knights of the left flank draw into one body, and prayed aloud as they charged the Turks at the base of the hills. The infidels made little attempt to meet the charge with their swords, but retired, shooting over their horses' tails; then, more quickly than he had expected, the Legate's foot were in position, and the Christian army, its flanks secure, filled the plain from river bank to mountain. A large force of Turks was cut off from their main body, and remained in rear of the pilgrims, but the Normans of Italy, who formed the rear-battle, faced west to keep them off. The Count of Taranto had a larger proportion of mounted knights than any of the other commanders, thanks to Count Tancred and the ponies he had captured in his dominions to the north, and he could safely be left to deal with the threat from the rear.

The morning had not quite lost its early freshness, though the sun was now getting high, when at last the Duke's trumpets sounded for the general advance. All the long line of men, stretching for more than two miles, marched forward with another shout of *'Deus Vult'*. It was impossible for such a large formation of undrilled men to keep their dressing, and Roger could see bulges coming forward and going back on both sides of him, while the inevitable but exasperating loss of the correct intervals between the files made the front continually expand and contract, so that he could seldom walk straight forward. But everyone was in high spirits, everyone felt the uplifting presence of the Holy Lance behind them, everyone hoped for good plunder from the Turkish camp that lay ahead, and the great wall of men, dotted with clumps of mounted knights as with towers, surged irresistibly forward.

When they came within range the crossbowmen discharged their weapons, but did not stop to wind them, and soon all were pressing forward together into a cloud of Turkish arrows. Roger kept his shield up and his head down, and stumbled over the uneven ground as fast as the weight of his armour would let him. The unarmed footmen could have gone faster, but they were kept in line by their natural desire to let the mailed knights reach the enemy first, and the whole force reached the Turkish van-battle in surprisingly good order. He saw a bulky-looking Turk, all bundled up in sheepskins, leaning forward on his pony's neck and fitting an arrow to his bowstring; he must knock that man over before the arrow struck him in the face, and he swung up his sword; but the infidel turned his pony with his knees, and trotted away, looking back and drawing his bow in the general direction of the pilgrims. The whole Turkish line had flinched at the last minute, and ridden out of reach just before the impact.

The pilgrims were in an ecstasy; the enemy fled before the Holy Lance without waiting for avenging sword-strokes; men on foot were chasing men ahorse, and all the Host of Heaven must be fighting on their side. The cry went up that Saint George and Saint Demetrius were leading the army, mounted on white horses and riding through the sky. There were white clouds passing overhead, driven before a west wind and seeming to beckon the pilgrims onward; Roger thought he saw a horseman clothed in white at the edge of one cloud, but he could not be quite sure.

They pressed on until they reached the Turkish camp. Here the infidels had arrayed themselves a second time, and stood to defend the tents that were their homes. The Christians paused, and the crossbowmen took the opportunity to reload. Roger gasped for breath, and wondered if he could do anything about his scabbard, which had skinned his left ankle already, and might trip him up at a critical moment; but if he threw it away he would never get another, for the Turkish swords were curved, so he resigned himself to the nuisance. He bent over and leaned on his shield to get his second wind. The pause did not last long. Soon the trumpets were sounding again, and the mounted knights were shouting to the foot to advance or get out of the way; the whole line moved forward at a brisk walking-pace. All the crowd of grooms and horseboys that mounted men need to wait on their horses had come out of the infidel camp with such weapons as they could find, and for the first time Roger saw Turkish foot; they were not very formidable, but they increased the solidity of the enemy's line, and some of them carried more powerful bows than a horseman could use. This time the Turks stood to await the shock, and he chose out a well-dressed, well-mounted infidel in the front rank as a worthy antagonist.

The two armies crashed together all down the line, with a final blast of Christian trumpets and a clatter of kettle-drums from the Turks; he swung his heavy sword down at his opponent's left thigh, the most vulnerable place on an unshielded horseman, and felt the jar as it cut through to the saddle-tree. Before he could recover an infidel footman jumped in on his right side, clutched at his knees, and began to fumble with the skirt of his mail, striving to stab him in the big artery of the crutch. But a crossbowman in the second rank leaned over and drove his knife into the infidel's back. Roger stepped over the body and swung his sword again. Facing him was the Turkish knight he had just wounded, who sat bowed in the saddle, weaponless, with both his hands on his pony's withers and blood pulsing out of his shattered leg; another blow at the man's elbows toppled him out of the saddle, and he pushed the end of his sword through the looped reins of the excited pony, and struggled to control it. The Turks were yielding ground, and for the moment there was no enemy within reach, but with shield on one arm and sword in the other hand, it was impossible for him to mount. Tom beside him had his foot in the stirrup of his crossbow, and was straining with both hands to bend it the quick way, by a direct pull on the cord, instead of using the winch. He straightened up with a grunt as the cord slid over the notch in the stock, and saw Roger with the pony rearing and backing away at the full stretch of the reins.

'Hold on, messer knight,' he said. 'Let me have a share in the pony, and I will see you mounted. My name is Tom de Oustrehem in the Duke's own following.'

He dropped his crossbow, and held the pony still while Roger hoisted himself into the blood-stained saddle. The pony was quite maddened with fear and rage, but he was able to turn it towards the enemy ranks, and was at once carried forward at full gallop. All the mounted knights were working their way through the mass of foot, to deliver the final charge on the demoralized foe. The Turks were not making a good fight of it; some of their barbarian allies from the interior of Asia were quite unused to combat hand-to-hand, and retreated constantly to get into position to shoot their arrows; the better sort among them stood to defend their gear in the camp, and the foot were prepared to die fighting since they had no hope of escape. But already the horse-tail standards were withdrawing to the rear, and the bravest men only made front for a little longer to give their lords a good start in the retreat. Roger was the first Norman to ride into the dissolving mass; it was safer than it looked, for none of the desperate grooms and camp followers had spears or pikes to keep off cavalry, and all were unarmoured. His pony knocked over a kneeling archer, and when it came to a halt he exchanged blows with a well-mounted man who wore some armour. Neither did the other any harm, and soon the last mounted Turks were flying.

The pursuit was pressed as far as the defile by the lake, the scene of their earlier victory; here the infidels were jammed together, and many of the rearmost were slain; but the majority made their escape unharmed, for their ponies were fresh and well-fed, and could easily outdistance the starved chargers of the Christians. The pursuers halted at the lakeside, and rode slowly back to the eastern end of the Turkish camp.

They found that the crossbowmen had made an end of the infidel camp followers; now the sack of the rich tents and pavilions was just beginning. Roger dismounted and sheathed his sword, but he kept his pony's reins over his arm, for it was the most valuable plunder he could hope to win. The beast was used to living in a camp, and followed him quietly into the pavilions without tripping over the guyropes. Many of the Turkish army had been nomads, who kept all their wealth in these moving houses, and their families also; now their families were dead, but there was a mass of domestic gear for the victors to choose from. Roger did not want cooking-pots, or dirty flea-ridden Turkish clothing; as a landless man with a wife to support, what he wanted was money or jewels, and they were not easy to find. The few locked coffers that lay in the furthest recesses of the tents had already been burst open, and in any case this particular Turkish army was poorer than their opponents at Dorylaeum, who had been robbing Asia Minor for twenty years. He remembered the advice his cousin had given him a year ago; these infidels kept their money in belts round their waists. He went back to the place where the dead lay who had fallen in the final defence before the camp, and looked for the richly-dressed man whose thigh he had laid open, and whose pony followed him. It was difficult to find the exact spot; nothing looked the same as the scene engraved on his mind, when the Turk had been spouting blood, and he had been grabbing at the pony. As he picked his way over the littered ground the beast whinneyed, and he saw that it recognized its dead master; hastily he turned over the bloody mess on the ground, and felt for the waist-cloth on the stiffening body. He was in luck; the corpse was so hacked about, and so stained with blood, that no one else had noticed its rich clothes, or bothered to search it; from the waist-cloth he drew out a long narrow leather purse, ornamented with embroidery in scarlet thread. It was divided into two compartments; one contained a necklace of large pearls, the other a good handful of silver coins, and five gold pieces. He bestowed these in his wallet, and decided he had taken enough plunder for one battle; his feet were beginning to hurt again as his blood chilled, and a ravenous hunger had taken possession of his whole body.

Some of the foot had already got a fire going, and were boiling great joints of horse and camel in the cooking-pots of the infidels. The main captured food supplies were guarded by armed sergeants pending their removal to the city, but this would serve his turn until he got back. A comrade disarmed him; how good it felt to get all his armour off after these long weeks! Soon he was sitting by a fire, gnawing at a joint.

In the evening the whole Christian army straggled back into Antioch in twos and threes, leading captured animals laden with their plunder. It was the most marvellous victory in the memory of man; weak with hunger, debilitated by sickness, nearly all on foot or at least very badly mounted, they had attacked an enormously superior enemy, had overthrown him in two separate charges, taken his camp, and sent him flying back to his homeland in Central Asia. Everyone agreed that this could only have been done by a miracle, and all talked of the wonderful virtues of the Holy Lance.

The infidels still held the citadel, but there was no hope of relief for them now, and they must surrender as soon as they could arrange terms; there was no other hostile force within miles, and the pilgrims might relax and enjoy themselves. The only cloud in this fair sky was that the Provençals and the Italians were still full of mutual mistrust. Different sections of the wall had been allotted to each contingent, and Count Bohemund's men had closed the doors of their towers, and threatened to attack the Provençal position, while the latter stood on their defence. But everyone was too joyful, too tired, and too full of food, to come to blows that night. Roger sought out Tom de Oustrehem, gave him three gold pieces as his share in the capture of the pony, and engaged him as groom at a wage of a silver piece a week. Organization was breaking up in the army, as it always did after a victory, and Tom said he would be able to leave his company of crossbowmen without asking anyone's permission.

Sleeping for the last time in the courtyard of Cemetery Castle, wrapped in his smelly old blankets, Rogers felt more cheerful about the future; tomorrow he would have a hot bath and wash his linen, then he would look for a comfortable house in the town; he could send for Anne to join him at once; he was rich and well-fed, and in no immediate danger; best of all, he was once again a mounted knight, the equal of anyone except a count or great lord.

Next day he fetched Tom, and together they inspected the city, looked for a convenient house. The lower town had been the poorer quarter, and also the first to be sacked when the Bridge Gate was taken; nearly all the houses had been destroyed, and the rest were already occupied, chiefly by the sick who could not man the defences or march out to fight. Farther up the hillside the destruction was less, but the leaders had sent their servants that morning to take over the large stone-built palaces of the rich merchants, and they were in process of moving in. There was no room here for a simple landless knight. At length, tired of wandering up and down the steep cobbled streets, he decided to take a chance; the infidels still held the citadel at the very summit of the climbing town, and the houses within reach of their arrows and catapults, though excellent in every way, had been left deserted; he installed himself in a stone-built house, only a hundred yards from the gate of the fortress; there was a small family of Syrian Christians sheltering in the kitchen, and he promised to leave them undisturbed if they would do the housework; then he made up a bed on the tiled floor of the principal room, and sent Tom down to the camp to fetch his pony.

That afternoon he lay in a patch of sunlight in the courtyard, surrounded by plundered cushions, and thought seriously about the future. They had won a victory, and the land was theirs, but it seemed there were not enough castles to go round. What was the best thing he could do for Anne and himself? The obvious

214

scheme, if he had no land of his own, was to take service with Count Bohemund or one of the other leaders who intended to settle in the East, once the Duke had gone home and left him his own master. It would not be like soldiering in England, there was no one to fight but infidels, or the schismatic Greeks who deserved anything they got for not supporting the pilgrimage. On the other hand the Count of Taranto was just as unscrupulous and unreliable as the King of England, and if he served him for a wage he might be ordered to take part in some very dirty business. Anne would not like her position; it was shameful to the daughter of a baron, even a robber-baron, to be the wife of a soldier. The alternative was to be a burgess of Antioch. It was not degrading for a Norman knight to go into trade, though he knew some of the southerners felt differently; he occupied a large house, in a good quarter of the city, and if his title to it was dubious no one else had a better; he had quite a large sum of money, and would probably get more if there was further fighting. On the whole, that seemed the best idea; but he did not trust his own judgement very far, and decided to look for cousin Robert to learn his advice. There was also the matter of sending a message to Anne; she ought to have the sense to come of her own accord as soon as she heard news of the battle, but she would not know where to look for him, and might even believe him dead. He strolled out in the late afternoon sun.

It was very pleasant to walk comfortably in his tunic, after all these weeks of wearing mail, and cheering to the spirit to see over the northern wall the deserted river-plain without a single Turkish scout. All the pilgrims were rich and well-fed, and even the local Christians, though they had been robbed of everything, were at least no longer in danger of death by starvation or the sword. He went to the Legate's lodging, near the Cathedral, where an idle clerk wrote a short letter for him in return for a few copper coins; he noted that the Cathedral was thronged with a crowd of worshippers, come to thank the Holy Lance for its victory, but he felt too restless and unsettled to go in and pray himself. The next thing was to find Robert de Santa Fosca, and get his advice about the future, but here he received a shock; it was easy to discover what part of the walls was held by the Normans of Italy, but when he approached a tower he found the door at the bottom bolted from the inside; a cross-bowman speaking from a loophole above warned him that no foreigners were allowed in, and backed this up by putting his weapon to his shoulder.

Roger wandered about the lower town, depressed and at a loose end; he had counted on seeing his cousin, and realized how much he depended on his counsel; but worst of all was the knowledge that the pilgrims had now broken up into mutually hostile groups. The lower section of walls, on the north, was held by Provençals and various other bands; but all warned him away, though he was unarmed and on foot. It did not seem that Antioch would be a good place to start a business in for some time to come.

He strolled back to his new home, and was disturbed to see knights in full armour watching from just out of arrow-range the towers held by the Italians. The miraculous victory had brought as many problems as it had solved. Before he got home his feet began to ache again, and he shed tears as he rolled his blankets round him, lonely, disappointed, and bored. Had his father felt like this on the day after Hastings? It seemed that the pilgrimage had done as much as it could accomplish, and that the feeble central direction of this army of volunteers from many nations had finally withered away.

On 5 July, exactly a week after the battle, the citadel finally surrendered. Anne arrived from Saint Simeon, and found her husband's house after inquiring at the Duke of Normandy's palace in the lower town. Roger was delighted to see her again; during her absence he had thought of her chiefly as a responsibility that must not be neglected; now he saw her again as a beautiful and intelligent person, someone in all this crowd of strangers who was his own to love. She was satisfied with the house, found the forced labour of the native Christians quite adequate, and saw to it that her husband had clean bedding and good meals. Roger settled down to a belated honeymoon, to rest and comfortable living, after the hardships of the past year. He could be idle with a clear conscience, for the leaders had met in council immediately after the surrender of the citadel, and announced that the army would rest until All Saints' Day, 1 November.

They had also discussed the future of Antioch, but the meeting had been stormy and they had failed to agree. The Count of Taranto claimed that the city had been promised to him; he had said this so often and for such a long time that it had become generally accepted as an article of belief, though in fact no one could remember a public promise by the Greek Emperor to this effect, and in any case most of them would have denied that it was Alexius's property to give. Undoubtedly Count Bohemund had been instrumental in the treacherous capture of the place, and the council had promised it to anyone who could take it, at a time when affairs were in a very desperate conditions; but many people argued that it was only an accident that he had been the first leader approached by the traitor, and all the great lords had taken part together in the actual escalade.

It was rather surprising that the chief champion of the rights of the Greek Emperor should be the Court of Toulouse, who had always refused to become his man, and had only taken an oath not to make war on his dominions. Public opinion condemned Raymond, for it was widely believed that his only motive was jealousy of the Count of Taranto. Meanwhile the various sections of the wall were held by different contingents, all under arms and with full military precautions.

A week later the council met to discuss yet again the government of Antioch, and the future plans of the army. A certain amount of previously unknown information leaked out at once; for one thing, the Greek Emperor had been in the field with his army, and might be said, by his friends, to have been coming to the assistance of the pilgrims; but at Philomelium, on the other side of the Taurus mountains, he had met the Count of Blois and other fugitives, who said all was lost, and the pilgrim army probably butchered already; so he had turned back to protect his own borders. It was known that the Count of Toulouse was making the most of this, as proving that the Emperor had done his best to bring help; but most of the pilgrims argued that the Greeks had been carefully keeping out of the way until the battle was decided. In fact, everyone would have been unanimous in telling the Emperor to come and take Antioch by force if he wanted it, if only they could have agreed on some other lord for the city.

The Count of Taranto had the best claim, but nobody trusted him, for the Normans of Italy were known to be unscrupulous; he was quite capable of making an alliance with the infidel against the Emperor, and then the Christians of the East would be worse off than ever. So argued those, like Roger himself, who had come on the pilgrimage out of genuine religious feeling. Of course the others, the landless adventurers who had come to win land from anyone too weak to hold his possession, backed Count Bohemund as a lord after their own hearts; this gave him enough support to persevere against the wishes of the majority. Even the disinterested pilgrims could not uphold with full conviction the Count of Toulouse, the Emperor's chief advocate; it was too obvious that his motive was not zeal for the Christians of the East, but jealousy of a better warrior than himself.

Every speech was recounted to the excited crowd in the square, by the numerous clerks and messengers who came in and out of the council hall; luckily, though the garrisons of the various towers were in full armour, the crowd was unarmed, and there was no more serious disturbance than cheers and counter-cheers. Long after dinner-time, when the most boisterous of the partisans had melted away to their meal, Roger heard a rumour that the Legate was proposing a compromise. He decided to stay and hear the fate of the city decided, though Anne might be anxious about him; if it was war between Provence and Apulia he would go north and take service with some lord in Edessa or Cilicia, rather than fight his fellow-pilgrims.

The Bishop's proposal at least prolonged the uneasy truce. Alexius was given another chance; the Count of Vermandois, the man of highest rank in the whole pilgrimage, was to go to the Emperor and bid him hasten to Antioch; if he came at once with his whole army he might have the city; otherwise the council would dispose of it. Meanwhile, for the sake of peace, the leaders were encouraged to send out their men on private expeditions; this would avert spontaneous clashes before the next council-meeting on All Saints' Day.

This was news, and good news too. Perhaps the Duke would ride out to win land in the east or the south, and there would be a castle for him after all. So Roger thought, as he hurried back to his wife. As he swung round a corner he was challenged by a crossbowman with a wound and loaded weapon. The man cried out in Italian for him to halt, and then repeated the command in bad French. Roger was taken aback; he knew that the various parties held portions of the wall by armed force, and strangers were not allowed near, but it was a bad sign if that state of affairs was spreading to the houses in the interior of the town. He brushed back his mantle, to show that he carried no sword, and asked the fellow whose man he was.

'I follow no lord,' answered the sentry in barbarous French. 'I am a citizen, and this factory is held by the Senate and people of Genoa.'

'Well, I don't want to take it away from them,' said Roger pleasantly. 'But how did you come by it? The council has just been trying to decide who the city belongs to, and they can't make up their minds.'

'The Count of Taranto, who took the city, has given us the whole quarter, and we shall hold it against his enemies and ours. If you want to buy our goods you can go up that alley there to the warehouse, but no strange knights may wander about in this street.' And he brought up his crossbow in menacing fashion.

Roger went back round the corner, and found another way to his house. It was clear now that Count Bohemund would have the city sooner or later. It also knocked on the head his earlier idea of becoming a merchant, for the Italian cities were close corporations of traders, all supporting one another under the leadership of a Bailey, and there would be no room for an independent competitor. His future was still undecided.

When he reached home he was pleased to find Robert de Santa Fosca finishing dinner with Anne; perhaps it was a little unconventional of her to dine alone with a man, but the servants must have been in and out of the room all the time, and anyway they were all campaigning together. He had not seen his cousin since the miraculous victory, and it would be interesting to hear his views on the political situation.

'I see your Count is not losing much time,' he began, after the usual greetings. 'As I was coming along the street I was stopped by a rude old Genoese sea-horse, with a crossbow; he told me his fellows held a quarter of the town from the Normans of Italy. You seem to have anticipated the verdict of the council, which still hasn't made up its mind, as a matter of fact. But I don't think anyone will try to turn you out by force, now you have the backing of the Italian fleets.'

'Our Count moves quickly,' answered Robert. 'But, of course, all this manoeuvring ought not to be necessary. Didn't the Emperor promise us Antioch, and didn't the council promise it to whoever managed to capture it? That is two good reasons why we should have it now. I was just telling Domna Anne what a pleasant place it will be to live in, when Count Bohemund is in control. The walls are still impregnable, and he is a good friend to all peaceful traders.'

'I hope you are right,' Roger answered. 'Those Italian sailors will be a help, too. They are the best crossbowmen and engineers we have in the army. Perhaps Antioch will be a good place to live in, but I don't see how Anne and I can go on staying here. Where is the money to come from?'

'Why not serve my Count? He always has room for more knights, especially Normans, and he has the money to pay good wages.'

'My oath to the Duke won't allow that; as long as he is on the pilgrimage I can't leave him. Now don't argue, Anne; we have had all this out before, and you know I have made up my mind on the matter.'

'Very well, cousin,' said Robert with a sly grin. 'Oaths must be kept, of course, if there is no way of getting round them. Your Duke is not good at winning land, and you won't grow rich while you follow him. When he goes back to Normandy there will always be a welcome for you with us. Now tell me what you saw of the great battle. We were in the rear, facing the other party of Turks; we had hard fighting and little plunder, and the camp had been sacked when I got to it.'

The conversation took a much more pleasant turn. Anne composed her face into the correct expression of rapt admiration, as her mother had taught her, and the two cousins settled down to a quiet bragging-match. Roger was hampered by the fact that he was eating his delayed dinner, but actually Robert had more to tell; for the Normans of Italy, facing the separated right wing of the Turks who had been cut off from the main body by the first Provençal charge, had had very much the hardest fight of the day. No one could deny that Count Bohemund, in supreme command, had chosen for himself and his followers the most dangerous task and the smallest chance of reward.

Robert was always a charming companion, especially when there was a lady present, and the afternoon was one of the pleasantest Roger had spent since he crossed the sea. That evening he looked round his neat little living-room, stone built, weather-proof, and clean, and he sighed with satisfaction. All this, and the constant companionship of an attractive wife, was a fair reward for all his troubles and dangers in the cause of God's Church; there was no justice in the world if he could not get enough money to keep it.

Though the weather was very hot during a Syrian July, Antioch was a pleasant place to live in, especially for a knight who could leave his armour hanging on the wall. It was true that at first the town was uncomfortably full of armed men, and sentries challenged at every corner; but the various contingents never quite got to the point of attacking one another, and each lord was content carefully to guard his own winnings. Later in the month the army began to disperse. The Duke of Lotharingia marched north to help his brother to enlarge the borders of the County of Edessa, the Count of Toulouse was campaigning up the valley of the Orontes and in the direction of Aleppo towards the east, and the Count of Taranto went back to settle his lands in Cilicia. Both Provençals and Italians left garrisons to hold their respective portions of the city-wall, and Robert de Santa Fosca was one of those who stayed behind. The trade of the town was beginning to revive. With Asia Minor utterly desolate after twenty years of Turkish raids the silk and spices of the East had to find some other outlet to a prosperous Europe, and Jewish merchants, tolerated and despised by both sides, brought caravans from across the Tigris to the Genoese factory. Provisions were cheap and abundant, for the harvest was already gathered in; the Turks seemed to have given up the struggle, and had retired to Iconium in Asia Minor, or to the uplands between the Caspian and the Black Sea; no one feared the lightly armed skirmishing Arabs of the desert, and there was no dangerous enemy nearer than the garrisons of Egyptian soldiers in Jerusalem and the coast towns of the south. Hunting parties rode out far and wide, though the contending armies had made game scarce in the Orontes valley; there were picnics by cool springs, and, to the annoyance of strict churchmen, tournaments outside the walls. Roger passed the time pleasantly sitting in his cool and well-built house, or riding with Anne on hired mules to some beauty-spot for dinner in the open air.

There was only one shadow on the season of gaiety; the Provençals and the Normans of Italy would not meet as friends. This was unfortunate, for Robert de Santa Fosca was liked by both the de Bodehams, and most of Anne's women friends came from Provence. Of course, they were really quarrelling about the possession of Antioch, but as that seemed to be rather a sordid question they took sides also about the Holy Lance. The Legate, a Provençal, had made the Count of Toulouse guardian of the holy relic, which increased his prestige among the devout; but the Normans of Italy, themselves rather lax in religion and anti-clerical in politics, mocked at the whole thing as a fraud. Everyone was drawn into the dispute, for it was the chief topic of conversation even among those who cared nothing about who ruled in the town. Anne, though a Provençal, came from a family that had long been hostile to the Count of Toulouse, and her friendship with cousin Robert made her a mocker. Roger himself was doubtful; he went once to adore it, and made a small offering, but the whole affair was too much mixed up with politics to satisfy his faith.

As usual, he took his difficulties to Father Yves. One day he found the priest outside one of the town churches; the good man was coming away in high spirits from the baptism of a family of hill-shepherds, who had been Orthodox Christians twenty years ago, infidels during the Turkish occupation, and had now been received into the Catholic Church; it was their simple rule to profess the same religion as the tax-collector who counted their flocks, but none of the pilgrims suspected that anyone could hold such a mercenary point of view.

'We shall really get a grip of this land,' the priest said, as they walked slowly uphill on the shady side of the street. 'These conversions are a most promising sign. The Greeks say that an infidel will never turn away from his idolatry, but it only shows that they don't try hard enough to convert them. They don't preach, and they won't trouble to learn the local language; in fact, I don't think they really want anyone to be saved who is not a subject of their Emperor.'

'I am glad you think it promising,' answered Roger, 'though I don't believe any of the converts I have seen so far will add much strength to our arms. Have you baptized a warrior yet?'

'Well, of course they find life easier if they don't have to keep to our morality,' Father Yves admitted. 'One prisoner had the impudence to tell the interpreter that it was the Law of Nature for one man to have many wives. Some of them seem to possess no natural conscience, and I am all in favour of killing out of hand those we find practising sodomy. They must know without being told by Revelation that it is very wrong.'

'It might be a good idea to tell that to the King of England,' Roger said with a laugh. 'One reason why I wouldn't serve him as a soldier was that his sins cry out to Heaven for vengeance, and I don't want to be involved in the bad end that must come to him. But seriously, Father, do you think we shall ever stamp out idolatry in Syria?'

'Of course we shall in the end,' the priest answered stoutly. 'It will take time, but the Truth must prevail. The Turkish and Arab fighting-men who are too proud to learn anything from us will go back at last to their deserts, and the humble peasants will do as they are told.'

'Well, that seems a very satisfactory end to it all, but who will hold Antioch while you are preaching to the heathen?'

'I haven't any very strong opinions on that point,' Father Yves said slowly, like one thinking aloud. 'The Greek Emperor has finally lost his chance; I suppose you heard that he led his army back to Constantinople? The Count of Vermandois went with him, and then right on back to France, which is really shameful. That is by the way. If the city is to be given to one of our leaders, then there is not much to choose between Toulouse and Taranto; they are both good warriors and practising Christians, and both have enough of a following to hold it. Our own Duke should have been given a chance; he has behaved much better out here than he used to at home, but I suppose the leaders felt that a lord who can't keep his father's inheritance would not be clever enough to hold this city. What about the Duke of Lotharingia? He sold his lands to fit out his men, and no one has fought harder or worked more earnestly to make the pilgrimage a success. I really don't mind who is lord, so long as he is of good birth and reasonably good morals.'

Roger saw the chance to put his question before they reached the house.

'Do you think, Father, that the position of the Count of Toulouse is strengthened by the fact that he is the guardian of the Holy Lance? And did the Holy Lance win the battle for us? Or is the whole thing a fraud, as the Apulians are never tired of saying?'

'That is three separate questions, my son. In the first place, we must reverence the Holy Lance since the Pope's Legate accepts it, always remembering that Rome has not yet pronounced, and the Pope may still decide against it in the end. Secondly, was our victory really miraculous? I was in the very back row of the foot, and I can't say that I had much serious fighting; but the Turks did not try very hard, for all that they outnumbered us so. As you know, I have been talking to the prisoners, and they tell me that the infidel army was disaffected. All these Turkish kings hate one another as much as they hate us, and some of their leaders were eager to betray the King of Mosul, who commanded them all. Then they had Arabs in their ranks, who won't fight hand to hand. Perhaps we won that victory only because we were all one mind, and our enemies were not. Finally, does the Count's guardianship of the relic give him any claim to hold the town? Here I say no. The possession of the most sacred relics gives no claim to dominion. Otherwise we ought all to obey the Greek Emperor, who owns the Crown of Thorns, and the greater part of the True Cross, both much better authenticated than the Holy Lance.'

The priest, trained in clear argument by the schools, had gone to the root of the question, and Roger felt relieved. Norman naturally supported Norman, but he had supposed uneasily that religion was on the side of the Provençals. As they reached the house he called out to Anne:

'Here is Father Yves. I have brought him to dinner, and he says that true Christians can stand up for Count Bohemund as much as they like.'

'Then you must get used to calling him Prince Bohemund,' his wife answered gaily. 'He claims that Antioch is a principality and that will be his title in future, so Robert was telling me yesterday.'

'Why not Emperor Bohemund?' put in Father Yves. 'For he will certainly recognize no temporal superior, and I believe that is the distinguishing mark of an Empire.'

They sat down cheerfully to a good dinner, and discussed the various failings of the Count of Toulouse.

At the end of August the heat increased. There was always a certain amount of disease when armies encamped for too long on the same ground, and those who were stricken with 'the sickness of the host', as it was generally known, rarely recovered; but now the number of deaths increased, and there were rumours of plague. By the middle of September this was definitely established, and all who could began to leave the city. Roger and Anne debated what to do; they had a comfortable house that cost them nothing, and plenty of servants, but it seemed foolish to risk the danger of infection; on the other hand the port of Saint Simeon, the obvious place to go for refuge, was overcrowded and expensive, and the plague was almost certain to follow them there.

They had made up their minds to stay in the house, which was high enough to escape the worst odours of the lower town, and to keep indoors as much as possible, when Robert de Santa Fosca called one day with another solution. He came in the evening after supper, when the sun had set with some promise of coolness. He was dressed all in light silk garments, and looked healthy, cool, and prosperous. When the Syrian servant had shown him into the living-room, he first kissed Anne, and complimented her on her beauty.

'But it is amazing how you keep your health in this foul city,' he went on. 'I have decided to get out while I am still on my feet, before they carry me to the burial ground.'

'You don't look ill,' answered Roger, 'and that silk is magnificent. The service of the Count of Taranto must be well rewarded.'

'The Prince of Antioch looks after his followers properly,' Robert corrected him, 'but I didn't get this silken mantle from him. I had a rather amusing and well-paid job under the Bailey of Genoa, persuading the Jews to go to his factory and not to the Provençals. We met them outside the gates, and if you are in armour they are quick enough to take a hint. But there is too much plague about now, and the Genoese will have to get along without my services. Have you any plans for getting out of the town?'

'We have been discussing that,' said Roger. 'It is a good idea to get away from the sickness, but living is cheaper here than anywhere else, and I can't think of any other place to go to. Anne and I have decided to stay, and bolt the doors; though of course they will always be open to you, cousin.'

'I have a better scheme than that to propose,' Robert said gaily. 'I didn't resign my duties with the Genoese until I had something else fixed up. There is a little castle out beyond Harenc, just an outpost, you know; but we hold it to protect merchants from the Arabs of the desert. Prince Bohemund has given me command of the twenty or so crossbowmen who garrison it, and authorized me to find another knight to act as my lieutenant. Would you care to take on the appointment, and bring Domna Anne?'

Roger looked at his wife to see what she thought of the offer. She nodded and smiled, much to his relief, and he gratefully accepted.

'I suppose that I shall be free to join the army on All Saints'

Day,' he added cautiously, 'and that I shan't be required to bear arms against anyone except the infidel? I am still the man of the Duke of Normandy, and I can't leave him permanently without his consent; though he doesn't want us until November.'

'Don't worry about your Duke,' answered Robert. 'No one is going to wage war on him, and he can't have the slightest objection. He need not even know what you are doing, unless you choose to tell him.'

So it was arranged, and Roger decided that since he clearly had leave of absence until All Saints' Day there was no point in worrying the Duke for permission.

A few days later the three of them set out. Their destination had no other name than the Black Castle beyond Harenc, and was the furthest outpost in that direction that was yet in Christian hands. They found it to be a small square stone fort, with higher square towers at the angles, and one gateway, just wide enough to admit a cart. The walls were patchwork of all ages, for it was placed on the edge of a valley leading south-eastward towards a crossing of the Euphrates, and a castle of some sort had stood there since men first began to build in stone; but the latest repairs had been done by the Greeks fifty years ago, and the towers were sheer and strong, though some of the roof-beams had rotted. The tower with the most watertight roof was cleaned out and arranged for the occupation of the gentry; the other towers were used as armouries and store-rooms, while the foot, their families, and the horses bivouacked in the courtyard. They found another knight in charge, also a Norman from Italy, but he was sick with dysentery, and eager to get away; Robert gave him money, and Roger understood that his cousin had bought the command.

The duties were simple and light. When a caravan arrived from the river it spent a night under the walls, and next day about a dozen crossbowmen escorted it as far as Harenc, riding on the pack-animals; then they would walk the nine miles back. One of the knights accompanied the escort as commander, and this was usually Roger's duty, unless Robert was bored and wanted air and exercise. Robert was tactful and easy-going, but Roger found it strange and rather irksome to take orders personally from an individual; hitherto he had obeyed the criers who transmitted the Duke's commands to the pilgrims of Normandy in the mass, and there had been nothing invidious in doing what everybody else did at the same time; now he felt uncomfortable while his cousin, smiling pleasantly, told him when to march out and at what time to be back.

On the other hand, Anne enjoyed herself immensely. She had to fulfil the duties of a chatelaine, since she was the only lady in the place, and was perfectly happy all day, inspecting the living-quarters and the well, giving out the food, and dosing the sick. She did not seem to miss the company of other ladies, and got on very well with the women of the crossbowmen, though many of them were of loose morals and all were dirty and stupid; after all, Roger reflected, in Provence there was no difference of race between the lower classes and the gentry, and she had not been brought up in the careful segregation of class-conscious and conquered England.

Life was healthy and simple, but his duties kept him away from Anne, through no fault of his own; her interest in housekeeping was something he could not share, and she was so often alone with Robert that they developed private jokes and memories that made him feel out of it. But she was his wife, and Robert was his cousin; both were well-born and trustworthy, and would not dishonour themselves by carrying on an intrigue.

One bright, crisp October day, when there were no merchants to escort, both knights had spent the afternoon outside the castle, trying to shoot partridges with borrowed crossbows, since the ground was too stony for riding them down on horseback. They came back to find a mule-train had arrived from Harenc. The escort were preparing to leave on their march home, but before they went the captain of the crossbowmen passed on a piece of news: Adhemar, Bishop of Puy, the Pope's Legate with the pilgrimage, had died suddenly of the plague. Over supper they discussed this sad event, and its bearing on the future of the expedition. Anne expressed the proper sentiments:

'He was a good man, and gave up his safe and comfortable bishopric to come out to these infidel lands; now he has died far from his home. God rest his soul. Will the Pope appoint another Legate to govern us? What do you think, Messer Robert?'

'It is, of course, sad,' Robert agreed with a sympathetic smile, 'though the poor man was really no warrior, and the expedition will be no worse off without him. The question is, do we really want another Legate, even if the Pope appoints one? Prince Bohemund is the best man to lead us in battle, we don't need a bishop for that; and the government of the land can be settled at this council that is fixed for All Saints' Day.'

'The government of the land will be easy to settle,' said Roger quickly, 'since you Normans of Italy hold all the castles and most of the city wall. If you are not too greedy, and leave Count Baldwin in Edessa, and the Count of Toulouse in his lands up the valley, no one will try to turn you out of this county, or principality, or whatever you choose to call it. But is there to be nothing more than a council-meeting on All Saints' Day? The Duke of Normandy has shown no sign of going home yet, and I thought they were going to plan another campaign, for the next cold weather.'

'What do we want with another campaign?' said Anne. 'Haven't we done all that we set out to do? The Christians of the East are quite safe, and we have reconquered hundreds of miles and scores of towns from the infidel. Now we only need a formal meeting, with plenty of parchment and sealing-wax, to give us a good title to the conquered lands.'

'You forget that none of us has any land as yet,' said Roger, seeing that the other two seemed to be agreed. 'I know that you, cousin, expect to get this castle or another when Count Bohemund is invested with his principality. But what about me, and all the other landless knights? We must conquer enough to make a whole kingdom if the East is to be safe. And since we are so near, it would be a pity to leave Jerusalem in the hands of the infidel.'

'What is all this about Jerusalem?' said Robert, rather angrily. 'We came out here to rescue the Christians of the East, and we have done so. It is rich fertile land round here, and the hills are cool enough for us to live in summer. Down south they say it is all desert, and the climate is too hot for our horses. If you want to increase our land and make it a kingdom, there is all the Empire of Romania to conquer.'

'No, we must not do that,' said Roger, with a firmness that surprised himself. 'We have just managed to avoid open war with the Greeks so far, though it has often been touch and go.'

'We cannot now avoid open war,' answered Robert fiercely. 'Haven't you heard what Count Raymond has been up to? You know he has been campaigning in the south? Well, he has captured Laodicea, on the coast, and handed it over to the Drungarius of the Greek Empire. He must have been bribed, that sticks out a mile; but if we are going to be hemmed in on both sides by the Greeks, we shall be forced to attack them when the next fighting season opens.'

'But this is fantastic,' said Roger. 'Are you proposing to make war on the whole world, Christian and infidel alike? That is to plunder like a brigand.'

'It looks as though the Pope should not send another Legate, but come over himself to command us,' put in Anne, who saw that the cousins might quarrel. 'We could have a cardinal in charge of each contingent, and we should be at peace until the Holy Father died; then we could start a war to see who should succeed him.'

'Our forefathers knew all about making and unmaking Popes, when they first came to Italy,' said Robert with a laugh; but he saw that Anne was worried, and did not want to make an enemy of her husband. He went on in a quiet, reasonable tone, as though appealing from one man of the world to another. 'You know, Roger, what we have done already is more than could have been hoped for; in fact I shouldn't disagree if you described it as miraculous. Most of us have fought our way from the Adriatic to the Orontes, and always, at the last moment, when things seemed hopeless, our enemies fled before our face. But it can't go on indefinitely. For the last eighteen months there have been no serious quarrels in the army, apart from those skirmishes in Cilicia. Would you have believed three years ago that Frenchmen and Lotharingians, or Aquitainians and Provençals, could have fought together in harmony for two long and bitter campaigns? But that won't last. The more different nations see of one another, the more they hate their allies; that is only human nature, and nothing can alter it. This pilgrimage has done all it can, and we should separate before we turn our swords on our fellow-Christians.'

Roger saw that his cousin was making an effort to be reasonable and friendly, so he answered gently: 'I suppose the Provençals could go home; the Count of Toulouse has wide lands in Europe. And you Apulians now have land here, enough for your needs. But that isn't what you really mean. You, and your Count, want to conquer the Christian lands to the north and west. Well, I think we should go to Jerusalem, and win new provinces from the infidel. However, it is not a thing that you or I can settle. The council of leaders on All Saints' Day will decide what has to be done. Meanwhile we are here in this little castle, and I am under your orders. Let us not discuss the future, but follow our lords loyally when the time comes.' They went on quietly to arrange the routine for the next day, grumbling about the short-comings of the native food supply.

The climate of the Orontes valley is pleasant for Europeans in October, and as the month wore on everyone's health and spirits revived; more important still, the horses grew fit and strong on their diet of barley and chopped straw. The two cousins agreed to differ about the future, and Roger compelled himself to carry out his duties cheerfully. They heard that the Count of Taranto had not been very successful in the north, where the Grand Drungarius with the Greek fleet had occupied many towns in Isauria and Cilicia; what had happened to Laodicea was not certain, but clearly there was a Greek force on the southern frontier.

As autumn drew on, and the rains broke, the Tigris and Euphrates began to rise and few caravans came from the east; on the Feast of Saints Simon and Jude, 28 October, they set out for Antioch, leaving the castle in charge of the local Christian inhabitants. This was risky, for the natives would never dare to hold it against the dreaded Turks, but Roger did not protest; he knew without being told that Count Bohemund needed all his force at Antioch, in case the council broke up in open warfare, and that Robert had probably received secret orders to bring every man with him.

At Antioch they found that Roger's old house had been taken by some important baron who was attending the council; but things had settled down, after four months' peace among a friendly population, and huts had been erected in the old camp of the pilgrims for those who could not get lodging in the town; even the Duke of Normandy had done a bit of organizing for once, and all his followers were grouped together at the east end of the camp, well away from any fighting that might break out by the Bridge Gate.

The council was prepared to sit for many days; everyone feared that civil war might start if no decision could be reached, and the leaders outlined their policies cautiously, with many delays and private interviews to win over the waverers. The first question to be decided was the disposal of Antioch. Though Bohemund held three-quarters of it he had the usual Norman longing for unassailable title-deeds, and the Provençals still held the remaining sector of the wall. They could not turn him out without a disastrous battle, and the real argument was as to how he should hold it and from whom. The Count of Toulouse spoke in favour of the claim of the Greek Emperor as overlord. Most of the other leaders were undecided. In a sense the discussion was rather unreal; nobody thought Bohemund would make a reliable vassal, on whatever terms he held from the Greeks, and he was in actual physical possession. But these matters of feudal law had to be settled with an eye to the future; Bohemund might be a rebel by nature, but his descendants would find any claims now incurred were a perpetual obligation. So the debate moved slowly on, with much hair-splitting about the treaty that had been agreed after the fall of Nicaea, and many disputes about the exact amount of help Alexius had given.

The fate of the town was only the open and visible sign of another question that lurked in the background: what were the pilgrims to do next? It was clear that an independent Prince of Antioch would need the largest army he could raise, menaced as he would be by Greeks and infidels alike; on the other hand, the

Count of Toulouse wanted to take as many pilgrims as possible on a further campaign towards Jerusalem, and this would be much easier if Bohemund's wings were clipped and he needed no more than garrisons for his cities. The general public could do very little to influence the conduct of the debate; they must follow their lords' banners, or at most take service under another commander. Roger was content to wait for a lead from his Duke, and did not often intervene in the violent arguments of the waiting crowd outside the Chapter House. Rather to his surprise, Anne also agreed that it was better to wait and see.

Another, parallel, dispute occupied the clergy and the more religious-minded laity; the everlasting debate on the merits of the Holy Lance. The death of the Legate had left the churchmen without an undisputed authority to appeal to, though the accident that he had himself been a Provençal had in this case weakened belief in his impartiality. The whole question really turned on the good faith and credibility of Father Peter Bartholomew; obviously, if he had invented the story of his midnight vision, he could easily have smuggled the lance-head into its supposed hiding-place under the altar while pretending to excavate it. So all these questions, the fate of Antioch, the proposed capture of Jerusalem, and the holiness of the Holy Lance, divided the pilgrims into the same two conflicting parties.

Taking their cue from the Duke of Normany, Roger's companions were not strong partisans. Most of them had a mild veneration for the Holy Lance, since it was not easy to find any other explanation for their surprising victory in the last battle; but they respected Count Bohemund as a brave and skilful warrior, though rather out of his element on a pilgrimage.

Meanwhile the council of leaders, after meeting daily for more than a week, broke up without coming to any decision except to meet again at Epiphany. It had not quite come to an open quarrel, though there had been a few scuffles between Provençals and Apulians round the towers on the wall. The de Bodehams lived in considerable comfort in a large hut in the Norman camp, went to a number of parties, and entertained frequently themselves; they still had their conscripted servants, and Tom the crossbowman looked after the horse.

That Christmas of 1098 was not a bad one, as far as food and lodging were concerned; better than the hungry winter of 1097 and at least as good as that of 1096, which had been spent in well-supplied winter-quarters in Italy. But the pilgrims could not help being dissatisfied. Even if they started back at once they would have been away for three years, while their rights were invaded by both tenants and lords at home; and they seemed to have accomplished very little in return for all the thousands of dead whose graves were scattered from Dyrrhaccium to the Orontes. It was true that a western state had been founded, or would soon be founded if the council could agree, in Cilicia and northern Syria; and the Greek Emperor had won back, with little fighting, a good many towns in Asia Minor. But the Normans of Italy could probably have done all this by themselves, and it seemed a small achievement for the united forces of Catholic Christendom. Although there were triumphant religious ceremonies in all the reconsecrated churches, and solemn processions to bless the walls that now kept out the enemies of God, it seemed that the Christian cause had gone over to the defensive. There was no longer a united army of the pilgrimage, but a collection of followers of different lords, hating their allies, and quite willing to draw the sword to prove it.

Roger went to the Christmas feast of the Duke of Normandy, and sat among the lesser knights; Anne sat at a different table among the other ladies, who all went home when the serious drinking began. He knew his companions well enough by now, and was not shy in their company, but their talk began to make him home-sick. All were convinced that this was their last Christmas abroad, and they spoke of what they would find when at last they returned. Occasional news had reached them from the Flemish and English ships that had put in to Saint Simeon since it had been in Christian hands, though laymen did not as a rule write or receive letters other than legal documents.

'I wonder if I have any villeins left,' said one. 'My poor old uncle believes anything that is said to him on oath, and they are quite capable of swearing they are all free men.'

'In that case you should hurry home,' said another, 'before next harvest. "Three times makes a custom", and if they dodge their boon-work next year you will never get them back. It isn't the tenants that worry me, but my lord. I hold from the Archbishop of Rouen, and now we are under King William. You know how the King treats church property, and I may find that I owe service to some promoted soldier from Brabant or one of the more scandalous clerks in the Chancery. Still, if I can get back to my manor, in a decent climate, where there are full rivers and green grass, I shan't complain whoever is my lord.'

'Has anybody any news from Sussex in England?' Roger asked. 'My father held there from the unfortunate Count of Eu. He was mutilated for rebellion, but they hadn't decided what to do with his fiefs when I left home.'

There was no news from Sussex, but the general opinion was that the King would keep forfeited land in his own demesne, unless he was very pressed for money; also that the vassals of a rebellious lord, even though they had refused to follow him in rebellion, would not be trusted by the royal court. Whatever the laws of England, they had certainly failed in their duty according to Norman custom, and so were unworthy of trust. It was not a family history on which Roger looked back with pride, and on the whole he was glad that he would never see Sussex again. Some other knights intended to live and die in the East, and many of these were still landless, but they hoped to be granted fiefs as soon as the Duke began his return journey. The Prince would need a large army for the war with the Greek Empire that everyone was convinced would come soon, and even if he made some sort of a truce with the infidels he could not trust them to keep it; his castles on the eastern frontier would have to be strongly garrisoned. Nobody spoke of going on to Jerusalem; that idea was quite dead among the Normans.

Roger drank his full share whenever the wine-pitchers came round, and presently he began to feel sorry for himself. After more than two years in the army, he had learnt to withdraw into self-made solitude and forget the companions who pressed against his sides as he sat at table; he could easily be alone with his thoughts in a crowd, a trick every warrior must learn if he does not want to acquire a hysterical hatred of his own side.

He thought of the future, which was not at all encouraging. His position was lower in the social and military scale than it had been when he set out; then he had been fully armed and well mounted, now with his little Turkish pony he was halfway between a knight and a skirmishing Turcopole. He looked to a future where he would always be just too poor to take his rightful place on the battlefield, and therefore in the world at large. In Sussex they had all been poor, but it had not mattered very much; there were so many other country knights in the same position, and none of them had attempted to live like the great de Clares at Tonbridge. On the pilgrimage, however, counts, barons, and simple knights were thrown together, and subsidies from the Greek Emperor and plunder from the captured towns had sent up the standard of living. He saw that this perpetual nagging worry about the future must always be the lot of landless men; if you had a fief, though you might be poor the land was always there, promising a better harvest next year; and even the poorest free landholder had a position in his lord's law-court. He must get hold of land soon. Well, the next campaign would solve that problem one way or the other. A page came round with the wine-jar, and he roused himself to get his cup refilled.

Different songs were always being started up in various parts of the hall, but the trouvères had finished the formal singing to the whole company, and these verses, most of them newly-composed and not yet widely known, were not taken up by the whole body of feasters. There was a great deal of shouting and gesticulation, but no one had yet quarrelled to the point of fighting, and it was unlikely that they would as long as the Duke remained in his place; for a man who drew sword in his presence could lawfully be mutilated on the spot.

Further down the table, where he could not hear all that was said, a tipsy clerk was boasting about the new benefice he had been given.

'It's a fine square stone church with a roof that reaches to the stars, I tell you,' he shouted, 'and it was stocked with gold and silver chalices. Of course, all the ornaments had been used in schismatical services, and I don't know how you are supposed to go about reconsecrating them; so I sold the lot for a very good price, and told my flock that they must buy me proper Catholic ones. Otherwise I shall make sure that their oaths are not valid in the Prince's new court. You can't have schismatics and heretics taking oath against honest Christians, can you? Well, I decide who is an honest Christian, and who is unworthy of belief, and I shall see that I am well paid for my services. I am in a more responsible position than the new lord, whoever he will be; for I must tame the souls of these Greeks, while he only keeps their bodies in order.'

It was not very edifying, but Roger reflected that it was true. The pilgrims would not be able to found an enduring state unless they got the support of the native Christians, and the only way to do that was to make good Catholics out of them. That priest at the lower end of the table (a lower place than his, he noticed with pleasure) might not be the best type of missionary, but the natives would soon come to heel if they found their oaths weighed nothing in the Prince's court.

A tough-looking, middle-aged knight sitting opposite listened and guffawed.

'That drunken old clerk seems to have the right idea, eh, Messer Roger? If these blasted Italian freebooters take all the best fiefs, and I expect they will, damn me if I don't get myself tonsured and look out for a nice fat job in the Church. That is where the best pickings will be. You're landless too, aren't you? You ought to do the same.'

Roger made some civil reply and returned to his private thoughts. Taking orders would be an obvious solution of his difficulties, for when the pilgrims went home there would be a shortage of Catholic clergy. It might not be a bad sort of life, with plenty of fighting as well as prayer. Then he remembered Anne. Of course, his marriage made any such scheme impossible. He had drunk enough to be full of self-pity; and for the first time he wished, rather hazily, that he was still a bachelor. His wife was very desirable, but always he must plan for her comfort, when he should be thinking of his own future. Everyone was against him, and he began to cry softly to himself, with mingled home-sickness and general despair.

After another two cups his mood changed from sorrow to anger, but there was no way in which he dared to show it. He sat hunched up on the bench, twirling the empty cup in his hands, while he silently hated everything; he hated the whole of Christendom, more especially the pilgrimage, the Duke, and all his companions in arms; he even hated his wife. If the Duke was far above his reach, and it was impossible to draw sword in his presence to attack any of these disgustingly cheerful and prosperous knights, he could at least teach Anne a lesson. He cheered up a little when he thought about the row he would have with her as soon as he got back to his hut.

The drinking continued, and presently all who were still conscious joined in the chorus of the song about Roland at Roncesvalles, which they all knew. At last Roger staggered out into the cold night, after a Christmas party that was long remembered in Syria and Normandy, though he himself had been miserable during the greater part of it. He woke up in the morning in a muddy alley of the camp. He felt very ill indeed, and lurched stiffly to his hut; he could not possibly face Mass on Saint Stephen's Day, though it was quite a considerable feast, and he fell on his bed, too tired to wash, and longing for a quiet sleep. Anne was looking provocatively healthy and strong, with her head tied up in a napkin while she superintended the work of the Syrian chambermaid. She greeted him with all the deference a wife owes to her lord, but he saw her smiling at his appearance, and he went to sleep in a worse temper than ever.

For the next few days he had a grievance against her, though he could not always remember the reason why; she, though outwardly polite, paid less attention to his opinions than before. Yet somehow he could not bring himself to quarrel with her in cold blood, and it was difficult to put her faults into words.

7

JERUSALEM

1099

At Epiphany, 6 January 1099, the council of leaders met again in the Chapter House of Antioch. The parties were still divided as they had been ever since the autumn; the Italians and the Normans of Italy for Bohemund, and the Provençals for the Greek Emperor; while the rest were undecided. But in one respect the Greek Emperor's case had weakened; everybody knew of the occupation of Laodicaea, and for the Greeks to hold a town to the south of the pilgrims' territory seemed to them all to be nothing but aggression and encirclement. This strengthened the party of Bohemund, and put most of the waverers on his side. It looked as though the council would invest him with his principality without further discussion, wind up the pilgrimage, and make arrangements for going home in the spring. However, there was a surprise in store; the Count of Toulouse had been concentrating on the clergy, and everyone who attended Mass that morning, which on such a great feast was practically the whole army, heard an impassioned sermon on the duty of going on at once to free Jerusalem.

Roger had been in the congregation of Father Yves, who celebrated at a little portable altar in one of the Duke's pavilions; and as he said to Anne when they came out, it was only what he expected to hear from the Breton priest. But at the great dinner held in the Duke's hall, in honour of the feast, he realized that everyone else had listened to the same exhortation. The knights were not very interested; preachers were always telling them what ought to be done for the welfare of Christendom as a whole, and they were used to disregarding these commands, unless they happened to fit in with their own worldly interests.

It was the duty of preachers to talk like that, and it would be very shocking if they did not, but it was for the great lords to decide what the army would do next. The general opinion was that the Count of Taranto would still get what he wanted, and that they would all be on their way home by midsummer.

But in the afternoon Roger went to the horse-lines to see his pony fed, and what he heard there brought home to him that the sermons had made a great impression on the lower orders. Tom the crossbowman was full of it.

'He told us pretty straight what we had to do, sir. He said there was no special virtue in Antioch, any more than in Carthage or any of those Spanish towns in infidel hands; but Jerusalem is different. He told us that we should lose all the blessing of the pilgrimage if we turned back now, with the Holy Land almost in our reach, and that it was only the covetousness and sloth of the knights, begging your pardon, sir, that was holding us back. He said that since the poor are always more pleasing to God than the rich, if we went on by ourselves Jerusalem would fall to our crossbows and pikes, without any need for the knights with their great swords. It was a very good sermon, sir, and of course there were not many gentry to hear it, for Father Peter is not well-born; in fact, they say his father was a villein.'

With the accurate memory of the illiterate, the groom was quite prepared to give a verbatim report; but Roger shut him up, for it was easy to reconstruct the whole story from these excerpts. He recognized the type of priest easily enough; a man who had come up in the world, and therefore spent his time attacking his superiors, and praising the virtues of the lower orders. There were many like him in country parishes at home, but it would be a serious matter if they began to incite the foot to disobey their natural leaders. He spoke severely to Tom.

'I hire you at a weekly wage to look after my horse; if you want to leave me you may, and I can easily get some Syrian to do the work instead. But you are also an oath-bound follower of the Duke of Normandy, and you must obey his lawful commands; or we shall see what you look like on the mutilation-block. As to the foot marching by themselves, remember what happened to those who first set out under Godescalc and Walter the Penniless. You can do nothing without knights in this land of bow-bearing horsemen.'

'I'm very sorry, sir,' Tom answered, putting his hand nervously to his eyes. 'I was only telling you about the sermon I heard this morning. Of course I would like to remain in your service, unless you intend to go home. I mean to stay here till I die.'

Roger dismissed the man, after making sure that the corn had really been given to his pony, and not kept back for sale later in the market. On the way back to his hut he thought over what he had heard. It was going to be very awkward if the foot became discontented and mutinous.

When he got back he mentioned his misgivings to Anne, but she was not inclined to take them seriously.

'These poor silly crossbowmen will never dare to take a line of their own. For one thing they haven't the slightest idea where they are, and they could never find Jerusalem by themselves if they tried to. Even the great lords have trouble enough getting guides to show them the way to the next town, in this land where everyone speaks an unknown language and the travelling merchants are infidels. If the foot do try to go off by themselves you must ride them down, and kill a few of the ringleaders; but nothing of that kind will happen. They may be reluctant to go home when the time comes; so much the better for us, as we are staying here. We shall be able to pick and choose our garrison.'

'I am sure you are right, my dear,' he answered. 'But it will be rather shaming if they set us a good example which we are unwilling to follow.'

'Oh, the poor are always setting good examples,' said Anne with a shrug. 'They haven't our temptations in the things of the flesh, and they are too stupid to think out pleasant ways of sinning.'

'That is quite enough of that, on Epiphany Day especially. But I know what you mean. I had thought of warning the Duke that there may be trouble coming; but I expect he will have heard all about it, and anyway it will blow over with nothing worse than talk. I shall go into town now, and listen for news outside the Chapter House. The council meets today, and it's time they decided something.'

But he was late. As he passed through the Duke's Gate he saw a rapidly growing crowd in front of him, pushing round a crier who was giving out some announcement. Evidently the council had come to a decision, and it was being published to the whole army. He saw a young knight he had spoken to sometimes at the Duke's table, and called out an inquiry.

'News enough, my friend,' answered the other. 'Count Bohemund has been given his princedom in absolute sovereignty.'

'Well, we all expected that, though perhaps not quite so quickly,' Roger interrupted.

'Yes, but that isn't the half of it. The Count of Toulouse was in a furious rage, of course, and he made a very violent speech. He says he will take the Provençals south on the Jerusalem road a week from today, even if no one else comes with him. That got them all excited, and God knows what will happen next. The Duke hasn't made up his mind, and we don't know whether we march or not.'

Without waiting to hear more Roger hurried back to the camp. So the split had come at last; now he must talk over his plans with Anne. As usual, this exciting news spread faster than a man could walk on foot, and Anne knew all about it when he reached her. She had already made up her mind, and told him quite calmly what he must do.

'Go to the Prince of Antioch in the morning and see what sort of promise you can get out of him. And it would be as well if we moved into the town as soon as possible. There may be fighting, and the quicker we join his following the better.'

The advice was sound, but it was going a little too fast for Roger, as he pointed out.

'I am afraid I am still the Duke's man, my dear, until he definitely decides to go home. I can't leave his camp now, when the leaders are quarrelling and may come to blows at any moment; this is just the time when he wants every one of his men to follow him loyally. It is quite possible he will make some bargain with the Prince, and sell his support for land, or even for a sum of money. That would be the sensible thing, though perhaps it's not quite in Duke Robert's tradition. But I will certainly go and see the Prince, and find out what he has to offer me.'

'Good heavens, Roger,' Anne said excitedly. 'Surely you are not still babbling about that oath you took in Rouen more than two years ago. Can't you see that everything has changed since then? Our whole future depends on our joining the right side now, while your support is still of some value. What can the Duke do to you if we leave him? I need not remind you again that we still have no land for him to harry, although that is a thing you should never forget. Even your family at home is outside his dominions. You are a free man, and your own master, and now is the time to get on the winning side.'

'Oh, leave me alone,' snapped Roger. 'Don't they have oaths in Provence? I am bound by my oath until the Duke leaves. I am certainly on Bohemund's side, like all sensible men. But I won't desert my lord at the very end of my service, after being faithful to him for nearly three years.'

'A fine faithful vassal you've been, I'm sure,' said Anne, her voice rising into a high nagging whine that Roger had never heard before, 'and how does he reward you? With your bare food, as though you were a scullion in his kitchen. But you are afraid to defy your lord openly, as befits a man of rank and honour. I suppose you think the Duke would have you beaten, like an insubordinate villein.'

It was an unfortunate choice of words, for of course it suggested to Roger what was the next thing to be done; he picked up a spur-trap that lay conveniently near, and thrashed her soundly. Then he walked out in a towering rage, without any supper.

It was already dark, and he was annoyed to find that he had left his purse at home. Now he could not go back to fetch it; though he was hungry and faint from the emotion that possessed him. He took himself off finally to the Duke's kitchen, where the butler would give him something. Munching bread and cold meat, as he stood in the crowd outside the kitchen, he reflected on the pigheadedness of Anne, and the insulting way she had spoken to him. He remembered what his father had so often said, that oaths were the framework and the foundation of Christian society; every Christian's right to the land he held was based on an oath, and it was because no one could trust a Jewish or infidel oath that Jews and infidels could not hold land rightfully. All that stood between Christendom and the horrid bloodshed of the reign of Antichrist was the sanctity of the vassal's oath. Of course, a lord might be unreasonable, or covetous, or try to interfere with his vassal's private affairs, and in that case rebellion was justified, after defiance openly given, though never by treachery. But the Duke had not done anything that he could rightfully complain of; his procrastination in setting out had actually given them the easiest journey to Constantinople of any of the pilgrims; and since then he had fed his followers as well as most of the army, and had led them bravely in battle. Perhaps it had been a mistake in the first place to follow a leader who had land in Europe, and intended to return; Roger now saw that that was the prime cause of all his troubles; but any knight ought to be proud to serve the natural lord of all the Norman race, and he could not blame himself for that. Anyway, he told himself, he was one of the most loyal knights in the army, he had every reason to be proud, and he would damn well teach that foolish wife of his to recognize his remarkable strength of character. Having reached this satisfactory conclusion he went home to bed; Anne pretended to be asleep, and refused to take any notice of him.

Next morning the whole camp was excitedly discussing the developments in yesterday's council. Anyone could see there was a serious danger of division between knights and foot. The Italians of course had nothing to worry about; the Normans of Italy would divide up the land into fiefs, and the crossbowmen from the Genoese and Pisan fleets would help them to man the walls of the city. The Provençals were in rather an exalted state; they had been despised as second-class warriors, not nearly as formidable as Normans, and their Count had been accused of malingering in the face of the enemy; now they were setting an example to the whole army, and if any others marched on

Jerusalem it would be under their leadership. All the other contingents were divided among themselves, and tended to divide on a class basis; the knights wanted to stay where they were, at least until all the fiefs of Antioch had been given out to new possessors; the foot thought more of their souls and less of their temporal welfare; of course, as Roger heard a jongleur point out, that was one reason why they were still poor and on foot, after all these opportunities for plunder.

There was no formal council, for everything that needed attention had been settled yesterday; but there was all the same a great coming and going of messengers from the various chanceries, and counts and dukes were busy calling on one another. Roger, carefully taking his purse this time, had gone out early, telling Anne that he wanted to find out all the news, and that he would buy his meals at a cook-shop. She seemed to have got over her beating, as all sensible wives must learn how to do; she was amiable enough, though subdued.

He went first to the Duke's pavilion, but found no definite news. The foot were thoroughly disturbed; they and their women were running about like ants, packing their belongings and bargaining with the Syrian traders for the hire of baggage-animals. As a knight he was greeted with black looks on every side, and heard a few shouted remarks behind him, though he was unable to catch the words.

He strolled into the city, where the streets were full of Provençals moving their plunder, and preparing to evacuate the positions they had held in the towers along the wall; he met patrols of Italian foot-sergeants, already policing the town in the name of the new Prince of Antioch. In the Cathedral Square a small crowd hung about, in case the council should meet after all. Roger leaned against a wall, sheltered from the cold wind that whistled through the streets, and settled down to watch with the others. This delay was extremely tiresome; if he wanted a fief he should offer his services to Prince Bohemund as soon as possible, while the new army of Antioch was still eager for recruits; yet he was impressed by the cheerful alacrity of the Provençals, and the undisguised hostility of the Norman foot. It was a big step to change his allegiance now, and an even bigger one to admit that as far as he was concerned the pilgrim-age was at an end. Also, there was still his oath; until the Duke finally made up his mind to go home he could not leave him.

Just when he was beginning to think of dinner there was a stir in the Cathedral itself, and a procession appeared from the great west door. Like the rest of the crowd, he uncovered and went down on one knee when he saw thurifers and a canopy emerge; it might be no more than some bishop going in state to pay a visit, but it might be the Blessed Sacrament; actually it turned out to be the Holy Lance, borne in procession from the High Altar to the Provençal camp. The Count of Toulouse was not going to miss the opportunity of reminding the army at large that he was the guardian of this holy relic. It was also a hint that those who stayed behind might lose the spiritual bene-fits offered by the Church to all true pilgrims. Doubtless there were various holy men and sacred objects in the procession, whatever might be the truth about the Lance, and Roger re-mained kneeling until it was out of sight round the corner of the street; though a few Italians in the crowd stood up and turned their backs, to show their contempt for the Count of Toulouse and anything that he might choose to call a holy relic. These Italians were only too willing to start a fight and give the Prince an excuse to clear the town of all who would not follow him; but no one believed so wholly in the Lance as to resent this lack of respect, and the rest of the crowd did nothing more than scowl. However, there might be trouble later on, and Roger, who was completely unarmed, thought it would be wise to go and look for an eating-house.

There were many of these in the lower town, for troops always think that what they buy is better than the rations issued to them, and most pilgrims still had money left from their plunder. Provençals and Italians avoided one another by mutual consent, and Roger, as a neutral, did not wish to find himself wholly surrounded by either; but in the end he discovered a sausage-shop kept by a Rhinelander from Coblenz, and patron-ized chiefly by Lotharingians. Since he had no wish to quarrel with anyone he was glad to be among people whose language he did not understand, and ordered what he wanted by pointing at dishes on the counter.

When he had finished eating he continued to sit there, musing drowsily over a pitcher of wine. The Count of Toulouse was due to leave in six days' time, and the Duke of Normandy, though he liked to put off decisions as long as possible, must make up his mind before then. Yesterday it had been pretty certain that he would go home, but already the temper of the whole army seemed to be growing more warlike and his foot might insist on continuing the campaign. For his own good name, Duke Robert might stay and lead his followers where they wished to go. In that case there would be no chance of getting a fief from Prince Bohemund. How strong was the obligation on a husband to provide for his wife, and how did it compare with the duties of the pilgrimage? All he could decide was that it would have been very much easier if he had remained a bachelor. He drifted into a vague reverie, seeing himself as a penniless knight-errant, fighting the infidel every day, and welcomed without question in rich and comfortable castles every evening; that was a better life than serving Bohemund as a soldier or worse, to satisfy the pride of a silly woman.

He came to himself with a start, for a messenger had put his head in the doorway, shouting something in German, and now all the Lotharingians were cheering and singing, and beating on the tables with their cups. He got up and walked over to a well-dressed young knight, who looked the sort of gentleman who must be able to speak French, though now he was babbling in German. The knight was eager to enlighten him, and explained the news in a barbarous Brabançon French. It was exciting enough; Duke Godfrey of Lower Lotharingia had decided to march with the Count of Toulouse, and all his men would follow him.

When this had been confirmed by a Latin-speaking clerk Roger decided to go straight home and tell Anne. The whole situation was altered. Duke Godfrey had a high reputation in the pilgrimage; his title was grander than his rather meagre possessions, for Lotharingia was a much-divided duchy, but he was known to have sold or mortgaged all his lands at home to equip his contingent; he had started on the Feast of the Assumption, 15 August 1096, the day appointed by the Council of Clermont, when many leaders had hung back to see what success the expedition might have; he had successfully negotiated his way by land through Hungary and Illyricum, without shedding the blood of fellow-Christians more than was absolutely necessary; and had played an honourable and prominent part in the discussions with the Greek Emperor about the release of the Count of Vermandois and the taking of the oath of allegiance; he was known to lead a good and Christian private life, better than any other leader, and he was single-minded to fight the infidel, without more thought for his own advantage than was fitting for a lord of many poor and hungry vassals. His adhesion to the Count of Toulouse would make an enormous difference. If the Duke of Normandy had made up his mind, he would have to do it all over again in these new circumstances.

In his excitement at the news Roger had forgotten that he was on bad terms with his wife, and he surprised Anne when he came in by embracing her heartily. Stuttering in his enthusiasm, he poured out the whole story, but she was not particularly impressed.

'Surely, my dear lord, we went into all this yesterday. You have a right to chastise me, and I don't want to provoke you again, but I hope you are not preparing to break your oath to your Duke so as to follow the Count of Toulouse. If your duty as a loyal servant prevents you from joining the Prince of Antioch, who would reward you well, it must also forbid you to leave your lord to go and sack Jerusalem.'

Roger was abashed by her calmness, and did not like to be reminded that he had punished her last night.

'Dear Anne,' he said, smiling as politely as though they were not married. 'Can't you see this alters everything? If the Duke of Lotharingia marches south he must become the leader, and the Count of Toulouse will fall into the background, with his convenient illnesses that keep him from the battlefield. No knight could ever be reproached for following Duke Godfrey against the infidel; it is quite a different thing from being led by that old nanny-goat Raymond de Saint Gilles. In fact, I shall march to Jerusalem whatever my lord does; if he goes I shall follow him, if he returns home I shall be free to follow Duke Godfrey.'

'Very well, my lord, it is for you to decide. I am sorry that we have no chance of a castle for ourselves, but we shall still be fighting the infidel, and doing our duty as pilgrims.'

Anne spoke quietly, with a smile of resignation. Roger felt more kindly towards her. When it came to the point she was willing to face her duty as a pilgrim, even though in conversation she still hankered after a life of brigandage in a castle.

They made a good supper, for Anne was clever at managing the kitchen. Afterwards, to show that they were friends again, she sat at his feet and sang love-songs in the langue d'Oc, while he threaded new thongs into his mail. All the proverbs were right; it was wonderful how a beating improved a woman's behaviour.

Quite late in the evening there was a knock at the door, and Robert de Santa Fosca came in so close behind the servant that Roger could not say he did not feel like talking with him. Anne was singing a sad little song about a lover who was killed because a husband stayed unexpectedly at home, and her voice was unusually loud; in fact it must have been audible outside the hut. Robert greeted the lady first, as good manners demanded.

'Good evening, Domna. I knew you were in, for I heard your voice, but I really came to see Messer Roger.' He was very smartly dressed, Roger noticed, but then he generally was.

'Good evening, cousin Robert,' he said. 'Do you wish to speak to me in private?'

'Oh no; there is nothing I can't say in front of Domna Anne. I only came to discuss the latest news, and to learn what you had decided to do.'

'I told my wife earlier this evening, and it is more or less settled. If my Duke goes to Jerusalem I shall follow him, if he goes home I shall be free, and then I shall take service with Duke Godfrey, and go south as his man.'

'What about my lord, Prince Bohemund?' said Robert. 'After all, he counts for something in this affair. The best warrior in the army, and leader of at least the second-best contingent. And yet as soon as he advises us to stop here, you all make plans to advance. I thought you were on our side, cousin. This is a very sudden change you have made.'

'The circumstances have entirely altered,' Roger answered firmly. 'When it was a quarrel between Count Raymond and the Prince I was all for staying; as you say, he is the better warrior, and I don't want to follow a Provençal. But the Duke of Lower Lotharingia is also a very brave and skilful warrior, of the blood of Charlemagne, and he will obviously command the expedition. Why doesn't the Prince come along too?'

'That is out of the question,' said Robert, frowning, and looking towards Anne. 'Antioch is a very great prize, and if we don't hold it for the pilgrims that low and double-dealing Greek Emperor will snatch it back from us. Do you think it is fair to desert us now? The Count of Toulouse is quite capable of making a pounce at the walls, when his men are gathered under arms prepared to march out. I really came to ask if you would arm yourself and help to garrison a tower on the day he is supposed to leave. I never guessed you would be under the Provençal banner. There is land to be had for the asking. That silly young hot-head Count Tancred, who has managed to lose most of Cilicia to the Greeks and Armenians, has made up his mind to march south with the holy knight-errants, and a number of our more foolish knights are going with him.'

'Will you forgive me if I speak, dear Roger?' said Anne humbly, so humbly that Robert raised his eyebrows.

'Of course, dear wife,' Roger answered quickly. A husband was entitled to beat his wife, but it was not a particularly heroic action; it was better for strangers, even his cousin, to think that he could subdue her by the force of his personality alone.

'Well then,' she went on, 'couldn't you look at it this way? The Provençals and the Lotharingians are quite right to march. I am not objecting to that at all. But are you bound to go with them? Here is the Prince of Antioch definitely offering you a fief, which you will have to defend against the infidel; surely that is in accordance with the terms of the pilgrimage? The Duke of Lotharingia is landless, and so are most of his followers; if they take Jerusalem there may not be enough land to go round, and when Duke Robert goes home you can be sure that a Norman of Normandy will be one of the last to be rewarded. Take what is offered you; you have been fighting for more than two years, and you deserve your pay now.'

'That is no good,' Roger answered sharply. 'You know that my oath to the Duke forbids anything of the sort. I'm sorry, cousin, but you will have to hold Antioch without me.'

'There is a way round this,' said Robert, speaking slowly, and trying to choose his words with care. 'You need not openly leave your Duke's banner. When the army marches you could be sick and unable to ride; God knows the Count of Toulouse has played that game often enough. Just stay behind for a few months, and quietly join the garrison of the city. These things can always be arranged without an open break, if you take your time. I shall tell the Prince what you intend to do, and see that he keeps a fief for you.'

This last proposal seemed to Roger a very dirty trick indeed; he was tired of this endless badgering, and his reply was shouted:

'Really, for the last time, I will neither break my oath nor evade it by pretending to be sick. If you go on like this, cousin, I shall think you are not worthy of knighthood. You must have picked up those ideas from your mother's side of the family.'

Robert's face blazed scarlet; the Normans of Italy were always touchy about their descent in the female line, for the early conquerors had sometimes taken over the harems of the Arabs.

'Take care that I don't prove on your body that I am as good a Norman as any tailed Englishman,' he shouted.

Roger sprang to his feet, his fists clenched and his lips drawn back in a snarl. As they stood facing one another, their whole bodies contorted with anger, the physical resemblance between the cousins was for the first time noticeable. Anne saw it with a shiver of apprehension; neither was armed, but in a minute they would fly at one another with the eating-knives they carried in their belts; and the survivor would face the Duke's justice.

'You filthy Gasmule!' shouted Roger. He was glad that he had remembered that expression, which he had picked up in Italy in his first winter abroad. (It was connected with the word 'mule', meaning a half-breed, and was used as a term of abuse to indicate the children of western fathers and oriental mothers.)

It certainly seemed to have touched Robert in a sensitive spot. He stepped back and looked round for a weapon. The armour-stand from which Roger had taken down his mail shirt stood in a corner of the hut; the helm and hauberk were still stuck on top, and the unscabbarded sword hung from two pegs supporting the hand-guard of the hilt. Robert took a stride towards it, but Anne was too quick for him; she had risen to her feet when the quarrel began, and now she moved swiftly and stood with her back to the sword and her arms outspread. Robert faced her for a moment, his right fist raised to strike, while Roger drew his eating-knife from his belt. All three were frozen motionless, each waiting for an enemy to move. Robert was the first to recover; he lowered his hand to his breast, and bowed to Anne.

'I cannot strike you, Domna. I am not one of those English woman-beaters. Now, sir, may I leave your roof in peace, or will you stick that knife into me when I turn my back?'

Roger came to his senses. He could not kill a fellow-Christian in his own hut; apart from the breach of hospitality there were no witnesses except his own wife, and the whole camp would call it murder. He sheathed his eating-knife, and folded his arms.

'You may go in safety, cousin. Do not ever come back, or if you must, first send a clerk to make peace between us. Now go.'

He turned his back on the door to show his peaceful intentions, and waited to hear it close. When it had slammed he went over to his wife, and dropped on one knee before her.

'God bless you, Domna,' he said. 'For I believe you have saved my life. If we had struggled for that sword one of us must have been killed, and the other would have faced mutilation. I am very sorry that I chastised you yesterday; though you deserved it then, and it was my right as a husband. In future I shall always remember your brave action tonight, and I hope we shall be such friends as husband and wife should be.'

He was still very young, and rather stupid, and he did not understand that it was no use asking for his wife's forgiveness if he still justified his beating of her; but Anne was glad to make friends for the time being.

'Don't worry too much, dear husband,' she said in her gentlest and most winning voice. 'As to my saving your life, as you are gracious enough to call it, why, that was nothing at all; I was only afraid that Robert would damage your arms. He is rather a scoundrel, but I don't think he would kill an unarmed man; and his manners are so good that I am sure he would never strike a lady.'

This reminder of the beating made Roger feel as awkward as it was intended to, and there was nothing for it but to spend the rest of the evening praising his wife's courage and devotion, and making courteous love to her as well as he knew how.

In the morning he found the whole camp packing and preparing to move. The accession of the Duke of Lower Lotharingia had made the Provençal party the stronger of the two, and the news that Count Tancred of Cilicia was prepared to bring some of the Normans of Italy to Jerusalem also had converted the last waverers. The Duke of Normandy and Count Tancred gave out publicly that they would march with the Count of Toulouse on 13 January; Duke Godfrey and the Count of Flanders would follow as soon as they had assembled their men from the scattered garrisons of Edessa and the north, and procured more supplies from the fleets that were expected in the spring. Only the Prince of Antioch and his personal followers would stay behind to hold the newly conquered land, with the fighting-men from the ships of the Italian merchant republics; these last were openly out for commercial advantage, and hardly counted as pilgrims at all.

All bustled about their work with a new purpose and cheerfulness. They had been stuck in one place for fourteen months, first during the starvation and counter-starvation of the siege, then during the long, purposeless and quarrelsome delay while the council was making up its mind; now they were off to capture the holiest city in the world from a foe much feebler than the Turk they had already defeated. The footmen sang as they packed their plunder into balanced loads for the baggage-animals, and the horse lines were full of knights fitting restuffed saddles and examining the horses' feet.

The short notice was a great nuisance to the Provençals and

the Normans of Normandy, but unfortunately the Count of Toulouse would not go back on the emphatic words he had spoken in council, when he had promised to leave Antioch on the Octave of the Epiphany. After all the arguments and discussions it left most people, including Roger, with only four days to pack their baggage and get in a supply of extra food and drink. Forage was bound to be scarce and expensive in an army of that size, and many of the horses were half-fed and unfit for battle; much of the plunder of Antioch had consisted of bulky goods of little value, though the foot treasured it all; now it must be disposed of for gold and silver, which was easier to carry. The Greek and Armenian merchants did well out of this, and out of the sale of the thousand and one heavy and useless objects of the countryside that an army always picks up when it stays in one place for a long time.

Roger's Turkish pony was in fairly good condition; it might have been fitter, but compared to some of the other horses it stood out as strong and well-fed, and would probably carry him to the end of at least one flight or pursuit without breaking down. His only follower was Tom the crossbowman, who would march on foot carrying his own pack, but he must have a mount for Anne, and something to carry his baggage. Of course the price of every sort of animal had gone sky-high now that the camp was breaking up at last, and in any case time was very short (in England most people took three months to buy a horse); but he managed to get hold of a tall and comfortable donkey for Anne, and a shaggy little baggage-pony from the Steppes of Central Asia, a vicious brute, all heels and teeth, but untiring, and used to scratching for its own food. By the time he had done this, and bought a skin of wine and a side of bacon for emergencies, his money was gone. Anne and he would be fed by the Duke, as they were entitled to be, but it was a sobering thought that after two and a half years campaigning he was still landless and penniless.

Jerusalem was more than two hundred miles to the south, and that would mean a long march through hilly country, though the worst of the mountains were behind them. It was expected that they would besiege Acre first, to win a secure seaport near at hand where supplies could be landed; but unless the town fell at once they would have a long campaign in cold weather before they even reached the Holy City. It was a bad thing to start without money, since native Christians were sure to come to the army with luxuries for sale, and Roger looked round for anything he could turn into cash. He at once thought of the many silken dresses he had bought for Anne, but when he suggested that she should sell them it led to a most unfortunate quarrel.

'I think you should remember, dear husband,' said she angrily, 'that I am the daughter of a baron, and the widow of a landholding knight. In France, where I was born, men do not sell the clothes off their ladies' backs. God knows I have had little enough out of this marriage; I have been hungry and cold many times and you still have not given me one foot of land. My dresses are my own, and I would rather go without wine than give them up. I don't know what laws there are in this camp, or whether there are any at all; but if you try to take them from me I shall go as a suppliant to the Count of Toulouse, whose born subject I am, and ask for his protection.'

'My dear,' he answered in a friendly voice. 'I know that I have not provided for you as I should; though you must remember that we are on a dangerous pilgrimage, which will very soon, please God, be ended. But you are a seasoned campaigner; think back to what it was like during the siege of this city. The Duke gives out what food he can, but when an army sits still supplies always run short, and he is not such a skilled administrator as the faint-hearted Count of Blois. The footmen and the Turcopoles go out to plunder the neighbouring villages, and sometimes they find more than they want at the moment. Then, if you are on the spot and offer ready money, you can often buy wine and meat from them as they come back to the camp. When we sack Acre I will make a point of plundering the best clothes I can find for you, so you won't be without fine dresses for very long. I certainly won't take them from you by force; that would be disgraceful indeed. But I wish you would do this to please me, and in your own interest as well.'

Anne was quite unpersuaded, and as angry as ever.

'Messer Roger,' she said formally, and with great emphasis, 'you will not take my clothes with my consent, and I give you credit for being a better knight than to steal them from me by force. That is all. I survived the hardships of the siege last year, hardships made worse by your incompetence, and I will somehow survive the siege of Acre. Now leave me to pack. We march the day after tomorrow, and I must fold my dresses properly, and get them sewn up in canvas.'

'You know I have only one little pack-horse, and he has to carry the extra food and the bedding. Don't give him too heavy a load.'

'I shall manage perfectly. I know all about loading pack-horses; my father was rich, and a landholder, and there were a great many pack-horses in his castle. Now go out and get your supper in a cook-shop; I am much too busy to look after you this evening.'

Roger remembered how she had helped him in that very hut during the quarrel with Robert. She was being very difficult, but she was within her rights, and somehow they must continue to live together; all married couples did, until one of them died.

Unfortunately supper at a cook-shop cost money which he could not spare; so he went to the Duke's kitchen, where there was bread and meat for all Normans of Normandy. There he found a great many foot and a number of knights, for much of the private baggage was already packed into horseloads and the huts were being dismantled. He listened to a discussion about the country to the south of them, and where they were likely to meet the first infidels; nothing was really known except that Laodicea was in the hands of the Greeks or the local Christians; no one would come out of it to attack them, though it was unlikely that they would be allowed to draw supplies from the port. Various lords had spent the summer raiding up the valley of the Orontes, and there were believed to be no important castles in the hands of the infidels nearer than Hama; beyond that all was a blank, though there were said to be independent Christian mountaineers in the Lebanon, who might or might not be friendly. The Egyptians held Jerusalem, that was certain; but no one knew the exact boundary between them and the

Turks, or whether they would find a Turkish army barring the way before they reached Egyptian territory. It was probable that they would be allowed to form the siege of Acre without a battle, since there was no news of the gathering of an infidel army in the south or east; the question was whether the power of the Holy Lance would save them from another year-long investment. The knights were dubious, for the Lance was popular only with the uneducated; in any case the upper classes hated all the dismounted sentry-work of a siege. But everyone was delighted that at last they were leaving that ill-omened camp of evil memory, where so many had died of famine or plague, and the whole pilgrimage had nearly broken up in civil war.

Roger spent the next morning fussing round his ponies and trying to rearrange the loads, which seemed to him more than they could ever transport; he could not dine in his own hut, with all cooking utensils already packed in the loads, and all the Normans of Normandy ate at long tables in the open, as they would on the march. He had not spoken to Anne since he had hurried out in the morning, and now she was with the other ladies, who ate at a table apart; there were one or two arrangements that he must still make with her, but he was not sorry that he could not discuss them now; it was better to leave as little time as possible for her to quarrel with him again. He sat a long time over his dinner, since there was nowhere else to go except his unfurnished hut.

Presently he went to the horse-lines, to try an experimental loading-up and see whether all his baggage could really be carried on the one pony available. It was about the eighth hour, two in the afternoon, when he reached the corner where his riding horse, Anne's donkey, and the pack-pony should have been tethered, with Tom the crossbowman keeping watch to see they were not stolen. As he approached he saw the donkey was missing, and Tom came running up and began to talk quickly and with agitation.

'I hope I have done right, Messer Roger. About an hour ago Domna Anne came here and told me to put her baggage on the donkey. She said she had found another horse to ride, and wanted her belongings moved to it. So I loaded up and asked her where she wanted it taken. Just then a fully-armed knight came up with three foot-sergeants and a led horse, Domna Anne mounted, and they all went away with the donkey. It looked like highway robbery to me, but I couldn't do anything against four of them, and Domna Anne never called out for my help.'

Roger was surprised and worried; he could not imagine what Anne was up to, though it hardly seemed like kidnapping. He did not want to raise an alarm, which would make him look foolish if there was some innocent explanation. He said quietly:

'I expect it is some friend of hers, who has got hold of a horse to offer her; you know she thought that donkey undignified, though everyone rides them out here. Could you recognize the knight?'

'No, Messer Roger. He wore his helm, and it had a broad nose-guard. And I'm certain I've never seen his horse before.'

'Well, how did he speak, and what sort of men were his followers?'

'He spoke good French, and yet somehow as though it was not his own language. The footmen never said anything, but they looked like foreigners to me. I'm quite sure I have never seen any of them among the Duke's Normans.'

'There must be some good explanation, though it does look queer. I will go and hunt for Domna Anne round the camps. Oh, and I might as well take my sword; I want to get it set by a smith before we march tomorrow. No, don't you come with me; stay here and keep an eye on the horses; and you had better wind your crossbow and keep it handy.'

He saw that Tom was not deceived by his casualness; but one crossbow would not be much help if there really was trouble, and he preferred to let the groom stay out of a quarrel among his betters.

He slung the baldric over his shoulder, and walked towards the Bridge Gate, where the Armenian and Syrian horse-dealers were encamped on the north bank of the river. To get there he had to cross the old temporary bridge that the pilgrims had built more than a year ago, when they were still besieging the city. As he walked down the north bank he suddenly gave a gasp of relief; he saw Anne on a strange pony, waiting for him beside an armed and mounted knight. As he drew closer he recognized that this was Robert de Santa Fosca, but wearing different armour and riding a strange horse. This was of course a pretty good disguise, for the nose-guard of the helm covered a good deal of the wear's face, and the hauberk came over his chin; Tom, who had seen Robert often enough at the castle beyond Harenc, might be excused for not recognizing him that afternoon. But why had he taken such pains to change his appearance (armour that didn't fit properly was hellishly uncomfortable), and, in any case, why was he fully armed the day before the campaign was to begin? He even had his shield on his arm, and his lance in his right hand. Robert walked his horse a few paces forward, and couched his lance. Roger stood still in amazement; had his cousin gone mad, and was he about to murder him on the open river bank, before thousands of witnesses? They had quarrelled three days ago, but not so desperately as all that. And what could be Anne's part in this strange business? Robert was speaking now, in a strained, unnatural voice, like a suitor pleading his claim in a law-court:

'Do not come any nearer, Roger de Bodeham. I must tell you that your wife, Domna Anne, has now sought my protection. She is coming with me to the citadel of Antioch; we shall live there together, and you will never see her again.'

Roger could find no words. He had married Anne for love, which in itself was unusual. Since then she had always been there, sometime a nuisance when he had to fight or make plans, but doing her duty admirably when he could provide a home for her. Surely she would not betray him after only one serious quarrel? Besides, honourable ladies just didn't leave their husbands; there was a law against it. Perhaps she was being carried off against her will, and was too frightened to admit it.

'Anne would never do such a thing,' he shouted. 'It is forbidden by the laws of God, and probably by the Duke's law as well. I won't believe it until I hear it from her own lips. Speak to me, darling Anne, and tell me that what this wicked and dishonourable knight says is untrue.'

He was taking a risk in insulting an armed man while he had

nothing but his sword, but he still thought too well of human nature to realize how dangerous this was. Robert shook his lance menacingly, and made his horse fidget; but he kept his self-control, and called over his shoulder to Anne in the background:

'Come here, my darling, and tell this horned idiot that you really love me, and that you leave him of your own free will.'

Anne urged her pony nearer, till she was sitting level with Robert; she was wearing her best silk dress, with a gold-embroidered white silk coif, and looking as lovely as Roger had ever seen her.

'My poor unfortunate little fool of a husband,' she said in clear, level tones. 'I have certainly made up my mind to leave you for ever, and to live of my own free will with this gallant knight. I was helpless and unprotected, and I married you because I thought you were a warrior who would win a fief. But your ridiculous scruples always hold you back, and you will die landless. The best solution would be for Robert to kill you now; but he is too honourable to murder you unarmed. So good-bye for ever, and I hope you meet an infidel arrow quite soon. Now run along, before my footmen beat you, in revenge for the beating you gave me.'

Thoughts flashed through Roger's mind of some eloquent appeal that would make Anne return, abashed, to his bed, or some flaming sarcasm that would send his cousin slinking away in shame. But his courage was not great enough to allow him to insult an armed man while he himself was in his tunic; at length he turned on his heel, and walked as slowly as he dared back to the bridge of the camp.

As he walked away, the blood pounding in his head and his legs jerking unnaturally from a mixture of fury and fear, he heard continued peals of laughter from the triumphant lovers. Tears were running down his face when he reached his hut and flung himself on his blankets. Tom would be wondering what to do about the donkey and Anne's baggage, but he could not possibly give him instructions now. His first thought was to get into his armour and hunt down his cousin, but he knew that the garrison on the walls would never let him into the city. He lay on his bed, calling down curses on the whore and her paramour.

As darkness fell he sat up and tried to pull himself together; whatever happened he must march in the morning. He could give out that his wife was sick, and that he had told her to stay in the citadel under the care of his cousin; but of course that was only a temporary expedient; all the pilgrims, and particularly his own acquaintances, would soon know of his shame. If they had all been on the march together he could have appealed to his lord for justice on the seducer, and asked the Legate for a sentence of excommunication on the guilty pair; but he knew that Duke Robert could do nothing against a knight who was sheltered by the city walls, and the Legate was dead and his office still vacant. Prince Bohemund, and all those plundering bandits from Italy, would admire their comrade for his exploit, and would not be bothered in the least by an excommunication that could not be published inside the city. He got up slowly, and lurched aimlessly about the darkened hut; he felt as stiff all over as though he had been beaten, and his hands still shook uncontrollably.

Of course, the conscripted Syrian servants had run off as soon as they realized that something was wrong. He could not join the crowd who would be supping at the Duke's tables, but he must eat something before the march tomorrow. With fumbling fingers he lit a torch and searched through the hut; in a corner was a small bag of mouldy dates, which the servants had not bothered to steal; he managed to swallow a few without being sick, and drank water from the flask that hung on a peg, already filled for the journey.

He could not bear to spend the night alone in the hut, which had been his married home for more than a year. Everything round him spoke of Anne, his darling golden Anne, who had betrayed him. With the tears still running down his cheeks, but with his breathing under control and a grim set to his mouth, he picked up his blankets and set off to find Tom at the horse-lines. At sight of the tough but familiar face he broke down again; he could not go through with his carefully thought-out story of Anne's ill-health, and he found relief in blurting out the truth.

'I shall spend the night here,' he said. 'Don't bother to look out for Domna Anne any longer. She is a whore who has left me for a richer man.'

Tom whistled with surprise; then he began to grin, as everyone does when he hears that a pretty wife has run away from her husband. But he hastily pulled his face into an expression of sorrowful concern.

'I am very sorry to hear that, sir. She was a kind and gracious lady, and it is a dishonour to us all. But you will find fighting comes easier when you have no family to worry about. Put your bedding down here by the fire, and I will fetch some more wood. You want to get some sleep tonight, for we shall have a hard day tomorrow. Have you eaten any supper, sir? There is cold bacon in this pack.'

He did his best to fuss over his master and make him comfortable for the night, but Roger had seen the beginning of that grin; he knew that everyone would feel the whole story made an excellent dirty joke, though some might be too polite to say so. That grin would follow him through the army; and Heaven only knew what sort of nick-names he would be called behind his back.

Very early in the morning, before it was light, the trumpets blew, and grooms started to load the horses. He scrambled out of bed, and let Tom tie him up in his armour, without bothering about a wash. All the hundreds of priests in the camp were beginning their Masses, and in a dazed and half-awake condition he wandered off to the pavilion where Father Yves was accustomed to celebrate. With murder in his heart towards his wife and her adulterous lover, he could not bring himself to confess to a priest who would demand forgiveness before absolving him; so he dared not take Communion, but even so it was unthinkable to begin a new campaign against the infidel without at least being present at the Sacrifice.

Most of the congregation were old acquaintances, and he thought they received him with curious glances and suppressed sniggers. He would have liked to stay afterwards and talk to the priest; but they were due to march in an hour, and already the footmen were waiting to strike the pavilion. He took a piece of biscuit from the Duke's pantry for his breakfast and walked slowly back to his pony, kicking the ground and muttering his grievances under his breath.

The wintry sun had risen on all the squalid disorder of the half-abandoned camp, and the Duke's criers were calling the order to mount. Thank God Tom was efficient, and as honest as a crossbowman could be expected to be; the pack-horse was well loaded, and his own Turkish pony properly saddled and ready for him. He mounted and rode to the eastern end of the camp, where the banner of Normandy was displayed. He caught a glimpse of his abandoned hut, where a squabbling crowd of Syrian peasants were already taking down the soundest timbers, and realized, with a shock to the depths of his heart, that all memorial of his married life would soon have vanished without a trace. The knights who rode beside him in the disorderly throng rejoiced that at last they were leaving the overflowing rubbish-heaps and barely-covered graves of this stinking suburb where they had been held up for more than a year, but he could only remember that Anne was somewhere inside that high and frowning citadel, and that he would never see her again.

At last they reached the open, and after a great deal of confusion and many lost tempers the Duke had them arranged in order of march. Roger was placed in the rearguard, since his pony was not good enough for the main-battle; he rode in the middle of that bad-tempered crowd, who knew that any decent plunder would be snapped up by those who marched in front, and that the winter mud would be poached girth-deep by the baggage-animals when they came to the many sloughs on the road. His head was sunk on his breast, and he pretended not to hear anyone who spoke to him.

As they endured the maddening delays of that first day's march, with untrained baggage-animals and incompetent drivers, his thoughts dwelt only on his broken marriage. The separation from Anne was very bitter, but the blow to his pride was worse. Endlessly repeating to himself Robert's and Anne's last words he found that his self-esteem withered and died; he was in truth an unworthy knight, too pusillanimous to win a fief in this large new country that the pilgrimage had conquered, and he deserved all that had happened to him. If only he had taken Anne's advice, and gone openly into the service of the Count of Taranto! Surely an oath taken in Normandy, all those thousands of miles away and more than two years ago, could not still be binding under these utterly different conditions; in any case, he should have known better than to become the man of such an undecided leader as Duke Robert. It seemed that no one else was bothered in the slightest by the scruples that had cost him his wife. Yet he had learnt from his father, and all England believed it, that Count Harold had lost a throne and his life because he was an oath-breaker. What should a man do? Even if he did not care for honour, there was still the wrath of God to contend with. Then another thought struck him. It was bad enough that his wife should openly leave his hearth for the protection of a better or more prosperous man; yet things might be very much worse than that. He began to wonder if Anne had been unfaithful while still under his roof. Robert, his cousin, had always been welcome at his table, as far back as when he had been freezing and starving in Cemetery Castle, and like the horned idiot that he was he had actually begged him to keep an eye on Anne; perhaps they were deceiving him then, when he was living night and day within range of the enemy's arrows, earning a little money to buy extra food for her sinful carcass. He cast his mind back over all the weary months that had passed since they first reached Antioch in October '97, and always he could remember himself busy on some irksome duty while the guilty pair were free to enjoy themselves together. He had been so blind as to think that his honour was safe in the hands of his own cousin, for a cuckold in the family reflected on all his relatives. But he saw now that Robert would not lose reputation, at least among the sort of friends whose good opinion he esteemed. It was one thing to be known as one of a family that were too spiritless to keep their wives, and quite another to be yourself a bold and successful woman-stealer, respected by every bandit and adulterer among the Normans of Italy – and most of them were damned and conscienceless brigands. He remembered the last time Robert had come to his hut, when they had quarrelled about his faithfulness to his lord. He saw it all now; he recalled how smartly his cousin had been dressed, and the ballad that Anne had sung, so loud that it might be heard outside the hut, about the sad fate of a lover when the husband unexpectedly stayed at home. She had sung that song as a warning. Then there was nothing open about the intrigue, they had been quite happy to go on as secret lovers, and Robert had come in to persuade him to stay in Antioch as a vassal of the Prince. It was only when he had announced his decision to march on this new campaign that they had made up their minds to brazen it out. Surely he was the blindest fool in Christendom, and trouvères would make comic songs about his stupidity until the end of time. He cursed aloud, and ground his teeth, as he thought of the funny stories that must have gone round in the quarters of the Normans of Italy. Why had he made a fool of himself by coming on this fantastic pilgrimage? What good had his coming done, anyway? When the real test came, and Hugh had been dismounted and helpless at Dorylaeum, his courage had failed him and he had left a fellow-Christian to perish miserably. The small part he had played in passing messages for the surrender of Antioch had done more harm than good, for the bloodless taking of the city had spread dissension among the pilgrims, and detained the whole expedition for more than six months. There was now less chance than ever of the Duke giving him a fief, since he would be known even to the leaders as a funny, ineffective little man. He was a cowardly warrior, and a husband who could not keep the respect of his wife.

He was roused from these mournful thoughts by an unusual commotion ahead. At last they were going to halt for dinner, and the baggage-guard were trying to get their baulky animals off the road. The rear-battle marched on to where the Duke's kitchens were set up, and he climbed stiffly down from his undignified little pony as the faithful Tom, always clever at picking his master out of the crowd, came up to take the bridle. It was given out that they would march no further that day, in view of the unfitness of all the animals, and he was thankful to be disarmed before going to look for his meal.

It was still quite early in the afternoon, and after the usual campaigning dinner of nameless stew and hard biscuit he went a little way from the others and sat down on a rock. He was tired out by the early start and the emotions of the previous day, but his thoughts still flowed too swiftly to allow him to go to sleep. He had sat for an hour, and the winter sun was low, when Father Yves came up to him.

'May God comfort you, my son,' he said, sitting down quietly beside him. 'I have heard of the grievous wrong that has been done to you. It is a foul and desperate sin, but you must be careful not to take it too hardly.'

'Oh, leave me in peace, Father,' snapped Roger; he could not bear to discuss this disaster which was not yet twenty-four hours' old.

'Are you in peace, my son?' said the priest, with his best professional smile. 'If you are I have nothing to do, but if you are still at enmity with some of your neighbours and mine I must try to get you into a better condition.'

'Of course I am not in a state of grace,' Roger answered angrily. 'But I am not in need of absolution at this moment. I hate Anne, and I hate her paramour; may they both rot in Hell for what they have done to me, as indeed they will. Don't tell me to forgive them, or I shall chase you back to the camp.'

'I am very sorry to find you in this frame of mind,' the priest continued in a quiet voice, disregarding Roger's interruption. 'Forgiveness is the most important, and yet the most difficult, part of the Christian life. You are in danger of death every day, as we all are on this pilgrimage. I beg you not to put yourself also in danger of Hell-fire. Just think of those foolish sinners; for a not very important gratification, that all religious men and women manage perfectly well to do without, they have lost their worldly honour and imperilled their souls. Try to be sorry for them. You may find it easier to have pity if you consider what is their position now. Domna Anne has no livelihood, except what Messer Robert gives her, and she will have to keep the love of that roving and gallant young man. I think she is nearly twenty, isn't she? She is past her first youth; her old age will be very pitiful. What about Messer Robert himself? He is tied by his sinful honour to live with a woman about whom he can only be certain of one thing, that she has already deceived her rightful lord; he can never be sure of her for one moment. Every time he rides out from the citadel he will wonder what she is doing behind his back. And always, when he couches his lance and prepares to charge the infidel, he will know at the back of his mind that he is in mortal sin, and that a Turkish arrow can at any moment carry him straight, without hope of salvation, to the gates of Hell. Don't you see that they are worse off than you are, and deserving of your pity?'

Roger had listened quietly, because he was too exhausted to get up and move away, and anyway the priest was only doing his duty. Now he began to picture Anne's hopeless old age, as she lost her beauty and took lower and more repugnant protectors in a desperate search for security; for Robert would not remain faithful all his life. As to Robert, he was not so certain; he had never noticed that knights were more careful of their lives because they knew they were in mortal sin. Father Yves was waiting for his answer, and he roused himself to speak.

'When you put it like that, Father, I see that Anne is to be pitied. Very well, I pity her, if that satisfies you; perhaps you can twist into forgiveness the contemptuous pity that I feel. But with Robert it is not so easy. He has won a beautiful leman whom he can shake off as soon as he is tired of her; perhaps he is a very lucky man. I hate that dishonourable seducer, and nothing you say will make me forgive him. So don't you try to absolve me now.'

The priest got to his feet, and prepared to leave.

'You are not a wicked man, my son. It is noble of you to forgive your wife, at least; and you are honourable enough, I am glad to see, not to pretend a forgiveness for the seducer that you do not really feel. But you have repented of at least half your hate, and it may be that when we talk again I shall win you to the proper Christian frame of mind.'

Roger suddenly knew that it was better to talk to Father Yves than to sit alone brooding over his wrongs.

'Don't go, Father,' he said. 'At present I need all the comfort I can get. It isn't only that my wife has left me for a better man; I may be able to bring myself to take the right Christian view of that. But everything seems to be so hopeless. I am poorer than when I left England, though many knights have won rich fiefs. I haven't even a decent warhorse. What is the good of a man like me trying to fight the infidel, when I can't keep a woman faithful to me. Why did I ever leave home to come on this wild goose chase?'

'Take care,' answered Father Yves, 'you are in danger of falling into the sin of despair, which is mortal. If everybody gave way to these feelings, which come to all of us at times, nothing would ever get done at all. Think of it in this way. You are a part, though a humble part, of a victorious army which has fought its way from Constantinople to Antioch, defeating the infidels by the manifest intervention of God wherever it has met them. Now we are on the last stage of the journey; when we reach Jerusalem, in a very few weeks, the pilgrimage will be accomplished. Your life has been safely preserved, by nothing but God's providence, and I am sure that you have killed as many Turks as you were able to, and as many as any knight should. Remember that we are now getting into the Holy Land, where the bodily influence of Our Saviour will be present to help us, and perhaps that spear-head we have to lead us is really the Holy Lance. So cheer up as much as you can, fight manfully as you did at Dorylaeum where I first met you, and give thanks that you have no family to cause you anxiety in battle. Now come and sit by the fire. You can't be a pilgrim and a hermit at the same time, and you will have to get used to being with your fellows in spite of what has happened. Take my arm, and we will see if there is any supper going.'

Roger walked back with the priest, still apprehensive of a jeering reception, but much happier than he had been all that day. If Father Yves was right he had a chance, by hard work and brave fighting, of regaining the respect of his comrades.

* * *

On the Feast of the Forty Martyrs, 10 March 1099, Roger was studying the fortifications of Acre, as he last year looked at the walls of Antioch. The little expedition of Normans and Provençals was a much less powerful force than the great pilgrimage that had sat down before the capital of Syria, and their camp was spread thinly over the plain, between the low but steep hills inland and the promontory on which the town was built. They were up against those crushing Roman walls again, and the memories of the last eight-month siege exercised a depressing effect.

The little army had wandered for a month before they reached their present position. The obvious route from Antioch to Jerusalem was by the great valley of Coele-Syria, up the Orontes and down the Litany until they reached the head-waters of the Jordan; but the strongly-fortified towns of Hama and Homs barred the valley of the upper Orontes. So they swerved westward, over the pass that led to the great port of Laodicea; but the Greek garrison of that town would not let them approach too closely, and they had to struggle on south by the coast road without refreshing themselves within its walls. Here their troubles were as bad as ever, for Tripoli and Beyrout were in the hands of infidel tyrants, either Turkish, Egyptian, or independent, but in all cases hostile; the enemy were cowed by their great defeats of the last two years, and they did not sally out to challenge a pitched battle, but it was necessary to skirt the towns, leaving the great coast road and travelling over difficult broken country. Finally, on Saint Valentine's Day, 14 February, the expedition had arrived outside Acre. The Count of Toulouse, always a cautious warrior, had refused to go any farther unless they could leave a friendly port behind them. So reluctantly and with sinking hearts, they had prepared for another doubtful and time-wasting siege.

The position was really worse than at Antioch; Acre stood on a promontory, and they could only approach the walls on one side, the south-east; it was impossible to starve out the inhabitants, for local boats could always bring in supplies from the other infidel towns on the coast.

After two years in the crowds and confusion of the main pilgrimage, the Normans and Provençals realized only too clearly the smallness of their own numbers; the siege was conducted by slow and careful approaches, with the object of saving as many lives as possible. Accordingly, everyone had been set to work to weave hurdles out of branches and scrub, and these hurdles were set upright in long lines as close to the walls as possible; they gave the besiegers cover at least from view, so that the infidels' machines must cast their stones at random; and if hides from the slaughtered cattle of their food-supply were thrown over them, they would keep out an arrow as well.

So it was that on the Feast of the Forty Martyrs Roger found himself peering round the edge of a leather-covered hurdle, watching the effect of a large catapult, whose engineers were trying to batter one particular patch of wall with each stone they threw. He was of course in full armour; his right shoulder was tender from the continued pressure of his shield-trap, so that he had taken off the shield, and propped it with stones against the inner face of the hurdle. As long as he kept behind it he was safe from arrows, and there was no more protection against stones cast from engines if he wore it than if he didn't. The Count of Toulouse was really a skilled and experienced warrior, though rather too cautious for such a desperate under-taking; he had given strict orders that all the look-outs should be grouped in pairs, and they were encouraged to talk for fear they should feel drowsy. Roger's companion was Eudes de Har-court, a Norman of Normandy, and each had already heard at wearisome length everything the other had to say about the prospects of the siege. Eudes sat facing the rear, with his legs straight out in front of him and his shoulders leaning against his upright shield; his job was to watch the catapult that was send-ing stones in a high arc over their heads, and warn Roger when-ever a missile was on the way.

'Here's another,' he grunted; they both heard the thud of the released spoon of the engine as it fetched up against its wooden stop. It was mid-afternoon and they were facing the south-west, so Roger only looked out at the last possible moment, with his hand before his eyes, to dodge the glare of the sun reflected from a calm sea. He saw the great stone, larger than a man's head, flashing out of the blue sky; it was hard to follow it when it left the sunshine and passed into the shadow of the town wall, but it seemed to hit the lower courses of masonry a glancing blow and raised a puff of dust and a few chips. The Christian engineers had the range perfectly, and all their projectiles were falling in the space of a few square feet; but the high trajectory lessened the shock to the perpendicular wall, which seemed little the worse for its repeated blows.

'A fair hit,' said Roger, 'but what's the use? There must be twenty stones lying there, and they all hit the right spot as well as you can expect from a catapult. Keep down! They are getting ready to send us an answer.'

Another great stone flashed in the sunlight; this time it came in the opposite direction, from a smaller catapault that the infidels had mounted on the city wall to reply to the besiegers. But the Christian engines were beyond its extreme range, and the line of hurdles was a very small mark to aim at; the stone hit the rocky ground behind them, and skidded away. Altogether the pilgrims had three catapults playing on the same length of the fortifications; the range of these machines was so short that it was impossible to concentrate more on the same object and keep the engineers out of range of infidel arrows. Obviously, if they continued long enough to hit the same spot the wall would eventually collapse; but it looked as though the besiegers would be dead of old age before that happened, at the present rate of progress.

Roger and Eudes settled down again to their monotonous occupation. Eudes, who was tired after a bad night, yawned long and loudly, and began to talk to keep himself awake.

'My God, we seem to have a life-work here,' he grumbled. 'Is there any sign of that cursed wall collapsing?'

'There is no hope of that for weeks to come, at this rate. The last shot but two knocked out a big chip, but these high-pitched stones come in at the wrong angle. At Nicaea the Greeks had engines that sent their stones more nearly horizontally; you saw some result from the day's work then.'

'Ah, those Greeks, clever chaps, always up to some new devilment in a siege,' Eudes answered lazily. 'It's a pity we haven't some of them to help us here.'

'Not much hope of their coming to help us,' said Roger. 'Those soldiers in Laodicea are more likely to be on the side of the infidels. It's a crying shame. I'm sorry Prince Bohemund couldn't get hold of that town last autumn.'

'He made a mistake all the same, picking a quarrel with the Greek Emperor just when we were going to need his help so badly.'

Roger gave a non-commital grunt in answer, and poked his head round the edge of the hurdle to watch the fall of another Christian stone. But Eudes wanted conversation, and soon he began to speak again:

'What were you doing this time three years ago?'

Roger thought back. It seemed so long ago that memory was dim; three years ago he had not met Anne, and now his married life was finished. Then a clear picture rose in his mind of the watermeadows beside the Rother, and his father coming down to say that his horse had done enough, and that they must get ready to ride to the Abbey of Battle.

'Three years ago,' he said dreamily. 'Do you know I think I was practising with the lance at a mark set up in a field. I remember I had to borrow my brother's mail because I hadn't any of my own. And I was learning how to manage a warhorse; of course, he died long ago. I don't suppose there are a hundred horses left that came out with the original pilgrimage. Digging and hurdle-making would have been more useful crafts to learn than all the swordplay and lance-exercises I did by the hour. I suppose war is never what you would expect, or like the songs the trouvères make about it.'

'Three years ago I was harrying Maine,' said Eudes slowly and comfortably, like one who settles down to tell the story of his life. 'That was a proper sort of war, and just like a trouvère's song. They had set up a wrongful Count, and it was open for all of us to raid, whether we followed King William or Duke Robert. Great fun it was too. You could ride out with a few friends, and perhaps joust with the same number of Angevins, if you would rather fight than plunder. Of course, there are strong castles in that country also, but we left them alone, or put the foot to blockade them, while we galloped about in the open and enjoyed ourselves. I tell you, it's the little wars that are fun. This pilgrimage is too serious and professional, and we never get away from our leaders. Besides, these infidels won't spare a knight who has a bit of bad luck in battle, and plundering by yourself is really too dangerous out here. I had a very narrow escape once when I left the line of march in Cilicia.'

'Yes, you told me about it this morning,' Roger said quickly. Perhaps this was another adventure he had not heard before, since Eudes, by his own account, had fought a great many desperate skirmishes with the infidel; but the conversation had made him homesick, and he wanted to think about his boyhood in Sussex. Truly that seemed another world altogether, where the rivers flowed in their appointed channels all the year round, with only a little mild flooding in the spring, and the pastures were green winter and summer alike. He suddenly longed to see his family again; his father was stern, and his brother had often bullied him and always treated him like a child; but they were home, the fixed landmark from which he had set out, and to which he would never return. He wondered if his father was still alive; he was ageing rapidly, and three years was a long time to an old man. His brother might even be dead also, in some obscure Welsh skirmish or by any other chance that could befall a king's soldier, and the manor of Bodeham might be rightfully his own. He tried to shut this out of his mind; by coming of his own free will on this pilgrimage he had left England for ever.

Now the stones came over at longer intervals; it was getting near sunset and the machines, as usual, were running short of missiles. The foot searched all day long on the rocky plain for suitable boulders, and others with crowbars tried to break up the reefs of the sea-shore, but transport to the camp was a difficulty, and they never seemed able to build up a reserve supply. Presently the sun set, and the engineers slackened off the twisted cables of the catapults before the night dew could do any damage; it was time for the knights in the front line to go back to the camp for supper.

Roger found all in order when he got back to his hut; Tom had been out with the pack-pony, carrying stones to the machines; this meant a lot of walking, but kept the animal fit. His riding-pony had been grazing with the horse-guard on the empty hills to the eastward, where the winter rains had kept the ground still covered with a little green. A European warhorse would have starved, but the pony was native to the country, and could pick up a living without corn throughout the year. Tom was still cheerful; he had not seen the wall from close to, and picking up stones was a definite job that could show results for a day's work. It was only the forward observers, who could see how well the city stood up to its battering, who were already disheartened.

Four days later the Duke of Lower Lotharingia and the Count of Flanders came into camp with all their followers. Now at last the main body of the pilgrims was assembled in front of Acre, and the siege could be pressed all along the accessible part of the wall. If only Acre could be quickly and cheaply taken other places would be cowed into surrender; yet a successful outcome was as unlikely as ever. The walls were too strong to be breached by such engines as they had at their disposal; the ground was so rocky that mining was impossible; and starvation was out of the question so long as the infidels held the other harbour-towns within easy sailing distance. There was one other desperate and bloody way of taking a city, by simultaneous escalade at so many points at once that the garrison could not gather to repel them all. The real question was: would the inspiration of the Holy Lance carry homesick and dispirited troops over that mighty Roman wall? That depended on what they thought of the Holy Lance, and the position of that doubtful relic had deteriorated since the day, ten months ago, when the whole army attributed their amazing victory to its virtues. Roger had long been a sceptic; now he found many to agree with him, even among the Provençals.

These doubts came to a head when the Count of Toulouse proposed that an escalade should be attempted on the seaward walls, by creeping along the rocks when the sea was calm. This was such a dangerous plan, and so certain to fail unless they were aided by a miracle, that public opinion demanded some test of the preservative powers of the relic that would lead them. Eventually it was given out that on Good Friday (8 April) Father Peter Bartholomew would walk through a fire carrying the Holy Lance, and if he came through safely its miraculous properties must be admitted by all. This shook the scoffers; it showed that the priest himself had faith in his own claims, and he was the one man who must know whether they were genuine or not.

Unfortunately the test was inconclusive. Peter Bartholomew came through the burning fiery furnace alive, but he was very badly roasted, and the two parties were more estranged than ever.

That afternoon Roger took his turn as a guard to the grazing horses, and tried to think the matter out. He could not make up his mind. Certainly Father Peter must have known whether he had really been granted a vision of the Apostle, and if he had lied about that vision why had he voluntarily faced searing pain and almost certain death? That was the inexplicable part of the affair. Roger was glad to turn over these inconclusive reflections, for they kept his mind off Anne, whose face still haunted his dreams.

He was depressed by a pervading feeling of universal failure. His wife was a very wicked woman, but she had left him because he was too feeble and undistinguished to provide for her as he should, and though the third year of the pilgrimage was well advanced he had not yet made a name as a warrior; his self-confidence was gone, and though if he had plenty of time to prepare he could brace himself to be as brave as the next man, his courage was not really spontaneous.

Then another idea struck him; perhaps he was too prudent because he was not in a state of grace; all the preachers, and at least some of the romances, held that a knight fought better with a clear conscience. In any case he must receive Communion on Easter Sunday, the day after tomorrow, and for that he must bring himself to forgive Robert de Santa Fosca, and then confess to Father Yves. Standing with his pony's rein over his arm, while the other horses grazed round him, he began to force his mind into a state of forgiveness. This is not really a very difficult thing to do, if only you try hard enough; in any case, all that had happened at Antioch seemed very far away now; at sunset, when it was time to drive the animals back to their picket-lines, he thought he had worked himself into the right disposition.

After supper he sought out Father Yves, and made a good confession. When he had received Absolution he stayed, at the priest's invitation, to drink a cup of wine and talk over the events of the day. Father Yves was upset about the ordeal.

'The leaders should never have allowed it,' he said. 'Though a miracle proves something, the absence of it proves nothing. It is presumptuous and temerarious to expect God to grant us a sign whenever we ask for one. Now we have been punished for our sins by being left in doubt when the trial is finished. The pilgrims must trust in their own swords.'

'In that case it doesn't look as though we shall capture this town,' Roger said sadly. 'If things had gone right, it's just possible we might have managed a sudden escalade. The army won't have the spirit for that now. We seem to have gone as far as we can by the power of our own swords.'

'That may very well be true, but it is no reason for giving in. If you die you still gain all the spiritual benefits of the pilgrimage, and no one has managed to beat us yet. I hope Father Peter recovers from his burns; it will have a bad effect on everyone's courage if he dies, and he was a brave man to face the ordeal, even if he was deceived.'

Nevertheless, on 20 April, twelve days after the trial, Peter Bartholomew succumbed to his injuries.

The siege continued, with an unwilling and disheartened army. With the coming of spring the grass grew thickly on the hillsides and there was plenty of forage. The warhorses were rested and fit, but from now on they would lose condition during the summer heat, and the knights clamoured that this was the moment to fight a pitched battle, not to hang about dismounted for a siege; unfortunately there was no enemy in the field for them to charge, and siege-warfare it had to be. The leaders were known to be divided; the Duke of Normandy and the Count of Toulouse were reluctant to give up the chance of capturing Acre after spending so much time and money on the investment, and Count Tancred of Cilicia was of the same opinion; men listened to him, although he was only a younger son with a small following, because he was really single-minded in his hatred of the infidel, and had a great reputation as a brave and successful warrior. The other side was led by Duke Godfrey and the Count of Flanders, eager to push on to Jerusalem; on the whole the army was with them, for anything was better than the way they were now wasting their time. But the wiser men had to agree that Jerusalem also possessed strong walls, and they would only be exchanging one siege for another. The result was that the army stayed in its camp and went through the motions of a siege, but listlessly, and without real drive.

It was really not easy to decide the best thing to do next. If the pilgrimage had been intended to rescue the Christians of the East from the yoke of the unbeliever, then probably the wisest thing to do was to go right back to Iconium, and turn the Turks completely out of Anatolia; or failing that, to build up Antioch and Edessa into strong and flourishing independent states; or there was the chance to found a principality among the Christian mountaineers of the Lebanon, who might be able to capture Damascus with the help of a Western army. All these would be useful objectives, that could pay from their own taxes for their own defence, and would safeguard the dominions of the Greek Emperor. Unfortunately these schemes were hardly considered. The more religious and uneducated of the pilgrims knew exactly what they wanted to do next. The headwaters of the Jordan were only fifty miles away across the mountains, they were on the threshold of the Holy Land, and they clamoured to be led straight up to Jerusalem. The lesser knights and the foot were united on this, and Roger felt the same as his fellows.

He talked it over one night with Father Yves.

'Do you realize, Father, that we are in the third summer away from our homes, and the pilgrimage still goes on interminably. In 1096, when I vowed to follow our Duke, I didn't think we should fight on and on, from Nicaea right up to Acre, and then to Egypt, for all I know. Does Duke Robert mean to carry on like this for the rest of his life, besieging these strong cities and then handing them over to someone else, so that his followers are never rewarded? Think of it; after three years' fighting, I have no money left, only a miserable pony to ride, and my armour is wearing out, though I shall never be able to replace it. We have fulfilled our duty to these Eastern Christians, ungrateful heretics that they are; now let us go on to Jerusalem, only a hundred miles away, and finish the whole thing. I'm not alone in saying that if we don't next year we shall have no army left.'

'Don't talk about breaking your vows, at any rate to me,' the priest answered, 'although I have a certain sympathy with you. When I left Brittany I did not think, either, that it would take three years. We have fulfilled our obligation to the Eastern Christians well enough. But a dash straight from Acre to Jerusalem will leave the boundaries of Christendom a very peculiar shape. If we go due south we shall leave infidel garrisons behind us on every side, and the peaceful pilgrims who come after us will find it difficult to get into the Holy City at all, even if it has a Christian garrison. We must take the coast first, and have safe harbours for the Italian ships to winter in, before we attack the inland. But if what you are telling me is what the whole army thinks, and I know you have been a conscientious pilgrim up to the present, I will send word of it to the Duke. It is better for us all to go together, even to the wrong place, than for the pilgrimage to break up.'

So it fell out. On 13 May the siege was raised, and the whole army set out for Jerusalem. It was the first open defeat for the pilgrims, and some were sullen and disappointed as they burnt their siege-engines amid the cheers of the infidel garrison; but most were too inflamed by the prospect of taking the Holy City, and ending their three years' wandering, to care about what nests of the enemy they might leave behind them.

*　　*　　*

At the first streak of dawn Roger was awakened by Tom the crossbowman, who came to arm him. He scrambled briskly out of the blankets in which he had been wrapped, for the whole camp was waking up, and the noise made further sleep impossible. It was 13 June 1099, and the seventh day of the siege of Jerusalem.

It was difficult to get barely enough water for the animals to drink, and no one had washed for the last four days; his whole body itched with dried sweat, his mail shirt stank abominably, and the clammy embrace of his hauberk round his head and shoulders nearly turned his empty stomach. The common people did not mind, for they seldom washed in any case; the great lords also could bear it, for they were obviously still great lords even when they were dirty; but for the lesser knights cleanliness was a cherished class-distinction, and they hated the foul smell of their bodies.

The sun rose over the mountains of Moab as he knelt outside the little pavilion where Father Yves said Mass at his portable altar; the whole army had been shriven the night before, and were to receive Communion this morning, for it was a great day of battle, and they hoped before nightfall to pray in the Sepulchre of Our Lord. After Mass came the scanty breakfast of biscuit and muddy water that all were accustomed to by now; he ate it standing in the crowd outside the Duke's kitchen, and then went back to his bedding to fetch his shield and sword. Fully armed, he strolled to the mustering-place, where the interminable and quarrelsome business of getting the pilgrims into the battle-order agreed on by the leaders had already begun.

The sun shone from a cloudless sky, and the day was already getting hot; by mid-afternoon armour would be glowing to the touch and helms would be burning into the skull. The walls of Jerusalem stood out black against the glare, sheer stone, perpendicular and uncompromising, the angles of the square towers sharp where they caught the sun; there were light-coloured, unweathered merlons and patches round the arrow-slits where the Egyptian garrison had made repairs in expectation of the siege. The black dots that clustered and shifted on the towers were the heads of the infidels, for preparations for the assault were being made in full view of the besieged, and the wall was manned in readiness. The Christian leaders had decided to rely on their prestige, and the memory of the victories they had won over great Turkish armies, to carry them over the unbreached curtain by the use of ladders alone. It might work; sometimes the defenders of a tower would flinch from their post when they saw a whole army advancing towards them, and if the pilgrims could gain a lodgement in the defences their heavier swords and stronger armour must carry them right into the town; but Roger reflected that none of this garrison would have been at Dorylaeum or Antioch, since they served a different lord, and that the last siege, at Acre, had been an unmitigated failure.

Now the ladders were being distributed. Storming-ladders should be strong and very heavy, so that the defenders cannot overturn them by wrenching at the head where it rests against the wall; but these were miserable little flimsy things, hastily made from the crooked timber of the low twisted trees that grew within reach of the camp. Lack of good timber was the chief reason why they could not batter the walls; no one ever tried to carry siege-engines on the march, they were always constructed specially when the siege was formed, and here there were no beams stout enough to make a good catapult. The ladders were so light that four men could carry them easily, and unarmed but able-bodied grooms and servants had been detailed for the work; each ladder-bearer was accompanied by an unarmed footman, carrying an enormous mantlet of wickerwork covered with leather or padded cloth. Behind each ladder was a little group of knights, fully armed, and each assaulting-party was linked to its neighbouring column by a thick line of crossbowmen; these also carried mantlets, spiked at the bottom, which they would plant in the earth when they came within range, so that they could cover the assault with their arrows.

At last, after long arguments and endless swapping of places by knights who wished to keep among their friends, the army was arrayed. Roger found himself one of a dozen Norman knights told off to one ladder, which was supposed to cover forty yards of wall. His objective was near the Jaffa Gate, where the approach was over fairly level ground, but in consequence the wall was stronger than on the precipitous south-east face. Presently, nearly two hours after they had first mustered, the trumpets blew and the leaders drew their swords; the whole body of pilgrims advanced in line at a steady walk, brandishing their weapons and making as much noise as possible, in the hope that some part of the defenders would panic at the last moment. Roger was glad to be on the move after his long wait; his feet suffered from corns, for he had done more walking in the last five days than he was accustomed to, and the rheumatism in his right shoulder, where the shield-trap pressed on the mail, was as bad as ever; but he knew that when he began to sweat these troubles would disappear. He had not slept properly for the last two nights (did anyone ever go into battle feeling fresh and rested?) and he was a little dazed, and unable to concentrate on what was happening. As he walked, he repeated to himself: 'That is the Holy City; this evening I shall be within it, and the three-year pilgrimage will be ended.' But somehow he could not key himself up to seize this wonderful moment, all he could think of was what a relief it would be to have a hot bath and a large meal, or even to sit down and take the weight of his armour off his tender feet.

The knights had been pushed into a formation of three ranks of four each, but they were not used to fighting on foot in close order, and they jostled and stumbled over one another's scabbards as they waddled behind the lurching ladder; he was the left-hand man in the centre row, and he found that he had to keep his eyes on the ground to avoid tripping over the heels of the man in front; the latter had insisted on wearing his spurs, so that his corpse would show his rank if he happened to be killed. Everyone shouted at the top of his voice, by order, and the crossbowmen waved their weapons in the air, but there was no genuine enthusiasm as they shuffed slowly nearer to the city; it was not like the usual opening of a battle, when you first saw the enemy face to face; they had all seen this view for the past week, and had been standing about for two hours before they moved off. A hundred and fifty yards from the wall the whole army paused, as the front ranks tried to pick up their dressing; but they were still in a sinuous and wavering line when the trumpets blew again for the final rush across the arrow-swept approaches.

Now the formation became a little disorganized. The ladder-bearers were not heavily burdened, and as they were completely unarmed they were anxious to get their ordeal over as soon as possible. They dashed forward at a quick run, and their protectors with the wide and cumbersome mantlets found it difficult to keep up with them. As for the knights, with their long mail shirts banging against their shins, and the points of their heavy shields just clear of their ankles, they could only stumble along in the rear of the ladder-party. A steady stream of arrows came from the wall, deadly to unarmed men, and two of the ladder-bearers were hit at the same moment. The remaining six foot-men halted and looked round, to find that their supports were still a few yards to the rear; then they dropped the ladder, and bolted back out of range. The knights halted, undecided what to do next. It was ridiculous to expect them to carry burdens when there were plenty of foot about, and in any case they could not manage their shields and the ladder at the same time, but it would be undignified for them to withdraw out of range; they stood in a clump, beside the abandoned ladder, while arrows thudded into the leather of their shields. Their commander, Geoffrey de Montclair, stood at Roger's right hand; he was shouting vague curses and orders, but clearly had no idea what should happen now.

Relief came from the crossbowmen, who had set up their mantlets in line with the fallen ladder, and were replying briskly to the archers on the wall. A few of them ran back from their shelter and rounded up the frightened survivors of the ladder-bearing party. Once more they advanced in a body, but this time with the knights in front, and as these were the slowest movers the little column kept together Roger glanced to his left, and saw that some other assaulting-columns were also stuck between the crossbowmen and the city; a few others had reached the wall, but so far no ladders had been reared into position; he could not see how things were going on the right, for his comrades obstructed his view.

At this point the town ditch of Jerusalem was not scarped steeply; it had been dug rather as an impediment to mines than as an obstacle to men on foot. All twelve knights scrambled down together; close under the wall they were out of reach of the archers in the town, unless the latter exposed themselves freely to the Christian crossbowmen; but a heavy block of masonry thudded down beside them as an earnest that they were still in deadly danger. Roger looked back with difficulty, under the cluster of bowed heads and upraised shields; he saw that the ladder had come to a halt again. The two rearmost of the four bearers were unprotected by mantlets, and though they had been safe behind the men in front so long as they were on level ground, they were exposed when the ladder tilted at the lip of the ditch; now one of them was on the ground, squirming round an arrow that stuck out of his belly, and the other was running out of range as fast as his legs could carry him. The remaining bearers left the ladder lying on the slope and jumped to the shelter of the wall. The knights were all warmed up at last; they could see the faces of individual enemies who peered through the embrasures of the wall, and hear their war-cries; this was no longer a question of advancing at a slow walk against an impersonal arrow-shooting wall, but rather the close-quarter fighting they were accustomed to. Two of them slung their shields on their backs and ran back to the ladder, which they began to drag closer to the wall; another great squared lump of freestone crashed into the ditch, without doing any damage, and now the ladder was lying with its foot at the base of the wall, in position for raising. A footman sprang to the far end, and began to hoist it above his head; it was too heavy for one man to raise, and they all clustered round to help, their shields slung. Just as they had the ladder nearly vertical another great stone was toppled from above, this time with better aim, for the foot of the ladder was smashed into kindling-wood and a knight lay dead beneath it.

There was nothing more to be done. What remained of the ladder was much too short to reach to the top of the wall, and there was no object in remaining in their present exposed position; Geoffrey de Montclair gathered them together in a compact body, with shields and mantlets raised above their heads, and they stumbled dejectedly back out of range.

Out of twenty men who had set out they had lost four in less than half an hour, but only one of these was a knight, and their fighting efficiency was little impaired. Behind the line of mantlets, where the crossbowmen still shot at the wall and made the infidels keep their heads down, the servants and non-combatants were feverishly improvising more ladders out of spears, tent poles and any bit of wood they could find; all along the wall the assault had come to a standstill, but many of the ladders had been withdrawn more or less undamaged, and everyone was eager to try again. The leaders rode up and down, marshalling their men for a new effort, and Roger's party was given another and even more flimsy ladder for the second attempt. But before they started out the line of mantlets was brought closer to the wall, only fifty yards beyond the lip of the ditch, and the crossbowmen shot at every infidel who showed himself. The leaders dismounted to take command of their own little columns, and the trumpets blew for the second attack; everyone was more exasperated than frightened, and all walked forward with a will.

As a matter of fact, the enemy was so occupied with the crossbowmen that they reached the edge of the ditch without being bothered by arrows. This time things seemed to be going right. The unarmed ladder-bearers planted the foot of the ladder in the right place, and began to hoist it into position; the knights stood close round it, their shields slung on their backs to leave their hands free; the ladder passed the vertical and clattered against the wall, ready for climbing; Geoffrey de Montclair was already on the second rung, while the others jostled one another for a chance to follow him, when a long pole with a hook on the end was thrust out from a slit-window in the side of a neighbouring tower. Everyone shouted warnings, and the knights tried to beat down the pole with their swords, but it was too high for their reach. Every crossbowman who noticed what was going on shot at the slit-window, but the target was very small, and the infidels who managed the beam were evidently standing to one side of the opening; nothing could be done to stop it; the hook soon engaged with the side of the ladder and sent it tumbling to the ground again. Geoffrey de Montclair jumped clear just before it fell, so the Christians suffered no more casualties, but it was clearly quite hopeless to attempt to rear the ladder again in the same place.

While they were gathered together all excitedly discussing what to do next, an earthenware jug full of blazing oil was dropped from the wall above. It broke squarely on the helm of a knight standing not six feet from Roger, who had to smother a few burning drops on his mail shirt while the wretched victim writhed in agony and begged his comrades to cut his throat;

actually two footmen carried him away to the shelter of the nearest mantlet, but his injuries were clearly mortal.

Since the wall was everywhere protected by the square towers, which projected for half their width from its face, Geoffrey decided that they must try to scale a tower, though it meant that they would step off the ladder into a cluster of defenders. First they used the remains of a broken ladder, which was raised against the slit-window on the first floor of the tower; a very brave crossbowman volunteered to stand on this ladder and hold the window against the enemy; but just as they were hoisting the longer ladder into position, he was shot by an infidel from the entrance to the tower room, and fell dead. Yet it was hopeless to try to climb to the top of the tower while an infidel at the slit half-way up could shoot at you from a range of three feet; they must find some way of blocking it up, if they could not hold it themselves.

At last, still using the short ladder, they got a dead knight's shield across the slit, and a hefty footman held it in position with his spear. The defenders had given up dropping large stones; these were too precious to be wasted, and they were held in reserve until things got more desperate. But the flaming oil-pots had been proved a good idea, and every few minutes another was lobbed from behind the battlements of the tower. Roger had long since been forced by the ache in his arm to lower his shield to its normal position, and he found that he must keep his face turned upwards all the time to dodge these blazing missiles.

When at last the unbroken ladder was against the face of the tower and Geoffrey again led the way, the long delay had effected a fatal change in the minds of the Christians. They had grown used to their place in the ditch, which was not so dangerous as it looked, but the tower, which they had previously regarded as a tiresome obstacle that prevented them from sinking their swords into the necks of the infidels, was now too obviously the boundary of their horizon, a boundary they could not hope to pass; they would have felt naked and exposed without its bulk reared in front of them. Geoffrey climbed fast, spurred on by his pride as their appointed leader, but the other knights hung back for a moment; for three long seconds Roger stood by the ladder, hoping with all his soul that someone else would push him aside and mount before him; but no one made a move, and he realized that he must start, or show himself publicly to be a coward. He clenched his teeth, slipped his shield on to his back, and clasped with his left hand the rung just below his leader's feet. As he climbed, he thought to himself what a silly way he had contrived of getting killed; the first man on the enemy's wall would win immortal fame, though he would probably lose his life in doing so; but who ever heard the name of the second man up, though the risk he ran was practically the same? However, he was not destined to use his sword that day; as Geoffrey de Montclair came level with the battlements a spear caught him in the front teeth, just below his noseguard, and penetrated to the base of his neck; he fell stone dead without a cry, knocking Roger off the ladder in his fall. Then the infidels overturned the empty ladder and the whole weary business had to be begun again, and this time without the inspiration of a brave leader.

The day wore on, in heat and dust and smoke; the knights were exhausted by wrestling with the heavy ladder in their cumbersome armour, and the foot could not be driven to leave the protection of the mantlets. Nowhere in the whole front of the attack did anyone succeed in scaling the wall and exchanging swordstrokes with the enemy. At last, as the sun was setting, the trumpets blew for a retreat; the sullen little groups who had been standing in the ditch, waiting for someone else to climb the ladders first, withdrew out of range, reeling with fatigue, hunger, and heat-exhaustion. Jerusalem could not be carried by a *coup de main*, there would have to be a formal siege.

Next day there were the usual recriminations that always follow the defeat of an allied army; each contingent was certain that they had done all the fighting and that the beastly foreigners had let them down. Luckily no one had the energy left to follow up words with blows and all could unite in cursing Prince Bohemund and his Italian Normans for their selfish absence. It was true that the pilgrims were now weaker in numbers than they had ever been; of course, they had been losing men by sickness and desertion ever since they left home, quite apart from their casualties in battle, and the reinforcements that had reached them in the Italian fleets hardly counted as warriors. Nobody ever counted heads accurately, not even the clerks who were supposed to give out the rations, but the leaders estimated that only about thirteen hundred knights had formed up for the assault, with about ten times as many miscellaneous foot carrying some sort of weapon; and the casualties had been heavy. In their earlier battles the Turkish arrows had not killed many of the knights; good armour was strong enough to keep them out, and the few who had died in battle had generally been first unhorsed and then murdered as they lay on the ground, too shaken to get quickly to their feet. In this assault it had been quite different; of course, the knights had led the way, and their armour had not saved them either when they were dashed from the top of the ladders or under the blows of the great blocks of stone. The losses in fully armed knights had been heavier than in any battle since Dorylaeum two years ago, and the pilgrimage could not survive another such costly set-back.

Meanwhile they spent 14 June resting, burying their dead, and grousing to one another. Roger was bruised and stiff all over as a result of the fall he had suffered when Geoffrey was killed just in front of him; he was too tender to wear armour, and thought it wise to spend the day very near the Duke's pavilion, where there would be no danger of getting into a quarrel with a Provençal or Lotharingian. He joined a group of the lesser knights who lay in the shade of a piece of canvas stretched on a few spears, and tried to rest in a position where his aching hip would be comfortable. To add to their unhappiness, they were all thirsty; there was only just enough water to be found to give them a very small allowance morning and evening, if the indispensable warhorses were to be kept alive, and for the time being there was only enough wine for Mass. Arnulf de Hesdin was resting near him; by birth he was one of the greater barons, but now that his lands in England were forfeit to the King his poverty often drove him to the society of his inferiors. It seemed that he felt that in his present company he was entitled to lay down the law.

'Good morning, Messer de Bodeham,' he said. 'I remember you at Antioch, and I see that you have changed your mind after all. It was you, wasn't it, who was all for staying behind and taking service under the Prince?'

'Well, Messer Arnulf,' Roger answered. 'I also am surprised to see you here. Surely in Antioch you were definitely one of Prince Bohemund's men. What made you follow the Duke? I had heard that your allegiance sat rather lightly on you.' This was a very cheeky reply, especially to one superior by birth; but Roger was in a bad temper, like everybody else, and they were all unarmed. Arnulf took it well; he smiled and shrugged his shoulders, then answered pleasantly:

'Now please, Messer Roger, don't begin to insinuate that I am a traitor. You were in England at the time of my trial, and you ought to remember that God himself proved me innocent of that accusation.'

He clenched his fist and flexed his right arm to show the muscle under his tunic. Everybody laughed; trial by battle was a privilege of Norman barons, but only the most obviously guilty underwent it, and all knights knew enough about fighting to realize that acquittal was the reward of strength, luck, and skill, and not a proof of innocence. This did not effect their belief in the other ordeals by fire and the red-hot iron, for somehow miracles are easier to believe in where flames are concerned.

Roger felt rather ashamed of his rudeness, and the other's soft reply had put him into a better temper.

'We are all loyal knights, Messer Arnulf,' he said, 'otherwise we would not be here, still following the Duke after three years of this pilgrimage. But you are a veteran warrior, and the best-born knight here. Tell me what you think of our prospects, and what we ought to be doing.'

'That's none of my business, thank God,' said Arnulf cheerfully. 'When in doubt, follow your lord's banner (which is all that I did in England). But if you want my opinion, I think we are in a very nasty place. To begin with, it was a mistake to plunge on here through the midst of the infidel castles, with the nearest Christian county as far away as Antioch. We are in no hurry; I have no home to go back to, and I believe that you haven't either. We could have worked our way south slowly all this summer, taking every town and castle in our way, so that we always had plentiful supplies in our camp; and then we would have reached Jerusalem some time next year, if it is God's will that we should have it. Above all, we should never have given up any enterprise once we had undertaken it. We cut our way from Nicaea to Antioch like a sword going through cheese, and the infidels at the end were too frightened to meet us in the open field. But our failure before Acre has ruined our record. Those devils sitting behind their wall know that we had to leave Acre untaken, and of course they think they may have the same sort of luck. As a matter of fact, it is only too probable that they are right. I don't see how we are going to take the town.'

'We could batter it, like we did Nicaea, or starve it out,' put in another knight, 'and there is always the chance of treachery.'

'I'm afraid none of those are any good,' said Arnulf slowly, with a frown on his brow. 'Treachery won us Antioch, but it is not the sort of thing that can happen twice. I'll wager anything you like that the infidel Count in command has made sure that there are no perverted Christians in charge of a tower or a gate, and keeps a strict watch for any negotiations. Blockade might work; there seem to be a lot of people inside the walls, and they didn't have much notice of our coming. But what should we eat ourselves while we were starving them out? This country-side is quite barren, and it would be difficult to draw supplies from the north, while there are so many infidel garrisons in the way. The odds are we should starve first, if it came to a fasting-match. Remember that a great army of relief will probably come from Egypt in the autumn, so we must keep our horses, and dare not eat them. As to battering, I am not very hopeful. At Nicaea we had those clever Greek engineers to help us, and the Emperor's ships brought us all the material we asked for; now that wily Emperor seems to be on the other side, blast him, and we haven't got the skilled carpenters to build catapults and rams. In any case, there isn't a tree for miles that would furnish a decent beam.'

This open pessimism fitted in well with the mood of the

others, for all were thinking of the defeat they had suffered yesterday, and of the friends they had lost under the walls; there was a general chorus of disillusioned agreement. Roger wanted to keep the conversation going; he was afraid that if he sat in silence and dwelt on the sad plight of the whole pilgrimage, he would break down and weep, or start planning to desert. Without much conviction, he began to put the other point of view.

'You can say what you like, but Jerusalem must be ours. It's only by a series of the most startling miracles that we have reached here at all. I thought all was lost at Dorylaeum, and I'm sure that all Normans thought the same. That was a miraculous deliverance. Then Antioch was betrayed to us at the very last moment, when we couldn't have carried on the siege for another week. God helped us there again. In the big battle outside the town we had to charge on foot against an enormous army of horsemen, and there again we won a great victory. I'm not saying it was the Holy Lance, I never believed in that very much, but some power in Heaven must have been on our side. Now finally, against all those odds, and after all those narrow escapes, we have reached the walls of the Holy City, and it must be God's will that we shall free the Holy Sepulchre.'

Arnulf gave an indulgent smile.

'That's right, Messer Roger. You keep on saying that to yourself and you will find that you fight all the better for it. But you have forgotten one thing, our failure before Acre. When we left Antioch I had the same belief at the back of my mind; I thought that with God's help we were bound to overcome all our enemies. But what happened? We sat down before a poor little fishing-port, and after three months we had to burn our engines and march away with our tails between our legs. That cured me of thinking that we could count on assistance from God. After all, though Roland did great deeds at Roncesvalles, the infidels killed him in the end, and the same sort of thing may happen to us.'

'Do you think we should retreat, then?' Roger persisted.

'It might be a good idea,' Arnulf answered cheerfully, 'if we had anywhere to retreat to; but we seem to be rather cut-off just now. Prince Bohemund won't be at all pleased to see us, since we left him after such hard words on both sides, and the Greek Emperor will set his soldiers on us if we try to go home by land. I haven't the money to buy a passage from Saint Simeon, or any other friendly port, and I have nowhere to go if I did get on a ship. No, I shall stay here until the pilgrimage breaks up, which may happen any day now. Then I shall try for a fief in the north, or take service as a soldier with some rich and generous master. You had all better make up your minds to do the same.'

'Nevertheless, Dorylaeum was a bit of a miracle,' argued a quiet elderly knight with a bandage over one eye.

'Nonsense! We should never have let them get into the camp if we had been properly arrayed,' objected another in an angry voice.

Soon the discussion of the past battle merged into reminiscence, and they were all boasting happily of the infidels they had slain, forgetting their present danger. So the time passed until nightfall, when it was cool enough to sleep.

Next day everyone was gloomy. There was plenty of scrub and brushwood on all the neighbouring hills, and the foot had been set to making mantlets out of the flimsy brittle branches. That had been useful as far as it went; the line of mantlets was thick and close up to the wall, so that the crossbowmen dominated the infidel archers; a crossbowman could shoot through quite a small loophole, with his weapon held to his shoulder, but an archer had to stick out his left arm and expose most of the upper part of his body. Mere arrows, however, could not harm a city wall, and the enemy had only taken cover behind the merlons of the battlements and left the crossbows with nothing to shoot at; they could still dodge out in plenty of time to beat back an escalade. If the pilgrims could not batter the wall for lack of timber to build siege-engines, the obvious alternative was to dig a mine. This was a well-known method of siege-craft; the gallery was driven right under the wall to be destroyed, the roof carefully propped up with stout timbers; then the chamber at the end was filled with oil and straw and set alight; when the props were burnt through the earth should cave in and bring down the wall above it. It was a foolproof method of taking a city, though it wasted time and cost much labour. But today skilled miners from southern Germany had been prospecting all round the city walls, and they reported that the ground was everywhere so rocky that a mine would take years to excavate; it would also have to be unusually deep to get under the city ditch, which had been dug with this very contingency in view. Accordingly, mining was out of the question. This had been made known to the whole army, and the leaders had invited suggestions as to what to do next; no wonder that the Norman knights, munching their biscuit and drinking a measured ration of water, were depressed about the future.

For two more days the pilgrims remained in their camp, or manned the line of mantlets, with no prospect of getting any further. The allowance of water was scanty, and much of it stank and caused dysentery in its consumers; the waterskins were old and foul, and it was hard to keep the multitude of warhorses and draught-animals out of the few and shallow pools. The town was impregnable to direct assault, and no one could think of a better way of taking it with the available materials. The army only kept together out of obstinacy, because they all knew they had reached the end of their journey at last, and would be able to disband when Jerusalem was Christian once more; and because it was so difficult to desert in small parties. The long ride north to the Principality through a hostile countryside was more than the faint-hearted cared to face. Roger, in particular, steeled his heart and determined to see the business through to the end, for he could not bring himself to go back to the city that held Robert and Anne. In any case, all agreed that this was the last campaign of the pilgrimage; when the weather cooled a great army from Egypt must come to drive them from the walls, and they would have to embark for home, unless they had first overcome the garrison.

He was beginning to face the fact that, if he survived the retreat and the embarkation, he would have to end his life as a soldier of King William. He had done his best to fulfil his vow to live and die in the East, but he could not serve Prince Bohemund while his wife lived, and it would be foolish to court death by staying behind if the main body of the pilgrims gave up the enterprise and went home. The Duke of Normandy ought to be grateful for his long and faithful service, but he knew that Duke Robert, probably a landless man at the present time, would be unable to reward him even if he wished to. He was very lonely, which increased his depression; there was no one, except Father Yves, that he could talk to openly about his private affairs and the disastrous tangle of his married life; and the priest was very busy just now, when so many other clergy were sick and the whole army in very great need of spiritual consolation. He was afraid to join with the other knights in their grumbling-parties during the heat of the day or after supper, for he knew that he was marked as an unfortunate and ridiculous husband, and he dreaded to hear some ribald joke that he would have to resent by single combat. Tom was a friendly soul, and he had long chats with his servant as they sat together scouring his armour, but his pride would not allow him to be seen walking about the camp with a crossbowman. There was no need for fully armed knights behind the mantlets, that was a job for the foot, and the five days after the unsuccessful assault were the saddest and loneliest he had spent since he started on the pilgrimage.

But on the morning of 18 June, the Feast of Saint Ephraim, the camp was buzzing with the most splendid and heartening news. A messenger had ridden all night from the coast with intelligence that Jaffa was in Christian hands. On the 17th a Genoese fleet had sailed into the harbour, the Christian townspeople had taken up arms, and the small infidel garrison had fled to the south. Best of all, the fleet had been equipped for a long siege of the seaport, and was laden with food, wine, and timber for building siege-engines. This was the nearest port on the seacoast, only forty miles away, and the presence of the Italians there meant that they could start at once to construct machines to batter down the walls. The leaders immediately held an excited and tumultuous council to plan the new operations, while knights and even footmen shouted their own views to anyone who would listen. In the afternoon a strong body of mounted men rode out to escort the first convoy into the camp, and when they saw the laden camels, swaying along with a great beam carried on each side of the packsaddle, all rejoiced and counted Jerusalem already won.

Next day they began to put into execution the plans of the leaders; it seemed that the council, in their joy and relief, had decided to try every trick of siegecraft at once. Mines, of course, were still out of the question, but the skilled carpenters from the ships were at once set to building catapults, while others were weaving and plaiting thin boughs and thorn bushes to make arrow-proof shelters for battering-rams and bores. The Duke of Lotharingia set an example by working with his own hands, and all the knights and nobles did their clumsy best to help. Once again, as at Dorylaeum and Antioch, the pilgrimage had been saved by unexpected help in the nick of time. After three years in the field they all knew something about making mantlets, and the shelters they were constructing were essentially the same thing, with a pent-house roof. Many hands made light work of it, and by dawn on the 20th they were ready to be placed in position.

The original line of shields for crossbowmen, that they had erected when all seemed hopeless, proved of great value now; the defenders dared not lean over the battlements to take long shots, and they could advance in safety to the foot of the wall. Roger had helped to make the covering for a battering-ram, and now that it was finished he got himself armed and joined in pushing it up. It consisted of a gabled roof, made in three layers; on top a sail filled with sand as a protection against fire-arrows, then a thick mattress of springy boughs to take the shock of heavy stones, and a stout framework of beams below. It was supported on sixteen vertical posts, each carried by four men, and all agreed that it was a splendid piece of machinery.

Roger was one of the fully armed knights who carried the poles nearest to the enemy. They reached the ditch without casualties, and managed to scramble down the steep slope without breaking the roof they were carrying; it was safely set up against the chosen part of the wall, and the stones and tiles that the infidels threw down on it only drove the supports more firmly into the soft ground at the bottom of the ditch. The carrying party then scuttled away, having suffered no more loss than one unarmed footman with an arrow in his buttocks.

The next job was to erect the gallows from which the ram was to swing. Roger did his share of carrying the timbers, though it was left to Italian carpenters to peg the framework together. The infidels had fully realized what was going on; they clustered thickly on the wall, and made a horrible noise with their kettle-drums. But they had no really big stones handy, and they could do no serious harm. Snug under the sheltering roof the sailors worked quickly, and by midday, when everyone went back to the camp for dinner, the framework was ready for the hanging of the battering-ram.

In the hottest part of the afternoon they began to bring this up to the wall; it was a mighty pine-tree from the shores of the Adriatic, a spare mainmast for a Genoese merchant-ship, and the shipwrights, working all night, had frapped the butt with rope, bound it in canvas, and covered it with wrought iron. It was already tied round with strong rope girdles, to which leather loops were attached, and on each side twenty men caught hold of it, and were just able to stagger forward under the weight. Roger was one of these; he had thrown down his shield and taken off his sword, for this dangerous part of the work must be finished as quickly as possible, and if one man stumbled the whole party might have to drop their burden. Nearly all the carriers were knights in mail shirts, for the enemy were certain to shoot hard and expose themselves freely to prevent the emplacement of the machine. A few footmen with very large light mantlets went on in front, to mask the carrying party, but these very large shields were too flimsy to stop a well-shot arrow, and served only to hide the men and prevent the infidels from taking good aim. A Genoese shipmaster hovered behind the ram, and with blasts on his whistle, and many shouted curses, tried to get the knights to heave all together.

With the leather thongs cutting into their hands they struggled sideways, the pine-tree between them, towards the pent-house in the ditch. Fewer arrows came at them than they had expected, for their own crossbowmen kept up a steady discharge over their heads, but the enemy had used the dinner-hour to bring up two moveable wall-balistas, and Roger heard

the new double sounds of the twang of the string and the crack
when the bolt-guide met the bow-arms, as both machines were
released together. One bolt went wide, close behind his shoulder-
blades (he was on the left of the pine-tree, and facing towards
it), the other was badly ranged, and whirred over their heads;
but these small wall-pieces were quick to reload when there
were plenty of men on the winches, and as they checked on the
brink of the ditch they were shot at again. This time the range
was too close to miss, and though one bolt again went overhead,
the other landed fairly in the short ribs of the foremost knight
on the left-hand side. With all the force of the steel and horn
springs that had impelled it, it penetrated its victim's mail shirt
as though it had been wool. He fell dead at once, and the knight
behind him let go with both hands, as he ducked instinctively
away from the missile. Roger was third on that side, and the
sudden increase in the weight of his burden was too much for
him; the thong was wrenched from his hands, and all the men
behind him were compelled to let go in their turn. He sprang
backwards in time to save himself from a crushed foot, and
there was the battering-ram lying on the edge of the ditch, with
its left-hand carrying-loops buried in the ground, and the right-
hand file of bearers leaning over it to catch their breath.

They were all in deadly danger, for all had discarded their
shields, and the bolts had shown that they could pierce mail;
but they were heartened by the memory of how God had sent
this fleet to help them when they were at the end of their tether,
and no one thought of running forward to the protection of the
pent-house, or back to the crossbowmen's defences. Doggedly
the eighteen who remained on the left, for one had broken his
leg under the fallen tree, scrabbled at the cords that went round
the trunk, while the right-hand file heaved to turn it over. As
they swung the tree clear of the ground the balistas shot again;
but now every crossbow within range was playing as fast as it
could be wound on the infidel engineers who stood in plain view
on the wall, and the latter dared not dwell on their aim. One
bolt buried itself in the side of the ditch, and the other killed
the rearmost man on the right; before the machines could be
loaded again, the tree trunk had been hauled under cover of its

roof, and the knights were congratulating one another that they had been successful with such a small number of casualties, only two dead and one injured out of forty who had taken part.

At once the carpenters got busy, attaching the battering-ram to the two chains which suspended from the framework they had built; when properly hung it would be depended about two feet from the ground; then a working-party would catch hold of the handles and haul it as far back as possible, and when they released it all together it would dash its ironshod butt against the wall. But sweating at machinery under the safe cover of a pent-house was not work worthy of the dignity of knights; plenty of the unarmed foot were eager to manipulate the ram, and others were even now making a zigzag corridor of mantlets so that the workers could get into the pent-house in safety. Another sharp volley from the crossbows drove the infidels round the balistas to take cover, and the knights scuttled safely out of range. Shortly before sunset, a muffled thud from the ditch told them that the engine had begun to beat against the wall, and relays of foot kept it at work all night long.

That evening the Normans were cheerful at their well-filled supper-table, and the veterans among them tried to calculate how long the wall could stand up to this new attack. Of course, this one battering-ram, though it was mightier than any other that the oldest of them had seen, did not represent the total effort of the attack, now well supplied with material. Elsewhere there were other rams, and also boring-picks; these last were slighter engines, thin strong spars with a pointed metal hook at the end, also slung from sheer-legs like a battering-ram, whose task was to pick out one stone at a time from the mortar of a rubble wall; the rams splintered by brute force large blocks of freestone where the defences were of shaped masonry. There was much argument which would penetrate the defences quickest, but with these unknown Eastern buildings it was all guesswork, though many knights and clerks could tell by a look at the outside how strong was a European castle.

The leaders had also decided to order the construction of three moveable towers, which could be pushed forward on rollers right up to the wall, after the ditch was properly filled in; this would be a lengthy and intricate business, needing perhaps more architectural skill than even the Genoese sailors possessed, and some of the bolder knights criticized it as faint-hearted, now that the rams were in position. The worst of it was that towers were always a chancy hit-or-miss sort of affair, for no one could calculate in his head how strong the bottom stage ought to be, and they often collapsed just as they were being finished. Still, a tower overtopping the wall, with its bridge in position leading to the rampart-walk, would be fatal to the defence, and the fact that the leaders were willing to incur the heavy expense of buying all this timber from the Genoese showed how much they were in earnest in the siege.

The 21st was an idle day for the knights. The rams and bores were busily at work, manned by the foot, but they could not be expected to produce a breach for several days yet; meanwhile they were adequately protected by the crossbowmen in the forward line of mantlets, and the infidels were unlikely to try a sortie until the damage was much worse. But although there was nothing for them to do, naturally they could not keep away from the siege-works; Roger had his armour put on, for it was stupid to take unnecessary risks, and joined the crowd of sight-seers, just out of arrow-range behind the battering-ram of the Normans. Once a minute they could hear the bang as its head was dashed against the wall, but no results could be seen as yet. This was not particularly disappointing, for the ram had not yet been at work for twenty-four hours, and in any case it was not supposed to work by degrees, like a bore. A properly battered wall would stand intact for a long time, until the final blow knocked out some vital block of stone on which the upper courses depended, and the whole thing came down with a run, leaving an easy sloping breach; when that happened, the storm-ing-party must be armed and ready, to dash in before the enemy could put up palisades on the mound of rubble, and that would probably mean many hours of waiting in column with shield on arm; but it could not come for several days yet. He waited until a shift of workmen were relieved, and dodged their way back along the zigzag line of mantlets; when he questioned one of them, all that he could learn was that the ram was standing up to its work splendidly, with no sign of split or fracture, but that the wall was doing just as well; not a stone had budged so far.

The pilgrims had other machines in action, at various places all round the city, wherever the defences did not look too solid, and the ground allowed them to approach. A number of catapults were nearly ready, though they were more difficult to make than rams or bores. But no one could hope to take this city by shooting at it with catapults; they could damage lightly built houses inside, and a lucky shot might kill some defenders on the ramparts, but the wall was obviously too strong to be broken down by throwing stones at it. The truth was, no one had ever found out a safe way of breaching well-made fortifications with any of the siege-appliances then known, or any combination of them. Starvation was the only certain way of compelling a city to surrender, and that was no good in this case, for the food supplies from the Genoese fleet would not last much longer, and the Egyptian army of relief was expected in the autumn. The pilgrims' best chance was still the battering-rams, but even they might take longer to breach the wall than the army could afford to lie in that ill-provided camp.

Next day the infidels let down mattresses in front of the damaged portions of their wall; these were either big sacks filled with straw, or the queer eastern tree-wool called cotton, or else hoardings of thick springy beams, criss-crossed and woven into a square. These cushioned the shock from the rams, which had made little impression as yet, though it was encouraging to see the enemy taking them so seriously. The obvious way to deal with these new devices was to set fire to them, but it was not an easy plan to carry out; oil and firewood were needed for cooking, and very little of either could be spared, while the enemy had plenty of water-pots ranged behind the merlons of the battlements, and continuously kept the mattresses dripping wet. Of course, if they ever did get properly ablaze, the heat of the fire would crack the stones behind them, and make the work of the attackers all the easier. Roger brightly asked a sailor why they didn't move the rams to an unprotected place, but the Genoese told him rather rudely that the mattresses could be moved much more quickly than the engines. Eventually it was found that the best way to deal with them was to attach grapnels and pull them down, but the defenders always seemed to have a new one ready when the old had been destroyed, and the battering-rams could only play on the walls for a very few minutes at a time.

On the Feast of Saints Peter and Paul, 29 June, all the engines had been at work for more than a week, and the wall was still completely undamaged. A week was not a long time, compared to the eight months siege of Antioch, but already food was running short again, the water supply caused perpetual trouble and anxiety, and no one had the heart to face staying where they were until the winter. The army was beginning to get discouraged; many of the barons had stood long sieges in their own castles in the wars of Europe, and they could appreciate what an extremely difficult task they had undertaken. They had all interpreted the timely arrival of the Genoese fleet as an example of direct Heavenly aid, but the sanguine hopes of ten days ago had already faded. They remembered the withdrawal from Acre, and some began to discuss the best way of destroying the engines if they finally decided to go home. Armies are creatures of habit; they always assume this battle will be like the last, and a remembered failure makes them ready to fail again.

Naturally, in these circumstances, the different contingents began to accuse their allies of not doing a fair share of the work. The Provençals had been unpopular for a long time, as too friendly with those heretical and cowardly Greeks, and what was much more galling, better fed and equipped than their neighbours; the Duke of Normandy and Count Tancred were not on speaking terms with the Count of Toulouse, and if the Duke of Lotharingia had not been there to act as a mediator the council of leaders would have broken up altogether. Even religious enthusiasm was at a low ebb, in spite of the holiness of the ground they were encamped on, and attendance at Mass grew thinner every day, while the bored and listless men lay in their beds long after dawn.

There was only one cheering development in the siege. Although the other engines were making no progress at the wall,

the building of the moveable towers was proceeding quite satis-
factorily. To dominate the infidel defences they would have to
be three storeys high, with a fighting-platform and drawbridge
on the roof. Already the carpenters were working on the second
storey, and so far none of them had shown any sign of collapse.
They were being constructed behind a spur of rocky ground, so
as to be hidden from the defenders; every day a curious crowd
watched the hammering and sawing, and came back to the camp
more hopeful of victory.

But there was no doubt that the spirits of the pilgrims were
getting very low, and the leaders cast about for something to
bring them into a better frame of mind. On 8 July they held a
religious procession round the walls, to mark the end of the first
month of the siege. The Blessed Sacrament was borne under a
canopy, with massed choirs and plenty of incense, and various
relics and holy images came behind. All round the sacred walls
they walked in due order, keeping carefully out of range of the
enemy's arbalasts and catapults. They were not exactly asking
God for a miracle (though that was a thing that was done often
enough, whenever anyone was tried by battle or ordeal), but
they were reminding him that they were pilgrims in the Holy
Land, fighting for his cause, and surely entitled to his help. The
infidels on the wall made a great deal of noise, and thought up
some quite ingenious insults, but probably their nerves were
a little shaken, for everyone believes that the other side controls
more magic than we do. When the procession was over, without
any serious casualties or other untoward incidents, all the pilgrims felt more at ease in their hearts. So many of them were
looking for good fiefs, so many others hoped for valuable
plunder to take home, the Italians were so anxious to settle in
good and profitable trading factories, that it was terribly easy
for them all to forget that they were engaged in a Holy War.
Three years' campaigning, much of it a sort of armed neutrality
against hostile or indifferent fellow-Christians, had dulled the
ardour with which they had first set out.

On the 9th, Roger was aware that the great procession had
altered the mood of the whole army. They had all got used to
picturing the pilgrimage as an unending road that stretched be-

fore them for some indefinite, but lengthy, period of their lives, and the feelings of urgency that had first possessed them had never recovered from the long halt at Antioch. Now they were all impatient for the end, and those in particular who had homes to go back to were ready to run any risk, however reckless, to capture the city and wind up the whole adventure. Instead of watching the progress of the battering-rams with a keen technical interest in the damage done to the wall, the knights were now hanging round the craftsmen building the moveable towers, or sharpening their weapons in their own quarters. He himself was not so eager for an assault; his future, if the city fell, held no promise of a secure life as a landholder, either in Syria or Europe, and for the present he clung to his oath of allegiance and dreaded the time when he would no longer be entitled to food and support from the Duke of Normandy. But the pilgrimage would not wait for him, and he knew that his only chance of a prosperous old age was to do a brave deed in the assault, so that some lord would be eager to have him as a follower.

In the afternoon the criers went through the camp, to announce that all footmen and camp-followers must try to provide themselves with baskets and shovels by next morning, the 10th; then they would begin to fill in the town ditch, so that the towers could approach the walls. That same afternoon the largest and most ambitious of the towers toppled over on to its side, and disintegrated into a pile of splintered beams; the workmen had been racing to finish it, and had put too much weight on the untested and insecure bottom storey. It was a disappointing set-back, but the other two towers were nearly finished, and only lacked the coating of green hides that would protect them from being set on fire, which was better added at the last minute. The plan was to fill in the ditch on the whole northwestern face of the town, a distance of some nine hundred yards, so that the enemy would not be able to guess exactly where the attack was coming; it had to be that face of the walls, for the ground was too steep and uneven on the other sides of the fortress.

Tom called him as usual a little before dawn, and he went up the hill to the line of mantlets that faced the city wall. The ditch was wide and deep and long; but the foot were working with a will, and said they had already raised the level appreciably. To begin with, they had taken all the rubbish and litter of the camp, which was a great improvement in living conditions, whatever effect it might have on the defences. Later they would put earth on top, and trample it down until it was firm; already a few cowards and weaklings were scratching with shovels at a safe distance from the enemy. But on that rocky ground even earth to fill the baskets was hard to come by; Roger reflected that Jerusalem had more subtle and ingenious defences than its walls; with no timber, little water, and now not even enough earth, the besiegers had met with one unexpected difficulty after another.

The infidel garrison was thoroughly roused by this menacing prelude to an assault; the wall was thickly manned, and in spite of the crossbowmen behind the mantlets, arbalasts and catapults were continuously in action. The foot were suffering heavy casualties, but they seemed to be bearing them well; in any case, the loss of a number of grooms and camp-followers would make no difference to the efficiency of the army as a fighting machine, and the enemy must be losing some of their warriors who worked the engines. The Duke of Lotharingia again set an example, by carrying a basket up to the ditch. Really, thought Roger, he was pushing himself forward more than was fitting, in an expedition that also contained the Duke of Normandy. But what he had done the other knights were obliged to copy, and Roger himself made three trips to the wall, though he took care to carry a basket of clean earth each time, not stinking rubbish from the camp. When he actually reached the brink and looked down, after a swift glance at the nearest arbalast (which was safely being wound up) he realized what an enormous job they had undertaken. His own little basketful was lost in the immense chasm of the ditch, and all the efforts of the whole army had only resulted in a dirty, evil-smelling streak at the bottom; at this rate it would take them weeks, if not months, to make level ground up to the wall. He crouched where he was, until the arbalast was discharged over his head, then hastily scuttled back to the mantlets.

The leaders also realized that the enterprise was too big for their powers, for that evening it was proclaimed that in future they should concentrate on two causeways, one at the north-east angle, the other in the middle of the wall; this would let the enemy know in advance where the towers were to be brought up, but nobody could prevent that.

The camp slept soundly, for the foot were tired out by their exertions, but next day at dawn they were toiling to and fro again. The excitement of dodging the missiles of the infidel, and the emulation of their hurrying companions, put them all into a frenzy of activity, and even clerks and women carried earth for as long as their strength lasted; the grooms jostled one another in their eagerness, and carried their burdens at a run. Naturally, the ardour of the knights took fire from this example, and everyone, without distinction of rank, toiled all day between the mantlets and the ditch. Roger took his turn with the rest, and had several narrow escapes from the infidel engines, for of course the mailed knights were the target of most of the missiles. But on the whole the casualties were less than might have been expected, since the enemy had to expose their whole bodies above the waist to shoot down at men so close to the wall, and the Christian crossbows would not let them take careful aim. The next day, and the next, the same dangerous toil continued from sunrise to dusk, and by the evening of 12 July the causeways were nearly completed.

It was announced that the assault would begin on the morrow. The Duke of Lotharingia was to command the tower at the north-east corner, and the Count of Toulouse the other, at the middle of the wall. All knights of the other contingents, including the Normans, could give their help to whichever contingent they preferred; since the Count of Toulouse was still unpopular, as a friend of the Greeks and a suspected malingerer, Roger and most of his companions chose to follow Duke Godfrey. Meanwhile, the other modes of attack had not been abandoned; battering-rams and bores still plied against the wall, and catapults lobbed their bundles of sharp stones on to the ramparts and towers; but this was chiefly to keep the garrison busy, to wear them out, and to stop them being quite certain where the blow would fall; for dummy towers, too light for serious fighting, were often built by besieging armies as a bluff.

Roger confessed himself that night to Father Yves, and then waited behind for a talk with his only intimate friend after he had finished with the crowd of other penitents. He was not looking forward to the battle; he had settled down into the lazy though ascetic life between the camp and the hostile wall, and he did not like to think that tomorrow it might all be over, and himself looking for another form of livelihood. He realized, with something of a shock, that though he had been very close to the enemy, both in this siege and at Acre, he had not used his sword in hand-to-hand combat since the great battle outside Antioch just over a year ago; now, out of practice, and never very thoroughly trained in arms even before he left England, he would have to take this last chance of distinguishing himself before the eyes of some rich leader. To make matters worse, the bad water had at last affected even his strong young stomach, and he was weakened by a touch of dysentery. He spoke rather gloomily of their prospects, but Father Yves was tired himself after carrying earth all day, and his answer was unsympathetic.

'You have nothing at all to worry about now,' he said rather crossly. 'It will be fair fighting against those loathsome infidels, in this holy place where God may be expected to give us his help. I don't say that I haven't sometimes been worried before, in some of the fights we had around Constantinople; I was not at all sure then that we were doing our duty as pilgrims. But now it's all as plain as the nose-guard on your helm. You can't go wrong if you try to kill infidels in God's holy city, and if they kill you, why, you have earned all the benefits of the pilgrimage. Tomorrow is the day I have been looking forward to for more than three years, ever since I first heard this pilgrimage preached by the envoys from Clermont; it ought to be the happiest and most glorious day in all our lives. Just do your duty, and don't fuss so much.'

Roger went back to his bed on the dusty ground, not at all cheered, and not in the mood for fighting.

At dawn the chiefs walked out, protected by mantlet-bearers, to inspect the ditch. The two causeways had been built up level

305

with the surrounding plain, but they were made of all sorts of light and flimsy rubbish, and had not had time to settle; a heavy weight would probably make them sink, and if they gave way even a foot when the front rollers of the towers reached them, that would be enough to capsize the clumsy contraptions. The camp-followers were directed to bring more earth, and build up the causeways until they showed above the edge of the ditch. Meanwhile the finishing touches were being put to the towers themselves; a herd of oxen and baggage-mules had been collected, and were now being slaughtered and flayed, and the dripping hides draped over the front and sides of the machines. This meant that if the army was unsuccessful, they would be unable to take their baggage with them on their retreat; but the enemy would certainly do his best to burn the towers, and it was well known that this was the safest protection against fire. The carpenters produced various convincing reasons for delay, and as so often happens, the army was not ready when the leaders had expected it to be. The assault was postponed until the afternoon, and they were all promised a specially good dinner, to encourage them to fight.

Roger spent an unhappy morning watching the preparations, for knights were not supposed to risk themselves carrying earth to the ditch just before the attack. The whole camp was in such a turmoil that the infidels must know exactly what was coming, and they had no chance of being helped by surprise; Egyptians and Saracens were crowded on the wall, shouting challenges to the besiegers to come on, and the infidels had brought up as many machines as they could move, to the towers and other emplacements where they could shoot at the causeways. Roger's dysentery was becoming troublesome, and he continually had to withdraw behind a rock, until he felt sore and empty. There was plenty of beef for dinner, thanks to the slaughter of the oxen, and every knight was given a cup of unmixed wine; this at least closed up his bowels, and he felt a little stronger as he moved off to the spot where the assaulting column was to form up.

Picked volunteers from among the Lotharingian foot were to propel Duke Godfrey's tower, and its complement of knights and crossbowmen were ordered not to climb inside it until the last moment, to make it as light as possible to transport. Unfortunately there had been no rehearsals, and the volunteers, though enthusiastic, were not united in their efforts. The great moveable building, sixty feet high, was mounted on four solid rollers, attached by iron brackets to the bottom floor, and turning in one piece like the axle and wheels of a country bullock-cart; this made the steering of the thing very difficult indeed, and the only way to get it round corners was to lift one side bodily off the ground. A great deal of time was wasted getting it pointed directly at the causeway.

At last, when the afternoon was well advanced, the tower reached the line of mantlets, and the storming party fell in at their appointed places. Some of the crossbowmen immediately ran up at the flat roof, to shoot down at the infidel engineers and drive them from their machines, but it was not thought advisable to add the great weight of the armoured knights just yet. Roger was ordered to walk on the right-hand side, with one of the parties that were trying to keep it straight; the unarmed foot were pushing with long poles from the rear, while others manhandled the rear-most roller. Roger was sorry he had been sent to the right-hand side, always considered more dangerous than the left, but he unashamedly slung his shield over his left shoulder, and put his right arm through the grips; he could not fight left-handed, but perhaps the Lotharingians round him would not know that. As a matter of fact, several of them quickly followed his example.

They were advancing south-east, towards the north-east corner of the wall, so that the enemy's stones and arbalast-bolts mostly came in from the right; as soon as the great machine had cleared the line of mantlets, and the men at its base were in full view from the wall, the infidels opened on it with every missile within range; long barbed javelins from the arbalasts, so fiercely propelled that they would pierce a mail shirt, whizzed among the guiding crew at the base of the tower, and mighty stones, cast in a high arc by catapults hidden in the streets behind the wall, dashed against the timbers of the upper storeys, while a cloud of arrows from the short stiff horsemen's bows flickered round their heads, too numerous to be dodged; luckily these arrows could not penetrate mail, which was why only knights were in that exposed station. But the arbalast-bolts were more than flesh and blood could stand; before the tower had advanced ten feet half a dozen knights were lying disabled on the ground, and the rest of the party on the right-hand side abandoned their task and crouched behind their shields. Luckily, Duke Godfrey at once noticed the trouble; he had been standing in the gap of the mantlet-line, conning the advance of the machine, and seeing that it kept straight for the causeway; now he called all the crew to come back, and for a moment the tower stood deserted. The infidels banged on their drums in high delight, but the attack had not been so easily repulsed; soon a wagonload of tall mantlets had been brought up from the camp, and workmen were sticking them in the ground in a line to the right of the path of the tower; canvas pavilions and sails from the Genoese ships were rolled up and placed behind them, and at the cost of a few unarmed men killed the pilgrims had a sheltered way right up to the wall. Roger had been badly shaken, seeing the knight next to him pierced by a bolt which spilled his intestines out of the back of his mail shirt, but he walked slowly back to his post when the order came to resume the advance. This whole method of fighting was quite new to him, and he found it hard to understand what was dangerous and what was safe.

The footmen at the back threw their weight on the poles and the great contraption crashed into movement once more. The ground was not quite level, and more rutted in some places than others, and as the rollers were all in one piece it was desperately difficult to turn the machine when it wandered off the true line; but after ages of hard work, when every man had lost his breath and his temper, at last they reached the brink of the ditch. Here the causeway was a little higher than the surrounding ground, to allow for the loosely packed earth to sink when the weight of the tower passed over it, and they all had to heave with redoubled efforts to get the rollers up the slight incline; the crossbowmen on the roof had driven the infidels from the only arbalast that could shoot straight at them, and they were so close under the walls that archers dared not lean out to take aim; but the great stones still arched up from inside the city, and bounced off the hides stretched over the upper stages; no wooden construction could stand such battering for long. The machine gave a great lurch to the right, as the rubbish of the causeway shifted under its weight. Roger and all his party obediently put their backs to it, to hold it upright, though they longed in their hearts to scamper from underneath that huge impending bulk. Then it came to a dead stop, where the front roller had ploughed up a moraine in the loose earth that supported it; the footmen at the back heaved and strained, but the whole thing threatened to topple over forwards, and they dared not use too much force. The sun was getting low, and if they left the tower where it was now the enemy would destroy it before morning; Duke Godfrey gave the order to haul it back out of range, and the survivors turned their backs on the infidel defences. They had lost more than a dozen good knights, besides crossbowmen and unarmed foot, and no one had delivered a single swordstroke at the enemy.

Roger was quite exhausted by heavy manual labour under the weight of all his mail; with a few other disconsolate Normans, he staggered stiffly to the Duke's kitchen, where the scullions sullenly gave out supper to the defeated champions. The tower of the Count of Toulouse had also failed to get into action, and the whole camp was murmuring that they had wasted their time on an impracticable stratagem. But nobody could think of a better scheme for taking the city, and it was given out by the criers that they would try again in the morning, and that relays of foot would work on the causeway all night.

Before going to bed, Roger sought out Father Yves, but the priest had a bad attack of dysentery and was lying in his blankets, quite unfit for conversation. Even Tom was not as cheerful as usual, when he came to disarm his master; he had been behind the mantlets all day, but he had been chosen to replace a casualty on the Lotharingian tower on the morrow, and he was full of forebodings about the dangers of the task.

Roger slept badly; his stomach had behaved itself all afternoon, when he had been working too hard to notice its complaints, but now the flux got him out of bed half a dozen times in the night. Many of the foot were kept at work all night, so that the army that mustered for the second day's assault looked much smaller, with workmen resting in the camp; but every knight who was well enough to wear armour was there, and they were what counted if only they could get to handstrokes. Roger heard Mass fasting, but he did not dare to take Communion, for he feared that he would be sick at any minute. Breakfast was the usual lump of biscuit, which he could hardly keep down, and he knew that he would be unable to take his place in the ranks unless he had a stiff drink to quieten his inside. Wine was scarce and expensive, and he had no money left, but a Greek sutler gave him a big cupful in exchange for his best blanket; it was thick sweet stuff from the islands, and he walked to his place with a comfortable glow under his ribs, feeling brave but a little clumsy in his movements.

The causeway had been levelled and strengthened in the night, and the tower had been repaired where the enemy's missiles had damaged the timbers. After the disappointment of the previous day everyone was in a state of frantic exasperation, but it was still exasperation against the infidel; it would only be when their rage was directed against their own leaders that the expedition would have been defeated.

When the time came to advance the tower, they had the usual maddening difficulty in keeping it straight; any experience that had been gained yesterday was wasted, for the working party of foot was composed of different men; but after several false starts they got it fairly heading towards the causeway. This time Roger managed to join the group of knights on the left-hand side, where the town wall curved away to the south-east and there were not so many infidel machines to shoot at them; also he could protect himself behind his shield worn naturally on the left arm. He left his place for a moment to embrace Tom, who was waiting nervously for his turn to climb the ladders to the roof, sixty feet up in the air; then they were all moving towards the gap in the line of mantlets, and he was leaning with his right hand against the side of the lurching bouncing pile of wood and hides. The enemy was ready for them, and the usual high-pitched quavering yells broke out from the wall; they rasped on Christian nerves, used to the deep booming warcries of Europe, and everyone knew that the noise would continue all day long. Arrows and stones twinkled in the sunlight as the tower came into full view of the defenders, but the enemy seemed to be running short of the specially-made javelins for their arbalasts, and the knights on the ground were not shot at as they had been yesterday. Things were going well; with a creak of working timbers the tower surmounted the slight rise on to the made earth of the causeway, and then a chain of men began to pass planks from the rear for the knights to lay down under the rollers. The strengthened causeway stood up well to the weight, and the tower boomed and rattled over its improvised road at a speed of quite two miles an hour.

There was a great cheer from behind them, and the tower ceased to move; it had been manoeuvred into position without a hitch, and now was the time for the knights to play their part. Everyone scurried round to shelter behind it, and Duke Godfrey, who had been directing operations on foot from a few yards in the rear, ran through the open back and began to climb the first ladder (for the sake of extra lightness, the rear face of the tower had not been planked over). This was the great moment, the culmination of their three years' pilgrimage, the goal of all those hundreds of weary miles of marching; Roger was as excited as the rest, and scrambled for his turn at the foot of the ladder.

The tower was in three stages, each twenty feet high, and each, with the exception of the hatchway, floored completely across, to strengthen the construction and brace the walls apart. When he got through the hatch on to the first floor he found himself in a milling, jostling crowd that threatened to sweep him over the edge at the back, for the footmen who had pushed the machine forward were now completely out of control in their excitement, and were swarming up supplementary ladders that they had placed against the open timbers. Naturally, the most active reached the top floor first, and these were not the fully armoured knights; soon the upper floors were clogged with a useless mass of unarmed men, and the Duke himself was still stuck at the base of the second ladder

It was very hot inside the packed staging, and the stench from the hides that covered the outside, exposed for more than twenty-four hours to the burning heat of a Syrian June, caught at the throats of the sweating knights in their airtight covering of iron and leather. Roger could not help himself; he was violently sick over the hauberk of a Fleming who was wedged up against him. Meanwhile the tower groaned and shook, as the men on the roof tried to hoist out the moveable gangway, and the stones from the infidel catapults crashed against the sides. It was a long time before the confusion sorted itself out, and then only because most of the unarmed men had been swept off the roof by the missiles of the enemy, since the crowd was too thick to allow them to climb down the ladders again to the ground; but presently the knights began to move up to the second floor. Roger felt weak and shaken, and his right hand trembled so that he could hardly grasp the rungs, but he managed to creep up the second ladder, and then leant against the wall to try and pull himself together. On this floor there were loopholes, each with a crossbowman shooting slightly upwards at the ramparts, and he thought he detected curious looks on their faces at the knight who withdrew to a corner when others were pushing to get into the fray. He swallowed a mouthful of saliva, clenched his teeth, and took his place at the foot of the third and final ladder. At last he got his head into the open air, where a fresh breeze blew away the stench of the rotting hides and immediately made him feel better. But the roof of the tower was a shambles. The infidel archers were shooting their arrows with a high curving trajectory, and they had got the range to a yard, so that every shaft thudded into the planking or into the unarmoured body of one of the wretched footmen; the crossbowmen on the roof had been hopelessly outnumbered by the concentration of much quicker-shooting bows on the wall, and those who were still alive were huddled behind mantlets or under the bodies of the dead; a few knights, dazed by the disaster round them and dizzy from the sheer drop at their feet, were fumbling with the gangway in an uncertain and half-hearted manner. There was no great leader present to give orders to the heterogeneous crowd from many different contingents; they learned later that Duke Godfrey was on the second floor,

keeping back the over-enthusiastic throng of half-armed reinforcements who only hampered the knights who really had a
chance of capturing the hostile wall. Just because most of the
knights on the roof were strangers to one another no one would
be the first to lead a retreat, and for some time they crouched at
the far side of the tower, safe from the arrows that could not
penetrate their shields, but nervously watching the great stones
hurtling up from behind the wall. At last the Duke of Lotharingia appeared at the head of the ladder, and by voice and
gesture got them all to heave together on the gangway. Yet, even
when the far end dropped into position, and the road seemed
clear at last into the Holy City, they hesitated on the roof with
it stretching down empty before them; the infidels were closely
massed at the place where it reached the wall, and a thick cluster
of spearpoints barred the way. The Duke was a great lord, and
it was not for him to throw away his life in a forlorn hope where
his men would not follow; perhaps if he had jumped down without a glance behind him things would have been different; as it
was the gangway remained there for a minute or two, empty, and
then the enemy worked loose the grapnels at their end and sent
the whole thing spinning into the ditch sixty feet below. There
was another gangway lashed to the back of the tower, ready for
just such an emergency, but they were slow and unwilling at
getting it on to the roof, and it would obviously be a waste of
time to push it out if no one felt brave enough to attack when it
was there. One or two tentative efforts were made, and then a
great stone smashed it up while it was sticking half way out.
There was no third in reserve.

As the tower was in such a good position they might as well
use it to kill some of the enemy, even though the attack was a
hopeless failure, and accordingly the knights withdrew, and the
two upper floors were filled with crossbowmen. They had an
excellent target, and did quite a lot of damage, though they
suffered casualties themselves from the catapult stones. The
knights stood around within call, in case the infidels tried a
sortie to destroy the tower, and then, in the evening, the
machine was drawn back out of range, and they were told to
go home and rest until next day.

Roger was in great misery. Up on that windy roof, looking over the wall into the very streets of the Holy City, he had seen his duty clear before him, and he had shrunk from performing it; his stomach had troubled him unceasingly, and whenever he looked at the enemy's spears he had seen a vision of Hugh's white face as he waited on his knees for his death-blow at Dorylaeum; he had been quite unable to force his trembling legs to carry him forward. He tried to imagine how his cousin Robert would have behaved; he could not see him either showing himself craven or leading a hopeless attack. Surely he would either have reached the enemy and used his sword, or disappeared quietly to some other part of the field, where he would not have been exposed in full view as a shirker; there must be some way by which more experienced warriors avoided these public humiliations.

He walked slowly back to his bivouac; his shoulders and back were covered with prickly heat and boils, where he had sweated into his thick leather mail shirt, and the supply of water was so scanty that he had no hope of a bath; he had eaten nothing since breakfast, and he had vomited frequently, so that he was faint with hunger though he did not desire to eat. When he reached the lair on the open ground that was all the home he possessed, he threw down shield and sword and sat on his rolled-up bedding, waiting for Tom to come and disarm him. He sat there for a full hour, until it was gradually borne in on him that Tom had also been on duty by the tower, and that now he must be dead. Feeling very lonely and friendless, he called to a passing groom to disarm him; the man served him sullenly, for the knights who had not dared to attack from the tower were disliked by the whole army. Now that he had no servant he ought to go and see how his pony was getting on, but he felt much too faint and exhausted; surely the beast would be watered by the horse-guard, and allowed to graze that night with the others. Instead, he slouched over to the Duke's kitchen, more because he wanted company than from any wish to eat.

When he arrived there he looked so woe-begone that one of the under-butlers insisted on giving him a bowl of hot porridge and a small cup of strong wine. The other knights were all angry and depressed by their failure, but two days' unsuccessful fighting was not long enough to take away all hope of victory, and after a hot supper they began to brag and take vows about what they would do on the morrow. Roger kept silent; his stomach had something to work on, and he felt much better at present, but he feared that the sight of the massed spearpoints of the infidels would bring back all his weakness again. Soon he left the loud-voiced gathering and looked in on Father Yves on his way to bed; but the priest was now delirious, tossing on his mattress and shouting a sermon in Breton; one of the Duke's servants was sitting up with him, and said that he had already received Extreme Unction, and was unlikely to last the night. There was nothing that Roger could do for him, and after saying a few prayers by the sick-bed he went off, more lonely than ever, to his solitary bivouac.

The next day was 15 July, exactly thirty-five months since they had first mustered outside Rouen. Roger had been so tired out by the previous day's exertions that he had been able to sleep soundly, and his dysentery was no longer so troublesome. Another knight fastened on his armour for him, since it was easier for a penniless man to ask favours of his social equals than of a footman who would expect a tip. He had been too tired to scour his sword the night before, and it was rusty from the dew; he got hold of a lump of butter, and managed to put that right, though the state of his helm and shield showed plainly that he was now without a servant. Of course everybody heard Mass before the battle, but Roger's mind was so dulled that he could not face the effort of making his confession to a strange priest, and his stomach would not let him fast for long, so that he did not receive Communion. Besides the usual lump of cold biscuit he had a drink of hot milk at the Duke's kitchen, which was recommended by the wise men as far better for dysentery than wine. He was used to a draught of wine or beer as soon as he woke up, and he missed the alcohol that usually settled his bowels; but he had no money to buy anything better than the butler chose to serve out, and he had often had to drink water during the march across Anatolia. He walked to his post by the gap in the mantlets, feeling feverish and light-headed and very depressed, but on the whole a little better than yesterday.

Various alterations had been made to the tower during the night. The chief cause of the previous day's defeat had been that the men on the roof were exposed to stones and arrows before they could begin the assault, so now an opening had been cut in the front wall of the second storey; it was closed by moveable mantlets, and at the last moment these could be taken down and the gangway pushed out. This meant that they would have to attack slightly uphill, and would also make it more difficult to fix the grapnels in the enemy's wall, but at least the storming party would be sheltered until they charged out of the tower. A number of sick or lightly wounded knights had been put in charge of the foot, with orders to keep them clear of the ladders so that their betters had a clear passage, and altogether it was hoped that the previous day's mistakes would be avoided. The leaders had put on cheerful expressions and the explanation on everybody's lips was that yesterday had really been a most valuable and successful rehearsal for the real attack today. The Count of Toulouse was also bringing up his tower again, though no one expected very much from his cautious leadership.

Moving the tower was now a well-worn routine, and there were enough experienced survivors in the working party to get it quickly going straight for the causeway. As Roger waited behind his mantlet it seemed to him that he had been watching the cumbrous machine sway and creak along for the greater part of his life; what was worse was that he also expected the attack itself to follow the usual routine; they would make contact with the wall and then in the evening pull the tower back again; the habit of defeat is very easily acquired.

The tower reached the gap, and Roger fell in on the left side. As they started across the causeway the infidel engineers discharged a steady stream of javelins and stones, and the Christian crossbowmen searched the wall with their arrows. The enemy had evidently spent the night tearing down stone buildings inside the city, and great capitals of columns and masses of Roman mortar crashed on to the roof of the machine; but the roof was empty, and the crossbowmen on the other stages so harassed the

crews of the nearer balistas that the exposed knights suffered
less than they had last time. Without any hitch, the tower rolled
on and settled into the grooves its rollers had made yesterday.
The knights ran round to the back, and stood by the ladders;
this time Duke Godfrey was the first man up, and he halted on
the lower stage, shouting to those he knew by name, and making
them file up in an orderly fashion. Now came the trickiest part
of the whole operation; the wall was slightly higher than the
second stage of the tower, and it would be difficult to sling out
the gangway so that the grapnels engaged with the battlements;
but ropes had been fixed to its far end, and led down over
pulleys from the roof; a few cool-headed men slackened these
off gently as the gangway was pushed out, and the grapnels
jerked and swayed in mid-air over the heads of the infidels. The
engineers at the defending catapults worked harder than ever;
mighty stones crashed on to the empty roof, and one of the
rafters broke right across. Roger was standing at the back of
the second floor, helping with the gangway as much as the
shield on his left arm would allow him; he saw the sunlight
flood in through the far corner; in a few minutes, if this kept
up, the tower would open out like an overblown rose, and they
would all be lying in the ditch under a heap of broken timber.
But now there was a great cheer from the watchers outside; the
gangway was resting fairly on the wall, and the way to the Holy
City was clear before them.

Nobody was eager to lead the rush across that dizzy bridge.
Roger leant against the wall, for the stench of the rotting hides
had upset his stomach again, and he wondered whom he would
vomit over this time. He suddenly saw Duke Godfrey waving
his drawn sword, standing in the blazing sunshine that flooded
the gangway; his back was to the foe; while he called into the
shadows of the tower for his men to follow him. The Duke was
very angry, and he shouted abuse in the north French tongue
that nearly all the pilgrims could understand; the quavering
warcries of the infidels and the hoarse cheers of the foot
crowded behind the mantlets made such a din that Roger could
not make out what he was saying, but at that moment there
was a sudden lull (both sides were craning their necks to watch

the flight of a colossal stone that hovered in the sky), and he caught the meaning of what the Duke was crying.

'Come on, you cravens, you dastards, you cowards, you bastards, you cuckolds,' their leader screamed, as he saw the chance slipping away, the precious seconds before the infidels rallied and cast off the grapnels. That last word pierced the fever-mists that enfolded Roger's mind, and rang through his head with throbbing insistent pain. There was that foreign Duke capering in the sunlight and calling him, Roger de Bodeham, a cuckold; it was quite true, and that made the insult all the more atrocious. It was not to be borne; he whipped out his sword, and pushed his way through the crowd towards the man who was abusing him.

Now in any battle more than half the men present only want to do the right thing; they will charge with their comrades, or run away if that seems to be the more popular policy; the knights in the tower were wavering, undecided whether to charge or not, and Roger's push to the front was all that they needed to make up their minds for them; the man in front of him, instead of getting out of the way, began to push too, and they all surged out in a solid mass, into the sunshine and clean air of the gangway. Duke Godfrey span round and let them on.

Roger was not in the foremost ranks; as he stumbled up the rough planking the shields and helms of those in front cut off his view of the infidels, and he concentrated on keeping his footing on that stage slung halfway to Heaven. There was a low railing on his left, no higher than his hips, and he stole a glance at the ditch far below; it made him dizzy at once, and he raised his shield to cut off the unnerving sight. Everyone on the gangway was terrified of being precipitated to the depths below, and this fear made them charge with all the more determination, to win the comparatively safe footing of the battlements; they ran with the speed of unarmed knifemen, rather than mailed knights. This was a more vigorous charge than even the celebrated dismounted attack outside Antioch, and the host of Egyptians on the wall could not hope to stand against it. Roger jumped from a merlon to the rampart-walk, and instinctively turned to his left to get out of the crowd. Every Christian within sight was yelling at the top of his voice, and the crossbowmen had left the shelter of their mantlets and were streaming down into the ditch. He saw in front of him a tall, slender figure in light mail, who brandished a little axe in one hand, and held out a shield to bar his way with the other; he noticed with dull surprise, through his fever-stricken brain, that his opponent's face and arms were as black as charcoal; he had never seen anyone quite like this before, but he supposed that he had to deal with a mortal man and not a devil, and he brought his sword sideways and down with a sweeping straight-armed swing, that should have cut the infidel in half. He had forgotten how much he was weakened with fever and dysentery; the other took his blow easily on the raw-hide shield, and then, quick as a cat, bent down and swung the little axe back-handed at his right ankle. It was a blow against which there was no defence, except to spring in the air over the blade, and Roger was too weak for such acrobatics; he felt the sharp axe bite through his chausse into the leg, and then he was toppling over to his right, on the unguarded inner side of the rampart-walk. With a scrape and a slither, he fell clear off the wall into the city street far below. He managed to turn over in the air, and landed with his shield beneath him. He did not lose consciousness, and for a moment thought he had escaped unhurt; he could not even feel the pain in his leg, but that was because his back was broken. Dazed, sick, and dying, he raised himself on his sound right arm and looked about him. To right and left the ramparts were black with pilgrims; someone had tied one end of a rope round a merlon, and was sliding down inside the city. He landed just beside Roger, waved his sword in the air, and uttered a great roar of 'Ville Gagnée!' Roger was scarcely conscious now, but that familiar triumphant cry raised a feeble echo in his mind; 'Ville Gagnée,' he groaned in answer, as his head fell forward and his spirit took flight.

The pilgrimage was accomplished.